EMINENT MAGE

BOOK THREE: THE MAGE AND THE BIRD CALLER

KAAREN SUTCLIFFE

Publisher: Inspiring Publishers,
P.O. Box 159, Calwell, ACT Australia 2905
Email: publishaspg@gmail.com
http://www.inspiringpublishers.com

A catalogue record for this book is available from the National Library of Australia

NATIONAL LIBRARY OF AUSTRALIA

National Library of Australia The Prepublication Data Service

Author: Kaaren Sutcliffe
Title: Eminent Mage
Genre: Fiction

Paperback ISBN: 978-1-922792-69-3
Hardcover ISBN: 978-1-922792-70-9
eBook ISBN: 978-1-922792-71-6

The author acknowledges that the Mage and the Bird Caller trilogy was written on the unceded lands of the Yuin Nation, and pays her respects to their Elders past and present and extends her respect to all First Nations people today.

ACKNOWLEDGEMENTS

I am thrilled to present the conclusion to Everand and Lamiya's meandering mission. I hope you enjoy reading the mayhem caused by the half-mage Malach as much as I enjoyed writing it. As the intended wild card in the pack, Malach exceeded even my expectations. Hang onto your paddles, you're heading for some choppy water!

My thanks go to Nature Coast Dragon Boat Club, who taught me to paddle in 2019 and still take me for awesome drills and training on the Moruya River. I didn't set out to put dragon boats in the story … but as well as providing fun and fitness you set fire to my creative inspiration.

I am further inspired by and eternally grateful to Dragons Abreast Australia and Dragons Abreast Canberra for encouraging me as a pink paddler and for providing such camaraderie as well as opportunities to paddle and have an unbelievable amount of fun. Special mention to Captain Annie, who gave me a seat with Team Hope to participate in the international regatta in New Zealand. A memorable and moving experience.

As always, I express heartfelt gratitude to everyone who so kindly and professionally helped me, Everand and Lamiya on our journey. A huge shout out to my trusted readers who waded through earlier versions, providing encouragement and constructive suggestions. Take a bow Annette, Natalie and glide extraordinaire, Susan. Thank you, paddler and editor Kellie for expertly polishing the final version. A humble bow of gratitude to Francesca Baerald, for the intricate, world-class map of Ossilis and the new business logo of my dreams.

I encourage readers to take five minutes to watch the awesome book trailer on my website, crafted by my talented brother-in-law and sister, Antonio and Phillipa Saraceno.

A huge, rib-cracking hug for husband Andrew for all his support — cooking dinner, putting up with my spiritual absences, sponsoring the matching bookmarks — and driving me to regattas.

A third round of thanks to the expert team at the Australian Self-Publishing Group for turning the story into another quality book that I am proud of.

Finally, dear readers, thank you for returning to Ossilis! I hope the story does the sport of dragon boating justice and inspires some of you to give paddling a go.

Kaaren Sutcliffe AE

www.kaarensutcliffe.com.au
https://www.independentauthornetwork.com/kaaren-sutcliffe.html

Cast of Characters

Axis

Everand	Mage, spy
Mantiss	Mage, Head of the Mages' Guild
Agamid	Mage, deputy to Mantiss
Beetal	Mage, deceased, former mentor to Everand
Tiliqua	Tiliqua, daughter of Mantiss, Inner Council
Inner Council	Saiphos, Menetia, Simoselaps, Neelaps, Pelamis, Caimanops
Hydrelaps	Mage, Guild librarian

Dragons

Mizukaze	Riverfall river dragon
Akachi	Riverplain lake dragon
Hanachi	Riverplain lake dragon, daughter of Akachi

Riverfall

Atage	Town leader
Tengar	Glide, team captain
Beram	Paddler 10 — irrigator, messenger
Mookaite	Pacer, healer
Lyber	Town second-in-charge, negotiator
Thulite	Atage's wife, cook, feast organiser
Vogel	Old man, historian
Paddlers:	Melanite, Selenite, Kunzite, Zeol, Persaj, Zink, Acim, Ybur, Ejad, Micate

Riverplain

Lamiya	Glide, team captain — bird caller
Lazuli	Pacer
Lulite	Drummer
U-Mali	Riverplain Guide
U-Lumin	Consort to U-Mali
Paddlers:	Larimar, Laza, Lopa, Levog, Lattic, Lapsi, Lepid, Luvu

Riversea

Cowrie	Glide, team captain — boatswain, carpenter
Paddlers:	Conch, Chiton, Limpel, Clommus, Summel, Pippel, Spirula, Charonia, Clama, Nawpra, Chella

Riverwood

Malach	Half-mage, glide, team captain, hunter
Torrap	Pacer — hunter
Paddlers:	Magle, Mahog, Kwah, Tiek, Perid, Melan, Meralb, Kerish, Folnak, Yosper
Chinfe	Mother of Malach (deceased)
Magrin	Former chief (deceased)
Hemma	Old woman
Fenchi	Young woman

The Island of
Ossilis
Mizuchi Falls
Hanaki Forest
Dragon Lake
Riverfall
Axis
Mages Guild
Riverwood
Zugari
Dragonspine River
Riverplain
Dragonfoot Lake
Riversea
N

GUILD LAW — AS ESTABLISHED BY MAGE LAPEMIS

Rule One — The key purpose of the Guild is to enhance and refine the workings of magic, and to impart knowledge and training to younger mages as apprentices.

Rule Two — The Guild will be led by an elected Head of the Guild.

Rule Three — The Head of the Guild will be supported by an Inner Council and an Outer Council, member numbers to rise over time.

Rule Four — The Guild will work 'to protect by sun and moon' the mages of Axis and the humans who work with us.

Rule Five — The Head of the Guild has overall authority, and the code words to access the Staropal are to be known only by the incumbent Head of the Guild.

Rule Six — The Staropal will be concealed and only accessed in times of dire need, as decreed by the Head of the Guild and with agreement from the councils. The stone must be used for honest purpose and for the greater good.

Rule Seven — The humans who reside in Axis agree to work with and care for the physical needs of the mages, such as food, water, clothing and labour, in exchange for shelter and protection.

Rule Eight — Mages must only breed with other mages to keep the lines of magic pure. Accordingly, the humans of Axis must only breed with other humans.

__Rule Nine__ — No mage or human shall pass outside the granite wall, unless ordered to do so by the Head of the Guild for special purpose.

__Rule Ten__ — Others from outside Axis shall not be allowed inside the wall of granite, unless authorised by the Head of the Guild for special purpose.

__Rule Eleven__ — Breaches of Guild Law will be judged by the Inner Council, with the final say by the Head of the Guild. Extreme digressions will be punished by obliteration or removal of power.

__Rule Twelve__ — Mage power must only be used for sound purposes with honest intent. Use for personal ambition or evil intent constitutes a breach of the direst magnitude and will be punished in accordance with Rule Eleven.

PROLOGUE

An eerie silence filled his room; a total absence of movement or sound. Goosebumps crawled along Everand's arms. He'd overslept! Groaning, he sat up and scrubbed at his face with both hands. Why did his parents always choose to start arguing after the sun-fade meal? Even ramming two pillows over his head hadn't muffled their bitter words and the moon was waning when they finally stopped hurling accusations. If he didn't get more consistent sleep the teachers would notice his lapses of concentration. At twelve season-cycles he was supposed to be fully focused on studying and preparing for an apprenticeship. No mage would agree to mentor a poor student.

Pushing down a curse, he shoved back the quilt, slipped out of bed and padded barefoot into the living area. Warm sunshine lit the wide space but his soft footfalls echoed ominously off the marble walls. The dining table was bare, no sign of any breakfast trays. His heart beat faster and his palms prickled. Something was wrong. He padded around the edge of the sofa and his feet snagged on his father's lanky ankles. Flailing his arms to right himself, Everand spun around. Why was Father sitting there? Shouldn't he be at a council meeting?

His breath caught and his heart raced. His father was sprawled against the back of the sofa, head on an unnatural angle, blue drool dribbling from the pale, slack mouth. The usually intense blue eyes stared sightlessly ahead, a milky film covering them. Everand froze. What? How? Was Father dead? With all his power? No, no, no … not possible. Heart hammering, he sprinted from room to room — greeted by one silent and empty space after another.

Skidding on the marble tiles, he yanked back to a stop in front of the body. Where was Mother? Acidic bile oozed into his mouth and congealed beneath his tongue. His mother often spat vitriol at his father, but surely she hadn't done *this*? His ribs were strangling his lungs and he dragged in shallow, painful gasps. An uncomfortable reprieve washed through him. Why hadn't Mother killed him instead? His throat knotted. Wasn't he, the unwanted brat she'd been 'saddled with for ever and ever', the one she really hated? Guilt seeped into his chest; Father's kindness to him had been a constant source of argument.

Fingers trembling, he reached out to touch the pale, lolling face in farewell — snapping his hand back just as he felt the brush of skin on his fingertips. *Touch nothing. The scene will be read.*

Someone pounded on the door to the family quarters.

'Tenuis! Are you there? Open the door!' Mage Agamid's voice.

Mouth dry as sand, Everand coaxed his feet across the cold tiles to open the door, leaping out of the way when Mage Agamid and Mage Mantiss charged in, their robes billowing around their ankles. By the time he'd closed the door the two mages were standing exactly where he'd just stood, gaping at the body with mouths open and eyes wide. Edging back into the room, Everand hovered to one side. What would they do?

'It is true then?' said Agamid, his voice strained with disbelief. 'I heard the arguments were getting worse, but this is unthinkable.'

'What, by the sun and moon, was Myopa thinking? At least she had the decency to send me a message, confessing.' Mage

Mantiss stroked his wispy blond-grey beard. 'The council will obliterate her. If we can find her.'

Mother had *confessed*? Is that what Mage Mantiss just said? Fear ripped from Everand's head to his toes. Would she come back for him? His throat clenched. Maybe, if he was lucky, she would stay vanished. Anger prickled him; he'd been saddled with her too, an aloof mother who dripped disdain and never love. No more sniping and criticism. Far better she was gone for good.

Mage Agamid leaned forward and sniffed. 'It smells like a form of poison. The blue froth suggests hemlock.'

'But why would Tenuis drink it?' queried Mage Mantiss. 'With his ability he would have either smelled or tasted it.'

A wave of profound sadness roared through Everand. Father must have known and had drunk the potion anyway. Had Father grown tired of the constant strife and seen no way forward? Of late, Father had seemed subdued. Blinking back a tear, he wished he'd hugged his father and expressed gratitude for his kindness, his gentle efforts at care. Pain lanced his heart. He should have done more. *Tried harder. Been better.* But these thoughts would lead to despair. Now he must be stronger. *Independent.*

Closing his eyes, he visualised protective, translucent shields sliding up to encase his heart. Flexing his fingers, he imagined courage seeping in through his fingertips. When not in class he spent most of the time by himself anyway, mainly in the Guild library. He would manage. *On his own.* Surreptitiously, he dragged the back of a hand across his nose and paid attention. What would the senior mages do now?

'What do we do?' asked Mage Agamid.

'We must summon the council and report Tenuis' death. Propose that a search be conducted for Myopa.' Mage Mantiss spoke slowly, as if he were thinking. 'Although what we will do if we find her … taking a life is a heinous crime and the council will seek her obliteration.'

'Then we will have lost two of our most powerful mages,' said Mage Agamid softly.

'Indeed,' replied Mage Mantiss. 'Myopa was so talented … such a waste. However, the Guild has rules and must be careful of precedent. This level of transgression can't be tolerated, as wasteful as it is. And no magic is allowed outside the Guild. She *must* be found.'

'You always understand the politics and strategy better than me,' murmured Mage Agamid. 'Let's seal these quarters and summon the council. The full Outer Council of Twenty?'

'That seems appropriate.' Mage Mantiss turned around and flinched when he caught sight of Everand. The mage lifted an eyebrow. 'Have you been standing there the whole time?'

Everand nodded.

The mage's look became intent. 'I see.'

The two senior mages stood looking at him. Agamid seemed to be waiting for Mantiss, who was thinking furiously by the way the hues in his green eyes were shifting. Taking a subtle breath to calm his racing heart, Everand waited.

After an uncomfortable interval, Mage Mantiss cleared his throat and said to Agamid, 'Why don't you go and summon the council and I will find a place for young Everand and seal these quarters?'

'As you wish,' replied Mage Agamid, turning and walking to the door.

After the door had closed and the sound of Agamid's footsteps had faded down the corridor, Mage Mantiss waved a hand towards Everand's bedroom. 'Come lad, let's get you dressed and discuss where you should go.'

Wishing his palms didn't feel so clammy, Everand walked into his bedroom and opened the wardrobe door. His hand went to his favourite azure robe. At least he could choose what he wanted to wear now. Embarrassed to be dressing in front of someone, he hurriedly tied the sash and retrieved his sandals.

Patting the end of the bed, Mage Mantiss said, 'Sit, Everand, and I will fetch a chair. Let's talk.'

Everand perched on his bed and listened to the mage's footsteps and then the scrape of chair legs across the marble tiles. The mage returned, placed a dining chair facing him and eased onto it. What could this senior mage want to talk about?

Mantiss sat with an erect spine and a sharp look in his green eyes. 'I won't ask you what happened here because the council will ask you those questions and I don't wish to influence your responses. What I do want to discuss is what we do with you from here.' The mage spread his hands in an open expression. 'You are twelve, so you're not a child but are still younger than a mage would normally start an apprenticeship and move away from the parents.' Silence stretched while Mantiss regarded him steadily.

Everand clasped his hands in his lap. He had the distinct impression the mage had a suggestion to make. The sun beaming through the window was welcome on his chilled hands. He calmed his heart rate, held the eye contact and waited.

A smile broke out on Mantiss' lean, lined face. 'As I suspected, your unusual upbringing has given you some strength, and perhaps useful skills.' He tipped forward. 'If you wish it, the council could find another mage couple for you to live with. You would continue your classes and be assigned as an apprentice at sixteen, as is customary.'

Acidic bile crawled back into Everand's mouth. Go to a strange couple and have to try to please them? What if they hated him too? His stomach roiled and his forehead tugged with the start of a frown. Forcing his face muscles to stay relaxed, he continued to wait. There had to be another option.

'By the stars, you are adept at concealing your thoughts,' murmured Mantiss. 'Or, given that you appear to be quite self-sufficient, we could allocate you your own rooms and begin your apprenticeship early.' Mantiss hesitated. 'Would you prefer this?'

Keeping his face neutral, Everand nodded economically. Several questions formed — such as who, where, for how long — but he held them back. The pensive look in Mantiss' eyes suggested this mage had more to say.

'Come, boy, surely you have at least one question?' probed Mage Mantiss.

'Who would I be apprenticed to?' He chose the obvious question, intrigued by the responding glint in Mantiss' eyes.

'Astute. Given the collective power of your parents, your mentor needs to be someone you can respect and who will coax your full skills to fruition.' Mantiss sat up and leaned against the chair back. 'There is a relatively young mage who shows extraordinary skill and who would benefit from having an apprentice. Having to explain and teach things to someone else is a good way to refine and hone your own skills.'

Quickly, Everand ran his mind over the mages who currently didn't have apprentices. The librarian Hydrelaps seemed pleasant but he had enough to do already. Mage Menetia, but she was vain and arrogant, and way too much like his mother. He repressed a shudder. Then there was the swarthy, bristly mage who he'd observed others tended to tread carefully around. As far as he knew, this mage had never taught an apprentice.

His eyebrows lifting in query, Mage Mantiss tilted forward. 'You have worked out who this is?'

'Mage Beetal.'

Mantiss sat up with a slow, calculated smile. 'You agree to be assigned to Mage Beetal?'

Why not? Everand shrugged. Then his shoulderblades prickled at the look of deep satisfaction crossing Mage Mantiss' face. What was Mantiss' interest in this?

'Excellent. Let me propose this to the council and suggest you be found some pleasant, sunny quarters of your own.' Rubbing his hands together, Mantiss leaned forward again. 'One more thing.'

Everand held his breath. Was this 'one more thing' the essence of this odd conversation? Adults rarely did anything without a motive.

In a measured voice, Mantiss said, 'Given that you no longer have parents, I propose you meet with me regularly to report on how your apprenticeship is progressing.' In a too-casual tone the mage added, 'And I will impart some additional skills to you. Would you like that, my boy?'

'Thank you, Mage Mantiss,' said Everand with a respectful bow to hide his surprise. Was he being asked to spy on his imminent mentor? It sounded that way. Inside, a smile formed. He was accustomed to sneaking around and observing undercurrents. If these were the skills Mage Mantiss proposed to extend, he'd embrace it. He could form a new identity and persona as an unreadable spy. The idea settled across his shoulders as comfortably as his favourite robe.

Rising, Mage Mantiss said briskly, 'Excellent, Everand. I'm glad we have a suitable arrangement for you. Let me take you to the library for your classes. Either I or Mage Agamid will look for you at the close of classes to take you to your new quarters.'

Standing too, Everand glanced around his room. Could he take his things? Not that he had much, although his gaze lingered on a pile of his favourite books. Even though he knew them almost word for word, he wanted those.

Mantiss said kindly, 'The humans will pack your things and move them, ready for you.'

After a brief, final look around his quarters, heart thumping but holding his head high, Everand followed Mage Mantiss' flowing green robes out through the door.

CHAPTER ONE

Everand traced circles on Lamiya's shoulder. Her skin was so soft, alluring, reassuring beneath his fingers. Being a fugitive mage had some good points. If only these peaceful moments could continue. Far nicer to be able to devise his own schedule, do what he wanted to do, with Lamiya at his side — instead of being at the beck and call of the Mages' Guild. And the location of Lamiya's hut, right beside the stunning, turquoise lake in the centre of Riverplain, was beautiful beyond compare.

'I need a swim,' said Lamiya, kissing his fingers then standing up and retrieving a drying cloth from a shelf. 'Coming?' She arched an elegant brown eyebrow at him.

He sighed. No way was he going into the cold water but he wasn't ready to let her out of his sight; he'd only just found his way back to her. 'I'll watch you.' Fetching and opening the bundle of clothes Beram had packed for him, he chose a fresh tunic and pair of trousers.

Lamiya wagged a finger at him. 'I *will* teach you to swim. Soon.'

'Agreed,' he said pleasantly, deflecting a shiver. 'Does the water get warmer during harvest season?'

'Hah! It's refreshing in the heat. You'll love it.' She smiled mischievously.

That, he doubted. But watching her splash around with not much on wouldn't be a chore. Not at all.

He walked barefoot to the lake with her, the water rippling with golden threads from a sun already past its zenith and arcing downward. Before long they'd be surrounded by others again. Beram, Mookaite and Tengar would arrive from Riverfall and, even sooner, Lazuli would bring Malach to him for further training in magic.

A frown burrowed into his forehead. Malach: the source of all the trouble. Could he successfully train the half-mage? More to the point, if Malach increased in ability could they trust him? One sun, perhaps two, before mages from the Guild would come hunting them both. His forehead throbbed. Despite the threat of obliteration by the Guild, Malach had been reluctant to hide in Riverplain. Did the half-mage have other ideas that he'd kept well concealed?

'Here!' Lamiya threw her cloth and over-tunic at him.

Catching them, he swept his eyes over her lithe, muscled body while she twirled around and ran into the water, splashing out to hip-deep before diving under the surface. His heart twisted and tumbled. She was infinitely gorgeous. Sitting down on the dirt beach, he watched her taking smooth, long strokes, cleaving through the water as elegantly as a fish. How was it possible she loved him?

He rested his chin on the top of his knees. The Guild would *never* sanction his relationship with her. Rule Eight stated non-pure mages were not permitted. *Never. No matter who.* Sadness welling, he swallowed. If only Mantiss would bless their union, show some smidgeon of warmth and joy that he'd finally found someone to love. But no, the Guild hid behind its warded granite walls and decreed there should be absolutely no existence or use of magic outside of Axis. His discovery of the half-mage Malach — during his supposedly simple mission that was anything but — was leading to an immediate confrontation. Two fugitives against the might of the Guild. Perhaps this was for the best. Get it over and done with — he'd make it clear he was leaving the Guild. *Or die trying.* As long as no-one else died on his behalf.

Cold water slopped into his face and he looked up just as Lamiya scooped another handful at him. Droplets ran down his cheeks, tickling.

'So serious!' she shouted from the water. When he didn't respond, she waded back out and came to sit beside him, leaning wetly against his shoulder. 'I know. We have much to plan.'

He slipped an arm around her shoulders. 'And so little time. But it's better to get this over with so we can go forward.'

'Maybe.' Lamiya slid her arm around his lower back and chewed at her bottom lip. 'You will be careful of Malach, won't you?'

Did she mean be careful as in protect Malach? No, her expression suggested she didn't trust the half-mage. He kissed her head, wet hair sticking to his lips, and refrained from telling her about the others he trusted far less than Malach, and who were significantly more powerful.

She shifted against him. 'Lazuli is bringing him now.'

Following her gaze, he saw the handsome paddler approaching with Malach beside him. 'So, we begin.' He kissed her head again and stood up.

Lamiya dried her legs and arms and slipped her tunic and trousers back on. 'Why don't you sit out here? I'll bring us some drink and food.' She jogged away.

Sitting in the waning sunshine would be pleasant but he hoped she hurried back. Lazuli's offer to hide Malach in his hut was courageous, but he and the paddler hadn't said much to each other since their brawl on the beach over Lamiya's affections. Still, this resentment between them was minor in comparison to the larger events.

The two men stopped a few paces away. Lazuli's left cheek was mottled with green and purple bruises and the knuckles of Everand's right hand throbbed in memory of connecting so hard with skin and bone. When Lazuli's expression tightened, Everand transferred his attention to Malach. The half-mage held a smug, expectant air, no doubt eager to advance his skills and power. Everand sighed.

'Let's sit there.' He waved a hand at a patch of grass in the shade and they both followed him and sat without comment.

Lamiya returned carrying a neatly-balanced tray of a jug, mugs and bowls and raised an eyebrow at the way they sat in silence. Putting down the tray, she said, 'Help yourselves.'

Everand poured a mug of water and selected slices of fruit.

Sitting cross-legged next to him, Lamiya asked Lazuli, 'Have you and Lepid finished your camouflage preparations?'

The paddler nodded. 'We've brought the hopeepa herd in close around our huts so there'll be energy from a hundred mingling animals. We're still deciding the best place to hide Malach.' Pausing, he looked at Everand. 'Any ideas?'

'I'll teach Malach how to shield himself and conceal his powers so it'll be harder for the mages to find his aura. Then we'll add the spell of invisibility.'

Malach gave him a sour look. 'These are defensive tactics. Tactics of a coward.'

Everand's spine stiffened. They'd be outnumbered when the Guild came! Did Malach expect to challenge several advanced mages head-on?

'Will you be sneaking around hiding too?' Malach added.

Glaring at Malach, Lamiya snapped, 'That's hardly fair. Everand is trying to help you! We all are.'

'I prefer a warrior's death. How long do we have to hide for? Will the mages only come once, or keep coming until they find us?' Malach gave Everand a flat stare. 'Tell me you have a better plan.'

Feeling as if the fruit he'd just eaten was trying to work its way back out of his mouth, Everand cleared his throat. Malach raised a fair point. His plan was flawed and based on … what? A futile hope that he could persuade the Guild to change its mind and relax rules that had stood for four generations. Perhaps he should describe the chamber of death that stood waiting in the Great Hall at the Guild, then Malach wouldn't be so bold. The back of his neck went cold at the memory of seeing the red disc at the top of the translucent chamber, where the Council of Ten would feed in their combined spell of obliteration to rain down on Malach.

'The plan isn't perfect, but challenging the mages is unlikely to go well.' He strengthened his tone. 'There are nineteen other mages in the Council of Twenty and much depends not only on how many come but also on *who* they send. Once I see this, I can judge whether there's any chance we can talk to them.'

Giving Malach a crisp look, Lamiya jumped in. 'U-Mali and U-Lumin only agreed to conceal you. The guides said they would yield you if there was *any* threat of violence and we are obliged to follow their decree.'

Malach looked at her with such distaste that Everand bristled. He should have left this unruly half-mage back in Riverwood and let him and his hunters die trying to deflect the ire of the Guild. What was he thinking?

Lamiya's hand stole onto his knee and her thoughts trickled into him. *Don't doubt yourself, my mage. Your intentions were honourable. This conflict will show us whether the son of your former mentor is worthy of such honour.*

Heartened, he faced Malach. 'You need to allow me to gauge whether I can reason with who comes.' The words sounded hollow, matching the emptiness in his chest. It was unlikely he'd be able to reason with anybody, not if Pelamis and Simoselaps came. Their ambition would drive them to be merciless.

Malach grunted and Lazuli looked justifiably worried. Hard to be responsible for hiding someone so unpredictable, not particularly likeable, and who could get them all killed. Everand felt a twinge of respect for the paddler, and besides, Lamiya wanted them to be friends. She said Lazuli now accepted that she'd chosen him, although he doubted the paddler's feelings had subsided. Her hand subtly squeezed his knee. Was she following his thoughts? If so, her abilities were developing with uncanny speed.

'We're making more bows and arrows.' Lazuli shifted uncomfortably. 'And slingshots. In case your mages don't wish to talk.'

'The guides won't like it.' Lamiya frowned.

Everand clenched his fingers and pressed his lips together. He couldn't tell them not to bother; the people of Riverplain had a right to defend themselves. Guide U-Mali was astute and she must know that weapons would be useless against mages and would only serve to provoke Pelamis and Simoselaps. When one of Malach's hunters had shot an arrow into Simoselaps' arm, Pelamis hadn't even blinked before felling the hunter with a single fire bolt. Worse was that Agamid, the senior mage present at the time, hadn't reacted or chastised Pelamis for murdering a province man.

His throat clamped tight — Agamid had also done nothing when Pelamis then turned on him, calling him 'a traitor to the Guild, just like his former mentor'. The fury and contempt on Pelamis' face while he hurled volleys of death strikes had been primitive and unsettling. If the dragons hadn't chosen to come to his aid, he'd have been forced to kill Pelamis. Then he *would* have been a true traitor.

A deep sigh floated from his lips. If only Agamid and Mantiss would realise the magnitude of the consequences of any violence. Perhaps wisely, the Guild had historically kept itself aloof from the river provinces. Everand curled and uncurled his fingers. Even so, Mantiss and Agamid would have to persuade the other mages, who didn't care what happened in the river provinces. If Pelamis made a bid for control of the Guild *anything* could happen.

Everand sipped at his water, his instinct nagging that he should act to buy time. But for what?

Lamiya tapped his knee. 'While you work with Malach I'll see if I can find the dragons. Now there are three, I'll ask them how they want us to interact with them.' She lifted her shoulders. 'And whether they plan to stay here, or whether they want to go back to Dragon Lake and the waterfall.'

Everand focused on her face. 'You'll be further along the lake, towards the hills?'

'That's where I found Akachi, so I believe she lives down the far end of the lake.'

'Should I come with you?' Lazuli asked.

'It'd be better if you greet our friends from Riverfall when they arrive,' Lamiya replied.

Disappointment passed over the paddler's face. 'I'll bring them to your hut?'

Everand felt hope returning. They all had a course of action, and Beram and the others from Riverfall would have good ideas to share once they understood what was happening. The blue flecks in Lamiya's grey eyes were dancing with excitement. Going with her to see the dragons would be wonderful, but the larger events, what she would say were the spirits speaking, seemed determined that she accumulate her own abilities. She trusted him; he must trust and believe in her.

With a tender smile, he said, 'See you later.' He turned to Malach. 'Shall we get started?' Ignoring the unfathomable look he received in return, he stood and brushed his hands down his tunic.

Malach had promised to learn fast. He'd better.

Chapter Two

Unease coiling in her stomach, Lamiya watched Everand and Malach heading along the lake shore. *Trust him. Everand knows what he's doing.* Her heart said otherwise. He was too generous with his willingness to help others, too courageous in taking on risks to himself. She sighed. *Yes, but that's why you love him.*

Lazuli rested a hand on her shoulder. 'Great glide, I know you see far more than us mere paddlers, but I hope your mage knows what he's doing.'

She brushed Lazuli's hand with her fingertips and turned to face him. 'Everand acts quickly when he has to. I too fear we're way out of our depth, but so far things have mainly worked out.' She shrugged. 'The dragon boat races were held successfully–'

'And the best team won overall!' Lazuli grinned.

'Indeed, the best team won. The dragon Mizukaze was called and made an agreement with Atage, leader of Riverfall, to bring rain for our crops. The dragon has already given us rain, with more promised, so our worry about our crops and pastures is over.' She flapped a hand. 'The trade discussions went ahead, despite Riverwood withdrawing, and Riverplain will host the next races and trade in just two seasons.'

Ignoring Lazuli's frown, she continued, 'We found the superior dragon Akachi in our own lake, Everand survived the trap for Malach set by his Guild mages, and not only did he make it here safely but he brought Mizukaze and Flight, who we now know is called Hanachi, with him. We now have all three dragons in *our* lake!'

She wagged a finger. 'And we're building a new, faster boat in the likeness of Akachi. We'll be the best team at the next races too! Which you, my trusty pacer, are in charge of.'

Lazuli held up his hands in defeat. 'When you put it that way … and no-one is sorry that Riverwood chooses not to trade with us.' He ran a hand through his hair. 'If we can dislodge Malach from our midst I'd be much happier.'

Lamiya tilted her head. 'Do you think we can trust him?'

His grey eyes serious, Lazuli considered her question. 'I don't like him. He's aloof and arrogant and I can't tell what he's thinking. As a hunter and warrior, he's ruthless.' He grimaced and shook his head. 'He'd set his raptors on your beautiful flock without blinking. I'm sorry, Lamiya, but I struggle to understand why Everand thinks we should save Malach.'

Touching the back of his hand, Lamiya said, 'You deserve to know more. It's complicated, but it's more than the principle of justice Everand tries to uphold. At the Guild he was apprenticed to Malach's father.'

Lazuli quirked an eyebrow. 'What does that mean?'

'Apparently the mages have to be taught how to summon and use their magical power. Everand told me the Mages' Guild works to research and refine their powers, and the senior mages teach the younger ones.'

'How many of them are hidden behind that massive granite wall?' Lazuli looked incredulous.

With a shrug, Lamiya said, 'I think over a hundred. Anyway, Everand told me he was assigned to Malach's father when he was twelve and studied with him until the mage was killed only seven seasons ago. That's a long time — nearly fourteen season-cycles. They must have developed a bond.'

She licked her lips. 'There's more. Everand was trained by the Head of the Guild to be a spy, and tasked to spy on Malach's father.'

'That's why the Guild chose *him* to go to Riverfall before the races? He's a spy? That's why he was in disguise?'

Lamiya nodded, admiring Lazuli's agile mind. 'Everand said the Guild doesn't want to interact with the province people so they sent him to find out what was going on and stop it, without anyone knowing they'd been involved.'

Lazuli gave a low whistle, then frowned. 'That doesn't make sense. If they didn't want to be involved, why send anyone at all?'

Smiling, she said, 'This is why you're my right-hand pacer! Smart as well as strong. Everand now thinks the Guild suspected someone like Malach existed and sent him to find out, but without telling him.'

'He was deceived?' Lazuli's frown deepened.

Worry niggling at her, she played with the end of a braid. 'Even more complicated is that Malach's father was a traitor to the Guild, so they have no reason to like his half-mage son. But, unlike the other mages, Everand regrets what happened to his mentor. When Malach was holding us captive in Riverwood, he accused Everand of betraying his father — and Everand didn't deny it. So, as well as believing Malach doesn't deserve to be executed simply because his mage father was entranced by his human mother, I think Everand is trying to make amends for what happened to Malach's father.'

'I wish you'd told me this earlier.' Lazuli rubbed at his jaw. 'It explains a lot, but it doesn't ease my concerns.'

'Nor mine,' said Lamiya softly. 'There are twists and currents to everything that's happening. But we're in it now, and I try to remind myself of the good things that have resulted. We now have three dragons and my bones tell me that's going to count for something. Maybe *everything*.' She bit her lower lip. If Everand looked like he would fail, she would call and command the dragons herself.

'Well, mighty dragon-caller, you'd better go and find them. And I will be nice to *your* mage.' Putting his hands on her shoulders, Lazuli looked into her face, a gleam in his eyes. 'And put up with the irksome half-mage for a little longer.' He kissed her forehead and stepped back. 'I'll bring Beram and the others to your hut when they arrive.'

Letting out a long, slow breath, Lamiya watched Lazuli stride away. He'd forgiven her and was trying hard to support what she and Everand were aiming to do. The two visions the spirits had revealed hovered in the back of her mind. If Everand hadn't arrived, she w*ould* have loved Lazuli. A chill crossed her shoulders and she shuddered, trying to dislodge the conviction that she and Everand were being moved around at the whim of unseen forces. The guides had implied as much. U-Mali had welcomed and accepted Everand but had said his spirit was not yet complete.

Turning east, she walked along the shore. When would Everand's spirit be complete? He'd chosen to leave the Guild and stay with her in Riverplain, a miracle, but deep in his heart he remained conflicted, obviously torn about Malach and his past with Malach's father.

What else? She replayed a recent conversation. His true master, Mage Mantiss, who'd tasked him to spy on Malach's traitor father, was the Head of the Guild. Thinking of the sorrow on Everand's face whenever he spoke of his master, certainty filled her. Mantiss was the deeper source of his angst. Did he now feel he was betraying his true master — on top of his guilt at betraying his former mentor?

Heart thumping, she stopped and stared unseeing at the lake. Everand *was* betraying his master. How would he get past this to become whole and free of guilt? Would her love be enough?

Raising her eyes to the cloudless sky, she murmured, 'Spirits of my ancestors, hear me. I love Everand and would see him whole. Help me to help him.'

A breeze lifted strands of hair from her face. The spirits were listening. Words tumbled past her lips. 'He must be whole, not just for me. Bigger events unfold and he is important.' She frowned, but the truth of this sat strong and secure. Her neck tingled and she closed her eyes, opening her mind to the vision.

The darkness behind her eyelids rolled aside. Everand stood clad in his azure silk robe, hands out wide, while storm clouds roiled and dust swirled around him. Lightning struck the air and earth, but he stood calm and focused. His robe flapped around his legs in gusts of wind. Buffeted, he lifted his arms higher, his lips moving with unheard words.

The gusts eased and the clouds slowed. He smiled, and the clouds softened into clumps of mist. The sun came out, sparkling on his starlight hair and making his robe glint with myriad colours, as bright as a precious stone. Something moved beside him and her heart galloped. She gasped as a version of her — standing tall, confident, fit — emerged. He gazed down at her and reached for her hand. *My rock. My reason for being.*

She flung open her eyes and looked around. It was as if he'd spoken from right next to her. Lake, trees and sky met her eyes. Her mouth ran dry. The vision confirmed what her heart said, what her heart yearned for. But her shoulders felt heavy. She must be strong and stand with him. What could she do to help? She could call birds and apparently dragons — and she could keep a more objective eye on Malach. *You've forgotten the most important thing,* teased her heart and she rolled her eyes. That was a given; she would love him for who he was. No matter what happened.

The chittering of birds reached her from the nearby grove of nut trees and she strode that way, reaching for her calling power. *Whirr! Come.* She'd only taken five steps when a bolt of jade and gold feathers whizzed past her face. Laughing, she held out her arm and Whirr perched on the back of her wrist, cheeping incessantly.

'Really? I'm sure you do have many females to choose from. Don't let it go to your head.' Whirr fluffed his wings and cocked his head. 'For now, you can come with me.' Bringing her hand up, she kissed his downy head and Whirr hopped onto her shoulder. She continued east, towards the hills at the end of the lake.

Glancing up, she gauged the sun to be two-thirds of the way to sun-fade. Already, shadows stretched away from the trees and bushes, and the outlines of the hills were softening. Striding faster, she didn't slow down until she reached the tree with the large red flowers, close to where she'd found Akachi. The vivid red petals had somehow made her just know the dragon was red and gold. The uneasy feeling of being positioned by unseen forces hovered again.

On reaching the small inlet where a still pond formed within the lake she stopped and faced the water. The lake was calm, the sun's rays forming a wide path of golden light across the middle. She tugged off her sandals and waded in up to her knees. Trailing her fingers in the water, she took a deep breath, pushed her aura into the water around her and visualised Akachi, Hanachi and Mizukaze swimming towards her.

Fear trickled through her. There was so much she didn't know about the massive creatures. Easing the frown tugging on her eyebrows, she imagined the dragons rising up from the water to greet her. She'd only taken a few breaths when small waves moved around her fingers. They were coming. Already. Everand would be impressed! Standing up straight, she tried to compose her thoughts.

Three swells of water surged towards her. She bowed respectfully when the dragons fanned out and all three rose up from the water right in front of her. Which one was the lead dragon? Akachi because it was her lake and she was the oldest? Or Mizukaze as the male dragon?

Akachi waddled forward, steam spiralling from her nostrils. A step ahead of the other two, Akachi was enormous with rivulets of water cascading down over her vivid red scales, bright gold spikes along her neck and back and a glistening golden chest. Lamiya swallowed. The red dragon was even bigger than Mizukaze.

The dragon fixed golden irises on her face and rich, deep words resonated in her head. *Lamiya of Riverplain, you brought the other dragons as asked. I greet you as a friend.*

Bowing to her waist, Lamiya said, 'Thank you, Great Akachi. I am honoured. Everand brought Mizukaze and Hanachi to us.'

Your mate? The one with magic who is friend to Mizukaze?

Flushing, Lamiya winced. Akachi had a way of getting right to the point. 'Yes, Mage Everand is my mate and friend to Mizukaze. He would be honoured to become a friend to you too.'

I care not for those with magic, but Mizukaze and Hanachi speak highly of him so I will hold my ire in reserve. The dragon's words rumbled in her mind.

Lamiya looked at the young orange-and-green-scaled dragon, who stretched her elegant, lithe neck forward until her head was close. Lifting a hand, Lamiya put it on Hanachi's nose, feeling the tough and warm scales under her fingertips. 'Your real name is pretty. Much more elegant than calling you Flight, after our boat.'

Hanachi's eyes glowed and her nose quivered. *I enjoyed our races. My name means flower.*

Removing her hand, Lamiya said, 'I would very much like to race with you again, Hanachi.' Her heart thumping, she looked at the red dragon. Wait! Had Akachi just said she didn't care for those with magic? What did the dragon mean? She hadn't even met Everand! Unease washed through Lamiya, making her arms and legs feel weak.

Not knowing how to tackle that subject, she resolved to address safer topics. 'Great Akachi, there will be more races in your honour and we are building a new boat. I would like to ask you …' She searched for the words to frame her question properly. 'On behalf of the people of Riverplain, I am here to ask how you would like the people to speak with you. Do you need anything from us?'

Akachi's hindquarters sank until she sat in the water. Mizukaze edged his blue-and-gold body closer and sat too. Lamiya breathed in slowly, the proximity of the beasts was overpowering and having three pairs of hypnotic golden eyes staring at her was making her truly dizzy. Should she be negotiating with these powerful creatures by herself? Perhaps she should have brought the guides.

Mizukaze shot steam from his nostrils and tilted his face, the sunlight catching his golden horns. *More races and beating of drums would be welcome.*

Lamiya hid her smile. Everand had said the young dragon was most persistent about racing the boats and hearing the drums. 'Of course, Great Mizukaze. Riverplain will host the next inter-province races in colour-leaf season. There will be many races then, and lots of training before.'

Mizukaze made a rumbling sound, which she assumed was approval. *Good. I will make lots of rain for the crops.* Lifting his head, Mizukaze said with a sly edge, *Offerings are welcome too.*

'More rain would be wonderful. I'm sure we can bring offerings for you. Often.' She moved her attention back to Akachi. 'May I introduce you to our leaders? Our guides speak with the spirits of our ancestors and direct our paths. They are keen to meet you.'

Akachi's eyes gleamed and the irises took on extra chasms of depth. She must have said something important! While the dragon stared down, the textured irises shifting and swirling, she noticed Akachi's horns were different. The golden spires were ribbed and curled, whereas the other dragons' horns were like short, smooth antlers. Her pulse quickened. The multiple rings around the horns reminded her of the rings that grew around the oldest trees.

Without being obvious, she peered intently at the dragon, noticing there were wrinkles in the leathery folds around Akachi's eyes, bestowing a deeper, wiser look. She swallowed. Was Akachi much, much older than the other two? Just how long had the dragon been secreted in the lake? Why had she hidden from them?

Bringing her head so close that Lamiya felt the heat radiating from the flared nostrils, Akachi rumbled, *Yes, Lamiya of Riverplain, I would meet with those who speak with the spirits. First, I will meet with your mate with power. I have many questions for him.*

Questions? Lamiya's breath caught. This sounded ominous. To do with the mages? Air brushed her neck and shoulders and she felt the spirits stirring around her. The idea that Akachi was a guide dragon popped into her mind. To hide the astonishment that must surely be reflecting on her face, she bowed. If she was right, this red dragon could indeed be the key to … everything. Whatever 'everything' meant.

She must establish trust. 'Great Akachi, I will bring Mage Everand at sun-up. And I will arrange a meeting with our guides.'

Very well, Lamiya of Riverplain. We will speak when the sun rises. Akachi dipped her gigantic head, turned around, waded deeper and then flowed under the surface. Mizukaze puffed steam at her before he followed. Hanachi fluttered her eyelashes, dropped her lower jaw open like a smile, then also disappeared under a bubble of water.

Her heart pounding against her breastbone, Lamiya stared at the fast-receding bubbles of water. Seeing the three dragons together … Akachi *was* different. She'd called a creature that made Mizukaze look tame; a creature that considered it held equal status to the Riverplain guides. She blew out a breath. The spirit of her deceased mother had said *she* was destined to become the next guide. Was this why Akachi had chosen to speak with her? The dragon *knew* they would eventually be talking leader to leader?

A shiver coursed down her back. U-Mali was old, but hopefully she wouldn't be passing the responsibility on any time soon. A stronger shiver chased down her spine: it would be soon. Very soon. Whirr poked his beak out the front of her tunic, his tiny body quivering, and she stroked the top of his head. 'Indeed, my little friend. What have we become immersed in?'

How many events were going to occur with the next rising of the sun?

Chapter Three

Malach waited until Everand stopped listing the spells of concealment he proposed to teach. Maybe if he learned these quickly, he could ask to be taught more offensive tactics. The mage was annoying, insisting on cowardice and stealth. His hunters would be appalled. He stopped the corner of his mouth from twitching up in a smile. Once he'd mastered the spell of invisibility, he could hide from Everand. How useful. If it looked as if they'd be captured by the Guild mages he could vanish, and then destroy Everand while he was distracted.

The memory of his father's final words slammed into his mind. Mage Beetal had spoken rapidly, his black beard bristling and bushy eyebrows slanted in a scowl: *'My son, I have been betrayed. By my own cursed buffoon of an apprentice. Thanks to Everand, the Guild knows what I've done and I must flee.'* *Father squeezed his shoulder with a firm hand.* *'If I don't return, you will know I have lost and am most likely dead.'* *Father squeezed his shoulder harder.* *'Chinfe was right; you were worthy of training. I'm glad she told me about you.'* *The brown-robed mage withdrew his hand and vanished.*

If only his mage father had taken him as the apprentice instead! Things would be different. Wanting to hurl rocks or bolts of power, Malach clenched his fingers.

'Did you hear what I said?' Everand asked sternly.

'I did not.' The frustration that flitted across Everand's face was satisfying.

'You need to concentrate. We don't have much time.' Everand positioned himself squarely in front of him. 'Tell me, how do you usually find and call your power?'

'Why?'

'So I can teach you how to hide it!' snapped Everand.

Good, he was getting to Everand. Malach frowned. 'I feel it as a pool of energy … located at the base of my stomach.' That sounded imprecise; analysing his magic was hard.

'What colour is it? What does it feel like?' Everand asked.

Focusing, Malach reached for his power and surprise eked into him. 'It is dark brown, like an ancient tree bark. Thick, like soup.'

'Hmm.' Everand looked thoughtful. 'So, your robe would be a chocolate brown, a shade darker than Mage Beetal's. Interesting.' The mage focused. 'I wonder why your power is thick? Mine is more like deep water. Maybe this is to do with you being a half-mage.'

'You digress,' said Malach. He was not a research topic. 'What's next?'

'Feel around the edges of your pool of power. Can you sense where your body ends and the power sits nestled within it?'

Malach probed internally, finally seeing that the pool of dark brown rested between the lowest edges of his hip bones, just below the bottom wall of his stomach. 'I feel it.'

'Imagine muscle, skin and blood closing over the top and front of it. Imagine the pool has taken on the colours and textures of your surrounding body and form a clear, hard wall over it.'

Taking a deep breath, Malach focused. His pool of power kept reverting to its usual colour of dark brown.

'Don't get annoyed. Keep trying.'

Malach sighed. 'Do you practise this at the Guild?'

'No.' Everand ran a hand over his hair. 'This is not taught.'

'Then how do you know how to do it?'

Everand flushed. 'Never mind about that. Do you want to be able to conceal yourself or not?'

Well, well. Judging by his discomfort, Everand had digressed even further from the Guild Law than he already knew about. He felt a grudging surge of respect. If other mages didn't know how to do this, he should pay attention. Half-closing his eyes, he tried again. Meticulously, he pieced together internal camouflage, then constructed a thin but unbreakable clear film and slid it over the top of his power. 'I've done it.'

'Good. Now hold it while I read you.'

Alarmed, Malach took a step away and his shield disintegrated.

Everand arched an eyebrow. 'Try again. You need to be able to hold the concealment despite what's happening around you.'

'You can do this? Who taught you? My father?' He felt a stab of jealousy.

'I taught myself. Stop worrying about it and master it.' Everand flapped a hand skyward. 'The sun is getting lower. Try again.'

Fuelled by irritation, Malach reconstructed his camouflage and shield. He grunted, and immediately Everand's power swept over him, the sensation unpleasant, like a thousand fingers poking and prodding. He fed more strength into his inner shield. His mind began to fatigue with Everand's relentless sweeps and he clenched his jaw. He must pass this test. The sweeps ceased.

'That was good.' Everand looked mildly impressed. 'Keep practising after you return to Lazuli's hut. As soon as you feel a probe like that, raise your block and hold it. No matter where you are and what you're doing.' Everand waved his hands. 'We're likely to feel these broad probes before any mages draw close. Learn to block instinctively.'

Momentary pride filled Malach. He'd mastered a complex spell — one that no-one else could do! Except Everand. He eyed his teacher, who was considering what to cover next. How did Everand contrive to look so harmless and meek and mild, when underneath he possessed these hidden talents? Slippery as a fish. There had to be a *lot* more to Everand than he presented. How else could he have bested his father, who had oozed power and confidence?

Perhaps they had a chance against the Guild after all. If Everand trusted him enough to impart these useful abilities, he should grab every single one. Fast. And consider Everand to be his mentor, at least for now, until he was positioned to drive his own destiny again.

In rapid succession, Malach absorbed the spell of invisibility, easy in comparison, learned to raise a protective shield, and then how to hold this and add the spell of invisibility. The muscles in his arms developed tremors, as if he'd had been out hunting from sun-up to dark-fall. He grunted, not wanting Everand to see his growing fatigue.

'You can drop your arms now,' said Everand, looking pleased. 'You've done well. Sustaining two spells at once is tiring and requires deep concentration.' Everand's gaze flitted away, then returned. 'Your hunting skills give you good base strength.'

Malach felt his jaw drop. Was that praise? He shut his mouth and thought about the mages cloistered in their Guild with humans doing everything manual for them. 'How do mages gain strength? They're not hunters or warriors.'

An odd collection of emotions passed across Everand's face, including discomfort. Malach stared. Had he found a weak point? Come to think of it, his father had only ever taught him one thing at a time.

'We practise. A lot.' Everand drummed his fingers against a thigh and appeared to be deciding what to do next.

Beyond, the lake was absorbing the darker hues of approaching dusk. He should push things along. 'What's the most useful thing I should know?'

'It would be better if we have another sun. You've expended much energy, but there is one more spell you need. Be warned, this spell takes considerable energy, which is why I left it to last.' Everand turned deep-blue eyes on him, with the smallest of frowns.

'What is it?' Malach's pulse quickened.

'Translocation.' Everand hesitated. 'Guild mages use it as a means of moving from one place to another … but it is entirely useful when you're being attacked.' He shifted his weight from one foot to the other.

'This is how you escaped the Guild's trap?' Malach's mind raced. So, *that* was how Everand had eluded four other mages! Yes, the dragons had something to do with it but from what Everand had said the creatures arrived at the end of the confrontation. Combine invisibility with a protective shield *and* sudden shifts of location when the others were using one spell at a time … He straightened his spine. Slippery as a fish wasn't even close. Trying to outmanoeuvre Everand must be like trying to snag a whole shoal with only your fingers.

Hope surged into his chest. He'd lost his father but now had a teacher just as cunning and inventive. Kidnapping the boatwoman so Everand would follow was turning out to be a decision of pure inspiration. *The Guild mages.* Everand referred to the mages as if he was not one of them. The boatwoman must have incredible lure. Regret rose. His mother had held Mage Beetal's attention for a long, long time but hadn't lured him away from the Guild. Lamiya might be more important than he'd realised.

'Are you with me?' Everand snapped his fingers. 'You're not too tired to proceed?'

'Of course not. I was thinking.'

'About what?' Everand looked curious.

'Managing multiple spells.' Watching Everand's face, he asked, 'How many at a time can *you* hold?'

Maintaining a bland expression, Everand said slowly, 'A number. It isn't easy.'

Malach's pulse raced. Everand was hiding something. If he bided his time, perhaps he'd find out what. He shrugged. 'So I am learning. Translocation, then.'

With a thin smile, Everand said, 'I can still remember how your father taught me this one.' He bent over and picked up a hand-sized stone. 'First, we'll move this.' Everand walked to stand beside him and put the stone on the ground in front of their feet. 'Note where the stone is now.'

Malach nodded.

'See that blade of grass bent sideways about two paces away?'

Malach squinted and nodded again.

'Between the stone and that blade of grass are hundreds of molecules of air. We're going to part them, creating a tunnel, and push the rock through the gap.'

'Sounds simple.'

'Not quite. First you have to perceive all the molecules, then part them with your will and generate a push of air. Focus now, reach with your senses and feel the air.'

It took a while, but then his mind suddenly grasped the perception of hundreds of bubbles of air clustered together. Once he saw them, it was easy to nudge some to each side, creating the tunnel. He grunted. 'Got it.'

'Good. Now give the stone a shove.'

Malach shoved — the stone shot forward and crushed the blade of grass. Myriad uses for this ability flooded his mind.

'A stone is a small thing,' said Everand, facing him. 'Moving a large object, such as yourself, requires handfuls of power, dedicated focus and significant mental and physical energy. And you must have a detailed image of *where* you are moving to.'

More grudging respect rose. Doing all this while you were defending yourself would take considerable ability, and an alert mind making rapid decisions. If you fatigued, the consequences would be dire. Malach's mouth ran dry and he licked his lips. 'Understood.'

The shadows leaned away from the hills and trees and Everand's patience seemed boundless. Increasingly, Malach's mind grew sluggish and tried to divert to thinking about simple things like food, drink and sleep. Everand kept pushing him until he moved himself from where they were standing to be poised by the edge of the lake. Tremors racking his legs as well as his arms, he blinked at the water lapping over the toes of his sandals.

'Well done!' shouted Everand, now behind him.

Spinning around, Malach raised both arms in triumph. He'd done it. No way could he summon another spell now, though. No wonder it took so long for the mages to learn their magic and master it. Without his fitness and strength, he wouldn't have got through four spells.

A small bird flew into the clearing and darted to Everand. Was the boatwoman coming? By the smile on Everand's face and the way he immediately looked to the east, yes. Sure enough, Lamiya was approaching with large, brisk strides. Malach waited where he was while she joined Everand and spoke rapidly, waving her hands around. For a moment Everand looked incredulous. The boatwoman must have achieved something.

Turning, Everand beckoned. 'Let's go back.'

Malach joined them, observing the static between them and Lamiya's pent-up excitement. Something momentous had happened, but Lamiya only gave him a polite nod.

'Beram and others from Riverfall will arrive soon.' Everand ran a hand over his hair. 'If they're not already here.'

When the two of them headed back along the shore, Malach fell into step behind them. So, they weren't going to tell him what she'd done. No matter, they'd tell the others and he would listen. Crimping his lips around a yawn, he hoped a meal would be included.

CHAPTER FOUR

Lamiya's hut came into view and Everand smiled on seeing the two hopeepa and cart standing out the front. Beram had arrived before dark-fall, as he'd asked. His pulse lifting, he strode faster. When he approached, the tallest of the hopeepa swung her long neck and fluttered her eyelashes. Crystal! He patted her neck, flinching when her purple tongue rasped up his cheek. The other hopeepa reached her neck under Crystal's and he patted her nose. Topaz, no doubt.

Beram, Tengar, Persaj, Ejad, Acim and Zink all tumbled out of Lamiya's hut and in a blink Everand's back was being thumped by multiple hands.

'Crystal pines for you, so we brought her,' said Persaj.

'Atage sends his regards,' said Tengar.

'For you.' Ejad thrust a cloth bundle at him. 'To thank you properly for saving me from that viper's bite.'

Returning the young man's infectious grin, Everand tugged the string open and lifted a flap of cloth to find a neatly folded azure tunic and a pair of gold-hued trousers. 'Thank you! These look wonderful.' Ejad's grin widened.

Lamiya patted his arm and disappeared into her hut. Hearing women's voices, he realised Mookaite must be inside.

The others stood in a small circle around him and an awkward silence descended. They were all looking at Malach, who hovered to one side. Of course! They weren't expecting to see the half-mage here. Not when he'd caused them so much trouble.

'I have much to tell you. I've brought Malach here to hide him from the Guild.' Everand paused while all their eyes slid to Malach. 'Let's go over everything while we eat.' Embarrassed, he wondered whether Lamiya would have enough food for everyone.

'Good idea,' said Beram. 'Lazuli has gone to fetch a few people and said he'd bring some food too.' He waved a hand at the cart. 'Kunzite packed a sack of loaves for us to share.'

Lamiya stuck her head through the feather curtain. 'Why don't you unload your things, Beram? You and Mookaite can stay here with us. The rest of you can sleep in Lattic's hut, which is the next one along.' Her lips twitched. 'He'll move into Lopa's hut to make room.' She disappeared back through the strings of feathers.

Everand eyed the group, wondering whether they'd all fit in Lamiya's hut. The curtain moved again and Lamiya and Mookaite emerged, carrying blankets.

'I thought we'd sit out here,' Lamiya murmured as she passed him. 'Can you create some of your pretty floating lights?'

While Lamiya and Mookaite spread four blankets on the grass, he created a number of orb lights and hovered them in an arch above the blankets so soft silver light shone down. On impulse, he turned a couple of them green and another couple orange, the Riverplain team colours.

Tengar and Beram laughed.

'Your true loyalty is showing, my friend,' said Beram.

Persaj tapped his elbow. 'Can you help me unhitch the hopeepa and settle them?'

'Of course.' Everand caught Lamiya's eye. 'Where should we put the hopeepa?'

'There's a patch of grass behind Lattic's hut. You could tether them there.'

Creating another orb light, given it was almost too dark to see, he helped Persaj lead the two hopeepa to Lattic's hut. Similar to Lamiya's, the hut also faced the lake.

Lattic rushed out. 'Good timing. I've just cleared enough space.'

Working quickly, Everand helped unload blankets, pillows, bundles of clothes and sacks of food and stacked them neatly in the hut. He and Persaj unhitched the hopeepa and led them to the grassy area. He held the head harness while Persaj expertly attached fetters to a hind foot of both animals, ran out lengths of rope and hammered the tether stakes in. Everand spread out piles of hay while Lattic fetched a wooden tub and filled it with water. Done, Everand gave Crystal a pat. Voices sounded in the darkness and he recognised Lazuli's among them.

Floating the orb light before him, he walked back to Lamiya's hut. The colourful space and blankets were crowded with most of the Riverfall team. Scanning the shadowy faces, he found Malach sitting next to Lepid. With a sigh, he chose to sit on the other side of Malach. After all, he had brought the half-mage here.

For a while, the mood was light and the paddlers bantered while they ate. Lepid produced a tall jar of feeja wine, which they passed around. Under the cascading silver and green light, Everand watched Lamiya chatting animatedly with Mookaite and Lulite. The lights sparkled off her rich mahogany hair and highlighted her cheekbones and fine features. His heart throbbed and he swallowed. This impromptu gathering was nice, but when would they be alone? Lepid thrust the wine jar at him; he wiped the mouth with a sleeve and took a long swig. Nothing would dull the ache of longing. Soon — surely events would slow down soon.

A natural silence stole over the gathering and when all the faces turned to him, eyes shining in the orb light, Everand took a deep breath. The air had turned crisp and cool and beyond the rays of his orbs the moon cast silver beams across the lake. He turned to Malach. 'Do you wish to speak?' When Malach frowned, he murmured, 'It would sound better coming from you.'

Lepid said softly, 'Remember, we already know. Just tell our Riverfall friends.'

Putting down his mug, Malach sat taller. 'I am here because the Guild of mages plans to take my life.'

Everand watched Tengar and Beram's faces, seeing the lifting of eyebrows and widening of eyes.

Lifting his chin, Malach continued. 'Everand tells me the Guild will not tolerate any non-pure mage.' His eyes glinted in the uneven light. 'I am fortunate that Everand told me this and, out of a sense of fairness, brought me here … I am grateful to Riverplain for their help. And now yours.' He pressed his lips closed.

Before the Riverfall paddlers could bombard Malach with questions, Everand spoke. 'I foiled the trap set by my Guild colleagues, but the result is that Malach and I are now *both* fugitives from the Guild's ire.' He flicked his glance to Lamiya. 'The Guild will never sanction my love for Lamiya. In effect, Malach and I fight for the right to live our lives the way we want to … as who we are.' That came out surprisingly eloquent and he averted his gaze from Lamiya's deep smile.

Lamiya leaned forward. 'The Riverplain guides agreed to conceal Malach and Everand, based on this principle. But our actions bring danger.' She waved a hand at him.

'The Guild will send mages.' Everand paused at the collective intake of breath. 'Riverplain prepares as best it can, but the reality is we could face anything up to ten powerful mages.'

'When?' croaked Beram, lines creasing his forehead. Mookaite leaned against his shoulder and grasped his hand.

'Next sun, or the one after,' said Everand.

Leaning forward again, Lamiya added, 'Lazuli and others prepare weapons and strategy. However, U-Mali and U-Lumin have decreed that we will yield Malach rather than resort to violence.'

Everand swallowed. She hadn't said whether they would yield him too. He took in her upright, strong posture. What was she *not* saying? Unease trickled into him. She was brave, confident and growing rapidly in her own abilities ... what might she decide to do of her own accord? How far would she go to protect him?

'We're so glad you have come, good friends.' Lamiya waved her hands. 'Next sun, our guides will call a gathering to agree what we will — and will not — do. We will welcome your views.'

Ejad yawned and everyone laughed.

Lamiya quirked an eyebrow, asking him if there was more to say. When he shook his head, she stood up. 'We should rest. Next sun will be busy and the guides will call an early meeting.'

'We should have come by boat,' said Ejad. 'Then we could have had a race.'

Tengar cuffed Ejad on the shoulder, then Lattic collected the guests staying in his hut and they set off into the darkness. Mookaite and Lamiya bundled up the blankets and Everand was left standing on the grass with Beram, Lazuli and Malach.

'I'll help set out bedding,' said Beram before ambling away to the hut. Lazuli blinked then hurried after him, leaving Everand alone with Malach.

Everand dissipated all but two orbs of silver light, observing the way Malach's face shifted in the shadows. 'Is there something you want to say?'

A breeze ruffled the lake and tiny waves lapped on the shore. The rushes brushed and hissed against each other. Foreboding needling him, Everand said brusquely, 'Ask what you want to know.'

Malach grunted. 'Will that mage come? The one that killed Mahog?'

Everand eyed Malach. Mage Pelamis would be the first to volunteer and had already demonstrated he had no qualms whatsoever about taking life. Mahog being felled by Pelamis' red fire bolt and crumbling into a charred mess flashed into his mind. 'Yes, but trust me, you do not want to challenge that mage head-on.'

By the way Malach's shoulders tensed he considered a warrior's death was preferable.

'You must not do *anything* to precipitate violence and unleash death on the people of Riverplain. Am I clear?' Everand stretched taller.

'Crystal.' Malach scowled.

Silence stretched between them and Everand's nape prickled. Lamiya didn't trust Malach … perhaps he shouldn't either.

Out of the gloom, Lazuli approached tentatively. 'Are you finished?'

Everand nodded. 'Yes. See you at the guides' gathering?'

'Unless anything happens before then.' Lazuli gave him a grim smile before he tapped Malach's arm and the two of them strode away, heading to Lazuli's hut.

His stomach twisting with unease, Everand gazed at the lake. The waters were still and clear, reflecting the half-moon sitting high in the velvet sky and the dusting of first stars. Soon, he and Lamiya could sit and watch this scenery every dark-fall. He had to hang onto that.

Detecting soft footfalls padding up behind him, he held up an arm and Lamiya slid underneath it and nestled against him.

He kissed the top of her head. She slipped her arm across his lower back and nudged him closer to the water, away from the hut. His pulse sped up.

At the water's edge, she turned to face him and slipped her other arm around his waist. Her expression serious, she said, 'There's something I have to tell you.'

'Now?' His mouth felt dry. What else could possibly happen? He groaned. She'd been speaking with the dragons. 'The dragons?'

Moonlight rippled over her hair, making the caramel threads stand out against the darker mahogany. She chewed her lower lip. 'They came to me. Akachi … Akachi is different. She is bigger, older, wiser. I think she is a dragon leader.'

Everand's chest grew tight. What were the implications of this? Lamiya looked worried and she wanted to tell him alone. 'What is it?'

Moonlight reflecting in her deep grey eyes, Lamiya said, 'Akachi wants to speak to you. At first light.'

'Me?' Fingers of fear gripped him. *First light.* 'Why the urgency?'

Reaching up to caress his cheek, Lamiya said softly, 'Akachi asked if you were the one with magic. I think it is something to do with your mages.'

The air left his chest as fast as if someone had punched him. Everything was complicated enough already! How could there be yet another twist, yet another layer? His vision blurred and Lamiya's words tumbled around him.

'We have to get up *before* the sun rises to speak with the dragons ahead of the main gathering.'

Thoughts exploded into his mind. How could they fit all that in? He could translocate them. But that would leave an energy trail. What if the Guild came? Did Akachi want to speak to him before any mages arrived? How old was this dragon? What did she know? How could the dragon know of the mages if the mages didn't know of the dragons? His instincts howled and screamed: the early mages. The granite wall. Was it to deflect the dragons? It was high enough.

Lamiya gently shook him. 'I'm sorry. Akachi's request was unexpected. Are you alright?'

Gazing down, he forced his eyes to focus on her beautiful face. She trailed her fingers down his cheek and hooked one under his jaw, pulling his face towards hers. Her eyes grew darker and she parted her lips. He anchored his mouth over hers, seeking her warmth and love. A shudder eased down his spine and he broke away to rest his chin on the top of her head, loving the way her hair tickled.

'Come to bed,' she murmured. 'We can hold each other until the sun wakes.'

That was true. He would hold her tight until the sun rose. Curse this mission. Curse its twists and turns. He closed his eyes and drew air into his chest. *Perhaps our reward for whatever we have to do is each other.*

It had better be.

Chapter Five

Mage Mantiss lay half-propped against the pillows, watching darkness creep down the windows. The chaotic events at sun-up seemed a lifetime ago. With each shallow breath his heart rattled and skittered. How had it come to this? Surely, Everand had some greater plan? His loyal spy *couldn't* have abandoned the Guild. Abandoned *him*. No matter how hard he tried to push these thoughts aside, despair flooded in.

Closing his eyes, Mantiss pressed deeper into the pillows, his muscles disconcertingly limp and shivery. His ears detected someone tiptoeing around in the dining area and the aroma of spicy stew teased at his nostrils. The sun-fade meal already? Other sounds reached him: Tiliqua conferring with Delma the cook, a distant knock at the front door, the rumble of Agamid's gentle voice. Footsteps approaching.

'Come along, my friend,' said Agamid. 'Time for some sustenance. We have much to discuss.'

Mantiss flapped a hand.

Louder, Agamid said, 'You are the Head of the Guild. We need your strategic mind on this. Let me help you up.'

Shards of pain criss-crossed Mantiss' body when Agamid slid an arm behind his shoulders and nudged him upright. His spine creaked with the effort and he couldn't supress his grunt of discomfort.

'Let me help.' Tiliqua rushed into the bedroom and came to his other side, a hint of violets wafting with her movements.

Mantiss let them turn him sideways and then tip him forward until he felt the cool marble tiles beneath his feet. He wanted to tell them he could manage, but his legs were ignoring his commands to push him upright. Leaning on both of their arms, he levered up.

'Take a breath or two,' advised Agamid.

Complying, Mantiss felt feeble strength seep into his legs and feet. He took a fumbling step. Then another. His heart gave a warning twinge and he stood taller. While the others helped him to the dining table, he encouraged his mind to focus. Saliva formed at the tantalising smells of the stew.

Once eased into his chair, he reached for his napkin, ignoring the usual tremor in his hands, and watched Agamid and Tiliqua sit and pick up their cutlery. Grasping his fork firmly, Mantiss speared some meat and chewed it carefully. More strength ebbed into him.

After another few mouthfuls, he waved his fork at Agamid. 'What is happening?'

Around a worried smile, Agamid said, 'Your collapse has stalled things, but Pelamis and Simoselaps are busy spreading the word of Everand's treachery. They aim to precipitate a sortie to capture Everand and call him to account.'

'The response is mixed,' said Tiliqua. 'Many mages remain loyal to you and wait for you to summon the councils.'

'Pelamis is gathering supporters,' interrupted Agamid. 'We can't afford to wait long. The upstart is strident in his persuasion. It doesn't help that Simoselaps was injured and is adept at describing the primitive hunter who shot him with an arrow.'

Putting down his fork with a clatter, Mantiss said, 'The fools have no idea of the greater risk.' His mouth twisted with bitterness. 'Neither does Everand.'

Tiliqua focused her clear, blue eyes on him. 'Just before you passed out again, you muttered something about a … water dragon?'

Fear shivered through Mantiss. So, he *had* spoken. He'd hoped that might have been a delusion. Across the table, Agamid was regarding him intently, both eyebrows raised and concern spilling from his hazel eyes. Mantiss' heart gave three jolting skips. Lapemis and all the preceding Heads of the Guild demanded secrecy, but could he afford to remain silent? If he didn't reveal the real risk, events would spiral further out of control. He sighed; maybe they would spiral regardless. Everand's simple mission had been fraught from the outset.

'Father,' said Tiliqua, a determined set to her jaw, 'you must confide in us. Events are escalating rapidly and we can't help you if we don't understand what you fear.'

'I concur,' said Agamid, stroking his neatly trimmed beard. 'Something troubles you sufficiently to affect your health. We want to help.' His hand stilled and his eyes grew sad. 'We also need to discuss what you think Everand is up to.'

Delaying them, Mantiss retrieved his fork and stabbed at another piece of meat, but the flavour cloyed in his mouth, mingling with the taste of failure. Struggling, he forced the lump of stew down and took a shallow breath. 'Since Lapemis founded this new Guild, each successive Head has been granted access to Lapemis' ancient notebook, which details the arrival of the mages on this island and their path to settling here.' He paused at Tiliqua's sharp intake of air.

'Go on.' Agamid nodded.

'One thing that was *not* scribed in the annals, and has been concealed from all subsequent generation mages, is that Axis — here — was chosen due to its distance from the river. And lakes.'

'We have the eternal spring,' said Tiliqua with a frown. 'We don't need the river.'

Mantiss sighed. 'You misunderstand me. The mages *fled* from the river and lakes.' He smiled at the way Tiliqua and Agamid both bolted upright in their chairs.

'Fled?' said Agamid sharply. 'Why?'

Flexing his fingers, Mantiss considered. How much should he reveal? The councils needed to be worried about the possibility of an irate water dragon, but did they need to know about the true origin of the Staropal? How much damage would be wreaked if the mages understood the extent of *that* lie? Perhaps he could tread a middle path.

'The annals state that before they found this island, the small group of refugee mages on *Wavestrider* encountered a massive sea serpent.'

'Yes, I remember,' interjected Tiliqua, her eyes bright. 'It tried to sink the ship and they deflected the beast with death-shards to its eyes.'

'Indeed. Then the boat was engulfed by a severe storm and was wrecked upon the rocky shore. The *eastern* shore.' As he anticipated, they both frowned, no doubt wondering why Axis was built on the western shore. 'They also encountered a serpent in the first lake they came to.' He took a swallow. 'They killed it.' He swallowed again. 'Then they found its mates.'

Tiliqua put a hand over her mouth, then hurriedly composed herself. 'The other serpent chased them?' Her frown cleared. 'It was another water beast, so they put as much distance as possible between the water and where they chose to settle.'

Not trusting himself to speak, Mantiss nodded. They would work the next part out for themselves.

Drumming his fingers on the table, Agamid spoke slowly. 'Let me see if I can guess correctly how we have reached this point … the contact from one of the provinces worried you. Even more worrisome was the fact the four provinces were organising to trade with each other.'

Mantiss held his breath.

'So, you were happy for Everand to go to the provinces and sort out their issue and, at the same time, you realised he'd be able to report whether there was any sign of these serpents? But you didn't tell him that?'

'You know me well, my friend,' Mantiss murmured. 'It seemed too good an opportunity to gather information to let it go by.' Vainly trying to quell the tremor in his hands he clasped them tightly together. 'The messenger man Beram said the river was called *Dragonspine* River. Why name it that unless there were serpents or dragons? I'd hoped the beasts were long dead, but at that point I understood the risk might be far greater than I first thought.'

Tiliqua leaned forward. 'Why didn't you tell Everand? I thought you trusted him implicitly?'

'I do. I did.' Mantiss winced, his heart throbbing painfully. 'On his previous mission, I didn't tell Everand I suspected Mage Beetal had transgressed so he would spy on his mentor with objective and clear eyes. I applied the same principle for this mission and, of course, I didn't want him to go *looking* for serpents!'

Sitting back, Agamid exhaled loudly. 'And you didn't want any possible dragons to encounter Everand outside the Guild. Alone. Everand didn't mention any serpents or dragons in his report, but he told us about the rogue half-mage. Were you expecting that?'

Sadness roiled through Mantiss. 'Beram's description of massive and aggressive moths concerned me. Something was clearly amiss, which I confided to you, but I wasn't sure what to expect.' He clasped his fingers together so tightly his knuckles turned white. 'I did indeed fear there'd been another breach of the wall. Already. But this time, I had no idea who it could be. I was worried about it being one of us again, from *inside* the wall.'

'I see.' Agamid rapped his fingertips on the table. 'Then when the trap went awry, Saiphos, Pelamis and I saw the dragons at the lake in Riverwood. The creatures clearly *knew*

Everand.' Agamid shook his head. 'The dragons even protected him. I don't understand. Why didn't Everand tell us he'd found dragons?'

Struggling to draw a breath through the tight bands snapping around his chest, Mantiss murmured, '*That*, I wish I knew.' The pain in his chest threatened to overwhelm him and, utterly exhausted, he leaned hard against the chair back.

'Enough,' said Tiliqua softly. 'We can see how much this pains you.'

Agamid shook his head rigorously. 'Nonetheless, we *must* work this out. What possible reasons could Everand have for concealing the dragons? He seemed reluctant to tell us about the rogue half-mage, but we managed to coax that out of him. Yet he said not one word about the bigger issue!'

Using the back of the chair to hold himself upright, Mantiss closed his eyes and recalled snippets of the notes Lapemis had made when he first encountered the water dragons. What were the precise words?

'Lapemis found a great red dragon in an underwater cave. These were the words he wrote: *Although similar to the sea serpent, these beasts were not the same. These had four powerful legs, a clear neck, body and tail and a longer face, shaped like that of a horse. The one before me felt sentient, graced with power and elegance.*'

Opening his eyes, he found Agamid and Tiliqua sitting with their mouths in an astounded O. 'Lapemis somehow negotiated with this beast. He granted it mercy, stunning it instead of killing it.'

Tiliqua frowned. 'Why flee from it then?' Her blue eyes grew intent. 'Negotiated what?'

Squirming, Mantiss muttered, 'Safe passage out of the cave? Across the land?'

Agamid blew out a breath. 'Are you thinking Everand has also negotiated something with these dragons? Following in Lapemis' footsteps, but unknowingly?'

Mantiss tilted his head. That made sense. But it still didn't explain why Everand hadn't mentioned them.

Tipping forward, Agamid spoke evenly. 'Everand told me to tell you he is sorry. He said he couldn't obliterate anybody, not even the rogue half-mage. I knew this was harder for him because not only had he met this rogue Malach, but the half-mage is Beetal's son.'

Speaking faster, Agamid waved his hands about. 'I think Pelamis got it right. Everand *had* hidden Malach! He knew our sortie would fail and that Pelamis would be a real threat. He must also have known the dragons were in that lake. Perhaps he hoped they would save him?'

Leaning forward too, Tiliqua said, 'This feels consistent with what we know of Everand. I *knew* he wouldn't let some half-mage outwit him to drop a sack over his head! He was lying about that. But why go with this Malach …' She tailed off, her gaze distant.

'He said he wanted to find out more,' muttered Mantiss, a bud of relief forming in his heart.

'Maybe he wanted to decide for himself whether this Malach deserved to be obliterated,' said Agamid. 'He knew the council would decree this fate. Sadly, I think he couldn't bring himself to condone it.'

'So,' said Mantiss, 'the good news is Everand does not intend harm to the Guild. The bad news is–'

'He's exposed the Guild to *two* significant risks,' concluded Tiliqua, eyes flashing with determination. 'Worse, he is colluding with both the dragons and the half-mage. He has to be stopped.'

Mantiss' heart shrank, as if squeezed by unseen hands. Stopped how? If only he hadn't sent Everand on this cursed mission.

He should have left things alone.

Chapter Six

Lamiya snuggled into Everand's chest, loving the way he immediately kissed her head and tightened his arm across her. He hadn't slept much. Each time she woke, she'd felt him lying tense, his mind churning with analysis. Beram's snores hadn't helped.

The darkness in the hut felt less dense; sun-up was approaching. She tenderly stroked his cheek. 'We should get up.'

He brushed her fingers with his lips, slithered from under the blanket and rummaged around retrieving his clothes. She reached for hers, folded neatly at the bottom of the bed. Once dressed, she grabbed a bag of bread and nuts and padded to the door. Outside, her breath misting in the greyness, she waited for Everand. As soon as he'd laced his sandals, she took his hand and squeezed it. He would need her. Taking a breath, she set off towards the lake.

'Wait,' said Everand. 'I'll take us. Visualise the place where the dragons will be.' He put his hands on her hips.

She brought to mind the image of the curve in the shore, the pond within the lake, the tree with the enormous red flowers. Her arms tingled when cold air moved around her and greyness swirled as if she were wading through a thick mist. The ground jarred against her feet and they were standing next to the tree.

Stretching up, Everand plucked an ornate, red flower and tucked it behind her ear.

'I suppose we have to get wet?' His crooked smile didn't hide his tension.

'Just to our knees.' How could she ease his nerves? She couldn't: she had no idea what Akachi was going to say, or what it would mean, only that it was going to be of fundamental importance. Her bones throbbed with the certainty of this.

Silently, they removed their sandals and she kept hold of his hand while they waded out to knee depth.

'It doesn't feel any warmer to me,' murmured Everand. 'Colder, if anything.'

Letting go of his hand, she trailed her fingers in the water. 'Refreshing,' she said, teasing. 'We could swim afterwards.'

'Very funny.' Everand trailed his hands in the water beside hers.

Closing her eyes, she projected her presence into the water. *Great Akachi, we have come. Everand is ready to speak with you.*

Everand's hands jerked and he looked sideways at her. 'When did you learn dragon-tongue?'

'I don't know. I just think what I need to say …' The sky and water tilted around her with the sense of being moved around to achieve things. Drawing in a breath, she thrust her fingers back into the water. If she could speak dragon-tongue then she'd be able to follow what Akachi and Everand spoke about! Excitement shivered through her.

'They're coming.' Everand tilted his head at three swells of water speeding toward them.

Joy and awe filled her; she'd never grow tired of seeing the dragons. Maybe later she could speak with Hanachi and find out how the dragon had attached herself to their boat, Flight. 'By the way,' she said quickly, 'Flight's proper dragon name is Hanachi.'

The water peeled aside with great swooshing waves and Akachi rose up to tower above them. Like last time, Mizukaze and Hanachi flanked Akachi from a little back. Everand straightened up and she saw his quick swallow when he realised how much bigger Akachi was.

She bowed. 'Great Akachi, thank you for coming. This is my mate, Mage Everand.'

Also bowing deeply to the red dragon, Everand said, 'I am honoured to meet you, Great Akachi.' He bowed to Mizukaze and Hanachi. 'Greetings, my valued friends.'

Holding her breath, Lamiya regarded the red dragon, which reared poised, textured irises shifting with suppressed eagerness as she stared down at Everand.

You are a mage from Axis? asked Akachi.

'Yes,' said Everand. 'I was a member of the Mages' Guild.'

Steam hissed from Akachi's nostrils and her pupils narrowed to black slits. *How many seasons have you walked this ground?*

If Everand was surprised by the question he didn't show it. 'Twenty-six full turnings of the seasons,' he responded. 'Our kind lives for around eighty season-cycles.'

Was this important? Lamiya stared at him. Oh! He was expecting Akachi to refer to something that had happened a long time ago. Before he was born. Perhaps before any of the current mages were born. She swallowed. Had he already guessed the issue?

Such a short span. Akachi lashed her tail and ripples curled past her legs. *Your Guild has something that belongs to me. I would have it back. You must fetch it.*

All colour draining from his face, Everand swayed as if he'd been struck. She just caught his look of devastation before he bowed low. 'What is this thing, and how did the Guild acquire it?'

Akachi wagged her head from side to side, steam spurting from her nostrils. *Do not play tricksy with me. Your kind has done enough damage. You must make it right.*

Behind Akachi, Mizukaze reared up and roared, his hot breath washing over her and Everand. Lamiya tipped her head down, waiting for it to pass. Her heart pounded so hard she could barely think. Glancing at Everand, she stiffened her spine and tried to emulate his calm demeanour. Although, for once he seemed lost for words.

She turned to Akachi. 'Great Akachi, may I ask a question or two? I'd like to understand what is happening.' Her knees trembled when Akachi swung her massive head around and fixed her in a baleful glare.

You may ask, but do not seek to dissuade me.

'Thank you, Great Akachi.' Lamiya licked her lips, working moisture into her mouth. 'May I respectfully ask if this thing was taken from you directly? I mean taken from *you*, not your ancestors?'

Akachi's lower jaw dropped open and a forked purple tongue swiped over jagged ivory fangs. *Yes. The stone was taken from my lair.* Steam spurted from her nostrils. *By mages seeking power.*

Questions rushing into her head, Lamiya slid her glance to Everand, who was frowning. 'Can I ask how long ago this was?'

A growl reverberated in Akachi's chest. *If mage-kind live for eighty cycles, then the people came four lifespans ago.*

This meant Akachi was four hundred season-cycles old! Trying to conceal her surprise, Lamiya clasped her hands in front of her. 'May I respectfully ask how long the lifespan of your kind is?' Out of the corner of her eye she caught Everand's grateful look.

Akachi's irises gleamed a burnished gold, and the textures shifted and glinted with deeper threads of gold. *My kind can live for five hundred turnings of the seasons.* She tilted her head. *My sister, Mizuchi, lived for almost four hundred cycles.*

Everand bowed, indicating his intention to speak. 'Great Akachi, at the time this thing was taken, was your lair here in this lake? Or was it in the lake by the waterfall?'

Akachi flared her nostrils, the lining glowing flame red. *This is my lake. The tricksy mages crept down the hills.* Flames flickered in her mouth. *They swam to our lair, killed our mate and took the power stone.*

Her mind reeling, Lamiya faced Everand. 'Do you know what stone she refers to?'

His eyes turning the deepest blue, he said sadly, 'I'm afraid I might.' Clearing his throat, he regarded the dragon. 'Great Akachi, is this stone the size of a human head, shaped like a star and filled with all the colours of a sky-arch?'

You have seen it? Akachi lashed her tail and lowered her head until her nose touched Everand's face. He flinched, but held his ground. *Yessss, I smell the stone on you. You have touched it!*

Mizukaze and Hanachi both pricked up their ears and stared at Everand.

Lamiya swallowed bile. Everand had *touched* this powerful thing? There was so much she didn't know about him. Was he a humble spy as he claimed, or was he something more?

'Regrettably, I confirm the Mages' Guild has the stone, although they do not often use it.'

Roaring, Akachi snaked her head alarmingly close to Everand's face. *You must bring it back. My kind needs it. We are now too few.*

Heart pounding, Lamiya held her tongue. This was between Akachi and the Guild. What would Everand do? Her throat constricted. To get this stone he'd have to go back to the Guild. If it held power, then the mages would hardly relinquish it! He'd surely be killed for even trying. Her forehead throbbed. If the mages lost the stone, would they lose their power? What did this all mean?

His face pale, Everand said slowly, 'Great Akachi, I will try. We younger mages did not know the stone belonged to you. We were told it was ours, found in the eternal spring in Axis, where we live.' He faltered at the jets of fire scorching the air just above his head. 'I won't hide from you that the Mages' Guild will not release this stone lightly.'

They'd be fools if they did, snapped Akachi. *But it is not theirs. You are different.* The golden hues shifted in her irises. *You are connected to the stone. I can feel it. You can bring it back.*

With a deep bow, Everand hid any consternation he might feel. 'I will try to find a way. It will take some time.'

Finding her courage, Lamiya waded forward a step. 'Great Akachi, Mage Everand always keeps his word, and I will help him. I request that you grant us some time.' She spread her hands in appeal. 'I will come to tell you of our plans.'

While Akachi tilted her head considering, steam coiling from her nostrils, Lamiya's mind reeled. How could Everand be connected to this special stone? Did he not know that? Behind the dragons, the water was becoming bluer and primrose light was rolling down the flanks of the hills. The water around her knees felt cold. She dared not look away but began to worry that the guides would call the gathering before they got back.

Akachi lowered her head until it was level with theirs. *Mage Everand of Axis and Lamiya of Riverplain, hold out your hands.*

Foreboding flooded her: the dragon was going to bind them to this task. But what choice did they have? Working some moisture back into her mouth, she straightened her spine and held both arms out straight in front her, palms down. Everand copied her posture.

When Akachi slid her head forward and took Everand's right hand into her mouth, Lamiya held her breath. Tears burned the back of her eyes at the way he inclined his head and stood proudly tall. *Such courage.* Her knees trembled. Could she show the same courage?

Akachi gently squeezed her jaw closed and Everand shut his eyes. The dragon's mouth moved subtly, then she opened her jaws and Everand slowly withdrew his hand. He opened his eyes and nodded to the dragon.

Lamiya wanted to examine his hand, but he dropped it by his side. A tremor set into her outstretched arms and, cursing under her breath, she forced her arms straighter and stiffer while the dragon shifted closer. Fixing her gaze on the dragon's chest of glistening red-and-gold scales, she admired the intricate alignment, noticing what perfect protection they provided with no gaps or weak spots. Her forehead pinched. What odd thoughts.

Heat enveloped her left hand when Akachi folded her jaws over it. Lamiya willed more strength into her spine. She must do this. She felt a sharp sting when Akachi sunk a single fang into the back of her hand, missing bones and sinews. A droplet of blood welled, and a leathery hot tongue rasped over her hand. Cooler air flowed over her skin when Akachi withdrew. Relief tumbling through her, she blinked. Was that it?

Akachi waddled three paces backwards. *I bind you both to this task. I have waited a long time for you. Do not fail me, Mage Everand of Axis and Lamiya of Riverplain.*

She and Everand bowed at the same time. When they straightened up, the three dragons dipped their noses then reversed and sank under the water. The back of her hand tingling, Lamiya waited until the bubbles of water were distant. When she turned, she found Everand looking at her, his expression tight.

Picking up his right hand, she twisted it. In the middle of the back of his hand was a faint white mark, like an old scar. Feeling her eyebrows lift, she looked up at his face. 'Are you alright?'

He gave her a tremulous smile. 'You mean aside from just having my world turned upside down?' His jaw clenched. 'I'd begun to suspect we were not being taught an accurate history at the Guild and Akachi has verified this.'

'Let's get out of the water. We have so much to talk about.' Keeping hold of his hand, she waded back to shore. While they were putting their sandals on, she said, 'As much as I'd rather sit and talk for a while, we should go back and get ready for the gathering.'

'Agreed, and besides, Beram and Mookaite are probably awake.' Everand stood and put his hands on her hips again.

On tiptoe, she reached up to kiss him. 'I'm beginning to feel like you do — so much to consider and so little time.'

The twinkle back in his eyes, Everand kissed her deeply. 'So little time for the really important thing — being with you.'

A warm glow coursed through her as the lake and shore dissipated into whirling greys and blues.

Chapter Seven

Everand set them down gently on the patch of grass near Lamiya's hut. He could hardly wish Lamiya hadn't found the dragon in her lake, he couldn't begrudge her achievement, but the task he'd been set was impossible. To even try meant he'd have to return to the Guild. He'd be lucky to escape twice.

Did Mantiss and Agamid know about the origin of the Staropal? How could they, if the stone was taken so long ago? Wait. Was *this* why Mantiss was suddenly keen to renovate the antiquity area of the library and remove the ancient texts? Did his master fear his time as Head of the Guild was drawing to a close and didn't want his successor trying to find out more about the Staropal? He yanked his mind back from the thousand questions forming; they had enough to worry about as it was.

'Explain later what this task means. Let's eat before the guides call us, and get through whatever this sun brings.' Lamiya gave his arm a squeeze and marched into her hut.

He trailed after her, pushing down the idea that if they didn't survive the events of this sun Akachi's task wouldn't matter. The aroma of warm bread seeping into his nostrils, he greeted the guests from Riverfall, already gathered around Lamiya's leaf-shaped table with loaves and mugs of brew. He snaffled two of the square loaves with snips of green and brown on top, the savoury loaf made by Kunzite that he so liked. Then

56

he wedged his way in beside Beram, and Mookaite handed him a steaming mug.

'You're up early,' commented Beram.

'We had to see the dragons. There are now three in this lake.' Everand bit into his loaf.

Tengar leaned forward and said, 'Will Mizukaze come back to our lake and river? How will we race him if he doesn't?'

Everand shrugged. Good question. Who knew what the dragons would do?

'Yo!' called Lazuli from the doorway.

'Come in, if you can,' called Lamiya.

Edging his way in, Lazuli stood just inside the door, Malach squeezing in beside him.

Everand dipped his head at Malach, taking in the half-mage's dishevelled appearance, clad in a worn and rumpled tunic with bits of hay protruding from his hair. They were at least taking the external disguise part seriously. On impulse, he flung a probe across the room.

Malach grunted and raised his block just in time.

Mookaite approached Malach with a mug of brew and Everand hurled another probe just as he reached out to take it. Malach shot another block into place but failed to grasp the mug, which dropped to the floor and bounced. Hot brew sloshed over Mookaite's feet and she jumped back with a yelp.

'Sorry!' said Everand. 'But better that he passed my test.'

Retrieving the mug, Mookaite gave him a sour look. 'Refrain while I make him another mug?'

Picking up a small loaf, Everand tossed it at Malach, following it with a probe.

Catching the loaf with one hand, Malach held his block up effectively and bit into the loaf with a smug expression.

Looking at the circle of curious faces, Everand said, 'Malach needs to be able to conceal his power. The mages from the Guild will probe for our presence before they appear.'

Lazuli's expression sharpened. 'So, we'll have some warning?'

'Maybe, and not much.' Everand thought of the slim book of tactical spells he'd stolen from the Guild library, currently concealed under his pillow. Were there other books with similar spells in the library? Hopefully not, or Pelamis and Simoselaps might learn how to conceal their advance probes.

Lamiya frowned and put down her mug. 'The guides have called us to the Meeting Place, ahead of the gathering.'

Wishing there was time for a second mug, Everand finished his drink. Everyone was already pushing up to their feet, but Lamiya paused mid-rise with a distant expression. Was U-Mali communicating with her further? He waited for her while the others filed out of the hut.

The focus came back in her grey-blue eyes and she twisted her fingers together. 'They also want to talk with just you and me after.'

She looked nervous, but now was not the time to press her. Everand moved around the table to give her a hug. 'It begins, my love.' He kissed her hair. 'We can do this. One step at a time.'

'I have noticed this is your style.' She gave him a challenging smile. 'I'd rather run and leap but we can plod, if you prefer.'

Smiling, he tugged her to the door and pushed through the feather thongs. A mind-numbing bolt hurtled at his head. Dropping Lamiya's hand, he raised a shield and the bolt bounced off. Shaken, he looked at Malach standing a few paces away.

'Two can play at that game,' said Malach.

'Good try,' said Everand, wishing his pulse would slow down. Thank the spirits that was Malach and not the Guild already! A timely reminder that he must keep his wits about him. *Constantly*. Seeing Lamiya's worried look, he said, 'Malach and I are testing each other. It's good practice.' The measured look she gave him was not reassuring.

He fell into step with her as she strode towards the Meeting Place, her shoulders set in a tense square. Could it be that she didn't like Malach gaining in skill? He exhaled a long breath. Yes, there was risk attached to this course, but there was also risk attached to Malach having insufficient ability to conceal himself when the Guild arrived. There were no easy decisions on this mission. Tickling sweat broke out along his nape.

They rounded the curve at the top end of the lake and the Meeting Place loomed above them. Facing east, the elegantly carved wooden slats of the entry to the shrine gleamed in the rising sunlight. The muscles in her legs bulging, Lamiya took the steps two at a time and Everand's breath quickened as he tried to emulate her feat. Behind him, Malach give an amused snort.

At the top of the steps, he briskly removed his sandals and purified his hands at the water bowl, then he and Lamiya padded across the woven rush mats with Lazuli and Malach at their heels. They all bowed to U-Mali and U-Lumin.

U-Lumin said, 'Lazuli and Malach of Riverwood, take these cushions before me. Lamiya and Everand, sit before U-Mali.' He waved a hand at the row of four cushions, and sat down.

U-Mali peered brightly at each of them before she folded forward from her waist, her tokens of office clinking with the movement. 'I see events continue to evolve around us, and time is passing rapidly.' She fixed keen eyes on Everand. 'First, I ask Mage Everand to tell how his plans of concealment are progressing.'

'Malach is a fast learner. We've been working on blocking search probes and how to bury, or hide, our power. This sun we'll work on invisibility and do more work on translocation.' He stopped. Would any of this be enough?

'Yes, Mage Everand, I *do* wish to know whether this will be sufficient,' said U-Mali firmly.

Trying not to wince, Everand took a breath. 'We can conceal Malach among your people, but this might not be enough. It depends how many Guild mages come, and how determined they are.'

'I like your honesty.' U-Mali sat back. 'You have been seen here by many of my people. What is your strategy if you are found?'

'If we are both found, our best option is to step away from any of your people and surrender ourselves.' Out of the corner of his eye he saw Malach's spine stiffen. His mouth felt full of gritty sand, but he should make the next point. 'I know honesty is important to your people, and the boat team know Malach is here, but it would be better if the rest of your people didn't know.'

Lamiya wriggled on her cushion. So did Lazuli.

Everand pressed on. 'If the people don't know, it can't be read from their expressions or their minds. Also, the mages don't know Malach because they have never met him. However, as you said, your people have seen me and if my presence is detected, the mages will know immediately who I am. I'm prepared to yield to the Guild and leave Malach concealed. There's no reason why he should be in this province, whereas the council will remember this is where they found me last time.'

Her throat moving with a large swallow, Lamiya tensely faced forward. Malach and Lazuli both scowled.

Deep creases forming around her eyes, U-Mali smiled. 'Your integrity is admirable.' Next, looking thoughtful, and somewhat sad, she twisted to look at U-Lumin, who responded with a faint nod.

Unsure what the guides were thinking, Everand added, 'There are some who respect me at the Guild and my fate is not yet determined — not like Malach's.' He slid a look to Lamiya. 'You know I'd try to find my way back.' Not that he liked his chances.

With a sharp nod, U-Mali turned to Lazuli. 'If the mages arrive with violence, what do you plan?'

'The boat team, and the guests from Riverfall, have been training with staves, spears and slingshots. But other than providing a distraction, I doubt we could achieve much. I don't like it, but Everand's plan is probably best.' Lazuli's fingers twitched in his lap, betraying his tension.

U-Mali next gave Lamiya such a long, considered look that she wriggled on her cushion. Lips pressed tightly together, Lamiya developed a deep crimson blush, put her hands in her lap and looked down.

A chill ran down Everand's arms. What were they communicating about? Knowing Lamiya, she had other ideas and U-Mali was endeavouring to constrain her.

Last, U-Mali turned to Malach. 'Malach of Riverwood, do you have anything to add?'

'I will learn as fast as I can and do my best to remain hidden, as much as this irks me.' Malach lifted his chin. 'I won't let myself be taken. I'd rather die fighting honourably.'

Frustration rising, Everand closed his eyes. But if he were in Malach's place, what would he do? The same — his stomach roiled at the very idea of the chamber of obliteration and standing trapped in there, being watched by impassive mages while death rained down. The best he could do was make sure no-one died fighting with Malach.

U-Lumin leaned forward to place a wiry hand on Malach's shoulder. 'We appreciate your honesty. Let's hope this doesn't come to pass.' He sat back.

For a long few moments U-Mali and U-Lumin sat with their heads tipped down and their hands composed in their laps. Assuming they were conferring by mind-speak, Everand glanced at Lamiya. She was frowning, but didn't have the focused look she would've had if they were including her. Malach looked as if he would rather be elsewhere, and Lazuli seemed subdued and downcast.

A clear horn note sounded from the base of the steps and Everand lifted his head. The horn sounded again, the notes echoing across the lake. His heart beat faster; they were calling the gathering.

The guides opened their eyes and U-Mali waved a hand. 'Lazuli and Malach, go now and conceal yourselves among the people. Lamiya and Everand, remain here.'

Lamiya gave him a faint smile while Lazuli and Malach rose, bowed and left with rapid steps.

'We have an announcement to make.' U-Mali turned bright eyes on them. 'Mage Everand, I sincerely hope you will not need to deliver yourself to the Guild. However, so many of my people already know who you are, it won't make a difference if the rest know too.'

Just as Everand opened his mouth to ask what announcement, two women rushed in from the side of the Meeting Place. The guides stood and the women moved their chairs forward several paces, to a spot where they would be visible from the lake shore. The sounds of hurrying footsteps and the chattering of people responding to the horn summons drifted up, echoing off the water. The women next moved two cushions to the right of U-Mali's chair.

'Lamiya, dear heart, sit on my right. Mage Everand, sit by her side,' instructed U-Mali.

His neck rigid with tension, Everand sat on his heels on his designated cushion, barely managing to return Lamiya's nervous smile. What was going on? While U-Mali and U-Lumin were accepting mugs of water from the women, he swept his gaze over the gathered people. The guests from Riverfall stood in the front row with the paddlers from Riverplain. The paddlers' usual banter was absent and Beram glanced up to give him a worried look.

Behind the paddlers, at least twenty rows of people were forming, including many children. Everyone wore brightly coloured tunics and trousers or skirts and, with the sunshine bouncing off the array of hair colour, the overall effect was akin to a vibrant garden adorned with myriad flowers.

Lifting his gaze beyond the people, Everand scanned the still lake stretching to where the hills were silhouetted green mounds at the far end. Would the dragons know something important was happening and come to listen? His forehead throbbed. Given what Akachi had said about the Staropal, nothing good would come from a confrontation between the dragons and the mages. Could he politely ask the massive creatures to stay away and let him try to sort it out?

With a rustle of cloth and a clinking of beads, U-Mali stood and took a wavering step to the edge of the matting. Focusing on the frail guide, Everand wondered how she would project her words to such a large gathering. Flexing his fingers, he readied a spell of enhancement to help her and when she gave him a clipped nod, he floated the spell towards her.

'My people, it's been a while since we've had a gathering.' The spell latched onto her words and spread them through the air to cover the massed audience. 'The spirits have blessed us with two generations of peace.' U-Mali lifted her eyes and arms to the skies, 'We thank you for this, great spirits, and request your guidance in the times to come.'

Everand shivered at the breeze hustling across the back of his neck and the eerie way the chimes and feather ornaments suspended from the roof swung and tinkled. Lamiya sat taller, strands of hair lifting from her face, and her chest heaved with a deep breath. He blinked: the breeze was not a coincidence.

U-Mali lifted her arms wider. 'The spirits hear us!' She lowered her arms, unable to stand fully straight due to the curve of age in her spine. 'You already know that Riverfall invited us to inter-province boat races and joined trade. You also know that our boat team was the overall winner of the boat races, captained by glide Lamiya.'

Lamiya bowed to touch her nose to the mats, while the crowd murmured and cheered softly.

'Riverplain has chosen to trade with the other provinces, and we will host the next races and trade markets at the start of leaf-fall season. Lazuli, pacer, will be in charge of the races and we now ask Luvu to be director of the trade.'

The paddlers all thumped Luvu on the back. The gruff older paddler looked pleased and gave a low bow. Lazuli turned a circle, waving at people, many of whom waved back and chanted, 'Yo!'

Please stand. The command from U-Mali snipped into Everand's mind and, blinking rapidly, he stood.

'Most of you have met Mage Everand from Axis. You might not know that he was instrumental in deflecting a threat to the Riverfall boat races and trade discussions.' U-Mali waved her hand at him and Everand winced at the way everyone fixed their eyes on him.

Flicking him a bright-eyed glance, U-Mali said, 'There is another reason we welcome Mage Everand to Riverplain.'

A blush staining her cheeks, Lamiya smoothly rose to her feet. Everand swallowed. What was U-Mali up to?

'It is unprecedented for a mage to venture out of Axis, but Mage Everand has proved to be a friend to the provinces. It is also unprecedented for a mage to choose to remain outside the mages' most imposing granite wall.' The guide's words were laced with humour.

'We of Riverplain have always known that Lamiya, daughter to Lestaya and Azuri, is special among us. Not only did Lamiya glide our team to victory at the boat races, but she and Mage Everand summoned the river dragon so the ancient traditions could be revived.'

The entire populace below applauded Lamiya until her face flushed a deep crimson. Fighting to contain a smile, Everand brushed his hand against hers.

U-Mali continued. 'Like her mother, Lamiya has exceptional talents. Her ability with birds is beyond compare, she can summon dragons and, apparently, she can also capture the heart of a mage from Axis.'

A wall of heat rushed up Everand's cheeks and beads of sweat erupted on his forehead. He couldn't look at anyone; especially not Beram and his friends in the front row.

'Lamiya has asked us, Guides of Riverplain, to approve of her union with Mage Everand of Axis.' U-Mali paused into the silence and allowed it to stretch for several heartbeats. The people waited, without a fidget or a murmur.

'I have soul-read Mage Everand. I deem him to be a mage and man of the highest integrity, with a pure heart. With great joy, I declare that I and U-Lumin approve Mage Everand to be Lamiya's consort. Her request is granted!' U-Mali stretched her cheek sideways to Lamiya for a kiss.

Eyes shining, Lamiya kissed the guide's cheek and bowed to the applauding audience. Everand looked at his toes and wriggled them, not knowing where else to look.

Raising and lowering her hands to quieten the gathering, U-Mali spoke again. 'I now explain that Mage Everand will be *consort* to Lamiya because I further announce that she is destined to be the next Riverplain Guide.'

Everand's breath caught in the back of his throat. No wonder U-Mali was beginning to communicate directly with Lamiya and more frequently! With effort, he smoothed his frown. Why was U-Mali announcing this *now*? Did she expect to pass the responsibility over soon?

His throat clenched. *The mages.* Would their arrival mean the demise of the guides? No, no, no … but why else would U-Mali so prominently proclaim their approval for him? They were making sure this was clear before something happened to them! His chest grew excruciatingly tight and he felt dizzy.

Arching an elegant eyebrow, Lamiya tapped his elbow. 'Look happy or I'll throw you in the river.'

Bowing deeply to the guides, Everand drew in a ragged breath. 'Thank you, U-Mali and U-Lumin. I am truly honoured.'

'Better,' whispered Lamiya.

Facing the crowd, Everand forced himself to nod and smile at people. If he were to be Lamiya's consort, he'd better get used to this. Perhaps he should ask U-Lumin for guidance. Beram grinned up at him and mimed having a drink to celebrate.

Clapping her hands twice to instil silence, U-Mali said, 'Our dragon-caller tells me there are now three dragons in our lake. The traditions have been renewed and we will respect the dragons, provide offerings to them in growing season, and race our boats against them.'

Thinking of Mizukaze, Everand was tempted to add 'and beat the drums'.

Flinging her arms wide, U-Mali called out, 'Thank you, my people. We will celebrate very soon.' U-Lumin came to stand beside her and they held hands and half-bowed to the crowd.

A mantle of sadness stole over Everand.

The guides looked as if they were saying goodbye.

Chapter Eight

Lamiya's heart pounded against her breastbone as if it were trying to crack the bone. It was done; not only was she formally approved to be partnered with Everand, but everyone knew she was to be the next guide. Emotions tumbled through her: joy, awe and trepidation. Everything was happening so fast! Her throat growing tight, she ached to go to her parents' shrine and confer with them.

Half-closing her eyes, she prayed. *Great spirits, please grant me this sun before the mages of Axis arrive, for I need to set my heart and mind in order.* The faintest of breaths washed over her head and dissipated. She peered at Everand, standing tall beside her but with his face cast down, not knowing where to look. He'd benefit from time to absorb everything as well.

'Take brew with us,' said U-Mali gently.

'Help me move their chairs back?' Lamiya picked up U-Mali's chair and Everand hurried to lift U-Lumin's chair. By the time they were placing the green cushions on the floor in front of the chairs, a woman was approaching with a tray of steaming mugs. Sitting down, Lamiya gratefully reached for a mug. There was also a plate of star-shaped, ginger energy cakes. Taking one, she smiled when Everand tentatively took two.

Dear heart, U-Mali's voice sounded in her mind. *Visit the shrine first, then walk with me. This sun. There is much we must talk about.* Ginger crumbs clustered in her throat at the wistfulness lacing U-Mali's thoughts, and inexplicable sadness welled inside her.

U-Mali's attention shifted to Everand. 'We know you will do your best. Whatever happens, we wanted you to know you have our blessing.'

Tipping forward, U-Lumin murmured to Everand, 'Later, let's talk about what being a consort means.'

'Thank you.' Everand dipped his head.

Desperately trying not to cough, Lamiya swallowed the ginger cake crumbs. She didn't have a vision of what was going to happen but the guides did — and they were saying farewell. Would a walk by the lake and a visit to her parents' shrine coax a forward vision? Her pulse raced. Did she want to know? Or maybe the future was not determined yet. She clung to the vision she *had* seen, of her as the future guide with Everand and their daughter by her side.

Hold tight to that vision, dear heart, came U-Mali's thought.

Handing her mug to U-Lumin, U-Mali leaned forward, wispy grey hairs drifting around her sunken cheeks and the beads of her necklace clinking. 'I want to tell you a brief history of the guides.' Her lips barely twitching, she flicked Everand a smile. 'You both need to know, for different reasons.'

Lamiya released the breath she was holding, her heartrate quickening when U-Lumin clasped U-Mali's left hand.

'You have heard how the people of Riverfall first came to land in the north, near Mizuchi Falls, some three generations ago,' U-Mali said, her eyes on Everand.

'Old man Vogel recounted the story for me, and I saw the tapestry in Atage's meeting room,' confirmed Everand.

'Vogel probably said that Aura, wife of Spinel, first spied the land after many suns at sea.' When Everand nodded, she said, her eyes twinkling, 'What Vogel didn't say, because he didn't know, was that Aura saw the land in a vision long before they approached it. It was she who charted the course of the boats, not Spinel.'

Excitement flooding into her, Lamiya sat straighter. She hadn't heard this, either.

'Aura had the gift of visions and calling. Spinel knew, but they didn't proclaim it widely.' U-Mali rasped a pale pink tongue over her cracked lips. 'It is not a coincidence that when the great blue-and-gold dragon in the lake appeared, roaring and terrifying the people, it didn't harm them.'

A jolt ran through Lamiya. 'Aura spoke with it?'

U-Mali tilted her head. 'Aura made a deal with the dragon, who said her name was Mizuchi, meaning great water beast. Aura knew the people would need to settle and grow crops to sustain themselves. It was she who asked the dragon to wield its powers to make it rain and, in exchange, offered to race their boats and ply the dragon with respect and offerings.'

Lifting a hand, Everand asked, 'Mizuchi was already there in Dragon Lake and came to Aura?'

U-Mali regarded him steadily. 'Without Aura, the creature would have remained hidden. But the reason for that is not my tale to tell.' She shook her head. 'You will work out whose tale it is.'

'So,' said U-Lumin, leaning forward. 'The people stayed for two full turnings of the seasons, enough to grow the relationship, and then moved south to find more suitable land. They settled by the widest curve in the river, and Zuqart was founded.'

Lifting his hand again, Everand said, 'But Riverfall doesn't have guides?'

A glint in her eyes, U-Mali said, 'No. Even before the split, there were disagreements about how things were to be done. The ability is passed from generation to generation and is only carried by women. Aura kept quiet about her abilities, and Spinel used her foresight to be a wise and proud leader.'

She turned twinkling eyes on Lamiya. 'The first formal guide was Hyalite — wife to Lode, the instigator of the division and first leader of Riverplain. But in reality, Lode was consort to Hyalite, my grandmother. The gift passed to Molda, my mother, and my father Geode was consort.' The guide flexed her fingers. 'Forty season-cycles ago, the gift passed to me, and I chose U-Lumin as my consort.'

'Sadly, we were not blessed with children.' U-Lumin gave U-Mali a fond smile.

'But why me?' Lamiya's heart pounded and the words blurted out before she could frame a more respectful question. Everand turned thoughtful deep-blue eyes on her.

U-Mali tilted her head to the other side. 'You are also descended from Aura. Your mother, Lestaya, could have been a guide with her deep calling abilities. We hoped and tried for children, but it seems the greater power had other ideas and has chosen you.'

'What?' Lamiya said, alarmed by the way Everand sat so still beside her. 'A greater power? Oh.' She thought of Akachi towering over her in the lake and commanding her with tasks.

Dipping her head, U-Mali said, 'Both U-Molda and I tried to reach out to the mighty red dragon. We could feel her presence, skulking under the distant hills. But we were not "the one".'

The room spinning around her, Lamiya opened and closed her mouth several times, her mind buzzing with so many questions she couldn't choose one to ask. Distantly, she felt Everand close his fingers over hers and give a reassuring squeeze. Pain lanced through her. Was *this* why she was so attracted to Everand? Because Akachi needed him? Did they not really love each other? The air around her grew close and sluggish and she couldn't draw any into her chest.

Next thing, Everand had twisted sideways on his cushion and she was crushed against his chest. 'Never, Lamiya. I love you because I want to. We were only given a nudge.' He kissed her hair.

She sniffed, gave him a brief hug and pulled away. Facing forward, she found both guides looking at her with compassion.

'The red dragon has chosen well,' said U-Mali. 'Lamiya, dear heart, you have more courage, insight and energy than most.' Her gaze skipped to Everand and back. 'And your consort will be *unprecedented* in his abilities.'

The smile slipped from the guide's lips and the wrinkles deepened around her eyes. 'We face troubled waters, but we must trust in the spirits and the red dragon. Things will be different on the other side of what comes … but with you two standing together, we feel confident.'

Lamiya bowed so low her nose brushed the mat floor and the scent of bamboo teased her nostrils. Air moved beside her when Everand matched the depth of her bow.

She failed to nudge aside the impression they were bowing at the whim of the red dragon.

Chapter Nine

Reluctantly, Mage Mantiss pushed open the doors to the Great Hall. Walking slowly across the large rug, he once more eyed the images woven into the silk. The idea of great battles and mages fighting for their honour and way of life sounded admirable, but the reality was horrifying. How had it come to this again so soon?

Taking his seat at the head of the table, he stared with dry, gritty eyes across the gleaming mahogany surface. Infinite sadness swirled through him, chased by an overriding sense of failure. This council meeting was unlikely to go well. Would he still be Head of the Guild by the end of it?

Everand's sincere face loomed in his mind and a torrent of emotions followed: anger, frustration, bitterness, despair, regret. Could he have predicted this? Should he have known he was stretching his spy too far? A deep ache rolled across his chest and when his heart thudded dully in response, he took three shallow breaths. Behind him, the door creaked, followed by brisk footsteps crossing the rug.

Agamid pulled out his chair, placed a furled-up map on the table and stopped it with a finger when it started to roll across the polished surface. 'You need not go,' he said softly. 'You know that Tiliqua and I will represent you and do our best for Everand.'

Not trusting himself to speak, Mantiss nodded. By not going, was he letting his spy down? Leaving Everand to his fate? But he couldn't bear to watch whatever unfolded. His heart gave another dull thud and, with effort, he ignored the tightness across his chest and sat straighter. Agamid was right; his role was to remain here and control the councils. To be ready for the sortie's return.

Voices sounded outside, then mages poured through the wide-open doors. The room became crowded in a colourful array of robes as the full Outer Council of Twenty filed around the table and pulled out their chairs. Most dipped their head in acknowledgement; Pelamis pulled his chair out with much confidence and noise and an annoyingly smug expression.

Once everyone was settled, Mantiss cleared his throat and began. 'Regrettably, we must make urgent and important decisions.' He pushed aside a twinge of irritation at the gleam of anticipation in Pelamis' eyes. 'I won't go over what has happened again. Suffice to say, we have significant breaches of Guild Rules Eight and Nine that must be dealt with.'

'And Rule Twelve,' interjected Pelamis. 'Everand acts for personal gain.'

'That would need to be proved,' said Mantiss firmly. 'Let us focus on what we know.' He steepled his fingers. 'We have a rogue half-mage, and now a full mage, outside the granite wall and wardspell. In sum, we have magic loose in the river provinces and the council must decide what course of action to take.'

'I insist we consider Everand's motives.' Leaning forward, Pelamis cast his gaze around those present. 'Yes, his travel was *sanctioned*,' Pelamis somehow curled distaste around the word, 'but Everand has deliberately failed to fulfil his mission and has deceived the Guild — for personal reasons rather than the greater good. He has *flouted* Rule Twelve.'

With a cruel smile, Pelamis added, 'Everand has *betrayed* our leader, Mage Mantiss, and the rest of us. In addition, he now has tame dragons, just like his traitor mentor.'

Bringing steel into his look, Mantiss forced himself to hold eye contact with Pelamis. Curse the impudent upstart for bringing the dragons into it straightaway! Ignoring the way the other council members were shuffling on their chairs, he said firmly, 'Be that as it may, the council will follow an agenda and make considered and ordered decisions. One at a time.' When he stared at each member present, gauging their reactions, Tiliqua gave him a faint smile of support.

'The council will address the decisions in this order: first, we will decide what to do about the rogue half-mage, Malach. We previously decided we would capture him and bring him here for obliteration. We must confirm or alter this decision.' When Pelamis opened his mouth, Mantiss held a hand up commandingly. For once, his fingers obliged and did not tremble.

'Second, we must decide what to do about Everand. I suspect this will be the longer discussion. Accordingly,' he glanced at Saiphos, the usual scribe, 'are you ready, Saiphos? Let's deal with the first matter. The half-mage Malach has fled from us. He now knows we will come for him, and capturing him will be more challenging. Those who wish to speak, put your palm face up on the table in front of you. We will speak in turn.'

Pelamis shot his arm out and thumped his hand on the table, palm upward. Beside him, Simoselaps did the same. Mantiss sighed when a further six mages, including Agamid and Tiliqua, indicated they wished to speak.

The discussion proved to be briefer than anticipated, all present considering that the original decision should be upheld on the basis that half-mages were unequivocally not permitted by Guild Law, and the rogue was the son of the traitorous Mage Beetal, as confirmed by Everand.

Mantiss nodded at Agamid, who obligingly unfurled the map of Ossilis.

Holding down a corner with one hand, Agamid spoke. 'The previous plan was to capture Malach at this lake in the north while Everand distracted him.'

A few mages shook their heads and Pelamis snorted.

'Logistically, finding and capturing the half-mage this time will be far more difficult.' Agamid waved his free hand over the map. 'The rogue could be anywhere.' He glanced at Simoselaps, who was injured on the previous attempt. 'And his people might be ready to defend him.'

'They won't be an issue,' said Pelamis smoothly. 'They are easily felled. It is Everand we need to worry about. And the dragons.'

Murmurs rippled around the table and Mantiss held up a hand. 'Perhaps we should discuss how far we are prepared to go to capture this Malach? Do we wish to start a war with the river provinces? Do we wish to battle with dragons again?'

While his questions hung in the air, Mantiss' breath hitched when a sudden insight landed. *This* was why Everand had faltered! Although his spy had suggested a covert way to snatch Malach, he must have been worried about the aftermath. Mantiss frowned. Or maybe not. The covert trap, if it had worked, should have prevented an aftermath because the province people wouldn't have known what happened. Yet Everand had sabotaged the trap. An eddy of nausea coursed through him. What *was* Everand thinking?

'Mantiss?' queried Agamid softly, his mouth twisted with regret. 'Pelamis suggests Everand be granted no favour or leniency, on the basis that he knew full well what he was doing and deliberately misled the councils.'

Slowly, Mantiss ran his gaze around the faces gathered. The majority of mages wore cold, determined expressions and only Tiliqua and Saiphos held a well-disguised air of discomfort. A large lump formed in his throat. His spy had abandoned him; he would now have to abandon his spy. Or abdicate his position.

Forcing his spine straighter, Mantiss clasped his hands together and rested them on the table. 'Very well. I move that a sortie be sent to the river provinces to capture the half-mage Malach and to bring Everand back.' He squeezed his fingers together, willing iron into his voice. 'I further move the half-mage will be placed in the ready-made cage for obliteration, as agreed previously.'

Pelamis smiled and the other mages gave clipped nods of agreement. Tiliqua arched an eyebrow and Saiphos held the pen poised, a frown pulling at his eyebrows.

'My third motion is that Everand be brought back to answer to the full Outer Council of Twenty. His fate will be determined by the full council.' When Pelamis opened his mouth, he snapped, 'Place your palm upward on the table if you wish to speak.'

Thumping his hand down, Pelamis growled, 'Why should Everand be given the opportunity to speak? His digressions are clear!' With agitated jerks, he tugged down one of his burnt-orange sleeves. 'You show favouritism where none is warranted. And what about his dragons? What if they try to protect him again?'

Eyes narrowed, Mantiss said, 'You referred to Guild Rule Twelve. At this point, we do not understand Everand's motives. He has not invaded the Guild or threatened us in any way, like his mentor, Mage Beetal, did.' When mages stirred around the table and colour rose in Pelamis' cheeks, he spoke more quickly. 'From what Agamid reports, the only mage the dragons attacked was *you* because *you* were attacking Everand. With lethal intent.'

He ground out the next part. 'As you also pointed out, Everand's mission to the province was *sanctioned*. By me. The Head of the Guild. Everand reported as requested, but not fully. I remind you all that he said we brought him back *before* he'd finished gathering his intelligence.'

Now he looked across the table at Tiliqua. 'At a dusk meal with Agamid, Tiliqua and myself, Everand proposed an excellent new research topic and agreed to work on it with Tiliqua.' He paused, giving her time to nod. 'These are not the actions of a would-be traitor. I move — no, I *demand* — that we bring Everand back peacefully and give him the opportunity to speak.'

Underneath the table, his legs began to shake and he clenched his jaw. *Just a little longer body, give me strength for just a little longer.* Seeing that he held everyone's undivided attention, some with their mouths open, he concluded with, 'Anyone who goes on this sortie *must* be prepared to aim for a peaceful outcome if at all possible. We *cannot* afford to take on the river provinces, nor any dragons. I strongly propose that we first resolve the matter of the half-mage and find out Everand's plan.'

In his mind he crossed his fingers, praying that Everand would indeed have more vital information. A whole lot more. Silence hung over the table like a brooding thundercloud, only broken by the furious scratching of Saiphos' pen.

'I volunteer to lead the sortie again,' said Agamid, breaking the sombre mood. 'A senior mage should go, and Everand may respond better to me.'

'I volunteer. We need *strong* mages on this mission,' said Pelamis with a sneer.

Simoselaps jumped as if he'd been kicked under the table and squeaked, 'Me too.'

His expression stern, Agamid said, 'Do you both swear to follow my commands? If not, I will not accept you in the sortie.' When they hesitated, Agamid said, 'Palms up and swear to follow my lead.'

Mantiss breathed shallowly while the two young mages held their palms up and, with surly looks, muttered their intended compliance. He doubted their sincerity but Agamid seemed prepared to take them. Perhaps their strength would be needed against Malach. On balance, if they lost a mage or two … he almost smiled.

'I wish to go,' said Tiliqua, and Agamid nodded immediately.

Roaming his gaze around the table, Mantiss hoped a few other trustworthy mages would volunteer. 'We'll need more than four mages. Who else will go?' His lips twitched at how several mages suddenly became fascinated by the table surface. He roamed his gaze more deliberately. Who was likely to help counteract any violence Pelamis could initiate?

'Mage Neelaps? I thought you might be interested in the unprecedented opportunity to observe the province agriculture.'

Shifting in his chair and licking his lips nervously, the moss-green-clad mage squeaked, 'Very well, Mage Mantiss. If you wish it, I will go.'

Saiphos quickly added Neelaps to the list.

'Add your name while you're at it,' said Agamid to Saiphos.

'That's six,' said Mantiss quickly, before Saiphos could argue. 'Will this be sufficient?'

An eyebrow raised, Agamid replied, 'Sufficient or not, I doubt we could transport a larger group. Not that far.'

Leaning against the back of his chair, Mantiss concluded Agamid was right; sending six mages would be taxing enough, and they couldn't afford to put at risk all of the Inner Council. With this selection in the sortie, perhaps he hadn't fully abandoned his spy, after all. A wave of fatigue washed from his head to his toes and the tremor in his legs intensified.

More abruptly than intended, he asked, 'When will the sortie depart? And where will we send it to?'

'*Before* first light,' said Pelamis quickly. 'While the people are sleeping. There's no point delaying. Who knows what Everand is plotting, and he could be training the rogue.'

Everyone around the table nodded, so Mantiss passed the resolution. The wave of fatigue grew heavier and he could feel his heartbeat becoming erratic. 'Last point. Where?' he croaked, looking at Agamid to cue him to take over the discussion.

Using the map as a prompt, Agamid herded the council admirably while several locations were proposed. Mantiss sat breathing shallowly, wishing the pain across his chest would subside. He must not show weakness. *Not now.*

After a while, Tiliqua asked, 'Where was Everand when we found him before? Surely, that is the most logical place to start? He must have been there for a reason.'

Agamid put a finger on the map near a turquoise lake to the south, towards the east coast. 'Here. He was in a hut by this lake.' Looking at Tiliqua, he added, 'I remember some of the details, so we can visualise this place to translocate to. Everand must know the owner of the hut, and if he isn't there, they might lead us to him.'

'If I may?' Pelamis snapped his arms forward to rest his hands on the table. 'I recommend no advance probe. No warning.'

Mantiss tried in vain to swallow the lump in his throat when all those around the table indicated their agreement. *No warning.* And wasn't that lake the very one that Lapemis referred to in his notebook? The one where the first mages found the red dragon and took the Staropal from the underwater cave?

A roaring filled his ears and his heart pulsed loudly. *Everand, my son, I sincerely hope you have some greater plan.*

A sense of impending doom crashed over him.

Chapter Ten

Everand sighed. Malach's mind was not on his training and the sun was already sinking towards the western hills, casting gold and amber light over everything. 'Something troubles you?'

Body held rigid, Malach said, 'My people. What if your Guild goes to my village?'

Frowning, Everand said, 'If you're not there, the mages will simply search elsewhere. Unless your people attack them.' He swallowed. That scenario would not go well for Riverwood. 'I don't think they'd go there first. Riverfall is more likely, given that's where they sent me. Or here, because that's where they found me last time.'

Alarm buzzed from his head all the way to his toes. Of course, the Guild would come straight to Riverplain. A cold shudder chased down his spine. Would the mages translocate directly to Lamiya's hut? They'd be able to magically recall the coordinates, given that the previous combined probe took him from inside her hut. He and Lamiya should stay elsewhere! Where, though?

A background noise intruded and he realised Malach was speaking. '… what do we do then?'

With difficulty, he focused on Malach's gruff face. 'What?'

'What will the dragons do? Will the mages kill them?'

'I'm not sure.' Everand thought of the history taught about how the first mages defeated a sea serpent when it attacked their ship, *Wavestrider*. But that had taken several mages, and would Agamid and the others have read about and remember how Lapemis and his crew had used death-shards to the serpent's eyes? Did the river dragon's eyes have the same vulnerability? A desperate longing to protect the dragons shivered over his whole being.

He scrubbed a hand over his face. Truth be told, his concentration wasn't much better than Malach's. 'Let's stop our practice. Don't tell me the details, but have you and Lazuli decided what you'll do when the mages arrive?'

Narrowing his eyes, Malach nodded sharply, his distaste at having to hide evident.

'Good. You go find Lazuli, and I'll go to refine my plan with Lamiya.'

'Very well. When do we next meet?'

Thinking quickly, Everand said, 'You and Lazuli should stay concealed until well after first light. Just in case.' He forced a half-smile. 'Don't practise anything we've been working on because that will leave an energy trail for the Guild to detect. Stay safe, so you can return to Riverwood to lead your people.'

After a brusque dip of his head, Malach strode away. Everand watched him go, observing the tension in the half-mage's shoulders and the choppy strides. Surely, Malach's sense of self-preservation would kick in and he would act to save himself. He rolled his shoulders to dislodge the uncomfortable tension tugging at them. What if the mages found Malach and not him? Would he reveal himself to continue to argue for Malach's right to live? He could almost hear Lamiya: *You know you would.*

His mind presented him with an image of the secret book on ancient tactical spells, neatly tucked inside the cover of the feather pillow in Lamiya's hut, and he set off with brisk steps.

There was one more spell he could usefully master. And two that he should be confident he could apply concurrently. If things went awry, this was a good back-up plan.

If things went awry … he glanced at the sun, almost kissing the tops of the western hills, sneaking purple shadows into the crevices and folds. His heart and groin throbbed. *Learn the spells then find Lamiya, spend time with her. And warn the dragons.*

Voices carried across the water and stopping short, he looked across the lake to see the dragon boat being carried out of the shed. They were training *now*? What was Lamiya thinking? Sadness flowed into his chest. Maybe the team thought they'd be fighting or fleeing by sun-up, when they usually trained. Conveniently, this meant her hut would be empty since Beram and Mookaite would take the opportunity to go in the boat.

He transported himself into the centre of the hut and snaffled a couple of cakes from the plate on the table before retrieving the slim book of spells. Sitting cross-legged and munching on the last cake, he skimmed the pages until he reached the spell he wanted, almost at the end of the book. The thin pages crackled and rasped under his fingers, the handwriting faint and cursive. It was amazing this book had survived the sea voyage and sinking of *Wavestrider*.

Pausing, he reflected that Lapemis had shown impressive foresight in taking some of the more advanced texts from the old Guild library when the few surviving mages fled. History told that the original Guild of a hundred and fifty mages had been outnumbered by *thousands* of warriors invading from the north. After a battle that reportedly raged for eleven suns and moons, the mages had lost due to exhaustion. Unable to summon any further power, the tiny group of survivors had fled their homeland.

Deflecting the idea of dead and dying mages, he realised the mages had lost that battle at a time when they didn't have the Staropal to help reinforce their power. Was this significant? Was their innate power not that strong, after all?

Adrift in the ship for several more suns and moons, the mages had become shipwrecked on the *east* coast of Ossilis. Frowning so hard his forehead ached, Everand realised the mages had settled as far to the *west* as possible. The annals said the Staropal was found in the eternal spring in the centre of Axis. But Akachi said the mages had wandered down the hills on the *east* coast and had taken the stone of power from her. His eyes refused to focus on the cursive writing on the page beneath his hand.

He sat straighter. This meant the Guild was stronger now. The new Guild numbered a hundred and twenty mages and had been refining and extending its magic for four generations, supplemented by draws of power from the Staropal. The stone was always managed and accessed only by the incumbent Head of the Guild. His master's face filling his mind, he ran his tongue over dry lips, dislodging a few cake crumbs. Mantiss *must* know more. A wave of nausea surged through him. This mission had *never* been simple, but the extent of possible deception... the tiny crumbs lodged in his throat felt like jagged shards of deceit.

Bringing the book back onto his knees and forcing his eyes to focus, he read the spell of deepest concealment of power. Three times. Feeling so cold all over that his breath misted before him, he visualised deploying it and overlaying it with a second spell that would stop his heart. If Mage Mantiss knew the true origin of the Staropal, there was not a chance, none at all, that Mantiss and the Guild would allow him, a fully trained and pure mage, to remain outside the granite wall within reach of the red dragon — no matter how much personal history had passed between them.

If he was correct about the extent of deception surrounding the discovery of the Staropal, there was also not a chance, not even a remote one, the Guild would let the dragons live. He *must* deflect the dragons from engaging with the mages — let the imminent sortie play itself out and then find a way to recover the Staropal. It was the dragons' best chance. Possibly their *only* chance now the Guild knew about them.

Wait. Lamiya's beautiful face in his mind, he drew in a ragged breath. The dragons had *two* chances. *If* Lamiya was right and Akachi was somehow manipulating events, then he and Lamiya were destined to meet and work together. Could the red dragon have *that* much power? He shook his head. If so, this was ancient magic, well beyond the grasp of the Guild.

The feather curtain flung inwards and Lamiya, Beram and Mookaite tumbled into the hut, clad in damp training gear and clutching their paddles. Everand slid the book back inside the pillow cover and stood up. 'You've been training?'

'Lamiya got to practise on our river before the festival, so we took the chance to get the feel of the lake.' Beram grinned. 'Only fair. We need to snatch back victory at the next festival.'

'Hah!' said Lamiya, wrapping her paddle back in its protective cloth and storing it behind her clothes rack. 'Brew, anyone?'

When she moved towards her small fire to light it and boil some water, Everand intervened. 'Actually, there's something we need to do, you and me, *before* dark-fall.'

'I can make the brew,' said Mookaite, prising the clay pot from Lamiya's hands.

'Can I change first?' Lamiya arched an eyebrow.

Everand shook his head. 'You're going to get wet again. Bring your cloak, though.'

Curiosity gleaming in her eyes, Lamiya fetched her cloak and handed him a spare one. To Mookaite she said, 'I hate to ask, but can you start the meal?'

'Of course.' Mookaite slid Everand a coy glance. 'You two do … what you need to.'

Warmth coating his cheeks, Everand ducked out through the feather curtain, Lamiya close on his heels.

'Well, my mage, where are we off to?' Lamiya slipped her hand into his.

Thinking of the first time they made love, Everand murmured, 'That special patch of grass beneath the willow tree …' Her fingers squeezed his. 'Then we must warn the dragons not to intervene.'

A tremble passed through Lamiya's hand. 'Are you sure? What if we need their help?'

Scooping his arm around her waist, Everand transported them to beneath the tree. Wispy willow leaves tickled his shoulders and the back of his neck.

'My, we are in a hurry,' whispered Lamiya, pressing against him.

Ignoring her question about the dragons, he planted his lips on hers. Her arms crept around his neck, pulling him closer. As one, they sank onto the grass. Still kissing her, he freed a hand and fumbled his cloak across the ground beside them. He felt her lips quirking into a smile, then she tipped sideways, tugging him down to lie on top of her. Feeling their time was precious, he propped up on an elbow and gazed down at Lamiya. Shadows flickered across her face from the leaves moving in the sun-fade breeze, and her hair and skin reflected the amber hues of the setting sun glinting off the lake behind them.

Reaching up, she trailed her fingers down his cheek. 'Whatever happens next sun, this was worth it,' she said, her voice cracking.

His heart swelled with painful, overwhelming love for her. It still seemed impossible that she wanted him; he couldn't think of a single thing to say that would do justice to what he felt. He kissed the fingers she was trailing across his lips and, seeing the desire in her eyes, leaned down to kiss her properly.

Breaking the kiss, he tugged off her damp tunic and short trousers, gasping when she ripped off her breast-cloth in one swift move. Wanting to savour the moment, he travelled his eyes over her lithe, muscled and gorgeous body. Goosebumps rippled over her skin.

'My mage,' she murmured hotly. 'Don't tease. Take me.'

Amid waves of rolling pleasure, he made love with her, savouring the sensation of moving against her silky skin, admiring her strength and ardour, breathing in the scents of her, feeling cool, crisp air washing over his back. Too soon, they were done. Goosebumps raced down his back and he fumbled for the edge of the cloak and tugged it over them. Lamiya burrowed against him while he planted kisses all over the top of her head.

'I'm so glad you thought of this,' she murmured against his chest.

Sighing, Everand planted a final kiss. 'We never have enough time to be together.' Pushing up, he drew the cloak around his shoulders and looked away across the lake. The water was a dark purple-grey, reflecting the twilight sky. 'Dark falls. We must warn the dragons, then get back.'

Efficiently tugging her clothing back on, Lamiya said, 'Are you sure? Didn't Mizukaze and Hanachi save you from the other mage — what was his name — last time?' She peered into his face. 'Isn't that mage likely to come again?'

'Pelamis. And yes, he will come. I am sure of it.' He focused on her face. 'Even more reason to keep the dragons away. This next part must be just about the Guild, me and Malach.'

Her grey-blue eyes flickered and she lowered her gaze.

Unease rising, he tipped her chin up and looked into her eyes. 'Promise me you will leave the dragons out of it. If they intervene, matters will become violent. Next sun is unlikely to be the end of it. We must get through whatever happens, and then I must address Akachi's request. Trust me, only then will the dragons have a fair chance.'

Stiffening, Lamiya said curtly, '*We*, my mage, *we* must address Akachi's request. I said I would stand with you, and I meant it.' Defiance shone in her eyes.

In the depths of her grey-blue eyes, he saw such fire and determination he was certain there was no way he'd be able to deflect her. 'I know, my love.' He caressed her cheek. 'And I will be glad of your help. But let's keep the dragons out of it until we can restore their full power to them.' When she looked sceptical, he added, 'It will not help my cause to have the dragons fight for me. Pelamis and his allies will be looking to brand me as a traitor and I must try to keep some mages sympathetic to me.'

The tension left Lamiya's shoulders. 'You'd better explain to me who is who then, before they arrive.'

'One more thing …' Everand waited until she arched an eyebrow. 'If things don't go well … remember Ejad and the viper, and how you helped me save him.'

Both of her eyebrows lifted. 'The viper?'

'The viper. It will make sense when the time comes.' Standing before she could ask more questions, he pulled her to her feet.

'Now, let's warn the dragons. Keep them safe.'

Chapter Eleven

Lamiya purified her hands, the glints of moonlight like crystal tears on the water tumbling into the lower bowl. The wooden ladle was rimmed with silver light. Everand's 'one more thing' had turned out to be 'oh, and another thing' when he suggested they shouldn't sleep in her hut because the mages would go there first. Not wanting to put others in any danger, she'd proposed they sleep on the floor in the Meeting Place. Everand had agreed. Too rapidly.

Alert from the cool water brushing over her hands, she wondered whether this was because the Meeting Place was well away from the dragons' cave. He was so adamant the mages should not find the dragons. Not yet. Frowning, she recalled the way Akachi's golden eyes had flickered with surprise at Everand's request they stay away until he could return the Staropal to them. The red dragon had agreed far too rapidly for her liking as well. Now everything rested on her and Everand's shoulders.

Warm fingers closed over hers. Looking at the wry smile on Everand's face, deep in shadow, she realised she'd drifted into reflection with the tumbling water.

'You are pure enough, my love,' he whispered.

Behind and above her, the wind chimes stirred and clinked. Feeling the presence of the guides emerging through a side door, she turned to greet them.

'Dear heart, welcome.' U-Mali glided across the mat floor and gripped her hands fiercely.

'Thank you for agreeing we can sleep here.' Lamiya tipped forward in a short bow and Whirr pushed his head out of the front of her tunic to peep at the guides.

U-Mali rubbed the top of Whirr's head with a gnarled hand. 'You protect your mistress,' she murmured. 'You too,' she said, angling her head up at Everand.

Lamiya swallowed. U-Mali seemed so certain she would need protection.

Shuffling closer, U-Lumin passed an armful of folded blankets to Everand. 'We didn't have time to discuss what being a consort means.' Lines of worry creased the old man's forehead, but when he slid his eyes to U-Mali the creases eased into a faint smile. 'You'll find it easier to just do as you are told.'

Taking the blankets, Everand said, 'Sound advice, I suspect.'

Grasping U-Lumin's hands, Lamiya thanked him. Dread flushed through her that this was the last time she would see them both. The way both guides held onto her hands and squeezed them only magnified the cold fingers of dread spreading across her chest. The air around her grew imperceptibly chill, the darkness a little denser.

'Sleep well.' U-Mali gave a bird-like dip of her head, then took U-Lumin's hand and they melted away into the gloom of the open space. Shortly after, a door clicked closed.

Clutching the blankets to his chest, Everand said, 'Where do you suggest we sleep?'

Lamiya looked out at the silvery moonbeams bouncing across the lake, fading into pitch black water lapping at the huddled shadows of the distant hills. Were the dragons asleep, safely curled up in their underwater cave? Or did they feed and hunt during dark-fall? A shiver ran across her nape. 'I think close to this edge, so we can see the water.' *See anyone coming.*

Everand backed a few steps and mimed putting the blankets down. Mouth dry, she nodded. They'd be partly concealed behind the support strut of the formal entrance but would be able to see down the slope and towards the water. Once he'd spread the blankets, he held out a hand. Closing the gap, she took it, allowing him to gently pull her down. It felt odd to be trying to sleep fully clothed, but she didn't want to face serious mages clad in her sleeping tunic.

She snuggled into Everand's strong, calming arms. Whirr climbed out of her tunic and marched up and down on top of the blanket like a sentinel on duty. She clicked her tongue and the bird hopped over to lie down next to her head.

'Better,' mumbled Everand, pulling her closer and kissing her forehead. 'Sleep, if you can.' He closed his eyes and took a few deep breaths, a frown pinching his forehead.

Her heart beat strongly against her breastbone, refusing to settle. Would the mages come while they slept? Why had Everand told Beram and Mookaite where they were going? Did he *want* to be found? Her heart beat faster. All their discussions had been focused on concealing themselves … but now, in this prominent, open space this didn't ring true. Malach and Lazuli were hidden — he wasn't.

She stared unseeing into the gloomy air stretching away from her. Was his strategy simply to remove himself from proximity to the dragons and those he cared about? That notion resounded with truth and her heart thudded unevenly. It was difficult to hide in the vast Meeting Place, but they were in the place of the spirits. Would that count for something?

Focusing on Everand's face, she committed each detail to memory: the chiselled, determined jaw, high cheekbones, fine blond eyebrows, hair like spun starlight, straight lips that could be so serious yet so loving. How could she go on if something happened to him? Her life would be bleak.

Blinking, she brought into her mind the vision she'd seen of him as her consort, with their daughter playing beside him.

In this very Meeting Place. *May this vision burn bright and true.* Forcing in deeper breaths, she became aware of insects clicking and buzzing, the croaking of frogs, the faint lapping of water over pebbles. All is quiet, she told herself. All is well.

Burrowing into Everand's warm chest, she sighed when his fingers traced circles over her shoulder. Nice. Calm oozed over her.

☪

'Peep! Peep!' Lamiya's eyelids fluttered. It was pitch dark. 'Peep! Peep!' Sharp talons scratched in her hair.

Forcing her eyelids up, she frowned at the coloured lights shimmering around her, as if a sky-arch was landing on the mats. Hazy purple, crimson, brown, orange, green and blue shapes shifted and blurred. Whirr pecked her shoulder and fear stabbed into her. Everand jerked upright then scrambled to his feet. The mages! What happened to the warning probes he'd said he would feel?

Dizzy with the speed at which she leaped up, she saw Everand's shield forming around them. Whirr dived down the front of her tunic, his talons scraping her collarbone.

The shimmering colours solidified into six tall, robed mages standing in a circle around them. Surrounded. No warning. Already, their plans were scattered like dead leaves in a wind. Gulping down her fear, she forced her mind to function. *Analyse!* Who has come? The older mage in purple with the neat beard must be the senior mage that Everand spoke of, Agamid. Next to him in the crimson robe was his former apprentice, Saif-something. Everand had hoped these two would come.

The angular, muscled mage in burnt orange robes glaring at Everand must be Pelamis. The violent one. The tall, thin mage in brown was his also violent ally. She swivelled to regard the two standing behind her. The mage in moss-green with curly chestnut hair looked as if he didn't want to be there. Everand hadn't mentioned him. Did he not expect this mage?

Her eyes moved to the sixth mage and her breath caught. The tall, elegant woman *oozed* power, intelligence and authority — and the way she was scrutinising Everand! Lamiya swallowed painfully. Everand definitely hadn't mentioned her, and there was an odd current passing between them. The way his mouth tightened and the slight nod he gave the woman — there was history there.

The woman turned austere, deep-blue eyes her way and she felt herself assessed and, by the way the woman's lips curled, found wanting. The woman arched an eyebrow at Everand, as if to say: *Really? You stayed here for that?*

Heat flaming across her face, Lamiya spun to face Everand. 'Who is she?'

Evenly, controlled, he said, 'Mage Tiliqua. Daughter of my master, Mage Mantiss.' His eyes held hers. *Hold firm,* appeared in her mind. *She is strong and her presence could prove useful.*

'Traitor, you are hereby called to account!' shouted Pelamis, his orange sleeves billowing as he wildly waved his arms. 'Your so-called friends gave you up in a heartbeat!'

To Agamid, Everand said, 'Tell me you didn't hurt them?'

When Agamid shook his head Lamiya released a breath.

'A simple mind-read revealed you had come to this place.' Agamid took a step forward. 'Explain yourself, and fast.'

'It is as I told you,' Everand said slowly and clearly. 'I could not condone, or bear to watch, *anyone* being obliterated for not being pure. Not without being given a chance. Can the Guild not at least hear Malach's side of the story? He didn't ask for Mage Beetal to sire him!'

Lamiya observed Pelamis, who was flexing his fingers, drawing power. Instant dislike flooded her. And for his snake-like friend in brown robes. These two were just how everyone imagined the mages to be — powerful, arrogant and cruel.

'You are weak!' snarled Pelamis. 'You know full well what Guild Law says. Bring the rogue half-mage to us.'

'Law that was created four generations ago,' snapped Everand. 'It is time for a review.'

'Says someone *consorting* outside the Guild,' sneered Pelamis, giving Lamiya a withering glance, '*and* keeping his own dragons!'

When the other mages glanced around uneasily, Lamiya chewed her lower lip. If only Everand *would* call the dragons. How did he plan to outwit six powerful mages? Did he really think he could persuade them with his words? What could she do to help him?

Lifting a hand, Agamid said, 'Enough, Pelamis.' To Everand, he said, 'As you are aware, the councils decreed that the half-mage was to be taken to them. This decree has not changed. I ask formally that you call this half-mage and tell him to accompany us.'

'I will not.' Everand stretched taller, flexed his fingers and the shield around them strengthened.

'Can you not do this for Mantiss?' Tiliqua moved smoothly around the circle to stand beside Agamid and opened a palm towards Everand. 'You *know* how much it would mean to my father to have your continued loyalty.'

Lamiya clenched her jaw. The woman's demeanour and voice were compelling. Everand was rigid with tension.

With a small, sad smile, Tiliqua said, 'I was looking forward to working with you on the new research project. Can you not return to the Guild?' She peered into Everand's face. 'Mantiss needs you.'

Nausea roiled through Lamiya. By the stars, this woman was clever. And she knew Everand well. Just how well? The senior mage, Agamid, seemed to be holding his breath, waiting to see if Tiliqua's strategy would work. Lamiya watched Everand's face, observing the miniscule muscle twitches that gave away his turmoil. Fight, her heart prodded. Tell him you need him too. Counter this woman.

Drawing upon her calling power, she brought to mind the vision of her and Everand seated together as the Riverplain Guide and consort. She layered the image with her blue dress, her hair rolling over her shoulders in rich mahogany waves, his azure tunic, the deep happiness in his eyes, and the beautiful young girl with hair like spun starlight playing with wooden hopeepa on the floor beside him. Curving her lips into a subtle smile, she floated the image towards him.

Is this not what you truly desire, my mage? To choose your own life? A breeze eddied past her cheeks and the chimes swung and tinkled.

With a massive shiver, Everand gasped then said, 'I'm sorry, Tiliqua. Under other circumstances, I'd welcome the chance to work with you. I do not make my choices lightly.'

He put a hand on Lamiya's shoulder. 'If the Guild is not open to some degree of change, not open to reconsideration of its policy of isolation and the Guild Rules, then I stand by my choice to live outside the wall. In Riverplain, with Lamiya.'

The reaction of the mages overrode Lamiya's rush of warmth at his declaration. Tiliqua snapped her head back as if she'd been struck, Agamid bowed his head in sorrow, the mages in crimson and green stared at her as if she were an interesting specimen of insect — and Pelamis and the brown-robed mage laughed.

Shaking his head, Pelamis said, 'You are the ultimate apprentice! Mirroring your traitor mentor's footsteps so closely it is laughable!' He lifted a hand and gave it a curious twist above his head. 'This folly has gone on long enough. Everand has rejected his chance! Can we get on with capturing him and the again curiously absent half-mage?'

A bolt of fire exploded against the shield right in front of her. Lamiya flinched. When Pelamis and brown-robe raised their hands to hurl further bolts, Everand put his arms around her. For several agonising heartbeats she couldn't see anything, surrounded by flames and smoke. She put her hands over her ears to block out the teeth-grating sounds of crackling and burning.

'Stay calm,' said Everand. 'They will not penetrate my shield.'

Heart pounding, she endured the crackling, sizzling and roaring.

The flames and noise stopped, and Lamiya blinked the candle-like afterglow from her eyes. The surrounding air held tinges of grey and outside the white pebble paths gleamed faintly in the approaching sunrise. At the edge of Everand's shield, the rush mats were charcoal and smouldered with a noxious smell. Anxiety rising, she swallowed: people would start to emerge soon. What would the mages do then?

The roof chimes rattled in a gust of wind and her heart shrieked in despair. *No! U-Mali! Stay away!*

'Who are you to desecrate our sacred place?' U-Mali's voice rang crisp and clear and the tiny guide emerged from the smoky air to stand beside the shield. At Everand's murmured words, the shield extended to cover the guide too.

'U-Mali! No! Please go!' Lamiya wrung her hands.

The guide gave her a glance. *Dear heart, what will be, will be. Hold to your purpose.* U-Lumin appeared and walked straight through the shield to stand by U-Mali's side. Lamiya gasped. How did he do that? The mages stared at U-Lumin, and even Everand looked surprised.

Together, the slight guides faced Agamid. 'State your purpose here,' said U-Mali. 'Why do you trouble our people?'

Agamid blinked and said, 'You are the leader here? We have come to reclaim one of our own and to take the rogue half-mage to the Guild for questioning. We ask that you yield Everand and Malach to us.'

Admiration rocketed through Lamiya at how U-Mali stood so proudly, despite being stared down at by imposing mages. The wizened guide reached only halfway up their chests!

'Malach of Riverwood has sought our protection,' snapped U-Mali, waving a crooked, bony finger. 'And Mage Everand, who is welcome among us, makes his own choices.'

U-Lumin stepped forward, his hands clasped before him. 'We will not yield those under our protection. But if you come seeking our friendship, we are happy to speak.'

Opening his hands wide, Everand said, 'Agamid, the people of the river provinces are good, honest people. The Guild would be wise to get to know them.'

'Hah!' Pelamis deliberately stepped in front of Agamid, his robe flapping about his ankles. 'The Guild does not need friends. Bring this Malach to us. Now.' He snapped his fingers, then narrowed his eyes. 'Still cowering behind your shield? Showing more weakness? The Guild is better off without you!'

Feeling as if time was moving at half-pace, Lamiya watched U-Mali and U-Lumin walk forward and pass out through Everand's shield. Her mind went into an endless shriek but her legs wouldn't move.

Ignoring Pelamis, U-Mali spoke directly to Agamid. 'If you have authority to speak for your Mages' Guild, we, and our people, would be glad to meet with you.'

'How did you walk through the shield?' responded Agamid, looking shaken. 'Do you have power?'

'They have power!' shrieked Pelamis. 'Forbidden outside the Guild!' He flung both hands out, and a crackling snake of fire circled U-Mali, hovering around her neck. 'Simoselaps, snare the other one!'

Lamiya's heart thudded into her mouth when the brown-robed mage shot a sizzling snake of fire around U-Lumin. The two guides stood calmly, hands clasped before them as if waiting, while the coils of fire hissed and spat sparks. Lamiya took a step but Everand grabbed her arm. She yanked it free. 'Relax the shield,' she hissed, frustration surging through her. 'Do something!'

Gripping her arm, Everand brought his face closer until he gazed right into hers, his eyes the deepest blue pools she'd ever seen. 'Are you sure? Things will escalate rapidly.'

'Save them!' commanded Lamiya.

Everand released her arm and at the same time the shield dissipated, a thousand tinkling shards of light spiralling to the ground. Flinging up both arms, Everand hurled massive bolts of incandescent blue energy at Pelamis. The air fizzed with heat and smelled like burning leaves.

The snake of fire circling U-Mali vanished when Pelamis diverted his power to block Everand. Lamiya ran to U-Mali, hunching into herself at the explosions of red and blue energy crashing around her. She pulled at the guide's frail arm, but U-Mali resisted, staring at U-Lumin, still held captive by Simoselaps' snake of fire. The other mages stood watching, but none seemed inclined to intervene. Did they intend to let Everand and Pelamis kill each other?

'You!' Lamiya pointed at Agamid. 'You are supposed to lead! Stop this.'

Agamid opened and closed his mouth.

Pelamis giggled inanely. 'You waste your time, woman! Agamid is no leader! That's the problem, isn't it? Mantiss is failing, his pet spy has abandoned him and there is no true leadership.' He hurled a black, spiked death bolt at Everand. Then another, and another and another.

Dissolving them, Everand flung a volley of blue, spiked stars at Pelamis' chest. Stepping sideways, he fixed his gaze on Tiliqua, who stood rigid with her hands clenched by her sides. 'If the Guild wants me back then show some honour.' He waved an arm at the guides. 'These people have done no harm. Who are you to come here and threaten them?'

'What would you have me do?' demanded Tiliqua.

'Stop Pelamis!' gasped Everand, sweat beading on his brow. 'So we can talk properly!'

Tiliqua turned pale. Next to her, Agamid was still opening and closing his mouth, like a fish gulping for air.

'You jest!' snapped Pelamis. 'None of these are strong enough to fight. You *will* fail here. Council's orders will be met. By *me*.' He hurled a massive red bolt at Everand's face and yelled, '*Now, Simoselaps!*'

Lamiya shrieked when Simoselaps' second fire snake flew at her and U-Mali, jaws of flame agape and heat radiating before it. Grabbing the guide, she threw herself to the floor and the crackling fire and wave of red-hot air passed over the top of them, crisping the ends of her hair. The second snake merged with the fire snake surrounding U-Lumin and the thickened python-like coils flung inwards. U-Lumin writhed and twisted amid a ball of fire, his mouth a dark O of soundless agony. Smudgy grey smoke billowed up from his clothes and the odour of burned flesh and bone cut the air.

Lamiya gagged. With inhuman strength, U-Mali threw her off and sprang at Pelamis.

Everand flung both hands out, hurling a shield at U-Mali but Pelamis' swarm of spiked shards reached her first. U-Mali's frail body jerked and spasmed when the swarm hit, piercing her flesh with nauseating squelches. The guide toppled face down onto the mat floor.

Covering her mouth with her hands and blinking back tears, Lamiya stared while the guides' spirits misted up from their charred and broken flesh and spiralled up to hover just below the lattice spars of the roof. *Farewell, dear heart. Lead our people wisely. You are strong, we have faith in you. Now save your mage.* A faint touch brushed her cheek, as if U-Mali had kissed her, before the grey mists seeped through the roof.

An invisible force snatched her and she flew, in Everand's arms, to land behind the group of mages. A brittle shield glinted in front of them.

His arms taut with anger, Everand shouted, 'Agamid! Tiliqua! Control Pelamis or we will have a war!'

Heart pounding so fast she could barely breathe, Lamiya observed the mages. The two in crimson and green were frozen where they stood and Agamid seemed undecided. Now she understood why Everand had kept insisting that what would happen depended on *which* mages came. For all their power and training in magic, the mages were not willing or adept fighters — except Pelamis and Simoselaps, who were both fast and ruthless — and who were now peering out towards the lake. *Oh no.* What were they looking at? She itched to move sideways so she could see out too.

Tiliqua cleared her throat and Lamiya spun to face the woman mage, who loomed beside Agamid, her face tight with annoyance.

After giving Agamid a look of disgust, Tiliqua addressed Everand. 'Many people are coming. There will be more losses. Give us the rogue half-mage and I'll tell the council, and my father, that we couldn't make you return.' Narrowing her eyes, she said smoothly, 'Give us Malach. Then the rest of us will go and leave you and Pelamis to fight it out.'

Lamiya stared at Everand. The woman was offering him a chance! Was giving him leave to kill Pelamis! Everand's jaw clenched and his eyes became dark with pain and sorrow. Swallowing her disappointment, she knew he would neither yield Malach nor kill Pelamis. Curse his integrity! Touching his arm, she murmured, 'My mage?'

Everand caressed her cheek with the back of a finger, his face an open apology. Relaxing the shield and standing tall, he turned to Tiliqua. 'I will yield. Take me instead.'

Great pain ripped through Lamiya's heart.

Chapter Twelve

The distress on Lamiya's face! Everand's chest constricted until he couldn't breathe and pinpoint stars whirled at the edges of his vision. But what else could he do? His plan to hide from the Guild had always been flawed. The lack of advance probes was a surprise, though. *Curse it.* He'd expected to lead the mages astray for a while, but if he let them take him now, he could continue to argue his points at council and the people of Riverplain would be safe. Perhaps Malach would not be found. Not this time.

Amid the dizzy stars whirled thoughts about the Staropal and Akachi's decree that he must recover it. If he let them take him back to the Guild, he could work out a way to access the stone — which was buried deep under the Great Hall. Once he held the Staropal *no-one* would be able to stop him from returning to Riverplain. Gasping in a ragged breath, he thought about how the Staropal had bobbed towards him once before. Would the stone willingly come to him again?

Unable to meet Lamiya's eyes, he mumbled, 'Sorry, my love. I will find a way forward.'

'You will yield?' Tiliqua's voice was laced with disbelief. 'You will return with us?'

'I will.' Everand squared his shoulders. 'On the condition there is no more violence, and the Guild swears to leave the province people alone to live their lives as they wish.'

Hurrying forward, Agamid gripped his hands. 'I am *so* glad. Mantiss will be most relieved.'

Neelaps and Saiphos gave him pleased nods, clearly happy that they hadn't actually had to do anything. Had Mantiss included these two in order to give him the ghost of a chance? So that Pelamis and Simoselaps would be alone in their proclivity for violence? Everand's pulse beat more quickly. Perhaps all was not lost.

Pelamis swung around from observing the lake. 'People are coming. Swarms of them. Who leads here now?'

'I do.' Drawing herself up and tossing her luscious hair over a shoulder, Lamiya glared at Pelamis.

'*You*?' Pelamis arched an eyebrow before throwing Everand an amused glance. 'Your woman is now in charge? How convenient. Tell her to deliver us the rogue half-mage, or do I need to persuade her?'

Fury balling in his stomach, Everand advanced on Pelamis. 'You'll do no such thing. We will leave. Now. Agamid, tell him.'

'Stop it! Both of you. Everand said he will yield.' Tiliqua stepped between them, her fingers crackling with turquoise lines of power. She looked over her shoulder at Lamiya. 'If we take the rogue half-mage with us, the council will not feel compelled to send more mages. Consider carefully.'

Stepping away from Pelamis, Everand watched Lamiya's face. As the new guide, although her people didn't know it yet, would she ask Malach to give himself up? He held his breath while an array of emotions flickered behind her eyes. When she looked to him, he spread his hands. 'You decide. Your people.'

Her expression cold, Lamiya faced Tiliqua. 'My people are coming, uncalled. We do not wish war with the Mages' Guild, but we are an honourable people who keep our word.'

Pride threatened to overwhelm him; she looked so assured, so wise. So beautiful.

'We have promised Malach of Riverwood safe refuge. However,' Lamiya lifted a hand and Whirr crawled out of her tunic and ran up her muscled arm to perch on her raised palm, 'if you assure me that you will leave, peacefully, I will ask — *once* — whether Malach wishes to join Everand and yield to you. If he does not reveal himself, you must still leave. Do you agree?'

Everand said, 'That's fair. What do you say?' Out of the corner of his eye he noticed Pelamis and Simoselaps were mind-conferring. They were not done yet and this event would play itself out one unexpected step at a time. For now, the way forward was in Agamid and Tiliqua's hands, and if Pelamis sabotaged things then he would be the one disobeying the current Guild directive.

Discreetly, he scrutinised Tiliqua. She was far stronger than he'd thought. Stronger than Agamid, she was on the cusp of assuming authority over this sortie. She fixed startlingly blue eyes on him and tilted her chin up, ready to speak. He gasped. In that pose, she looked just like his mother! His heart hammered wildly. Why hadn't he seen it before? *This* was why he couldn't warm to her overtures. How could he? He'd be constantly reminded of his childhood pain. *Finally*, he understood why he couldn't bring himself to consider a relationship with Tiliqua. If he could explain this to Mantiss, perhaps his master would forgive him for placing his love elsewhere.

Tiliqua arched a fine blonde eyebrow at him and then dipped her head brusquely at Lamiya. 'We agree. Summon your people and give Malach the opportunity to yield. Now.'

Mouth dry, Everand observed Lamiya. What was she thinking? If Malach and Lazuli were following the agreed plan, they wouldn't be here to answer her request! What should he do? Stand beside her or just get out of her way? If anything, the steel in her eyes had hardened and the blue glints in her hair had become deeply cold, like ice under pale blue sky.

She flicked a curt look at him and sniffed. Unease wriggled in his stomach. He'd let her down. As the new guide, would her uncanny abilities have mysteriously magnified? What would happen if Lamiya and Tiliqua ended up challenging each other? That must not happen.

With swift strides, Lamiya grabbed his arm then led him to the edge of the mats to look down at the people collecting on the shore. 'Well, my mage,' she murmured, 'it comes to this. We'll find out what mettle Malach has. I, for one, do not hold my breath that he will behave with honour.'

She sounded furious. Every muscle taut, Everand waited while Agamid and Tiliqua came to stand on his left, and Neelaps and Saiphos came to hover on the far side of Lamiya. Pelamis and Simoselaps chose to stand on the far side of Saiphos, and moved closer the edge. Swallowing, Everand realised they both had a clear line of sight of the people gathering below — and of him.

Forcing his mind to focus, he scanned the lake, seeking any hint of the dragons. He eased out a breath; the water was tranquil, not a ripple in sight.

'My people,' Lamiya's words rang out without any assistance from him. 'Mages have come from the Guild to reclaim Mage Everand, and to seek a fugitive who is under our protection.'

The paddlers had gathered in a knot to the far left of the crowd. Fervently hoping Lazuli and Malach had exhibited the good sense to stay away, Everand glanced to the right so as not to cue the other mages to look there. He resolved to keep an eye on Pelamis instead.

Lamiya lifted her hand higher and Whirr let out a series of high-pitched cheeps. 'My people, with profound regret I tell you that with the rising of this sun, the mantle of Guide of Riverplain has passed to me. The spirits of U-Mali and U-Lumin now dance with the sky spirits.'

The people murmured, and several started to cry and wail. Husbands hugged wives and children clung to their parents' tunics. A bleak hollowness crawling over his body, Everand bowed his head. Riverplain had already suffered because of his decisions. He would miss the guides with their bright eyes, boundless wisdom and compassion.

The air became dense with the sound of beating wings, chirps and bell-like calls. Forcing his chin up, he stared in amazement at the clouds of brightly coloured birds zooming towards the Meeting Place. Around him, the mages shifted uneasily.

When Lamiya raised both arms and emitted a bell-like cry, the clouds of birds swirled in circles above the crowd, chattering and dipping their wings. 'We praise Guide U-Mali and her consort U-Lumin and thank them for their wisdom and guidance!' The birds circled faster, blurring into long ribbons of assorted colours.

The hairs on the back of Everand's neck lifted at the easy thrall Lamiya held over the birds, and the uncanny energy humming around her.

'We escort the spirits of beloved U-Mali and U-Lumin to the sky and bid them fond farewell. We wish them boundless joy in the spirit world.' Lamiya arched her arms upwards and outwards and the birds formed a massive arrow, spearing up into the pink-and-yellow dawn sky.

'U-Mali and U-Lumin!' chanted the people, flinging their arms high above their heads and tilting their faces skyward.

'What is this sorcery?' Agamid leaned in to mutter in Everand's ear.

His words thick with pride, Everand said, 'Lamiya is a bird-caller. She has abilities that we can't even imagine.' Louder, so Tiliqua would also hear, he added, 'The Guild would be wise to learn about these abilities.'

Tiliqua bestowed him an impassive look. 'And the rogue half-mage?' she mouthed.

With a shrug, Everand looked back at Lamiya. Face tilted skyward and eyes closed, she was distant, absorbed in her role. He glanced at Pelamis, who was systematically scanning the rows of people. Did the mage think he'd be able to recognise Malach? Watching the arrow of birds dispersing, Everand tried to convince himself that Lazuli and Malach were far away on the hopeepa plain and Malach had effectively concealed his power, like he'd taught him. By his side, Lamiya elegantly lowered her arms, as if she were dancing.

Taking a half-step, Lamiya shouted, 'My people, Mage Everand has yielded to the mages who have come to collect him.' When her people shifted and muttered, she held up her right hand and Whirr peeped shrilly from her palm. 'He does this to prevent any more violence.'

Reaching her left hand behind her, she waggled her fingers until he moved forward and took it. 'I wish it were otherwise because Everand's heart is with us,' her voice wavered, 'but I respect his honour and integrity. I trust his judgement on this.'

Warmth flowing through him, Everand squeezed her hand.

'The mages came with the intention of capturing and taking the fugitive concealed among us. Due to Everand's honour and self-sacrifice, we have agreed that I will *ask* the fugitive to reveal himself and submit to them. The mages have further agreed to leave peacefully, even if the fugitive does not declare himself.'

Releasing his hand, she held both arms out straight, palms upwards, and Whirr faced the crowd and fluffed up his wings. 'I now give our fugitive the opportunity to surrender himself.'

Everand held his breath until his chest hurt. Against the lightening sky, tinged with blues, yellows and pinks, long lines of tiny and unusually silent birds flew loops above the lake. On the adjacent slope, the people of Riverplain muttered to one another with confused frowns. It was good that they didn't know who the fugitive was, and Lamiya had cleverly avoided mentioning Malach by name or province.

The knot of paddlers surreptitiously closed up tighter and Beram and Mookaite cast him anxious looks. He sighed. That wasn't Lazuli's square jaw he'd glimpsed at the rear, was it? Surely not. They couldn't be that stupid.

Turning sad eyes upon him, Lamiya said wistfully, 'I fear Malach does not possess your courage or honour.'

He sensed her unspoken words: *Now let's see how much honour your fellow mages have.*

Forcing a breath in, he looked at Pelamis and then Tiliqua. Both were staring at the knot of paddlers.

Tiliqua was faster. 'You!' She pointed at the boat team. 'Come forward.'

Instead, the group squeezed closer together. Tiliqua's eyes narrowed and furrows formed across her brow. Everand's pulse quickened; she looked so determined.

'Yes,' she growled, 'you hide your ability but I see you. You *are* indeed just like him!' After a cross sideways glance at him, she pointed sternly at the group. 'Malach of Riverwood, son of Mage Beetal, I see you. Submit to us now.'

Nobody moved. Everand's heartbeat boomed in his ears. Before he could decide what to do, a snake of fire shot out from Pelamis' hands, chased by another one from Simoselaps, and a ring of lurid red, sizzling fire circled the team of paddlers. The group huddled into each other and Beram slipped an arm around Mookaite. At the rear, Lazuli and Lepid reached behind their backs. For weapons?

'No!' yelled Lamiya. 'Malach! Show yourself.' She tilted her face to the sky and cried, 'Spirits, protect us!'

With a spine-tingling howl, a wall of wind raced across the lake, whipping up choppy waves, bending the trees and gusting into their faces. The swirling birds scattered, fleeing towards the trees with shrill cries and Whirr dived head-first down Lamiya's tunic. Unease shivering from his head to his toes, Everand swore under his breath. *Anything* could happen! Agamid, Tiliqua and even Neelaps and Saiphos, were all curling their fingers and murmuring low words, summoning their power.

Thunder rolled across the water, bouncing off the waves in hollow, booming echoes and his eyebrow raised at the broiling dark clouds massing over the pale-green hills to the east. The dragons! This was their doing!

Grabbing Lamiya's hands, he pleaded, 'Don't call them, my love. Malach will yield; he'll have to. Wait. Their time will come.'

'How do you know?' she hissed, her eyes grim and flashing with determination.

'I don't! But we still have a chance. Let it play out. Please.' For what seemed an eternity, she gazed at him like a stranger, the grey-and-blue flecks in her eyes shifting, her lips pressed in a thin line.

'Very well. But the storm is their idea, and I like it.' Snatching her hands from his, she snapped, '*Anything* to unbalance your mages will help.'

Feeling chastised, Everand spun around. The crowd had broken apart into huddled clusters. The paddlers had somehow melted backwards out of the snakes of fire and Malach was on his knees, alone and surrounded by crackling, sparking snakes, just like U-Lumin had been. Thank the stars the paddlers had come to their senses! How could he protect Malach? He ran barefoot down the steps.

'Everand! Stop!' Tiliqua's command chased his back.

Unheeding, he ran down the pebbled path and across the dirt shore, ignoring the pricks and jabs to his bare soles. While he ran, he flung spells of dissolution at the snakes of fire, satisfied when they dissolved like the dying embers of a bonfire and flakes of ash fell to the pebbles.

Panting, he reached Malach and hauled him to his feet. In a red cloud of anger, he bit his tongue, the taste of blood fuelling his fury. 'What are you doing?' Grabbing Malach's shoulders so hard his knuckles hurt, he shook him. 'You were supposed to conceal yourself!'

Malach punched his arms away. 'I'm no coward!'

Swinging his arm hard, Everand smashed Malach across the face. Malach spat and tried to hit him, then followed up with a bolt of fire.

'Don't be stupid!' yelled Everand. 'Pelamis will fell you. Who will lead your people then?'

'We are warriors! I will die a warrior!' screamed Malach, his face as dark as the hovering thunderclouds. Head lowered, he charged.

Dancing aside, Everand swung his fist at Malach's back and his whole arm jarred with the connection. Malach grunted then spun, fists held in front of his face ready to box. Everand clenched his hands into fists. So, *another* brawl! But better than using their power, which would bring a swift and deadly reaction from the mages. He pranced a half-circle, desperately trying not to worry about what Lamiya would think of him now. Shaking sweat from his eyes, he bounced on his toes, ready.

The air glowed, crackled and shimmered while the six mages took form in a circle around them. Still dancing on his toes, Everand glowered at Malach.

'How perfect,' said Pelamis with a sardonic grin. 'They can't even agree with each other.'

'Enough,' snapped Agamid. He stepped forward, hands held aloft with lines of purple power poised between them. 'Do you submit?'

'Never!' yelled Malach, waving a fist at Agamid.

Roaring with laughter, Pelamis said, 'He's as stupid as his father. Not worth saving.'

Everand intercepted the death shard that Pelamis flung at Malach's chest and snapped a protective shield around the two of them. Agamid and Tiliqua were shouting at him, but the roaring in his ears obliterated their words. Or maybe it was the overhead thunder splitting the air. He must move Malach away from everyone! Away from disaster. Frantic with haste, he fumbled the spell of translocation.

Malach sprinted — out through his shield — and charged at Pelamis. 'You killed Mahog!'

A mighty bang rent the air and Malach dropped face-first in the dirt.

Heart pounding so fast he thought he'd throw up, Everand gaped at Pelamis.

'He's only stunned,' snapped Pelamis. 'Like I said, a *strong* mage will deliver the rogue to the council. For the public obliteration he deserves.' His brown eyes glittered with malice. 'Now, what shall we do with *you*? You are hardly yielding, are you?'

Juggling orange balls of fire, Pelamis advanced. 'I say you are resisting us.'

Acutely aware of the crowd of three hundred people forming a wide ring around them, Everand heaved in a breath. *Calm down! Focus.* He dared not take his eyes off Pelamis to talk to Agamid or Tiliqua. In an uncanny sense of having lived this scene before, it felt as if he were back by the shore of Dragon Lake, fighting with Pelamis.

Except this time, he didn't want the dragons to save him.

Chapter Thirteen

Disbelieving, Lamiya stared at Everand's back while he sprinted, barefoot and arms flailing, towards the kneeling Malach.

'I don't believe it,' said Tiliqua. 'What *is* he thinking?'

Wishing she knew, Lamiya faced the woman mage. 'We must stop him.'

'That, we agree upon,' retorted Tiliqua, giving her a grim smile. 'He is too valuable to waste like this.' Turning to Agamid, she said, 'We must go down there.'

Before Lamiya could say anything else, the six mages dissipated and she saw their translucent robed forms shimmering in a circle around Malach and Everand — who were now brawling! What was *wrong* with them? Whirr peeped inside her tunic. 'I know. We must go there too.'

She grabbed her sandals, laced them on and bolted down the steps. The lake was a flat mirror of pale grey with hints of blues and pinks below a clear, crisp sky, silver-primrose rays of light fingering the tops of the hills. Were the dragons hiding in their cave? With the water this still, the creatures would have a clear view of the shore.

Her breath misted with each exhale at the end of every long stride. When she drew closer to the ring of mages, her paddlers rushed to intercept her, Beram grabbing at her sleeve.

'I know,' she said, gently plucking Beram's hand off. 'Nothing is unfolding as we hoped.'

Lazuli loomed in front of her, a sharp knife in one hand. 'What do you want us to do?'

'Just wait.' A hard knot formed in her throat when she noticed all the paddlers held a knife or a stone or a slingshot. Shaking her head, she said firmly, 'Wait. Let's see how the mages handle this first.'

Grumbling, the paddlers nodded and hid their weapons in pockets or tucked them into their belts. Mookaite patted the back of her hand and, looking into the healer's strained face, Lamiya remembered the conversation she and Mookaite had just before she took Everand to Riverplain. It seemed a lifetime ago, rather than a mere six suns. In vivid clarity, she visualised the earnest expression in Mookaite's brown eyes and her wise words: *A powerful mage he might be, but he's also a young man, caught up in events just like you. Treat him like a man, and be kind to each other.*

'Follow me. I have an idea.' She'd only taken two strides when the ground bucked with an almighty thud and the air vibrated in a resounding bang. Whoa! She flung her arms out to steady herself. Regaining her balance, she scanned ahead. Power crackled and writhed around Pelamis' hands. She almost swallowed her tongue; staring defiantly at the other mages, Everand stood protectively over Malach, who lay in a distorted heap at his feet.

With a groan, she strode forward, the team forming up behind her. Rapidly crossing the expanse of dirt, she thought hard. Six mages, four of whom appeared to like Everand. However, they were utterly bound by their Guild Rules, not at all accustomed to thinking outside of these. Except for Everand, who was prepared to be flexible for the greater good out of his highly-developed sense of fairness. How could she use this?

Aiming for the small gap between Agamid and Tiliqua, she called, 'Desist! I, Lamiya, Guide of Riverplain, would speak with you. You are under *my* authority here.'

An astonished silence fell. Everand and the mages gaped at her, their expressions akin to naughty children who'd been caught out.

Pelamis grinned and opened his mouth to speak. Mustering every particle of courage she could find, she rounded on him, pointing accusingly. 'You. You are on my land. You two …' She swung her finger at Simoselaps and back, 'have committed murder. You will both be judged, so be quiet while I talk with the *senior* mage.'

Growling, Pelamis lifted a hand but Agamid and Tiliqua both raised their arms, power crackling, and the orange-robed mage froze, his mouth half open.

'We will hear what Lam– … the guide has to say,' commanded Agamid, for once looking like a senior mage.

'Speak,' said Tiliqua to Lamiya. 'I will watch Pelamis,'

Her heart battering against her breastbone, Lamiya drew courage from the team standing behind her. She imagined Lazuli, expression fierce, poised ready to protect her. They all would. An all-out confrontation must be avoided. What would Everand do? She eyed him standing immobile in the centre of the circle of mages, hands folded neatly in front of him, appearance submissive, awaiting judgement.

Her eyebrows tugged into a frown. Judgement against unbreakable rules … what would he do? He'd play for time by asking for the *exact* nature of the rules and then seek a way around them. *Yes, dear heart. You have a path.* U-Mali's spirit hovered behind her eyelids, shadowy figures blurring behind her. Pulse lifting, Lamiya perceived the spirits of *all* the previous guides, and her mother, standing with her.

Schooling her features into a bland expression, as she had observed Everand do countless times, she faced Agamid. 'State for me the *exact* Guild Rules that have brought you here. I would know what transgressions you claim Malach and Everand have committed.' Out of the corner of her eye, she saw the tiniest flicker cross Everand's face, followed by an imperceptible dip of his chin.

Taken aback, Agamid merely raised an eyebrow at her.

'Fair question,' said Tiliqua promptly. 'Guild Rule Eight states that mages must only breed with other mages.' Pausing, Tiliqua gave her an uncomfortable, meaningful look. 'Rule Nine states no mages must travel outside the granite wall and wardspell.'

Ask for the full words, Lamiya imagined Everand saying. Or had he sent her the thought? She flicked a glance at him, sure his head moved in a subtle nod. 'Please recite the *exact* words of the rules for me, and any other rules relevant here.'

Gleefully, Pelamis jumped in. 'Guild Rule Eight states: *Mages must only breed with other mages to keep the lines of magic pure.*' He grinned. 'You're wasting your time if you think Everand could ever stay with you.'

Pushing down the instant rush of fear, Lamiya gave Pelamis a cool stare. 'And Rule Nine?' She transferred her attention to Agamid.

Regarding her pensively, Agamid said slowly, 'Guild Rule Nine says: *No mage or human shall pass outside the granite wall, unless ordered to do so by the Head of the Guild for special purpose.*' He opened his hands. 'Everand did not breach this rule when he arrived on his original mission because Mantiss and I sent him, but his return here was not sanctioned.'

Holding her gaze, Agamid added, 'Possibly also relevant is Guild Rule Ten, which states: *Others from outside Axis shall not be allowed inside the wall of granite, unless authorised by the Head of the Guild for special purpose.*'

'And,' said Pelamis loudly, 'the council would never grant the likes of *you* permission to live among us. Unless you'd like to wash floors or–'

'Enough!' Agamid made a chopping motion with his hand. 'Does this answer your question?'

Tilting her head to ease the growing tension in her neck, Lamiya considered. Not really. She'd been hoping the rule said no *magic* outside the Guild rather than no mage or human. But they hadn't described the punishment yet; she should press on.

A flicker of movement caught her attention. Had Malach just opened an eye? No, his eyes were closed. Wait. His face was turned her way, whereas before he was facedown. A ball of unease formed in her stomach. She must hurry. If he stood up, chaos would follow.

Extending a hand towards Agamid, she asked, 'So, who decides when the rules have been breached and what the punishment is? Are there more rules?'

Tiliqua put a hand on Agamid's sleeve. 'Let me answer. Yes, two more rules are relevant,' she said, with a long, cool look. 'Rule Eleven states: *Breaches of Guild Law will be judged by the Inner Council, with the final say by the Head of the Guild. Extreme digressions will be punished by obliteration or removal of power.*'

Lamiya held up a hand. 'Wait. Let me absorb that one.'

She thought rapidly. This explained why they wanted to take Malach, and now Everand too, back to the Guild. Decisions had to be made by the Inner Council and the Head of the Guild. No, wait, hang on. The council had already decided! That was why Everand hid Malach and then fled himself. This group was here to carry out decisions already made. Hurry, hurry. She already knew that. There must be something else of importance.

Pebbles and dirt scattered as the team shuffled impatiently behind her. Meanwhile, Everand was staring blankly at his feet. Did he have any idea how annoying he was when he did his bland, unreadable thing? Flattering that he was leaving it up to her, but what did he want her to do? The sky grew brighter, the lake mirroring pale yellow hues. *Her* lake. Maybe this wasn't about what *he* wanted her to do. What if it was about what *she* wanted? What outcome did *she* yearn for?

Peace and … she ran her eyes over Everand — still waiting, still trusting her — the early light making his hair glint like a thousand stars. Her heart gave a mighty beat; she wanted her mage. Another throb from her heart and she roamed her gaze over Everand's tall frame, the lean, angular, kissable face, the deep azure eyes that could convey so much, the warmth of his lips on her skin … Desire flared. She yearned to be with Everand the man. Mage or not.

Blinking, she scrutinised Agamid and Tiliqua. Could they vary a council decision? Did they have sufficient authority? Wanting to rub at her temples, she wished U-Mali was still the guide. This was complex beyond belief. *Dear heart, you are doing just fine. Be strong. Continue.* Lamiya looked down to hide her consternation.

'You need to hear Rule Twelve.' Tiliqua's voice broke her concentration.

Lamiya looked up. Was Tiliqua trying to help in some way? Her pulse raced. 'Go on.'

Slowly and distinctly, Tiliqua said, 'Rule Twelve decrees: *Mage power must only be used for sound purposes with honest intent. Use for personal ambition or evil intent constitutes a breach of the direst magnitude and will be punished in accordance with Rule Eleven.*' She pressed her lips closed.

For several breaths, no-one moved or said a word. A breeze gently lifting her hair away from her face, Lamiya wished time would slow down so she could reason this through. The alertness on Tiliqua's face was cuing her that the last two rules were significant. The answer lay there. Everand was studying his bare feet and wriggling his toes in the dirt. *Help me work it out!* she wanted to shriek at him. But he was busy remaining impartial, avoiding a confrontation for the greater good.

The greater good. Her heart thudded loudly. Honest intent. Her heart gave such a massive thud, she felt the blood pulsing away from it. Hurry, hurry, hurry. Piece it together! *Save your mage*, U-Mali had instructed, saying that was her purpose. U-Mali's image blurred into indistinct colours and then reformed as the face of Mookaite, lips moving soundlessly. *He is also a young man ...*

Her heart galloped. *Yes*. What if he were *only* a young man? Didn't Rule Eleven offer a choice of punishment? Whirr wriggled out of her tunic and flew across the short gap to perch on Everand's shoulder, then peered back at her with beady eyes.

Lifting her chin, Lamiya looked at the group of mages, who were all regarding her with curiosity and a hint of impatience. Next, she glanced over her shoulder at the team hovering close behind. Lazuli nodded, his grey eyes intent. *Go on.* Beram nodded. Mookaite smiled. They all seemed confident she had the solution. She ran her tongue around the inside of her dry mouth. *Order the words.* She must make sense.

Facing the mages, she addressed Agamid and Tiliqua. 'I wish to present a way forward.'

Pelamis glanced down at Malach's inert form and Everand stopped wriggling his toes and straightened his shoulders.

Frowning, she forced herself to focus on Agamid and Tiliqua. 'I understand it is important to you to uphold your Guild Law.' She took a breath. *Go on, out with it.* 'I put to you that Mage Everand has *always* acted with honest intent and has *never* acted for personal gain. He completed his assigned mission by saving the boat races and trade discussions.' The mages shuffled impatiently and she lifted a hand. 'Hear me out.'

When they stilled, she continued. 'However, he did leave the Guild unsanctioned, which is, as you said, a breach of your Rule Nine.' She couldn't look at Everand.

At the edge of her vision, Pelamis started to tap a foot and the other mages' shoulders tensed. She needed to make her main point, and fast, before they started to argue. Everand was annoyingly pulling his best bland face again.

'I understand the intent of your Rules Eight and Nine is focused on there being *no mages* and *no magic* outside of the Guild.'

Tiliqua's blue eyes became piercingly sharp, like a raptor on the hunt, and the woman's gaze seared into her. Surely, if this woman was a friend at all to Everand, if her father Mantiss cared at all for Everand, she would support what she was about to propose?

Tilting her chin higher, Lamiya said firmly, 'Your Rule Eleven says punishment is to be by *either* obliteration *or* removal of power.'

With a groan, Malach stirred and when one of his legs kicked out, Everand took a hasty step backwards. No, no, no. Let Malach stay out of it! If only she could tell Everand to kick him in the head to knock him out again. Slowly, purposefully, calmly, Everand dipped his chin in a tiny nod.

He'd guessed her plan! Better, he was telling her he'd go along with it! Emotions tumbling through her like the river currents after a wild storm, she spread her hands palms up and rushed on.

'I propose that Mage Everand and half-mage Malach be allowed to live — and that their punishment be the removal of their power. Further, if they have no power, then they are no longer mages and should be allowed to live outside the Guild.' She pressed her lips together so she wouldn't babble on or plead.

Her proposal was clear enough.

Chapter Fourteen

A deep, deep calm flowed through Everand, mingled with awe and pride. *She'd done it.* Lamiya had found what was probably the only way forward to avoid a confrontation between the mages and the provinces. So clever, so astute and far-seeing, his love had found the way they could be together. If this played out as anticipated, she'd also have gifted him the opportunity to tackle Akachi's task.

He smiled at Lamiya, adoring the way she held herself so tall and composed, silken, wavy hair falling over her shoulder, grey-blue eyes alert and challenging the mages. The utter stillness in the air and water surrounding them reinforced his conviction this was meant to happen. The lake stretched away in such a flat, blue mirror that he felt invited to walk across the surface; the crisp, clear sky shone bright with anticipation. His pulse throbbed in a slow, strong beat of satisfaction. If only nobody would move or say anything to break this precious moment.

'Outrageous!' spluttered Pelamis. 'Who are you to challenge our decrees?'

At Everand's feet, Malach pushed up to all fours, then reached out a hand and grabbed unsteadily at his knee. Curse it! What bad timing! Pushing aside his dismay, Everand leaned down to take Malach's elbow and hauled him to his feet. 'Shhh,' he hissed.

Blinking groggily, Malach slurred, 'Whassh happening?'

Yanking Malach beside him, Everand mumbled, 'Just listen. Lamiya has proposed a solution.' He gave Agamid an urgent nod; he must convey that he would go along with the proposal so the mages didn't dismiss it out of hand.

Agamid tugged at his beard with shaking fingers, his hazel eyes troubled.

With a warning glare at Pelamis and a frustrated glance at Agamid, Tiliqua took charge. To Lamiya she said, 'A creative proposal, but one that could fall within our rules.'

Everand held his breath while Tiliqua's eyes lingered on his face and she said, 'We must consult with Mantiss. Wait there and do not move.'

Agamid stopped tugging at his beard and pulled a communication orb from his robe pocket. 'Tiliqua is right. Wait while she and I confer with Mantiss.' He held his arm out with the green-veined orb balanced on his palm.

Her eyes still not leaving Everand's face, Tiliqua placed her right hand over the top of the orb. Everand continued to hold his breath while they both bent their concentration to the orb, which flared green, then the veins pulsed with moss-green light.

Subtly scrunching his toes on the dirt beneath his feet, Everand thought of Mantiss, silently thanking him for his extensive training, care and support, and mentally asking that his master now let him go. Perhaps they could remain friends. His chest panged with sorrow. It was unlikely that he'd even be allowed to enter Axis, let alone mingle with the Guild mages. Warm tears prickled the back of his eyes and he blinked to dissuade them from falling.

From under his eyelashes, he peered at Lamiya, her face aglow with hope and her loyal paddlers fanned out behind her. His heartbeat thudded slowly through his veins. Beram, Mookaite, even Lazuli … his new friends. Warmth radiated out from his heart; he could do this. Power wasn't everything.

Lifting his chin, he observed the mages. Agamid and Tiliqua were still conferring, their lips twitching while they conveyed their mind-speak. Saiphos was watching him with lines of worry creasing his forehead. At Everand's small smile, he looked astonished before returning a tentative smile. Next along, Neelaps was twisting his head this way and that, taking the opportunity to absorb the landscape. When he realised Everand was looking at him, he gave a happy nod.

Slowly, Everand brought his attention back to Agamid. Better to not make eye contact with Pelamis or Simoselaps at this point. Not while things hung in the balance.

'Thank you for your counsel,' Agamid said aloud, before he looked up directly into Everand's eyes. 'Mage Mantiss, Head of the Guild, has agreed to vary our instruction. If you formally accept the removal of your power, he will sanction this as your punishment instead of obliteration.'

Removing her hand from the top of the orb and frowning, Tiliqua fixed intent, sad eyes upon him. 'Mage Everand, on behalf of the Guild I formally ask whether removal of your power is a punishment that you will accept?'

Acutely aware of Lamiya's held breath and the eyes of all the paddlers, all the mages and the gathered crowd upon him, Everand drew courage from the pale, infinite blue sky above and said clearly, 'I formally accept removal of my power — as long as it means I can choose to live in Riverplain as a non-mage and be consort at Guide Lamiya's side.'

After a hurried breath, he bowed to Agamid and said, 'I formally ask Mage Agamid to be the one to take my power.' Ignoring the horror that spread across the mage's face, he said, 'Mage Agamid, my friend, will you perform this crucial act for me?'

His voice husky, Agamid said, 'I will. As long as you are sure.'

'What are you doing? I won't let anyone take my power!' Malach swung around, wide-eyed and pale, with bits of grit stuck in his chin. He looked on the verge of trying to bolt for it.

Curse the idiot! He could undo everything! Gripping Malach's arms and shoving his face so close their noses almost touched, Everand snarled, 'You didn't hide. We're outnumbered. Don't you want to live and lead your people? You can do that without your power!'

Rigid with fury, Malach spat back, 'No! I want to be like my father!'

Grinding his teeth, Everand glared at Malach until Agamid gave a loud cough. Abruptly, he realised that Agamid hadn't said whether Mantiss' decision included Malach and had chosen his words carefully to only convey that Mantiss had agreed to *his* future. Curse it! He felt the saliva running away between his teeth until his mouth was bone dry. Once they removed his power, he wouldn't be able to protect Malach. And if they tried to take Malach back to the Guild, or tried to take his power, the determined idiot would resist and Pelamis would kill him.

What to do? Think! Lamiya would say call the dragons. No. They'd be right back at the start with a major confrontation and even if the mages left, they'd vow to come back. A long-term answer had to be decided now. He couldn't look at Lamiya. She would have to trust him, believe he had a plan. Releasing Malach's arms, he took a step away. *Lamiya. Do this for her, for you. Nothing else matters.* If he didn't ask about Malach's fate and let them take his power, then he couldn't be held responsible for what Malach did.

After another step away, he said distinctly to Agamid and Tiliqua, 'I am ready.'

Arching an eyebrow, Agamid gave a tense nod and began to curl and uncurl his fingers.

'Wait.' Heart hammering, Everand said, 'Let me say goodbye to Tiliqua first, and give her a message for Mantiss.'

'Very well. But hurry,' urged Agamid.

In two quick steps, Everand reached Tiliqua and grasped her hands. Her eyes widened in surprise. 'Tiliqua,' he whispered,

'I'm sorry things could not have been different. In many ways, it would have been wonderful to join your family. You will be a great mage, I can tell.' A faint blush adorned her cheeks. 'Please convey my deepest gratitude to Mantiss, for *everything* he did for me. Including this. No, *especially* this. If possible, I wish to remain a friend to him, and to you.'

Tiliqua squeezed his hands with her slim, cold fingers. 'I too am sorry things are not otherwise, but I wish you well, as I'm sure my father does.'

'Bind the half-mage until this is done,' snapped Agamid sharply.

Releasing Tiliqua's hands, Everand stepped sideways to stand before Agamid. Refusing to look at Malach, he now wanted Agamid to hurry, to get this over and done with. *Lamiya.* Think only of being with her. Forever. In this beautiful place.

'Are you ready?' Agamid asked kindly, purple power crackling down his arms and bouncing around his fingertips. 'Tiliqua, you will witness?'

Taking a deep swallow, Everand squared his shoulders and said, 'I thank you both.' Closing his eyes to make it easier for them, he drew in a long breath, called his power to sit coiled in his power well at the base of his stomach, and slid the tiny walls that looked like internal muscle and tissue over the three azure droplets he buried so deep in his groin he couldn't even feel them. He was ready. No doubt this would hurt.

'Wait.' Lamiya's voice. 'Let me stand closer.'

He heard her tunic rustling and the light slap of her sandals crossing the pebbles and dirt. Briefly opening his eyes, he waited until she stood between Agamid and Saiphos. 'My love,' he mouthed. 'It will be alright.' With his foot, he scuffed a wiggly line in the dirt, satisfied that it looked a bit like a snake.

After peering down at his feet, she gave him an undecipherable look.

'We begin,' intoned Agamid. 'Mage Everand, the Guild has decreed that you should be punished for unforgiveable breaches of Guild Rules Eight and Nine. In recognition that your actions intended no harm to the Guild, you have been allowed to choose your punishment under Guild Rule Eleven. As a punishment defined under Guild Rule Eleven, you have granted us leave to remove your power. Release your power upon our call and allow us to take it from you and absorb it into our power.'

'Proceed,' croaked Everand, scrunching his eyes shut and straightening his spine to deflect the trembles threatening to overwhelm him. Drawing measured breaths, he concentrated on thinking about waking up with Lamiya entwined in his arms, birds singing outside her hut in bright sunshine and the turquoise lake stretching away to distant colourful shores. A new life.

The air around him filled with crackling and warmth until a cloud of energy hovered just above his head. His hair lifted with static, then his skull tingled and prickled, as if a thousand tiny needles were being stabbed into it. Breathing deeply and evenly, he fought to keep his heart beating at a steady rate. *Relax. Let it happen.* The prickling and crackling moved its way through his head and edged down his neck, like a spreading bout of pins and needles. Behind his eyelids, purple-and-turquoise energy shifted and shimmered, forming into grasping fingers of purple light resting near his collarbone.

His stomach and torso wrenched with a sharp tug, as if he were about to throw up. Despair threatened to intrude as his azure power uncoiled from his well and flowed up into the outstretched fingers. A sob sounded in his ears. More vivid blue power gathered and streamed upward, disappearing into the purple fingers and flowing up out of his head, following the lines of crackling purple power. Without opening his eyes, he perceived his beloved blue power flowing across the gap and receding into Agamid.

Gradually, his pool of power emptied, leaving a bone-deep ache bordering on pain. Weakness spread out from his centre and oozed down his arms and legs; his head weighed heavy on his neck.

His blue power became a trickle, reluctantly spiralling upwards, leaving behind an immeasurable sense of loss, a chasm of absence. Another sob escaped. Sorrow washed through him, chasing the tail end of his power, and he allowed his sadness to seep into the grasping purple fingers. The final miniscule tail of blue flickered, then dissipated. The prickling purple fingers remained, joined by slender turquoise ones. Pushing all thought away, he let them check, probing and niggling, that they had it all. Bursts of nausea followed their probes and he gagged, then schooled his face to show no expression.

Sure enough, the purple fingers tugged a few more times, demanding, calling for any residual power, scraping at the edges of his power well. The tiny, translucent walls held. *Lamiya. Think of Lamiya.* Everand filled his mind with her grey-blue eyes sparkling with mischief, her velvet kissable lips, her luscious mahogany hair. The turquoise fingers rapidly retreated and he felt Tiliqua's energy leaving through the top of his head. Agamid lingered, probing, digging for any sign of power. Everand let the trembling, fatigue and loss wash in. Finally, the purple fingers retracted and Agamid's presence departed.

His heartbeat booming in his ears, his teeth chattering with shock and fatigue, Everand perceived he was surrounded by a crowd of silent, horrified people below heavy air that stifled all sound, all thought, all reason. He couldn't bear to face the expressions of pity. Or the glee on Pelamis' face. All remaining strength evaporating, he sank to his knees, the dirt and stones digging into his skin to add to his pain.

'I declare it is done,' said Agamid, sounding weary.

'I bear witness that it is done,' said Tiliqua strongly. 'We have removed Mage Everand's power and he is no longer a mage of the Guild. No longer a mage of Axis.'

The slap of approaching sandals made him force his eyelids apart, the overbright light made his eyes water. Through blurry tears he saw Lamiya.

'My love. Are you alright?' she asked tenderly, clasping his fingers, urging him to get to his feet.

His mouth too dry to form words, he gripped her hands and tried to use her strength to help him rise. His legs and body would have none of it.

'I love you so much for doing this for me. For us.' Lamiya sounded close to tears. 'Please, try to stand.' She leaned in closer, the ends of her hair tickling his cheek. 'Stand, my love. I fear Malach is about to erupt.'

Everand exhaled slowly. The next phase. It would be far better not to be on his knees. Holding Lamiya's hands, he leaned on them and dragged his right foot into position beneath him. When his body wobbled annoyingly, Lamiya braced, ready to take his weight. Forcing pressure onto the sole of his bare foot, he grunted at the stabs of sharp stones, put his weight onto that leg and swung the other leg beneath him.

'Excellent,' Lamiya murmured, light dancing in her eyes. 'Some swimming and paddling will make you stronger, my love.'

'Indeed,' he muttered, squeezing her fingers in gratitude, then looking over her head. Straight into Agamid's gaze.

With a curt nod, Agamid broke eye contact and looked to where Malach paced in agitation, constrained by Pelamis and Simoselaps within two snakes of fire, one hovering around his waist and the other around his neck.

'Malach of Riverwood. I will now advise your judgement and punishment.' Agamid's face was stern.

'You can't judge me!' roared Malach. 'I am not of your Guild!' He took a step and the crackling, hissing snakes of fire magnified and sparks flew at him. Batting these away, he snarled at Pelamis.

Letting go of Lamiya's wonderful, warm, reassuring hand, Everand whispered, 'My love, go and stand with your paddlers.'

Reaching for his hand, Lamiya shook her head. 'Together, my love. We face this together.'

'Not yet,' he whispered urgently, feeling weak energy seeping into his legs and arms. 'One more thing will happen. After that, we'll be together.' Ignoring her astonished gasp and the way she peered searchingly into his face, he gave her a nudge. 'Go. Trust me. I need you away from me for what comes.'

It took a further two nudges before she walked away, displeasure oozing from the set of her shoulders and the way she tossed her hair over them. His mouth feeling like he'd just eaten a bowl of sand, Everand crept his awareness into his groin and plucked one of the azure droplets. Cradling it in his deepest subconscious, he set the droplet to activate on a sudden impact. Then he looked down to make sure he was standing a few paces back from the S he had scuffed in the dirt.

'Your Guild has no right here!' shouted Malach, bristling just like Mage Beetal used to and shaking a fist at Agamid.

'Can I subdue him?' asked Pelamis with a smug grin. 'I assume we *are* taking him to the Guild?'

With a guttural roar, Malach tried to charge out of the circle of fire. Laughing, Pelamis and Simoselaps strengthened their flow of fire and heat, singeing Malach's tunic and skin until he lowered his arm and stood still, panting.

His pulse beating faster, Everand ground his teeth and commanded his feet not to move. Behind him, he heard the paddlers muttering uneasily. *Lamiya, my love,* he thought, *keep them calm.* He made a shushing motion with one hand, hoping she or Beram would notice.

Malach spun to shake a fist at him. 'You tricked me! I should have stayed in Riverwood! We would have fought for our right to live in our own province.' Flexing his fingers in and out rapidly, Malach spun around and hurled a fire bolt at Pelamis.

Tiliqua intercepted the bolt. 'Enough! Stand still and hear your fate.'

With lips curled into a cruel smile, Pelamis planted his gaze upon Everand. 'Let's make sure you really have given us all your power. Watch your friend dance.' Pelamis twisted both wrists and hurled massive bolts at Malach. One took the half-mage in the shoulder, the other in his thigh.

'Aggh!' screamed Malach. 'You coward! Release me and fight like a man!'

'Enough!' shouted Tiliqua, drawing up to her full height.

Ignoring her, Pelamis played lines of crackling fire all over Malach, watching Everand's face the whole time. 'Can't save your precious rogue now, can you?'

'Stop it, Pelamis,' snapped Agamid, stepping forward. 'Malach, the Guild instructs us to bring you before the council. Do you submit willingly or do we need to subdue you?'

'Never!' screamed Malach, puce in the face, jumping up and down and fiercely waving his fists. 'Grant me a warrior's death!'

Lifting his chin, Everand caught Lamiya's eye, twitched his lips in a hint of a smile — and took two long steps — towards Pelamis.

'Finally,' Pelamis yelled, glee smeared over his face. 'He attacked me!' He hurled a massive death bolt at Everand.

The bolt flashed through the air. Incredible pain smashed into Everand's left shoulder and an excruciating force spun him completely around. With an imperceptible click, the hidden spell activated.

A tidal wave of blackness gushed up to drown his heart.

He plummeted into a dark, endless void.

Chapter Fifteen

'No!' Lamiya screamed. Why, by all the spirits, had Everand done that? A torrent of anger tumbled into her. How could she trust him, when he did *this* with no warning? No goodbye? A growl reverberated in her chest. The mages were hateful. Scorn filled her at the way Pelamis and Simoselaps were teasing Malach, making him dance to avoid their fire snakes while Agamid and Tiliqua stood frozen in shock with the other two mages cowering behind them.

Using the energy of the roar that began in the soles of her feet and flashed through her body, she flung her arms up in a V. 'To me!' she commanded, sending her summons far and wide. 'To me!' Thousands of tiny voices answered, and before she had lowered her arms the sky was blotted out by birds zooming towards her.

In the gathering darkness, she rounded on Agamid. 'Leave immediately. You are not welcome here.' The birds swooped and whirled, a broiling feathered thundercloud above her. She flung her arms towards the mages and thousands of birds flew at them, screeching and squawking.

The colour drained from Agamid's face. 'Gather around!' He frantically tugged the green orb from his pocket and it instantly flared to life. 'Bring Malach!' he snapped at Pelamis and Simoselaps.

Lamiya called Whirr and immediately he hovered before her face, his feathers fluffed with excitement and eyes bright. 'Tell the dragons we need a storm,' she snipped and he sped away, flying low across the lake.

More anger than she thought was possible rammed into her at the sight of Tiliqua kneeling by Everand's inert body. Sprinting across the dirt, she slammed both hands into Tiliqua's shoulder and the woman mage fell backwards. Lamiya gritted out, 'Leave. Now.'

Sitting up, Tiliqua dusted the dirt off her hands. 'We're going! For what it's worth, I'm sorry. This shouldn't have happened.' Stiffly, the woman stood, nodded curtly then backed away, watching her warily.

Lamiya stared at Tiliqua's receding turquoise robe, part of her mind chattering about how foolish it was to shove a mage. The rest of her mind raged. *How dare they*. And they were being far too slow to leave, milling around, with Malach yelling insults and trying to charge at them. A gust of wind tugged at her hair, the icy blast following it raising goosebumps down her arms. She tilted her face skyward. *Great spirits, help me now. Akachi, bring me chaos.*

Huge black clouds formed out of nowhere and shards of hail flung earthward. A tongue of crackling lightning bit the ground only a few paces from the mages. *Yes*. Revelling in the wild static in the air and the turbulence beating at her, Lamiya threw her cry again. *Help me.*

Thunder boomed and crashed, the air whipped erratically, lifting her hair and moulding her tunic to her skin. Next breath, she was soaked by the pebble-sized raindrops pelting the ground. Thousands of birds wheeled in a chaotic blur of colours and cacophony of beating wings and shrill cries. Blinking water from her eyes, she saw amid the chaos that the circle of mages was shimmering and dissipating. Malach hung limply between two of them. *Good riddance*. Rubbing her eyes, she blinked again to be sure the mages had actually gone. No sign of them.

Slowly, she brought her mind back into focus. Her people stood in a large circle around her, huddled against the rain and shivering but all watching her, waiting for her command. Humbled, she lifted her face, the rain sluicing over her washing away her doubt and sorrow. *Thank you. You can stop now.*

The birds slowed their flight then wheeled away across the lake, heading towards the trees, cheeping and chattering. The rain abruptly ceased, leaving her cloaked in damp and heavy air.

Closing her eyes, she took two slow breaths. *Everand.* She blocked the tidal wave of sorrow. *Check, before you grieve.*

Sunlight breathed gentle warmth over her cheeks and she opened her eyes to fresh and clear blue sky. Footsteps hurried behind her. Just knowing they belonged to Mookaite, she turned to face the healer's tear-streaked face. 'We must check Everand.'

Uncertainty crossed Mookaite's face, chased by a glimmer of hope. 'You think … he isn't dead?'

Lamiya sank to her knees beside Everand. He looked so broken, twisted awkwardly, clothes and hair sodden, pale face smeared with dirt, those wonderful blue eyes vacant. His tunic was torn across his left shoulder, blood and the edge of a bone showing. 'Help me turn him over.'

Gently, she and Mookaite straightened Everand's legs, then rolled him so he was face up. Bands of dread bound her heart, strangling her breath; he was so absent, so still. What if he really was dead? Her throat ached with a rising sob and she clenched her teeth against it. Be confident. Shuffling around, she sat by his chest, indicating Mookaite should kneel on his other side. Lips compressed, the healer cast her a worried look.

Tenderly, Lamiya traced Everand's eyebrows, then his cheekbones. *My love. What am I supposed to do?* With a peep,

Whirr landed on her shoulder and nuzzled her neck with the top of his head. Shutting her eyes, Lamiya allowed her mind to see-but-not-see. The scene rang familiar; she'd been here before. Blanking out thought, she waited.

A heartbeat rolled through her, then another, and she and Mookaite were in the boat dome with Ejad sprawled before them, his face turning blue from the viper's poison. Her heart beating faster, she thought of Everand tracing an S in the dirt with his foot before his power was taken. He was telling her to remember the viper. To remember what he'd done to save Ejad!

Opening her eyes, she said, 'We must save him the same way he saved Ejad.'

'How?' whispered Mookaite. 'We don't have his magical ability.'

'No,' murmured Lamiya, 'but he showed me what to do. Let's try. We have to somehow travel along his veins, sensing his life force.'

Mookaite arched an eyebrow. 'We'd better hurry, he feels cold.'

Cringing at the blue tinges around Everand's slack lips, Lamiya took a breath to calm her racing heart and reached deep within for her calling power. Then she put both hands on his chest, grateful when Mookaite promptly placed warm hands over hers. Bowing her head, she pleaded, *U-Mali, aid me. Mother, strengthen my call. I must not lose him.* Mookaite's fingers twitched atop hers.

Another breath passed then, with a puff of lily-scented air, Lamiya felt the spirits of U-Mali and Lestaya hovering by her shoulder. Whirr peeped a greeting before flying down to perch on Everand's chest. Clutching at these signs of encouragement, Lamiya gathered her courage and visualised her essence flowing through her hands and entering Everand. A shiver wracked her. His flesh was so cold! Mookaite's gasp reached her ears.

Dear heart, keep going, came U-Mali's nudge.

Yes, agreed Lestaya. *I wish to meet him properly, daughter dear.*

Focusing, Lamiya pushed her essence deeper, finding the large blood vessels leading to Everand's heart. Nothing was moving. No heartbeat, no pulse of blood, no air flowing into the flaccid lungs. Someone sobbed. Had that come from her? Whirr chirped twice and Mookaite scrunched her hands in a squeeze of reassurance.

'We can do this,' the healer murmured.

Lamiya let her mind roam. Fleeting images came of the dragon Flight peeling away from her boat, of Akachi rising from the lake to greet her, of Everand sitting opposite her in the flickering light of a feast bonfire and saying, his expression earnest, 'You can call more than birds, my love.'

Hanging onto the intensity in his blue eyes, she sent forth her presence, systematically pushing it along the blood vessel until she felt her fingertips caress the wall of his heart. Nothing happened. Yet Everand had scuffed an S in the dirt. There *must* be a clue in what happened to Ejad! She replayed the incident in her mind. Everand had drawn out all the poison, but there was no poison here. Afterwards, Ejad had sat up. Wait, at first Ejad couldn't stand and said he felt weird, like he was asleep.

What happened then? Oh. Everand had gone to stand behind Ejad, saying he'd forgotten to restart his heart properly. Excitement buzzed through her and her fingers tingled. *Yes.* Everand had stopped Ejad's heart to slow the spread of the poison. Had he stopped his own heart so he'd look dead? If so, he'd fooled Tiliqua and the other mages. 'So clever, my love,' she murmured, feeling a gush of anxiety — he had a plan that involved needing the Guild to think he was dead. If she didn't succeed, his plan would fail.

Bending her full concentration, she methodically probed around the walls of his heart. Wait, her mind fingers paused.

There. A tiny, translucent wall was snicked across the main blood vessel, stopping the flow of blood. She felt a flush of fear. How was she supposed to undo that? 'Ouch!' Her finger stung where Whirr pecked it. 'I am hurrying!'

She stared at Everand's pale face. 'I see what you have done. Tell me how to undo it.'

Cold air washed over the back of her hands when Mookaite sat up. Using the extra space, Lamiya tipped forward and put her ear to Everand's lips. Did she imagine the subtle intake of air? She brushed her lips over his cold ones. Could she breathe life into him?

Try it, urged U-Mali, pushing at her shoulder.

Brushing her lips over Everand's again, Lamiya fumbled for his hand and clutched it. His fingers were damp and limp in hers but it felt right. She brushed her lips back across his, then sealed her mouth over his, visualising her energy and love as a bright golden light flowing into him, travelling down his throat and pouring into his heart. Her heart gave a mighty throb. She imagined his heart filling with golden light and throbbing in response, the golden blood warming, pulsing, and dissolving the tiny wall blocking the flow of blood and opening the connection to his body.

Mouthing ancient words she didn't understand, she thought of the heart sluices opening and vivid gold light, chased by incandescent blue light, coursing through him like a river and spreading along a thousand tributaries to every part of him.

Everand's body twitched. Then he took a great gasp that sucked the air from her mouth. She'd done it! Pulling her mouth away, she watched him take two deep gulps of air before crunching her lips back over his. His hand gripped hers, and his other arm flung over the back of her neck, crushing her against him.

'By the spirits, he lives!' Mookaite said tearfully. Scrambling to her feet, the healer shouted, 'He lives!'

Revelling in the warmth returning to Everand's lips, Lamiya heard the great cheer that went up. Whirr ran up her arm, peeping and chattering. Breaking the kiss, she peered into Everand's fathomless azure eyes. 'Don't scare me like that again! Ever.'

With a crooked smile, Everand croaked, 'Sorry. I had to make it look real.'

Lamiya sat up. 'Are you strong enough to stand?'

'Maybe. Help me up?'

'Since you asked nicely, I might.' Tossing her damp hair back over a shoulder, she said, 'You have some explaining to do.'

Tilting her head, she wagged a finger at him. 'Make that a *lot* of explaining.'

Chapter Sixteen

'I knew you could do it. That you'd work it out,' Everand said to deflect Lamiya's outrage and trying to kiss the finger wagging too close to his nose for comfort.

'Hah!' Her eyes flashed a steel grey, but she stopped wagging her finger. 'What if I hadn't?'

Pushing away the thought that she'd still be the Riverplain Guide but she'd have partnered with Lazuli instead, he said, 'I think I can stand up now.' Letting Lamiya and Mookaite take an elbow each, he gingerly sat up then pushed his feet beneath him. His legs refused to support him and he wobbled annoyingly, but Lamiya's concerned glance made him straighten his spine.

A massive cheer went up and he flinched at the crowd of people rushing towards him with Beram, Tengar, Persaj and Ejad racing at the front. Multiple hands clapped his back and shoulders, making him wobble again, while voices cried out their joy that he was alive. Humbled, he felt utterly ashamed for making his friends fear for him like that.

Tucking his chin down to hide his emotions, he wondered what the Guild reaction would be. Would Mantiss grieve for him? Or would the councils carry on without missing a beat? Agamid and the others! Alarm ripped through him and he scanned the area. His alarm faded; no mages. 'The mages have gone?' he asked, wanting to be sure.

'You should have seen Lamiya!' said Beram, his face alight with wonder. 'She frightened them away.'

Around him, with nods and grins, numerous people muttered praise to Lamiya. Everand felt an eyebrow twitch. What, exactly, had she done? 'It seems I'm not the only one with some explaining to do,' he said, tempted to wag his finger at her nose. Plucking at his damp tunic, he added, 'Are you the reason I'm wet, on top of everything else?'

Those nearby laughed, and Beram clapped his shoulder. 'Traveller, you really are priceless.'

Lazuli approached and shook his hand. 'I'm glad you are alright.'

Unable to think of a suitable reply, Everand nodded. Wait. Lazuli and Malach hadn't hidden like they were supposed to. Snippets of memory flooding back, he grew still. 'Malach?'

Shuffling his feet, Lazuli said, 'The mages took him. I'm sorry.'

'Alive?' Everand swallowed his rising disappointment.

Lamiya came to stand beside Lazuli. 'The Guild approved removal of your power, but didn't grant Malach the same concession. He fought well, but the mages have taken him. We had no way of stopping them.' She touched his arm. 'This is better. Now they have no reason to return.'

Conscious that everyone was watching, anxious for his reaction, he bit down his frustration and curbed his desire to yell at Lazuli for not sticking to the plan. 'That's true.'

Looking uncomfortable, Lazuli turned to Lamiya. 'What do you want to do now?' He looked up at the sky briefly. 'It's still early. Can we paddle?'

Before Lamiya could agree, Everand said, 'Can I suggest the team rests?' When they both narrowed their eyes at him, he faltered. 'We need to do a long paddle, a really long paddle, before dark-fall.'

'Why? To where?' asked Lazuli, his eyes lighting up in anticipation.

Putting her hands on her hips and tossing her hair back from her face, Lamiya said, 'I see. So, the explaining you will be doing includes a plan?'

Warmth sliding up his neck, Everand said, 'Could we possibly eat while I explain?'

Sensing the conversation had turned to important matters, the rest of the paddlers crowded in with such eager looks that Everand felt humbled again. Was there no limit to their courage? With friends of this calibre, perhaps his wild plan had a chance. But first and foremost, he had to persuade Lamiya. After all, she now led these people. When he looked at her, she arched an eyebrow.

'Akachi's task?'

He nodded, then waited for her to decide what they should do.

Roaming her gaze around the group of paddlers, Lamiya said crisply, 'Gather in the boatshed, just my team and the visitors from Riverfall. Everand can enlighten us about his plan.' She flicked him a dry look. 'While we eat, we'll work out the details together.'

Relieved, Everand said, 'Could someone prepare two suns' worth of food and water for us to take when we, er, when we go.'

'I can do that,' said Lulite. To Lamiya, she said softly, 'If you agree, I'll remain behind.'

'Of course, and thank you,' Lamiya grasped Lulite's hands. 'Lapsi will stay too.'

Everand saw how Lapsi flushed and the others exchanged confused glances. Lamiya clearly knew something he and the others didn't. No matter, with the guests from Riverfall there would be enough paddlers for the distance. His damp tunic was chafing his armpits but he suspected Lamiya and the others would head to the boatshed without bothering to get changed. Catching her eye, he plucked at his damp tunic and she frowned.

Lifting her arms, Lamiya shouted, 'People of Riverplain, thank you for your support and bravery. Go about your duties and I'll call a meeting when we've worked out a way forward.'

Everand was impressed by the respectful bows everyone gave before heading off in various directions. Would there be a special ceremony to formally instate her as their guide? Busy watching the crowd disperse, he jumped when Lamiya slipped her arm through his.

'Yes, my love, there will be a special ceremony involving the spirits past and present, followed by a large and noisy celebration.' She fluttered her eyelashes at him. 'Where you will formally be named as my consort.'

'Did you just read my mind?' he asked.

'Try not to shout, it isn't necessary,' she replied pertly, then reached out her free hand to snag Lulite's sleeve. 'Can you bring fresh tunics for us?' She turned back to him. 'Come, tell us what you have in mind.'

Tempted to ask whether he needed to or whether she'd already read his mind to find out, he gave a meek nod and let her lead him towards the boatshed. The paddlers quickly fell in behind them.

Halfway across the pebbly beach, Beram drew alongside. 'How do you feel? Do you feel … different?'

Mookaite hurried to catch up and peered at him too.

'Yes,' he admitted. 'I feel somehow smaller, weaker. But,' he rushed on when they both started to look sad, 'I hope this won't be for long. I'll explain at the boatshed.'

They both looked hopeful and Lamiya flicked another dry glance his way.

While they walked the last part, he assessed his body. In truth, his limbs did feel as if the strength and energy had been sapped from them, and his mind felt as if a fog had descended. No, maybe more of a mist. His intellect was there, it just seemed slower. Putting his hands over his lower abdomen, he tried to locate the two droplets of power. His heart thudded in his ears when he couldn't find them. Wait. There they were, dormant like flower seeds buried below cold-season ground. A shiver crawled across his nape.

The grating of the shed's wooden doors being heaved open brought his mind back. Quickly and efficiently, the paddlers lifted Flight and carried the boat out onto the beach, then gathered cushions and threw them in a circle on the shed's dirt floor. Lamiya chose her cushion, and in a fluid movement the paddlers all sat cross-legged and watched her expectantly.

Everand sank onto the vacant cushion beside her and murmured, 'You lead. Ask what you want to know.'

Blowing a wisp of hair away from her mouth, she fixed grey-blue eyes on him. 'First, we're all most glad to see you are well.' The others mumbled agreement. 'We're also relieved the mages have gone. I'll tell you what happened later, but I must tell you the Guild mages are not welcome in Riverplain.'

'I understand.' He dipped his head, red-hot embarrassment sliding up his neck.

'We will listen to your plan, but consider carefully whether it is one that is likely to bring the mages back.'

Feeling as if she'd tipped a tub of cold water down his back, Everand shifted on his cushion, realising that first and foremost she was now the leader of her people and he could no longer assume her unconditional support. He wanted to trace a finger down her cheek and tell her he did understand, really. For so long, she had followed him, but now he must negotiate. 'Do you want to tell our visitors about Akachi? Then I'll explain our task and my plan.'

'Yes, a good approach.' Her expression animated, she told the Riverfall paddlers about how she'd summoned Akachi, the massive red dragon from the distant end of their lake. Rapidly, she explained the dragon had been there for generations, concealed, but had revealed herself now because there was something she wanted her and Everand to do. She flapped a hand at him.

Sitting straighter, he said, 'Akachi wants me to return to her the magnificent stone of power known as the Staropal. It seems the early mages, who arrived four generations ago, might have taken it from her.' Shame flooding his veins, he spread his hands open. 'I didn't know this when I came on my mission to help you protect the races and trade discussions.'

He paused at the surprise on their faces. 'I confess, I worried that the true reason I was sent had not been declared, but I had no idea it would be a matter of this significance.' Conscious of the flush crawling across his cheeks, he took a breath. 'The current mages, and possibly the previous three generations, have all been taught that the Staropal was found in the eternal spring in the centre of Axis.' His cheeks grew warmer. 'We were also not taught anything about there being any river dragons in Ossilis.'

Looking at Beram, he said fondly, 'When Beram threw rocks at the protected granite wall to gain the Guild's attention, he started an adventure far bigger than any of us anticipated.'

Now Beram flushed, and those near him clapped his shoulder or patted his knee.

'Put simply, Akachi has asked me …' He glanced at Lamiya. 'I mean, me and Lamiya, to recover the Staropal for her.'

'But you'd have to go to the Guild in Axis to get it!' spluttered Lazuli, casting an anxious look at Lamiya.

'How will you get through the death wall?' asked Beram, his mouth hanging open.

Acutely aware of everyone's attention drilling into him, Everand said, 'I know of a secret tunnel.'

'Is that how you got back here?' asked Lamiya.

'Yes. Malach's father created and then used a tunnel to sneak out of the Guild to see Malach's mother. It is in Riverwood.'

'You want us to paddle to Riverwood?' Lazuli caught on quickly. 'That's the long paddle?'

'And the mages don't know about the tunnel?' asked Luvu gruffly.

'They do not. It is in a barren area a long way north of the Guild buildings and they have no cause to go there. I found it only because I let Mage Beetal's former transport mount take me there.' Everand shrugged. 'I guessed the creature would remember the way.'

'Clever.' Lazuli shook his head in admiration.

'So that's how you retrieved Malach and brought him here?' Lamiya regarded him thoughtfully.

'Yes. I should have said, but the fewer people who knew about it the better because then the mages couldn't extract the knowledge from you.' A chill pelted down his spine. 'Did you say the mages took Malach alive? We'll have to hurry then because Malach knows his father came through the wall there!' *Curse it.* Would the Guild interrogate Malach or just obliterate him as quickly as possible?

Another chill scurried down his body. If Malach hadn't yet been obliterated, could they rescue him? Then there would be two of them with power to help with the escape!

Lamiya groaned. 'I can see what you're thinking, my love. Do we have to?'

Thinking rapidly, Everand swallowed. 'My plan is that we paddle all the way to Riverwood and reach there just on dark-fall. Three of us will go through the tunnel into Axis.' He looked around the circle of paddlers and, as he anticipated, Lazuli quickly leaned forward and gave him a nod. Yes, if Lamiya agreed, Lazuli would be his choice. No-one else would protect her so fiercely.

'We can't take more than three because we'll need to use the transport beetles to escape, mine and the staghorn that belonged to Malach's father. They can carry two riders apiece.'

'That's four,' said Beram. 'Can I come?'

Noticing how Mookaite reached over to grip Beram's hand, Everand said slowly, 'I appreciate your courage, but if Lamiya agrees, I was thinking Lazuli. And we need a space to bring Malach back. If the mages haven't killed him.'

Silence bouncing off the boatshed walls, he eased in a breath and waited. Through the open shed doors, it seemed that even the lake outside was holding its breath, the water still and not lapping at the pebbly shore.

After what felt like an eternity, Lamiya said, 'Very well. I do not like Malach but we will rescue him if we can. To the main task, though, how do we obtain the stone of power? Won't this be protected?'

'Yes. The Staropal is buried beneath the floor of the Great Hall and only the Head of the Guild knows the secret words to access it.' He winced at the way Lamiya's eyebrows quirked upwards. 'My plan is that we sneak in through the tunnel, walk to the Guild, and first go to Mage Mantiss' dome.'

Lamiya's stare was penetrating. 'You think he will help you? Why would he?'

Never ever having felt so weak or so vulnerable, Everand swallowed around the lump clogging his throat. 'I rely on his integrity. Mage Mantiss is fading and wants to hand over the leadership to someone he trusts, a mage who can uphold the Guild vision. In the past, all the trouble has arisen when ambitious mages have tried to take the stone.' Running a hand over his jaw, he added, 'Because Mantiss is under a real and current threat from Pelamis, he has incentive to act.'

Looking deep into her eyes, he said, 'If we give the stone back to Akachi, the temptation of additional power will be removed, the Guild will be more stable without it and the dragons will be protected, my love. If Akachi has the stone, the mages wouldn't dare go anywhere near them.' He swallowed painfully again. 'And I could use the stone to restore my powers.'

His heart gave a full ten beats before the frown lifted from her brow and the blue flecks in her eyes danced. Tentatively, he touched the back of her hand. 'This is a long-term plan, to forever protect the provinces and the dragons. If we rescue Malach on the way and return him to his people, we'd also improve relations with Riverwood.' Grasping her fingers, he said sincerely, 'If Malach causes trouble, I will remove his power myself and he can lead his people without it. Can we at least try?'

Her fingers tightened around his and her hair tickled his cheek when she leaned in close to whisper, 'Are you sure about this? You want to do this?'

Feeling as if the boatshed was tilting around him, he anchored himself to her gaze. 'It's not that I *want* to do this, it's more that we *must*. I feel compelled. We need to finish everything, complete all tasks and missions and bring the natural order back. The stone belongs with Akachi and this is the only way I can see to get it. We have a one-off opportunity while the mages think I'm powerless. No, better, they think I'm dead.'

Extracting her fingers from his, Lamiya smiled. 'Another stealth mission. What you do best.' She addressed the gathering in a ringing voice. 'I will stand with Everand and this new mission! Are you all with us?'

The cries of 'Yosh!' and 'Yo!' ricocheted off the boatshed walls and roof.

Chapter Seventeen

Gritting his teeth, Malach endured, wishing his arms and legs didn't throb so painfully where Pelamis and Simoselaps held him with invisible bands. As he became accustomed to the swirling mists and perception of being weightless, his stomach mercifully started to settle. He refused to gag or vomit. *Show no weakness*!

After a while, the group of mages hovered high up in cold and vacant, pallid blue sky, robe sleeves and hems flapping in the air currents. With a faint crackling, wavery lines of purple, turquoise, green and blue etched a large, oblong doorway just in front of them. Pulse racing, Malach realised they were about to pass through the wardspell and enter Axis. Curiosity bubbled through him. *Finally*, he would see the famous Guild his father came from — even if only briefly. Bitterness edged out his curiosity.

His stomach lurched when his body was yanked forward and he clenched his teeth again at the intense prickling and stabbing sensations when he passed through the wavery door. Around him, the mages gave grunts or gasps. So, it was unpleasant for them too. *Good*. His stomach churned when they flew at speed, and the ground flitting past brought on a bout of dizziness. After a short time, the group slowed and dropped height and his dizziness ebbed.

A large, formal building made of white marble and glinting in the light rushed at them. Next breath he found he was inside it, with marble walls and a high, wood-beamed roof around him. An ornate rug slapped the soles of his feet at the same time the mages released their bands and he pitched onto his knees. A shockwave passed up his legs and the air left his chest. Immediately, he was surrounded by a solid circle of mages, all staring down their noses at him with mouths curled in distaste.

Looking down at the rug, he heaved in ragged breaths, wishing his thoughts would cease scattering in all directions like a flock of startled birds. He must be stronger. Die with courage and honour. Make his father proud.

With a faint humming, a translucent shield formed around him and his throat clogged with sour bile. Over and over, Everand had said that the two of them wouldn't stand a chance against a group of mages. He should have listened instead of using a mind-spell to compel the reluctant Lazuli to take him to watch what happened when the mages arrived. But then again, surely the mages would have found them eventually anyway?

'You are Malach of Riverwood?' asked a stern voice.

Pushing up off his knees, he stood as tall as his quaking limbs would allow and lifted his chin to look into the face of the older mage in green robes standing before him. 'I am.' His voice came out strong, but he'd be more imposing if he wasn't clad in a grubby tunic and didn't have grit in his hair and scratches all over his arms. Not the impression he'd prefer to make.

The mage's green eyes flickered with thought before he asked, 'Do you confirm that your father was Mage Beetal from this Guild and you are a half-mage?'

'I do.' He ignored the murmur that passed around the circle of mages.

'I am Mage Mantiss, Head of the Guild. You understand you have been brought here for judgement because your existence is a breach of Guild Rule Eight? Mages must only breed with mages.'

Tilting his head, Malach assessed the older mage. Power and authority didn't ripple off him the way it roared off the obnoxious Pelamis. Was this because the mage was older? Or was his power waning? Was that why Agamid hovered protectively nearby? If the older mage was weakening, that would explain why he hadn't come to Riverplain. He looked a tad familiar. Glancing to the side, he realised that the woman mage was so similar in appearance they must be related.

Both Agamid and the woman mage were raising their hands and opening their mouths, trying to catch the attention of the older mage. But the mage ignored them and continued to stare, the lines around his mouth and eyes deepening at his failure to respond.

'I await your response,' Mage Mantiss prompted.

Averting his eyes, Malach looked around the circle of mages. What would Everand do if he were here, in his place? The slippery mage would argue, sow doubt, sow dissension, play for time. The expressions around him varied, displaying a mix of distaste, anxiety and in Pelamis' case a smirk of satisfaction. Perhaps he need not embrace death so quickly. He would not beg, but he could try to stall the inevitable. An image of Lamiya standing tall and proud and hurling her authority back at the mages came to mind. If she could do it, so could he.

He squared his shoulders and glared at Mantiss. 'I, Malach, leader of Riverwood province, do not accept your judgement. I am not a subject of Axis and hence am not subject to your Guild Rules. I demand that you return me home.' *There, take that.*

'The arrogance!' spluttered Pelamis. 'He should be obliterated immediately!'

'I concur!' shouted Simoselaps, rubbing at his upper arm and looking irritated.

A number of other mages murmured agreement and in the periphery of his vision, Malach saw their nods. Far more interesting were the reactions of Mages Mantiss and Agamid, who both looked troubled. And the woman mage, who moved subtly closer to them while a younger mage dressed in crimson robes also nudged closer to Agamid. Were these the mages that Everand had hoped to influence? Only four out of a roomful. How could he make them argue among themselves? He thought of the way Everand had dropped like a stone when Pelamis struck him with a death bolt.

'Before you think to judge me, you should judge the murderer in your midst.' Yes, that struck home by the way Mantiss' mouth opened in shock. 'Did you say you are the leader here? I thought you agreed that Everand's punishment was to be removal of his power. Yet,' he tipped his head towards Pelamis, 'that mage killed him.'

Mantiss faltered backwards a step as if he'd been struck, and the woman mage hurriedly moved to support him with her hand under his elbow.

Seizing the opportunity, Malach pressed on. 'You sent mages to a land not under your control and on that land your mages took me by violence — and *that* mage killed one supposedly under your protection. He also killed the two leaders of Riverplain province, their revered guides.'

Seeing Mantiss' rising distress, he waved a finger accusingly. 'Not only did *that* mage,' he curled his lip and glanced with distaste at Pelamis, 'murder the revered guides and Everand on Riverplain soil, he killed the intended *partner* of the now new guide and appointed leader of Riverplain. You think there won't be consequences for that?'

'Is this true?' Mantiss rasped at Agamid, the colour leaching from his face and leaving a ghostly sheen.

'It is,' said Agamid tersely. 'I was trying to tell you this. Pelamis and Simoselaps disregarded your instructions to avoid violence. You have four witnesses.'

Breathing in through his nostrils, Malach worked hard to keep his expression bland, like Everand would. He'd sown the seeds of dissension; let them ferment.

'He is deflecting you!' shouted Pelamis, turning puce in the face. 'You told us to fetch the rogue half-mage and without my intervention that wouldn't have happened!'

Simoselaps stepped forward. 'Pelamis is right. This half-mage would never have come without force. The others would have failed you.'

Spinning around and spreading his hands, palms up, Pelamis addressed the circle of mages. 'There was magic outside the Guild! Mantiss has failed to keep us safe. Who do you wish to lead you? Strong mages who will continue to keep us pure and safe? Or weaklings like these?' He flapped a hand at Mantiss and Agamid. 'Worst of all, Everand, Mantiss' pet favourite, is a traitor, just like his former mentor! And these,' he sneered, 'would have let the traitor live and consort with humans!'

Now glad of the containment shield around him, Malach felt glee bubbling inside. Mage Beetal's swarthy face hovered in his mind's eye, black beard bristling and dark eyes glinting in amusement. *Father. I now understand what you fought for. Died for.* A giddy elation surged through him: *Maybe I can finish what you started and bring down the Guild council!* He almost laughed. Almost.

More soberly, he observed Pelamis exuding fury, spitting and spluttering while he exhorted his colleagues. A victory by Pelamis was not in his best interests, for that path would undoubtedly confirm a punishment of obliteration.

Tuning out the chaotic shouting and arguments spreading among the mages, he analysed Mantiss. *This* was the master who held Everand's loyalty? The older mage might not be impressive now, but he shouldn't forget that this was the mage who outmanoeuvred his father to gain the coveted position of Head of the Guild. Beside Mantiss stood Agamid. Loyal, somewhat boring and not at all leadership material, based on his observations so far. On his other side stood the related woman mage. Was her name Tiliqua? Standing so tall, clenching her fists, her striking blue eyes blazing. Now *there* was strength and power, and she seemed to be a friend to Everand. His groin tingled. She'd be a challenge worth pursuing. *Focus.* Who should he support?

'Enough!' commanded Tiliqua, her voice with augmented volume booming off the walls and even the vaulted ceiling. 'Control yourselves.'

Dipping his chin down submissively, Malach watched Tiliqua. Surprisingly, the mages all turned to regard her and a brooding silence descended. What would Mantiss do now? He felt an eyebrow lift when he realised Agamid and the mage in the crimson robe were supporting the older mage who was even whiter than before and had a hand clutched at his chest. Was his heart about to fail? It looked that way.

Drawing himself up and straightening his sleeves, Pelamis said in a ringing voice, 'I move that we convene the councils to vote for a new Head of the Guild. Mantiss is clearly unwell and no longer fit to lead.'

Several mages murmured agreement and shuffled to stand near the orange-robed Pelamis. With interest, Malach observed others move around the circle to stand near Agamid. At a quick count, the mages appeared to be divided into two almost equal factions. Excellent. This should slow things down. But what would they do with him while they voted? Deliberately, he caught Tiliqua's eye and arched an eyebrow. She frowned then murmured something to Agamid, who turned and whispered into Mantiss' ear. The older mage gave a weak nod.

Clearing his throat, Agamid lifted his hand that was not supporting Mantiss. 'Very well. Mantiss decrees that the full Outer Council of Twenty will convene next sun. The summons will sound straight after the sun-up meal.' When the mages began to chatter excitedly, he raised his voice. 'First, we must replace Everand on the Inner Council so there is a full council to vote. Be quiet, Pelamis,' he snapped. 'Then we will vote on the position of Head of the Guild.'

'And the rogue half-mage?' asked Pelamis eagerly.

'The half-mage will be put into the prepared cage as planned. His fate will be voted on again once the new councils are formed.'

Malach lifted his chin when Agamid looked squarely him.

'The judgement will likely remain the same, but should a new Head of the Guild be elected it is just that he has the opportunity to confirm or alter a decision of this importance.'

'Or *she*,' said Tiliqua. 'I will stand against Pelamis.'

The looks on the mages' faces! Sorely tempted to clap, Malach flexed his fingers by his sides. This was growing more interesting with each breath he took. In his mind, his father was laughing and saying, *Look at them! They have no idea.* Then he caught the vicious smile on Pelamis' face. Staring back with his best haughty expression, he willed the mage to lose the vote. Pelamis' grin widened and he nudged Simoselaps, who also grinned. Malach's pulse raced. Definitely not in his interests for Pelamis' faction to win.

'On behalf of Mantiss, I dismiss the councils,' called Agamid. 'Except Saiphos, Caimanops, Neelaps and Hydrelaps, who are to stay to prepare the Great Hall for the meeting and votes. The rest of you may go.'

His legs tiring, Malach remained as still as possible while the mages formed into pairs or threes and moved around his shield to make their way to the door.

Pausing to glare, his nose close to the shield, Pelamis said softly, 'Don't get your hopes up. You have merely gained an entire sun and dark-fall to contemplate your pending obliteration. Hmm. Let me see … shall it be free from pain? I think not.'

'*Excruciating* pain,' added Simoselaps, sticking his face close and peering with disdain.

'You are cowards and idiots,' growled Malach before he could stop himself. 'My shade will exact revenge from the life beyond.'

Simoselaps took a satisfyingly hurried step back, whereas Pelamis gave him a level look, then spun on his heels and strode away across the large rug. Malach watched them exit through the door. Fatigue coursing down his legs, he felt a vicious stab of satisfaction at how the mages would be busy arguing and negotiating until the next sun-up.

'Malach,' said Tiliqua, approaching the shield. 'We will now transfer you to the cage made ready for you.'

Noting that six mages stood ready to handle him, Malach nodded.

'The shield around you will move. You must move with it towards the back wall.' Looking to the others, Tiliqua added, 'Add your weight and follow my path.'

She placed her hands along the side of the shield and when four others gathered around the shield and leaned onto it, the translucent dome began to glide slowly across the floor. Over his shoulder, Malach saw Agamid help Mantiss to a chair, where the older mage sat slumped, taking shallow breaths. The back of the shield bumped him, as hard as rock, and he concentrated on moving with it while they crossed the rug, went around the edge of a raised wooden dais with a solid, long, shiny table and many chairs around it. The shield glided towards the back wall.

At first, he thought they were heading towards two enormous, thickset bookshelves but when they drew close, he saw the high, square cage nestled between them. Its walls were as thick as his arms and although they were transparent, myriad colours refracted like the facets of a gemstone. Peering up at the roof of it, his throat closed with a rush of dread. A formidable red disc rested in the centre, right above where his head would be once he was inside. Was that where they would feed in his death? His mouth became annoyingly dry.

With a squidging, squelching sound, the shield he was within merged through the wall of the square cage, and he was stood inside it, facing the rear wall. Reluctantly, he turned around.

'Don't try to escape,' said Tiliqua. 'It isn't possible.' Her lips tightened as if she wanted to say more, but with a clipped nod she turned away.

Breathing evenly to calm his racing pulse, Malach watched the mages traipse across the Great Hall. Tiliqua stopped to help Agamid lift Mantiss and, half-carrying the older mage, they disappeared through the ornate, wooden doors. A breath later, the two massive doors swung inwards and closed with a solid click. He was on his own.

The sound of his breathing loud in his ears, Malach inspected the cage. If he stretched his arms either in front of him or out sideways, his fingers brushed the smooth walls. There was no chair, just wooden floorboards below his feet with a hard shield across the top of them. He rapped the walls, soon concluding that there was, indeed, no escape.

Wait. They hadn't removed his power! Could he hurl a bolt or use a spell to dissolve the wall to make an exit hole? Closing his eyes, he reached for his dark-brown pool of magic. There, it sat like a deep pond in the base of his stomach. Flexing his fingers, he tried to draw power into his arms and hands. Nothing. Not even a ripple. His pond of magic was stagnant and unresponsive. Curse it! A shudder travelled down his spine and his legs trembled. Was this how Everand had felt when he'd made him drink the magic-quelling potion?

Serious trembling set into his legs and he slid down to sit on the floor, leaning his back against the wall and resting his forehead on his bent knees. Everand and Lamiya had been rescued by loyal friends. His people didn't even know what had befallen him nor where he was, and they lacked the means to rescue him in any case. His eagles might be able to help. Hope rising, he tried to reach out with his mind to the birds. The echoes of his mind summons bounced off the translucent walls and wheeled mockingly around him.

With a sigh, he rested his head on his knees again, his mind presenting him with the fleeting glimpse he'd had of Everand's inert form lying broken on the pebbly shore while Lamiya hurled a storm at the mages, forcing them to translocate. A jolt of grief hit him.

The only one who could save him, who might actually try, was dead.

Chapter Eighteen

Head pounding and his shoulder throbbing where Pelamis'
bolt had struck, Everand traipsed behind Lamiya along the
narrow, winding path. Without the inner strength of his power,
everything required so much more energy and concentration.
Watching Lamiya stride out, a bounce in her step, he appreciated
anew just how fit and strong the paddlers were.

An eddy of nerves shivered through him. Before they
embarked on the fresh mission, Lamiya had insisted he
accompany her to a shrine to meet the spirits of her parents.
Although clean after a dip in the unpleasantly cold lake, and
clad in fresh clothes provided by Lulite, he felt unworthy. What
if her parents didn't like him? Would she change her mind?

Slowing her stride, Lamiya reached for his hand. 'So sad,
my mage.' A frown marred her face. 'Can I still call you this?'
Her face brightened. 'Yes. You will be a mage again. I am
sure of it, as I'm sure my parents will approve of you, so stop
fretting and hurry up.'

'Yes, great Guide of Riverplain,' he said. 'Although I
respectfully point out that my body would be better able to
hurry if it were provided with more regular food.'

The blue flecks in her eyes dancing, Lamiya laughed. 'Well,
if you stop arranging for one mission after another that would
be easier to achieve!'

'Good point,' he conceded. His humour departed. He had no control whatsoever over the presentation of missions. Once the dragons were appeased, would life become straightforward or would some other random assignment materialise?

'You're overthinking again,' said Lamiya pertly, linking her arm around his elbow. 'Come along, it's not far now.'

Trying to calm his still-racing pulse, Everand said, 'Tell me about your parents, and this shrine.'

'My mother Lestaya was a bird-caller of exceptional skill.' Fluttering her eyelashes coyly, she said, 'I'm told I look like her. But she was less energetic than me, preferring to tend to the birds, grow flowers and herbs and impart wisdom to the other women.'

'She didn't hurtle across the water in a dragon boat then?'

'Very funny. No, my father Azuri, however, was a proud and talented paddler and also a fisherman. He was happiest when he was out in a boat.'

Uneasy, Everand said, 'Do I need to learn to adore boats?'

'It would help!' Although she gave a quick smile, her arm tensed around his. 'My father was close to Lazuli and he will ask questions so he can measure you.' She shrugged. 'It is the role of a father to protect his daughter. Just be yourself.' Falling silent, she walked more slowly.

The path became even narrower, weaving through the dangling branches of weeping willow trees adorned with countless newly-budded leaves. The fresh, scented air and tranquil greenery helped calm his heartrate, but his palms were growing clammy. She spoke as if her parents would actually be there to meet him. What did he have to offer Lamiya now? He had no power and no Mages' Guild behind him … he was adrift with nothing except the clothes he wore, and even those were given to him by others.

His steps faltered while his chest burned with a deep ache and grew tight, as if being strangled by bands of tension. Why had he ever thought his strategy would work? All he'd done was leave Mantiss and Agamid at the mercy of Pelamis and his colleagues, raised Tiliqua's hopes then let her down, allowed Malach to be captured while his people didn't even know where he was, thrust Lamiya early into her role as the Guide of Riverplain and right after he'd been proclaimed as her future consort — when he had nothing and didn't even like boats. He was a liability. She should choose Lazuli.

Something fluttered across his nose. Focusing, he saw it was Lamiya's finger, trying to get his attention. 'You should choose Lazuli,' he croaked.

'What?' Her eyes widened. 'Why?'

Staring at her beautiful face, he clenched and unclenched his fingers. 'I … I … have nothing!' Tilting her head to one side, she looked at him steadily for so long his heart hammered against his breastbone and his head began to feel thick and fuzzy. Perhaps he should sit down.

Caressing his cheek, Lamiya said gently, 'My love, you give me you. That is what I desire most, whether you are an all-powerful mage or just a handsome, kind and occasionally funny man.'

'Are you sure? You now lead a province!'

'Is this a ploy to get me to kiss you?' She tipped her chin up.

Leaning down, he planted his lips over hers, a sigh travelling through him when she slipped her arms around his lower back and pulled him close. Putting his arms around her shoulders, he deepened the kiss, groaning when desire instantly flooded his body.

'See?' she mumbled, breaking for air. 'It doesn't matter whether you restore your power or not. You are still you.' Grabbing his chin with her fingers, she made him look at her. 'My parents are waiting.'

Kissing the top of her head, he said, 'Already so wise and clever, my love. Lead on.'

Even without his power, he sensed the change in the atmosphere when Lamiya led him towards a small copse of trees with elegant branches and leaves dangling like long, shapely fingers. He felt anticipation creep into the air, heard the subtle whisper of small waves lapping at the shore, became aware of the power and strength in the water stretching away to distant colourful shores. Further east, the green hills loomed in a comforting embrace, protecting the lake and its people. Nerves jangling, he licked his lips.

Tightening her fingers around his, Lamiya stepped daintily into a small, grassy grove with hints of lily wafting in the air. Soundlessly, they crossed the short verdant lawn and stopped in front of a mound of stones, piled to waist height in a solid and deliberate pattern. Runes were carved into the smooth granite faces. The tinkling of water teased at his ears.

When Lamiya released his hand and gave a deep bow to the cairn of stones, he bowed too. Next, she moved to the left side and his eyebrows lifted at the perfectly round stone bowl filled with crystal-clear water. There was a crimped lip on the far-left edge and water trickled over this to tumble into another perfect stone bowl below. Watching for a few breaths, he noticed that the top bowl remained full, although he could see no water entering it. The surface glinted greens, blues and golds, reflecting the trees and glimpses of sky.

'I know,' murmured Lamiya. 'I don't understand it either, just accept it is so. The spirits provide pure water for us to cleanse ourselves.' Kneeling down, she retrieved a long-handled wooden ladle and tipped water over both hands, just as she did at the Meeting Place.

Kneeling beside her, Everand copied, marvelling at the purity of the water and admiring the way it glinted with greens, golds and blues as it trickled over his hands. His mind cleared, his heartrate slowed and he felt refreshed. He gave Lamiya a brief smile.

Turning to face the stone cairn, she clasped her palms together before her chest. 'Spirits of my mother and father, I bring Everand to meet you. Please grant us your presence and guidance.'

Finding his eyes drawn to the two uppermost stones, Everand saw the carved names of Lestaya and Azuri briefly glow like molten silver. A breeze eddied past his neck and cheeks and the fingers of leaves brushed together, murmuring and whispering, while the scent of lilies grew more pungent.

'They're coming,' whispered Lamiya, her lips quirking into a smile.

Currents of air shifted around him and invisible hands touched his shoulders, getting the sense of him. A shiver travelled down his body, leaving a wake of tingling skin. There was so much to learn about the people outside the Guild, so many wonders to be uncovered. He felt a stronger pat on his right shoulder, as if his thought was approved of.

'Peep!' Whirr flew into the clearing and hovered before Lamiya's face.

'There you are! Sit and join us.' At Lamiya's command, the bird fluttered down and perched on a small twig lying on the ground near her.

Smiling, Everand allowed his mind to calm and be open again, pleased when Lamiya's hand stole across to rest lightly on his knee, warmth seeping through her touch. Was she connecting him so he could hear her parents?

Welcome, Mage Everand. A woman's voice, like Lamiya's but gentler, washed into his mind. *We are glad you found our daughter. You give her great joy.*

Taken aback, Everand stumbled, seeking a suitable response. How would he convey it?

'Just think what you want to say,' came Lamiya's whispered advice.

Thank you, Lestaya. I am honoured Lamiya has chosen me, and honoured that the people of Riverplain will let me live with them. Would this suffice? Where was the presence of her father?

He is polite and sincere, isn't he? It felt as if Lestaya directed that at Lamiya.

Boats, came a gruffer presence. *Young man, boats are important in Riverplain. Can you learn to love the water and our boats?*

Greetings, Azuri, projected Everand. *Truthfully, I respect and admire the paddlers' prowess. Perhaps over time when I gain in physical strength, I can better appreciate the joy they feel too.* He thought of his wild ride on Mizukaze when trying to protect the dragon from Malach's crossbow bolts at the end of the long race in Riverfall. *I did enjoy my experience riding the dragon in the river.*

The air swirled around him and Whirr emitted short, sharp peeps.

You rode the river dragon? Daughter, you should have told us this! Now he has my respect and approval. The presence of Azuri seemed pleased.

Thank you, mother. Thank you, father, sent Lamiya. *Will you grant us your authority to partner? I choose Everand to be my consort.*

You will guard her with your life and love her for eternity and beyond? Azuri's clipped question snipped into Everand's mind.

Instinctively bowing low, Everand said, *Yes. I promise to guard her with my life for eternity and beyond. Lamiya is most special and I love and adore her with all my being.*

I approve, said Lestaya, a smile in her words. *He has already made great sacrifices for our Lamiya. Besides, U-Mali and U-Lumin have approved of him.*

They did, but that was before my powers were taken. Everand felt compelled to be honest. *The depth of my love has not changed, but I am perhaps less able to guard and protect Lamiya.*

We still trust that you will protect her better than anyone, *said Lestaya. The key thing is your love for her.*

Azuri grunted. *Indeed.*

Humbled, Everand sat with his head bowed. The air grew chill about him and another shiver coursed down his body. A tiny pressure nudged his knee and he peered down to see Whirr rubbing his head affectionately against his kneecap. Lamiya's fingers squeezed his other knee. The air grew a notch colder, small waves raced across the lake and the sibilant hissing of water over pebbles magnified.

His knee grew cool when Lamiya removed her hand, clasped her palms together and bowed so low her nose almost touched the grass. What was happening? His shoulders felt multiple pressure points, as if many hands touched and poked at him, and he gasped at the impression of a crowd of spirits surrounding him. By his bended knee, the feathers on Whirr's head kept flattening as if several hands patted the top of it. Nervous now, he sat straighter. Lamiya looked shaken too, her eyes wide and alert with expectation.

Releasing the breath he hadn't realised he was holding in so tightly, he sat as still as possible while grey wraiths shifted and blurred around him, forming into the outlines of slender people, then becoming fuzzy again. Blinking carefully, he was certain they formed into four pairs of wraiths, each pair drifting to stand before Lamiya, mist-like arms reaching out to clasp her hands, shadowy figures tipping forward to kiss her forehead. A glint of silvery moisture rolled down her cheek. Was she crying?

Next, the wraiths floated before him, and he perceived wizened women and men, tendrils of hair drifting adorned with feathers and beads, hollow eyes peering at him. With the approach of each outline, he felt a light brush across his forehead.

The final wraith hovered, more substantial than the others, and U-Mali's voice accompanied the feathery brush across his skin. *Welcome in your new form, Everand. We wish you well on this mission. May you and Lamiya find true joy and peace afterwards.*

Inclining his head, he said, 'Thank you, U-Mali. I wish you and U-Lumin well in the afterlife.'

Still so formal and polite! U-Mali's tinkling laugh lingered in his ears while the wraiths drifted away to the lake-side edge of the grove and passed through the trees.

His skin tingling and prickling with alertness and life, he realised the lake surface was building into waves that were curling, swelling and rolling towards the nearby shore. The branches and shapely leaves around him jiggled in a stiff onshore breeze and the air grew so cold his breath misted. Through the leaves, he watched the shadowy outlines all turn to face the lake. A gasp escaped his lips. The dragons were coming!

Dizziness surging through him, he realised the union of him and Lamiya was bringing about a meeting between the dragons and the spirits of *all* the previous Riverplain guides. Had Lamiya known this would happen? No, judging by her serious and anxious expression she hadn't known. So, they faced this together. Surreptitiously clearing his throat, he stood when she did and followed her to the shore, wishing his heartbeats would cease booming in his ears.

With a mighty roar, Akachi rose from the lake and stomped from the water on massive, powerful legs, stopping once fully on the pebbles. Waves tumbled over the pebbles, creating bubbles and foam, when Mizukaze and Hanachi emerged and came to flank Akachi. Acting on instinct, Everand gripped Lamiya's hand and stepped forward to greet the dragons, surrounded by the eerie shades of the past guides following them.

He halted ten paces away from the dragon, trying to be respectful without looking too deeply into the textured golden eyes. 'Greetings, Great Akachi.'

Akachi turned to regard Lamiya, beside him. *Well met, Lamiya Guide of Riverplain and Mage Everand. You are ready to commence my task?*

'Yes, Great Akachi. We begin the task this sun.' Twisting slightly, Lamiya flapped a hand behind her. 'The ancient spirits have come to greet you, given the momentous nature of our task.'

Mesmerised, Everand watched the three dragons concurrently lower their noses and blow gentle puffs of steam while the shadowy mist people swirled across the pebbles and gathered before them. Blinking, he tried to bring the shapes into focus but they remained wraith-like impressions of wizened men and women with flowing tunics and feathers in wafting long hair.

'They're *all* here,' Lamiya mumbled to him. 'My parents, U-Mali and U-Lumin, U-Molda and Geode, U-Hyalite and Lode and even Aura and Spinel.' Her voice cracked. 'I can't believe it.'

Stunned, Everand mutely patted her hand. Four generations of guides were present, including the first arrivals! A thought occurred. 'Should I now call you U-Lamiya?'

'After the ceremony, yes.'

The skin on his arms tingled again when the shadowy wraiths brushed back past them, melting into the grove behind to leave him and Lamiya facing Akachi. His pulse raced when the red dragon trained her enormous eyes on him and brought her face close. Heat radiated from her nostrils and washed over his cheeks.

You will bring me the Staropal? Soon? Akachi's irises shifted and flecks of gold glinted.

'Yes. I promise to do my utmost best to recover the stone for you.'

Steam coiling from her flared nostrils, Akachi said, *You, I believe. You have touched the stone and it will come with you.*

When all three dragons lowered their heads and fixed him with piercing gazes, Everand's vision swam in giddy loops. His head and chest tickled and tingled, as if he were being mind and soul-read. An image of the Staropal snapped into his mind, offering itself to him, twinkling with the allure of power and its many hues of colour swirling enchantingly. *Take me, take me*, the stone whispered, bobbing closer and shifting with myriad shades of his favourite blues and jades.

His soul sighing in admiration for the stone's beauty, he imagined reaching up to clasp his hands around the Staropal, carrying it, and then bowing gracefully before he held the pure stone out to Akachi. A gust of warm air buffeting him, he shook himself, feeling muzzy as if he'd just woken from a deep sleep.

Yes, you will bring it to me. You are the ones. The red dragon's face remained alarmingly close to his, but she tilted her head to include Lamiya. *For a long, long time we have waited for you two. Together, you will restore the natural order; you will bring dragons back to the rivers. Do not fail.*

With Lamiya's hand in his, he bowed low. Working saliva into his mouth, Everand gulped down the lump of fear that had lodged in his throat.

They must bring the Staropal back — or die trying.

Chapter Nineteen

By the time her hut came into view, Lamiya's forehead and chest were taut with concern. Her parents had approved of Everand; they had told the dragons they were about to commence the task of retrieving the magical stone; and the spirits of all the previous guides had come to bless them! Yet Everand had uttered barely a word all the way back, intent on withdrawing so deep inside himself that he was like the aloof and closed mage he'd been when they first met.

Chewing her lower lip, she considered. How she could bring him back out of himself? This would be difficult without first working out what was bothering him. Was he still worried he had nothing to offer her? Or that this new mission would fail? Perhaps it was both.

Watching him lower his lean frame onto a cushion and rest his elbows on her table, his eyes focused inward, it occurred to her that this was not a win-win mission. If they succeeded, he would be taking from the Guild a valuable artefact that the mages relied upon. And if they didn't succeed, they failed the dragons and, from what Akachi implied, doomed the survival of the species.

Sitting opposite him, she reached across the table to take his hands and began stroking the back of them with her thumbs. 'My love, we can only do our best. Your plan is bold, and only you know all the factors involved, but we trust you. The dragons trust you.' She squeezed his hands.

'I understand you must feel conflicted. You have to choose between your mages and the dragons. I know you, my love, and you always act for the greater good. In this case, saving the river dragons *is* the greater good. Your Mages' Guild will survive and continue without the Staropal.' Finally, his eyes blinked into focus. 'Besides, as you have noticed, we appear to be obliged to undertake these great missions, whether we like them or not.'

His frown dissolving, he gave her a crooked smile. 'What would I do without your clarity and wisdom?'

'I'm sure you would muddle your way through, great mage.' When he promptly started to frown, she asked, 'Do you truly have no power left? Can you get it back?'

'I concealed a couple of drops from Agamid. Before you ask how, I stole an ancient text from the Guild library with special spells in it that aren't taught anymore.'

Astounded that he had stolen anything at all, let alone a valuable book, Lamiya said, 'How did you know you would need this book?'

Everand shrugged. 'I overheard Pelamis and Simoselaps plotting to discredit me. I'd hidden Malach and I knew they'd brand me as a traitor. I suspected my best-laid plan of concealment would go awry, and I'd be forced to let the Guild either obliterate me or take my power.'

His eyes gleamed a deep azure. 'You were brilliant, working out for yourself that the rules allowed for a choice and then convincing them to take my power and let me stay. I asked Agamid to be the one to mete my punishment, hoping that if he even faintly suspected he hadn't got all my power he'd let it pass. And he did.'

Around a deep swallow, he said, 'I'm sorry I gave everyone such a fright, but I also thought I might need to end up being dead, so I prepared a spell for that too. Back to your question, I must conserve the two drops of power I have, but if I reach the Staropal, I can ask the stone to restore it.' A flush etched up his neck. 'I think the Staropal likes me. Akachi is right and I have touched it before. I am hopeful of becoming a full mage again.'

'So, this mission will be like when you first arrived in Riverfall with a lot of sneaking around and not using your power?'

'For the first part, at least.' His mouth formed another crooked smile. 'You and Lazuli will need to do your very best sneaking. No crying yosh or yo or showing off.'

Giving him her driest look, she said, 'We'd better eat and get ready.' Extracting her hands from his, she added, 'We'll do our very best *sneaking* and you need to do your very best *paddling*. All the way to Riverwood!'

When he pulled a sour face, she laughed. 'Going by boat was your idea, not mine.'

Pleased to see he looked more relaxed, she went to her clothes rack and stood contemplating what to wear. They were going to do a long paddle which suggested a short-sleeved tunic and shorts, then sneak about during the dark which suggested warmer attire, and also possibly meet some mages, suggesting decent attire. Hmm.

Hurrying, she slipped on her team outfit and chose a dark-green long-sleeved tunic, a scarf and her cloak for when it grew colder.

On turning around, she found Everand dressed and rummaging in the bundle of clothes Lulite had brought for him. Seeing the cloak draped over her arm, he pulled out a long dark-grey cloak and rummaged further until he found some storm-grey trousers.

'Good thing we left the food bundles at the boatshed,' she said, then rushed outside.

From fifty paces away, Lazuli stopped and waved. 'Are you ready?'

'Almost.' Sticking her head back through the curtain, she asked, 'Can Whirr come?'

Before Everand could answer, Whirr flew at him and dived down the front of his tunic. He squirmed and gave her a resigned look.

Lamiya cast her gaze over her hut, lingering on the intricate leaf-shaped table, the colourful cushions and her favourite jars. Would she see these again? Everand was watching her, compassion on his face. Had he said farewell to his home at the Guild? She began to have an inkling of how he must feel, stepping out of a known and comfortable life to meet the unknown. Shaking off the building melancholy, she reversed out of the hut, vowing that she would be back. Soon.

In almost no time, they were at the boatshed and she was pleased to see the others had Flight out ready and were piling their bundles of extra clothes under their seats. Lulite was tying down the last of the bundles of food at the front of the boat, where the drum would usually be. When her friend looked up and waved, Lamiya noticed Lapsi approaching, carrying water jars and his paddle. Frowning, she worried he was going to refuse to be left behind. Ready with a statement about how Lulite and their unborn baby needed him to stay safe, she snapped her mouth closed when Lapsi walked past her and handed his paddle to Everand.

'Thank you,' said Everand, looking surprised and humbled.

Lapsi came to her. 'Good luck, Lamiya. May the spirits bless and guide your journey and return you to us safely.'

Now it was her turn to feel humble as she mumbled her thanks. Then she thought of how the spirits of the past guides had blessed her and besides, they had the blessing and resolve of the dragons! 'We'll be back soon,' she replied, hoping she sounded confident.

Water swished behind her as the others pushed Flight onto the lake. Clutching her cloak and spare clothes under her arm, she told Everand to follow her to the back seat and waded out to step into the boat. The glide oar lay ready and she slid it into the slot and held the boat steady while the others climbed in. Lapsi and a handful of others waved farewell from the shore while she worked the oar to turn the boat's nose towards the tributary.

'Paddles up. Go,' she sang, energy zinging into her when Flight glided forward.

While the crew paddled steadily, she ran her eyes over the mix in the boat. Right in front of her sat Everand and Beram, where she could keep an eye on Everand to make sure he didn't fatigue, and so Beram could rotate with her to take turns to steer the boat. In front of them sat Luvu and Tengar, some strength at the back of the boat and two other steerspersons to take turns. Before them were Acim and Zink, Ejad and Mookaite. It was good to have the healer with them, in case anyone was injured. As usual, Lazuli and Larimar were the pacers, setting a strong and steady rate.

A solid team for an epic-length paddle. Flicking the ends of her hair from her cheeks, she wondered whether they'd be written into the annals for this journey. Hearing Clommus' rich voice in her mind, she imagined the opening to a new ballad:

> 'In a risky, bold and audacious move
> ten mighty paddlers and renowned glide did hove
> in an epic paddle all up the Dragonspine they strove,
> to sneak under darkness into a warded mages' cove ...'

Humming, she imagined the motley crew of Riversea musicians and their stirring beat. Her hum became a gurgle when both Beram and Everand stared over their shoulders at her, their paddles clashing awkwardly.

'Alright there, glide?' called Luvu, without missing a beat in his strokes.

'Just imagining how Clommus will sing of our deeds,' she called, her cheeks stiff with the depth of her smile when the whole boat laughed.

Even as the crew's laughter died, they neared the opening to the tributary and she nudged the boat straighter to align it for the narrow entry. To her right, the slope rolled up to the silent and empty Meeting Place and her heart panged with grief, the faces of U-Mali and U-Lumin filling the space before her eyes. Their guidance and keen insight would have bolstered her confidence. She eased in a deep breath. The guides were gone. This was down to her and Everand now.

Refocusing, she lined the boat up. 'Paddle slow and steady, take us through,' she called, taking another slow breath to bring her attention to the narrow tributary with its uneven currents and eddies. Any breeze tended to bounce small waves off the banks to create a band of choppy water. Flight slid under the narrow footbridge and the opening to the main river loomed ahead.

Larimar and Lazuli reduced their power. The boat slowed and she veered them to the left bank preparing for the turn to the right. The sun was in her eyes as it sank towards the western hills. Squinting against the glare, she manoeuvred Flight and they swung into Dragonspine River and headed north.

'We'll paddle for a thousand strokes then swap sides,' she told the crew. Several nodded, and she heard Everand's sigh.

Observing him for a while, she was pleased to see his timing and rhythm were good. He'd be too proud to tell her when he was getting tired, but he ought to be able to paddle the first few sets of a thousand strokes. She could reduce his contribution once they reached the waterwheels north of Zuqart, unless he obviously fatigued earlier. It would be better to let him rest more often when they drew nearer to Riverwood.

The countryside slid past smoothly while the crew maintained a steady rate, the paddlers chatting lightly to the person beside them. Every now and then, Lamiya called for only the front half or the back half of the boat to paddle for fifty strokes, giving everyone a brief respite. Working the oar gently, she admired the way the onset of dusk was giving the hills hazy outlines, blurring the trees into huddled shadows and casting gold flecks across the water. Occasionally a fish jumped in a flash of silver and spray of twinkling droplets.

Coming up on the right were the pinkish walls of the town of Zuqart. On the left, the grasses rustled together, hiding a veritable chorus of insects buzzing, chittering and clicking.

'Swap sides from the front,' she called. 'Keep paddling but slower. Take a drink when you're swapped.' The boat jiggled while the paddlers changed sides and she firmed up her hold on the oar.

When the whole boat had swapped, she leaned forward. 'Are you okay, my love?' Although Everand nodded, when he glanced over his shoulder his mouth was set in a tight, tired line. 'How about you take a rest after this next set? I'll swap with Beram and we can talk more about our plans.'

'Sounds good,' he said, and beside him Beram nodded.

Soon, the hazy hills were merging into the mauve sky. The faint breeze faded altogether, and the air brushing her cheeks was fresh and cool. Lamiya felt as if she were blending with the river and landscape. A harsh cry jostled her back to awareness. Craning her neck back, she could just make out a dark speck circling above them. The bird gave another screech. Was this one of Malach's raptors? Reaching out with her mind, she sensed it was a falcon. *Plummet?*

The bird dived down to hover above her head, wings beating the gloomy air and shrilling anxiously. Conscious that Everand and Beram had tensed their shoulders, she said, 'It's alright, the bird is friendly. Keep paddling. The raptors want to know where Malach is.'

Setting the boat's nose straight, she conveyed to the bird that Malach had been captured and they were going to try to recover him. In exchange, Plummet told her that the villagers had searched far and wide for him in vain and Torrap now led Riverwood. The raptors were roaming free and directionless.

Wait, she told the bird when it began to drift upwards. *We go to Riverwood. Collect as many raptors as you can and perch in Hanaki Forest near the great grey wall in case we need you next sun.*

With a final screech, the falcon dipped her beak and spiralled away, swallowed into the haze, her cries fading to echoes from the hilltop.

'Stop the boat while I swap with Beram,' called Lamiya. Her arms aching and feet growing numb, she was glad to release the oar into Beram's hand when he stood perched next to her.

Lowering herself into the last bench, she leaned against Everand, pleased when he put a warm arm around her shoulder and kissed her hair. 'You'll make a paddler yet,' she told him. 'Even Azuri will be impressed by your efforts.'

'I hope so,' he murmured back. 'My body is not so impressed!'

'Think of the muscles you'll grow,' she said, running her fingertips down his arm, delighted when he shivered in response. 'More seriously, you must rest more as we pass through Riverwood. We need you full of energy for the sneaking part.'

'I don't suppose you brought any of those fire cakes with you?' he said, looking hopeful.

'I see your legs are still hollow! I'll get you some after the next set.'

'Paddles up!' called Beram. 'Go.'

Lamiya plunged her paddle deep into the water, enjoying the pull along her muscles and the instant rush of energy. The white balls of bubbles flowing from the paddles were distinct under the rapidly darkening river water. Flicking a glance up, she saw the first stars peeping out from the inky sky. A shiver tingled along her neck underneath her hair.

This dark-fall she would get to see Axis.

And understand more about Everand's past and what drove him.

Chapter Twenty

The next thousand strokes seemed to take far longer than the previous sets. A slow burn was spreading from the back of Everand's neck down across his shoulderblades and creeping down his arms. His fingers were stiff and swollen from gripping the paddle, the palm of his inside hand was stinging, and he'd swear the water washing over his hand and wrist was getting colder. Or maybe that was because it was dark. Beside him, Lamiya paddled smoothly and strongly, a small smile playing over her lips.

Risking a peek far ahead, he saw the mountains rising, the craggy tops mere silver-laced outlines under the wan light of the rising moon. Perhaps he wasn't imagining it; perhaps nearer the river source the water was indeed colder. Did the dragons prefer the warmer water in Lamiya's lake or did Mizukaze miss the brisk chill in the water at Dragon Lake? Did the dragon miss the cascading, thundering Mizuchi Falls?

Distracted, his timing slipped and Lamiya clucked her tongue. He flexed numb fingers and gripped his paddle harder. His palm stung like crazy and he felt some flesh tear. What the? Clenching his jaw, he fumbled for a more comfortable grip. Difficult around the unexpectedly sore spot. On top of this, his lips felt dry and cracked — a drink, food and rest would be welcome.

'Pull your paddle in for a while,' suggested Lamiya. 'I can see you need to think.' When he hesitated, she said, 'Go on. Rest it upright so it's out of the way. Like this.' She lifted her paddle, put the handle on the boat floor between her feet and held the dripping blade upright.

Copying, he grimaced when cold water dripped over his knees, but he could lean lightly on the haft for support. He took the opportunity to inspect his palm. Was that blood? He brought his hand close to his nose, squinting at it.

'Something wrong?' asked Lamiya.

'I'm bleeding!' That sounded too much like a wail. He shook his hand and peered at it again.

'Show me.' Lamiya rested her paddle across her knees and held her hand out.

'Has something bitten me?' he asked, a knot of anxiety forming in his stomach. 'Will it get infected?'

Lamiya kissed his palm. 'My mage, you have a blister. Sorry, I should have anticipated.'

'A blister? Is it serious? How will I paddle?'

Beram, Luvu and Tengar all laughed with Lamiya.

'It's from lack of training,' said Tengar in a kind voice. 'The rest of us are just getting calluses on our calluses.'

Lamiya tore off a strip of cloth from her trouser hem. 'I'll wrap it for you. I'm afraid it will still sting though. You'll need to paddle on the other side, so that hand is in the water.'

Everand stared at his wrapped hand. If he had his power, he could heal it. Curse it. This was inconvenient … and annoying. How often did humans have to deal with irritations like this?

'Rest for a bit.' Lamiya picked up her paddle and resumed paddling.

Rocking gently with the rhythmic movements of the boat, Everand let his mind drift. Within the next thousand strokes, the boat would reach the ruins of the bridge. Just as well he and the dragons had cleared a channel through the middle, although at the time he hadn't anticipated anyone paddling this way so soon.

Thinking back to when Malach had kidnapped him and Lamiya, he tried to remember how much longer it had taken the Riverwood boat to reach their village. A wave of fatigue coursed over him. They still had a long way to go, but they needed to take the boat as far as possible and not cut across country, as they had done during their escape. Taking the boat would be faster than toiling uphill on foot, but even so, the moon would be high in the inky sky by the time they landed Flight. Which left only half a dark-fall to go through the tunnel, reach the Guild and persuade Mantiss to help them. Without any magic.

'My love,' he said to get Lamiya's attention. 'I hesitate to ask, but is it possible to paddle faster? We have a lot to achieve before the sun rises.'

Arching an eyebrow, she gave him a look of disbelief. Then she sighed. 'You're serious.' Twisting, she called up to Beram, 'We need to break out food and drink, paddle front half and back half to eat and then speed up.'

Amazed, Everand watched Mookaite and Ejad take over as pacers while Lazuli and Larimar retrieved and broke open the bundles of food and drink and started to pass small parcels back through the boat.

'I have a better idea,' murmured Beram before calling out, 'rolling rows! Lazuli and Larimar, eat and drink, swing back in as soon as you're ready. Then Mookaite and Ejad take a rest, roll it through each row and keep it snappy.'

Everand took the food Luvu handed him, Lamiya insisting that he eat now. Prising apart the tightly bound leaves, he found a savoury loaf and two zesty fire cakes. Clever. Easily digested, these would give a burst of energy.

'You can eat the leaves too,' said Lamiya, passing him a flask of water.

Eating quickly, Everand watched the rows of paddlers coming in and out in smooth intervals down the boat, the extent of their training and skill evident. Quicker than he would have deemed possible, Lamiya was brushing crumbs off her lap and the whole boat was powering forward.

Flight's nose slid around the bend and a collective gasp rose from the paddlers at the sight of the yawning, empty space where the bridge had been.

'Are you sure we want to rescue Malach?' said Luvu sourly. 'Unless we make him rebuild the bridge single-handed.'

'I agree,' said Tengar, rolling his shoulders. 'The idiot has a lot to answer for.'

The crumbs of the second fire cake threatening to stick in his craw, Everand swallowed carefully. Just as well it was Lazuli coming into Axis with him and Lamiya because the others would possibly refuse to help Malach. If the half-mage was still alive. Propping his paddle between his knees, he dangled his outside hand into the water to rinse off the crumbs, scooped a handful to rinse his other hand, then wiped his palms along his trousers, careful not to rub the blister.

'Log ahead!' shouted Lazuli.

'And another on our left,' called Larimar.

The pacers continuing to call out alerts, Beram navigated the choppy water around the debris from the bridge with the whole boat paddling strongly as Flight's nose rose and fell over the criss-crossing waves and eddies. Occasionally, Flight's nose bumped against a broken slat of wood or drifting piece of bridge railing. Then they were clear and Beram called for a lift in rate.

If he wanted the paddlers to speed up, he'd better join in. 'Swap sides so I can paddle too?'

Lamiya gave him an approving nod and quickly half-stood and shuffled across in front of him. Tentatively, he gripped his paddle and took a few strokes. It was better with the blistered hand in the water, and the cold water soon numbed it. Clearing his mind, Everand persuaded his arms to rise and plunge in an endless cycle, his breath coming in gasps and then easing as Beram set the pattern of calling for a hundred stronger strokes, letting them take a thirty-stroke breather, then calling for a further lift. Sweat trickled annoyingly down the back of his neck, sliding down his back and making his tunic progressively sodden. His feet were in a shallow puddle at the base of the boat, and his toes felt swollen and numb. Unbelievably, Lamiya was still smiling and humming softly. Gritting his teeth, he hoped Azuri was indeed impressed by his efforts.

The others swapped sides on the move twice more, and then Everand noticed the trees were denser on the left-hand bank. Surely, they were almost at the tributary into Riverwood. His arms and feet felt like blocks of wood and he doubted he could keep up for much longer.

Sitting taller, Lamiya called up to Beram, 'Swap with me. The next part is tricky, but I took note of how Malach steered his boat through.'

'Fair enough,' said Beram. 'Slow the boat … stop the boat … take a quick drink while we swap glides. Change sides if you want to.'

Everand took a drink, then gave Lamiya a grateful smile when she patted his knee and passed him a fire cake, murmuring, 'I saved this for you.' Brushing his lips across her forehead, he took the cake.

Beram dropped onto the bench beside him with a grunt and took several swigs from the water flask Lamiya had left there. Wiping his mouth, he mumbled, 'Nearly there. Lamiya's right, we need Clommus to sing a ballad about this.'

'Perhaps it could be a new event at the next festival? Racing the whole river would sort out the best team,' said Everand, keeping his face serious. He couldn't help but laugh when Beram gulped and then choked, coughing and spluttering.

'Most amusing, my mage,' said Lamiya, leaning forward so the ends of her hair brushed his neck. 'Let's see if you still have good humour when we paddle all the way home again.'

He started to grimace, then remembered that if things went well he'd be holding the Staropal and wouldn't need to paddle home. Keeping that thought to himself, he hefted his paddle ready. He jumped when Lamiya's hair tickled his neck again.

'No more paddling for you, my love. You focus your mind on sneaking.' She kissed his head. 'Can't have you distracted by blisters!'

'Very funny,' he murmured, glad to stop paddling. Placing his paddle along the floor of the boat by his feet, he took the opportunity to roll his shoulders and flex his fingers to coax back some circulation. In the darkness the Riverwood bank slipped by, the trees like a shadowy crowd monitoring their approach and the sporadic clumps of granite like huddled shapes waiting to pounce. What would Torrap and the hunters do when they arrived? Tension pulled at his already tight shoulders. What if the hunters attacked? He had no magic to shield them. They'd need to be alert, make lots of noise and declare their intentions early.

Twisting, he asked Lamiya, 'Do you have any lamps for the boat? It might be best if Torrap sees us coming.'

The oar clunked a few times before she replied, 'No. We don't train in the dark, but I see your point.'

'Once we enter that final narrow channel, we need to call out then.' Flexing his fingers, he wished he could draw on his two drops of power to create an orb of light, but he was more likely to need his tiny reserve once at the Guild. Shouting would have to do. Judging by how much this simple blister throbbed, being injured in an attack would be unbearable.

The paddlers maintained their solid rate, the only indication of the extra effort the lack of banter between them. The banks surged by and Everand admired the balls of white bubbles from the paddles speeding past the boat's side. This was a mighty team for a mighty effort. He closed his eyes briefly: may he bring them all home safely.

The change in rhythm rousing him, he realised he'd dozed off and the boat was turning into the tributary into Riverwood. Sitting up straighter, his nerves ramped up at the way the narrow banks made the tree foliage tower above them, blocking out the light. Had the hunters noticed their approach yet? A ghostly blur flashed past his shoulder and he grabbed the side of the boat before he realised it was the falcon.

Lamiya's words came out of the darkness behind him. 'Plummet will warn me when we're noticed and the hunters are coming.'

'Good.' He realised Whirr was no longer tucked down the front of his tunic, and probably hadn't been for a while. 'Where's Whirr?'

'With me, hiding.'

Unclenching his fingers from the rim of the boat, Everand squinted into the darkness and tried to extend his senses. Frustration rose: everything was so much harder without his power. All he could sense were countless shadowy shapes and leaves brushing together in a mild breeze. But he had chosen this path, chosen to be with Lamiya. Holding that thought, he kept peering into the darkness.

The boat slowed and veered hard to the right as Lamiya aligned the path to enter the narrow channel on the left leading to the lake where Riverwood kept their boat. His heart skipped a few beats. During their escape they'd blocked this narrow run with a fallen tree trunk. Would they hit this in the dark? He turned to remind Lamiya.

'I remembered,' she said before he could utter a word. 'Plummet says the tree trunk has been moved.'

The boat glided amid the shadows, and the prickling between his shoulderblades intensified. The air split with the falcon's shriek, followed by a zinging sound. Thunk! An arrow pierced the boat's dragon forehead and stuck out, quivering. Lazuli and Larimar yanked their paddles up. Silence. They resumed paddling, sitting hunched.

'Blood's oath!' swore Beram.

Another arrow whizzed out of the inky trees and thunked next to the first one to also protrude quivering.

'Torrap!' yelled Everand. 'It's Everand and Lamiya. We come in peace! We need to talk.' Fear rushed through him at how vulnerable Lamiya was, standing up behind them. Should they stop the boat?

'Slow the rate,' called Lamiya, 'but keep going.'

'Torrap!' Everand yelled again. 'We bring news of Malach. Meet us at the landing beach.'

Silence oozed from the dense, dark trunks, although he sensed wraith-like shapes flitting along the right-hand shore. By the stars, the hunters were skilled. His stomach squirmed with unease. Torrap was intensely loyal to Malach, and he must use that to negotiate safe passage. Quickly. Dark-fall was passing.

For an eternity, Flight glided across the brackish small lake and finally her nose slid onto the muddy flat shore. 'Wait in the boat,' suggested Everand, certain the hunters would appear.

Sure enough, the darkness slipped and moved and twenty hunters clad in black or grey tunics fanned out to approach the boat, the whites of their eyes glinting in swarthy faces and arrows nocked ready in bows. A few held knives with cruel curved blades.

Everand tried to stand up but his legs quaked so much he thumped back down. 'Need help,' he muttered to Beram, who put a hand under his elbow and pushed him upright.

'I would speak with Torrap,' he called. 'I bring news of Malach.'

A lone shadow moved out from the fan of men. 'What do you want, mage?' came Torrap's burly voice.

Wishing his legs would cease wobbling, Everand tried to make his words strong and confident. 'We seek passage through Riverwood. We must go to the Mages' Guild on a mission, but you should know the mages have captured Malach. We must hurry because they intend to kill him.'

'You have come all this way to rescue Malach? I don't believe you!' spat Torrap.

Another arrow flew at the boat's head.

'Hey!' shouted Lamiya. 'Stop that.'

'Would you prefer we shoot you to shut you up, boatwoman?' snarled Torrap.

Before Everand could counter, raptors of all shapes and sizes flew from the trees and hovered around Lamiya.

'Malach's birds trust me, so should you,' said Lamiya boldly. 'We owe Riverwood no favours — none whatsoever — but we are going to the Guild on our own mission and will do our best to recover Malach while we're there.'

'You can hinder us or choose to help us,' jumped in Everand. 'But while we argue time passes that we and Malach can ill afford.'

'Let us disembark,' called Lamiya. 'Only three of us are going to the Guild, the others will remain here with you.'

'This will guarantee our return,' added Everand. 'Choose quickly. We need sustenance and a swift forward journey.'

The air throbbing around him, Everand forced his legs straighter and clamped his mouth shut, but kept his gaze on Torrap. *Come on man, decide.* The raptors continued to hover around Lamiya. A dim beam of moonlight shone down and he saw Torrap frown at the birds.

Torrap lowered his bow. 'Very well. But first you will explain how Malach came to be captured.'

Grateful for Beram's support under his elbow until it was his turn to disembark, Everand clambered stiffly from the boat and went to Torrap. Giving a respectful nod, he said, 'I understand you lead here now. You should also know that Lamiya is now the revered guide and leader of Riverplain. Treat her with more courtesy.'

Torrap glared at him. 'Understood. Walk with me and explain.' The hunter spun around and started to walk.

Persuading his leaden legs to walk, Everand lifted and lowered his shoulders and swung his arms trying to work circulation back into his body. Assuming the others were following, he rapidly outlined to Torrap his attempt to conceal Malach and the Guild's reasons for wanting to obliterate the half-mage. Every now and then Torrap would grunt.

The trees thinned and the rings of stone-and-wood cabins came into sight. 'So,' said Torrap, 'if you are not in time, you will bring back Malach's body?'

Everand snagged Torrap's elbow. 'Stop. Look at me.' The hunter turned dark eyes filled with distrust on him. 'There won't be a body. Malach will be … disintegrated.'

The hunter's eyes widened and he gasped. 'You must stop them, then.'

'I'll do my best, but the mages have stripped my powers, otherwise I'd have been captured too.' Everand released Torrap's elbow. 'We must hurry. Lazuli, Lamiya and I have to run all the way to the Guild from here. I beg you, give us food and drink and let us go.'

The paddlers stopped, waiting, the hunters hovering in a pack behind them.

Lamiya came to Everand's side and said softly, '*You* must decide, Torrap. There's no time to consult your people. I too am making rapid and unlooked-for choices. Decide. Choose to help us.'

In the dark, Torrap's eyes glistened. 'Very well. Food and water, and I will go with you.'

Before he could think about it, Everand shook his head. 'We can't take you. The means I intend to use to flee once we have Malach will only carry four. And if we're found, we must not appear threatening. This will be a battle of wits and words, not strength and might.'

'Besides,' said Lamiya, 'the people of Riverwood need you. In case we fail.'

Everand watched anger ripple across Torrap's face and the man's lips compress. Then he ventured, 'We might need your help once we come back into Riverwood. If you and your men can wait in the woods at the edge of the forest from first light, you could protect us while we flee across the grasslands. We'll emerge from the wall on the far side of the grass.'

Bushy eyebrows lifting, Torrap rasped, 'Reluctantly, I agree. The rest of your team remaining here will guarantee your swift return.' He turned to the young hunter with the odd white streak in his hair. 'Tiek, run and find Hemma. Get the women to make three parcels of food immediately, and prepare a meal for the others remaining here.'

Tiek brushed past and ran off into the gloom, his footsteps fading rapidly.

Torrap gave Everand a sour look, his expression still one of distrust.

Sweat prickled on Everand's brow.

What would happen if they returned without Malach?

Chapter Twenty-one

Lamiya shuddered when they strode past the raptor cages, her mind replaying unwelcome memories of being captured and humiliated by Malach. Her nose itched as if the coarse, stinking sack they'd used had been put over her head once more. Rubbing her nose, she squashed her irritation. They were free and she had far greater things to worry about.

In front of her, Everand was striding out, not saying a word. He obviously knew the way, having rejected Torrap's offer of guides, and perhaps he didn't wish to reveal the exact location of this secret tunnel. That made sense. A hand landed on her shoulder and she jumped.

'You alright?' queried Lazuli, looming close behind her.

'Yes,' she said, briefly running her fingertips over his hand. 'You?'

'So far,' he replied. 'I'm honoured to be going to Axis with you, but nervous. Will this be the end of this epic adventure, do you think?'

Smiling despite everything, she said, 'Let's hope so. As Ejad would say, this is seriously disrupting our training!'

Lazuli laughed. 'What, you think the longest paddle undertaken in history is a *disruption* to training? You are a tough glide! No wonder we're the best.'

Laughing with Lazuli, she saw Everand's amused glance over his shoulder and could imagine his thought: back to boats, *again*? Her spirits buoyed, she ran over the plan. Sneak into Mage Mantiss' place, persuade him to help them raise the Staropal stone thing from a secret hiding place and give it to Everand, who could then use it to restore his powers. She'd feel safer then, but they'd still have to get out of Axis with the stone, past Pelamis and Simoselaps. Really, *everything* depended on cooperation from Mantiss. Who Everand had let down. Deserted. Betrayed. Why would Mantiss give him the stone? Why would *any* mage let Everand take it and give it to a dragon?

Drumming her fingers on her thigh while she walked, she thought of Tiliqua. Everand said she was Mantiss' daughter. Under other circumstances, she'd have admired Tiliqua, who displayed more courage and intelligence than the other mages who'd come to Riverplain. An uncanny belief crept into her that *Tiliqua* was the key. Her stride faltered when she sensed the spirits of U-Mali and Aura drifting above her shoulders. Inside her tunic, Whirr peeped.

In what way could Tiliqua be important? Because she could influence her father? Because she liked — her brow furrowed — no, more than that, she desired Everand. Her breath shortened. Having been rejected by Everand, would Tiliqua seek to block him? Whirr peeped again. No, the mage-woman seemed to have more integrity than that. She hoped. Only partly concentrating on following the narrow, winding track through the trees, she inhaled the pungent scent of pines to clear her head and considered what she knew. What outcomes could Tiliqua want from this? Would she help them if their actions protected her father somehow?

Everand stopped and raised a hand. Her momentum carrying her to stand beside him, she saw the trees had ended in an abrupt, severe line and they faced a flat sea of grasses, the seeded heads glistening faintly in sparse moonlight. Lazuli came to stand on her other side.

'Let me get my bearings,' muttered Everand. 'Can you see anything untoward?'

After squinting at the grasses until her eyes grew blurry, she said, 'Nothing except insects and bunya scuttling around.'

His expression serious, Everand said, 'We're exposed while we cross the grass, but as far as I know the mages have no reason to expect us from here.' His lips twisted into a half-smile. 'Actually, they don't have cause to expect us at all.' He waved an arm at the wall. 'Let's cross swiftly, heading directly to that segment of the wall.'

She and Lazuli nodded simultaneously, and after a brief twitch of his lips Everand set off in long, measured strides.

'You next, I'll follow you,' said Lazuli.

Hurrying, she caught up to Everand, wishing the grass heads didn't tickle and scratch so at her legs. A baby bunya hopped away from almost under her foot and she bit down a yelp. No doubt Malach's raptors enjoyed hunting these small creatures during dark-fall. Ahead, the great granite wall towered higher and higher. She could just discern the mages' warded shield above it, reaching up into the sky and gleaming luminously as it reflected the slip of moon. When the shadow of the wall fell across her, her shoulders hunched in. Trust Everand, she told herself.

They stopped beside a dark, yawning mouth into the wall, and Lamiya's pulse skittered.

Lazuli grunted in surprise and ran a hand through his hair. 'The mages don't know about this? It's bigger than I thought.'

Everand shook his head, and said, 'As you'll soon see, there's nothing but barren dirt on the far side. We have a long way to run to reach the Guild proper and we're only just going to make it before first light. Not ideal.' He grasped Lamiya's hand. 'Hold hands and let's move through the tunnel as fast as we can.'

Lamiya barely had time to grab Lazuli's hand when Everand tugged her forward into pitch darkness. To her relief, the floor seemed smooth and she didn't catch her toes on any edges. Everand was stooping, so she guessed the solid darkness a handspan above her head was the rock roof. She counted her paces, and after sixty felt squeamish at the press of darkness, nudging aside her fear that it was squeezing inward to entrap them. When Everand gave her fingers a squeeze she realised she was pinching his.

After another sixty paces, Everand slowed. Were they nearing the end? Another twenty paces and he stopped, a wavery outline against clear space beyond him. Rushing forward, she stopped and inhaled the cooler, fresher air, revelling in the flat space rolling away from them.

Peering around with interest, she saw only bare dirt and rocks rising some distance away. How odd, such a bare and useless space. Pulling her water flask from her belt, she took a drink and tipped some into a hand to refresh her face.

Realising Everand had moved away, she twisted her head and her eyebrows rose. He and Lazuli had retreated back into the mouth of the tunnel. What were they doing? Then Everand's low words reached her ears.

'You know why you are here, don't you?'

'Yes,' came Lazuli's hushed reply. 'If you fall, I am to bring her home safely.'

'Good. I'm counting on you.'

'Wait … despite everything, try not to fall. You make her happy.'

Her eyes smarting, Lamiya bent over and retied her sandal laces so they wouldn't realise she'd heard. They had become friends, after everything. A bundle of nerves and emotions erupting, she breathed out. *Lestaya. Mother, did you hear them?*

A hollowness surrounded her and she stood up quickly, her pulse racing. Whirr climbed up her tunic and rubbed his head against her chin. Heart still racing, she reached out again.

Lestaya. U-Mali. Are you with me? Utter silence and emptiness, as bleak as the bare dirt shadowy landscape.

'What are you doing?' Lazuli stood there, looking at her with concern.

'I …' she swallowed, 'I can't feel the spirits.'

Approaching too, Everand arched an eyebrow at her, then glanced up with a frown. 'The wardspell. The spirits can't reach through it.' Understanding flashed in his eyes. 'They haven't deserted you, Lamiya. They just can't hear you.' When she twisted her fingers together, he added, 'Remember, the dragons are with us. This is their task.'

That was a good point. Lifting her chin, she said, 'Are we going to run now?'

'Sadly, yes,' said Everand. 'I'll need a whole bag of fire cakes just for me afterwards.'

With a snort of amusement, Lazuli said, 'I'll set the pace. Follow the wall?' At Everand's nod, he set off, hugging the base of the wall and setting a medium-paced lope.

Glad she'd tightened her laces, Lamiya secured her water flask and broke into a run, wishing they didn't have to stick so close to the towering wall. After three thousand steps, she stopped counting. When Everand had said it was a long way, she hadn't thought it would be quite so far. Peering past Lazuli, her heart lifted at the sight of tall, white buildings ahead. The elegant domes stood out against the darkness, and whatever stone they were made of caught the dim light in hinted threads of silver and gold. She reckoned they were running due south, meaning the sun would rise to the east, behind the granite wall on their left. Shame the tunnel wasn't further south.

Her hair was clinging to the back of her neck and her tunic felt damp and clammy when Lazuli dropped back to a walk for a breather. 'We should take a drink and eat,' he murmured, waving a hand at the buildings which were distinctly closer.

Going towards the wall, he turned around to sit with his back against it.

'Don't touch it!' gasped Everand, leaping to grab Lazuli's arm and yank him away from the rocks. 'It's warded. An alarm will sound if you touch it.'

A cold shudder rippled down Lamiya. Didn't the rock wall also bestow death? How had they passed through the tunnel then?

'You could have said,' growled Lazuli, looking pale.

'How did we get through the tunnel?' asked Lamiya. 'That's not warded?'

With a shrug, Everand said, 'I have no idea how Malach's father managed to create the tunnel without anyone knowing. All I know is that the ward covers the surface of the granite rocks both inside and outside the wall, but it doesn't seem to extend into the tunnel. Maybe Mage Beetal blocked the wardspell somehow.'

Both *inside* and outside the wall … another shudder rippled down Lamiya's back. The Guild was serious about keeping the mages contained. Deadly serious. It was a miracle they'd agreed to remove Everand's power rather than forcibly escort him back to Axis. Hope beat in her chest. He did have allies. Tiliqua's face hovering in her mind, she pulled out a small loaf and forced herself to eat it.

Everand said, 'I'll lead from here. We have to pass the senior mages' country estates and although the mages should still be asleep, I don't know how early the humans who work on the estates rise.' He took a step, then stopped. 'We should put on our dark cloaks.'

Fumbling in her pack, Lamiya drew out her dark-grey cloak and shook it out. A glimmer of light was creeping along the top of the granite wall. To her right, several hundred paces away, were what looked like homes and a really long cocoon-shaped grey dome. 'What's that?'

'The grey dome?' Everand followed her gaze. 'That's the beetle training arena. It's on Mantiss' estate.'

'What do you mean by train the beetles?' asked Lazuli.

'In Axis, we use beetles for transport rather than waste our power,' said Everand. 'They are massive, almost as large as your hopeepa.' He smiled. 'If things go well, we'll take two beetles for our escape. No more running.'

Lazuli gave a low whistle. 'You must tell me more about the training.'

'Later,' agreed Everand. To Lamiya, he said, 'If we get separated for any reason, don't go wandering into any forests or fields of flowers. The snakes and spiders are also large.' He broke into a jog.

The more relaxed pace afforded her the opportunity to observe the landscape. They passed along the edge of what looked, in the ghostly light, to be multiple fields of various crops and small clusters of houses. Beyond these, she discerned four-floor-high white stone buildings, surrounded by what she guessed were lush lawns and flowerbeds. Only the senior mages had estates? As in Mantiss and Agamid?

Slowing to a walk, Everand reached for her hand. 'We enter the Guild grounds,' he murmured. 'Walk on the grass beside the pebbled paths rather than on them.' Pointing with his free hand, he said, 'Mantiss lives on the far side of the Great Hall. The hall is where Malach will be, but we'll go to Mantiss first.'

She nodded, relieved he wasn't going to let his desire to rescue Malach override their main mission. Crossing the fingers of her other hand, she hoped Mantiss was in the mood to talk. Lazuli flashed her a nervous smile and she inhaled deeply. This was it.

Holding tight onto Everand's hand, she tiptoed with him as they wove between buildings and cut across short, spongy lawns. Everything was ordered into neat squares with crisp edges. Even in the pre-sun gloom she observed how the colours and flowers all complemented each other. An exotic scent wafted past and she breathed it in. Small wonder Everand was so controlled and systematic; the lifestyle here shouted rigidity and order.

Feathers tickling, Whirr peeked out of the neck of her tunic and it occurred to her that there were no bird calls or twittering, like she'd hear in Riverplain with the rising of the sun. Everything was silent and still, as if waiting. She shivered.

The building that Everand said was the Great Hall was imposing, and the woodwork in the ornate flight of steps and elegantly carved doors was impressive. Everand scurried across three more lawns, and then made for a dome of white stone with a short flight of reddish wood steps. Releasing her hand, he virtually leaped up the steps and knocked lightly on the polished redwood door.

Lamiya briefly closed her eyes. *Akachi, send us your magic. Bring us good fortune.*

Nothing happened and muttering a curse, Everand ran a hand over his hair. Making a fist, he knocked again, louder.

Lamiya stared hard at the door. *Come on. Come on.* Her back prickled with the sense of being exposed on a doorstep so deep within the Guild. Then she heard footsteps approaching from inside. The door creaked open a handspan.

It flung open and Tiliqua stood there, gaping at Everand.

Chapter Twenty-Two

Mantiss grumbled at the deep ache pressing across his chest, willing it to ease so he could breathe properly. Blinking away the whirling pinpoint stars from lack of air, he brought his room into shadowy focus. Curse it. Still well before sun-up. Sinking deeper into his pillow, he squeezed his eyes shut. There was nothing to look forward to this sun. Everand was dead, at the imminent meeting he'd be deposed and that upstart Pelamis would be victorious, and the half-mage would then be obliterated. Hardly a fine moment in Guild history.

Yearning to hold Lapemis' notebook against his chest, he wanted to apologise to the first mage. Such auspicious beginnings for the new Guild, all undone. Under *his* leadership. If only he could burn the notebook rather than pass it into Pelamis' greedy outstretched hand. Maybe he would. Why should he hand it over? Trying to sit up, he let the notion take firm hold. The handing over of the notebook assumed it was passing from one worthy Head of the Guild to another worthy mage to lead. He snorted. The likes of Pelamis did not qualify. How could he prove it?

Pushing with both hands, he levered himself into a half-sitting position. The notebook, there was some clue in there, a reference, something Lapemis had written about the Staropal rejecting someone … Both his arms started to shake. Curse it.

He'd have to ask Agamid to help him walk to his study alcove so he could retrieve the notebook. Opening his mouth to ask Tiliqua to fetch Agamid, he found the chair beside his bed was empty. Where had she gone? Just when he needed her. He tried to call out, achieving a croak.

Voices and footsteps. Had Agamid arrived already, also unable to sleep? That would be convenient. Instead, a veritable crowd rushed in through his bedroom door and he gasped in dismay. Had Pelamis arranged an assassination? His heart throbbed in warning.

'Father,' Tiliqua came to his bedside and gripped both of his hands. 'Everand is here!' She sounded close to tears.

His mind spun. What nonsense was this? Why remind him Everand was dead? No need. Bitterness washed over him. A tall, lean figure came to the other side of the bed and kneeled down.

'Master, forgive me.'

The surge of dizziness made Mantiss close his eyes. That sounded like Everand. What sorcery was this? Was the onset of death mockingly presenting what his heart wished for? When his heart panged in earnest, he eased in a shallow breath.

'How long has he been like this?' asked the Everand-like voice.

'Since we came back without you,' replied Tiliqua, as if she were talking to the real Everand. 'Pelamis has challenged for the Head of the Guild. We vote this sun.'

'Get Agamid,' croaked Mantiss. 'Need notebook.' Whatever this delusion was, it could wait. An idea was forming.

'I'll summon Agamid,' said Tiliqua, adding, 'I don't know what notebook father refers to. I fear he won't survive the council meeting.'

Irritated, Mantiss leaned back, letting the pillow absorb his aching neck and head. Wait for Agamid to come. He listened to the swishing of Tiliqua's dress as she hurried out of the room.

Half opening an eye, he grunted. People were hovering around his bed. Dressed in bizarre clothes. Ghosts come to gloat?

'Master.' Someone sat on the bed. 'Master, it *is* me, Everand. I'm not dead. I tricked Pelamis. I need your help.'

Mantiss tuned the voice out. Agamid would be able to tell him what was really happening.

'Let me try,' came a woman's voice. Not Tiliqua. 'I think I know what's wrong. Move away, my love.'

The pressure on the bed eased, and was replaced by a lighter pressure. Two gentle hands grasped his. Such silken skin. A subtle aroma of wild grasses, trees and flowers surrounded him, and his heart gave a steadier beat. A bird chirped and he felt tiny feet hopping up the bedspread and soft feathers brush his cheek. The delusion was becoming stranger with each unsteady breath.

'Mage Mantiss,' said a melodic voice. 'I am Lamiya from Riverplain.' The pressure on his fingers increased and his hands began to tingle. 'I call your spirit back from death. It is not your time. Everand *is* here with me. He loves you, and he needs you.'

His soul gave a sigh and a warm tear seeped under his eyelashes. Everand loved him? Could this be true? But Everand was gone. Murdered. The tingling in his hands increased until it felt like the onset of pins and needles. The tiny bird peeped and rubbed soft, downy feathers against his cheek again. The woman's words washed around him.

'You and Everand need to talk. Properly. You are a beloved father to him, but he also loves me, as much as I love and adore him. He didn't want to leave you, but your Guild Rules forced him to choose between the Guild and me. Between serving you and being with me. You *know* Everand. You *trust* him. He intends neither you nor the Guild any harm; he merely wants to be happy.'

Strong fingers squeezed his. 'With his honour and integrity, and after everything he has done, Everand deserves to be happy. You know this.'

Another warm tear slipped from Mantiss' eyelashes. There was a background kerfuffle and he heard Agamid and Tiliqua's voices in the doorway. Someone hushed them. This dream was blissful; he could slide into death amid these thoughts.

'Mage Mantiss. Come back.' The woman's voice was sharper. 'Everand needs you, his master, now. This sun. You must forgive him and you must help him. Your Guild depends on it.'

The pins and needles intensified, crawling up over his wrists, and a strange energy crept up his arms. His whole being felt compelled to open his eyes, listen to this woman, obey this woman. He opened his eyes. A beautiful, exotic woman smiled at him, light dancing in grey-blue eyes in a heart-shaped face framed by luxurious, wavy mahogany hair that tumbled down over her shoulders.

'There you are,' she said. 'Please speak with Everand.'

An acute sense of loss washed over Mantiss when she released his hands and moved aside. Everand's face loomed, brows furrowed in concern, an unusual stubble covering his chin. Tentatively, Mantiss lifted a trembling hand to touch Everand's cheek, gasping when a small, colourful bird ran along his arm and hopped onto Everand's shoulder. Was any of this real?

Passing the small bird to the exotic woman, Everand took his hand with slim, cool fingers. 'Master, we need to talk, as Lamiya said. But more urgently, I need your help. *Before* the council meeting and the vote. We must hurry.'

The space around Mantiss' bed became crowded when Agamid and Tiliqua materialised in the circle.

Giving Lamiya a wary look, Agamid said tersely, 'Why are *you* here?' Glancing at Everand he said, 'Why are *either* of you here? You made your choices clear. Abundantly so.'

Tiliqua put a hand on Agamid's arm, saying, 'Our last interaction was … unpleasant, but let's hear what they have to say.'

'How?' croaked Mantiss, staring at Everand. '*How* are you here?'

A frown crossed Everand's face. 'How? I anticipated Pelamis would attack me and deployed a spell to mimic death.' Smiling wryly at Tiliqua and Agamid, he murmured, 'Sorry to give you a fright. It was indeed … unpleasant.' Then the azure eyes latched onto his again. 'Agamid has removed my power, as you agreed.'

Mantiss flapped a hand. 'Not what I meant. *How* did you get into Axis without anyone knowing?' At that, Everand hesitated and exchanged a glance with the exotic woman. So, however they had snuck back into Axis was significant.

Everand rubbed at his nose before saying slowly, 'We found the passage that Mage Beetal created for his forays into Riverwood. We used that.'

'Are you saying *anyone* can sneak in and out of the Guild? We must put a stop to this.' Agamid stared at Everand.

Tilting his head in the so familiar sincere way, Everand said, 'When we go, I'll reveal where the gap is. You can destroy it then.'

Stepping into Mantiss' line of sight, Tiliqua said, 'I think we should all sit at the table to talk. I'll ask Delma to bring the sun-up meal.' To Agamid she said, 'You can bring father?'

As soon as Tiliqua moved away, Mantiss found his arms being grabbed by Agamid and Everand. Lurching him upright, they swung his legs around so he was perched on the edge of the bed. He looked up into the mesmerising face of the exotic woman, who stood before him with her hands held out. Transfixed by her intense eyes, he grasped her hands, stood up by himself and took a step.

She stepped backwards, and he took another step. Energy tingled through the touch of her hands. Feeling strength ebbing into him he straightened his spine and took a bigger step. He almost laughed at the expressions on Agamid's and Everand's faces. 'Thank you, er …'

'Lamiya,' the woman said with a delightfully warm smile. 'Of Riverplain.'

By the sun and all the stars, he could see why Everand liked her. Some of Everand's odd comments about how they could learn from the provinces drifted into his mind. Perhaps his spy had a point. Letting go of Lamiya's hands, he wavered his way to the desk in his study alcove and murmured the words, 'note-scrawl-Lapemis'. The tile in the wall dissolved and presented him with the ancient notebook.

Clasping it to his breast, he turned and met Everand's questioning gaze. 'I intend to explain.' Hustling past, on legs that felt surprisingly steady, he took his seat at the head of his dining table and commanded the wall orbs to light.

Chairs scraped as Tiliqua and Agamid took their usual places. Everand brought over the desk chair for Lamiya to sit on, and only then did Mantiss realise there was yet another person hovering, waiting for a seat. Someone else attired in province clothes.

'This is Lazuli, also from Riverplain,' said Lamiya. 'He is a pacer.'

'A what?' Mantiss felt his eyebrow quirk, and then lift even higher when Everand laughed. He'd never heard his spy laugh like that, so carefree.

'It's a boating term,' said Everand with a fond look at Lamiya and waving a hand at Elytra's empty chair for the boatman. Then he sat down and asked, 'This notebook is important?'

Not wanting to discuss the notebook yet, Mantiss solemnly regarded everyone. So much had happened since Beram from Riverfall had arrived to seek the Guild's help. *No meddling …* yet here he was, seated at his table about to discuss the fate of the Guild with unknown people from another unknown province. Within the passing of less than one season! What had it been? Some twelve or thirteen suns. It felt like a hundred times that.

He drank in Everand's face. His spy was here to help, after all. With unexpected allies, like last time. Why had he ever doubted his trusted, loyal spy? Warmth and gratitude rushing into him, he curled his fingers around the edge of the notebook. Would Everand now accept the notebook and the position of Head of the Guild? Was that why he'd come back when given the choice not to?

'He will not,' said Lamiya, fixing grey-blue eyes upon him. 'You must find another solution.'

Startled, Mantiss' gaped at Lamiya, whose hand was underneath the table, perhaps resting on Everand's leg. Had she read his mind? Did she have magic? How much magic was already outside the Guild? First the half-mage, and now this.

Amused, she said, 'No, I read it in your face, and Everand confided in me that you might wish to pass the role to him.'

Conscious that the others were watching, mouths open in disbelief, Mantiss cleared his throat, searching for appropriate words. How could this woman possibly see so much?

'Master,' said Everand gently, 'Lamiya is now the revered guide and leader of Riverplain province. The guides, including Lamiya, have abilities that we have not encountered. One of them is being able to read people, combined with a blinding clarity about matters of importance.'

'I see.' Mantiss cleared his throat again, feeling uncomfortable. Sadness welling, his fingers gripped the notebook. As the woman said, Everand deserved to find happiness. Besides, his spy had relinquished his power and thus he could not pass the notebook with all its cursed secrets and responsibility to Everand. But it must not pass to Pelamis. So why were they here?

His face earnest, Everand said, 'We must raise the Staropal. I need it.'

Alarmed, Mantiss said, 'So do I.' The room and faces spun around him. Had he misjudged? Would Everand take the

Staropal, something he never thought his spy would desire or seek.

Shaking his head sorrowfully, Everand uttered the fateful words Mantiss never, ever wanted to hear.

'It is not for me. The red dragon wants it back.'

Chapter Twenty-Three

Everand feared Mantiss would topple from the chair! His master was hunched over, breathing ragged, all colour drained from his face.

Eyes flinty with anger, Tiliqua snapped, 'Look what you've done! What are you talking about?' Moving her chair next to Mantiss, she eased him upright. 'Breathe, father.'

Sadly, Everand eyed his distressed master. 'You know about the red dragon?'

With trembling fingers, Mantiss pushed the ancient, crumpled notebook across the table.

'Wait.' Tiliqua slammed a hand on top of the notebook. 'What is going on?'

'Lapemis' notebook,' croaked Mantiss, sitting straighter. 'It passes from the outgoing Head of the Guild to the incoming one.' He stared at the crinkled cover. 'It describes the arrival of Lapemis and the foundation of the Guild. The *true* foundation.'

A shiver tingled across Everand's nape. He was right; the mages were not told the truth. Not the full truth. 'It speaks of the red dragon?' He frowned. So, he could apparently now freely discuss the dragons? Had Akachi or Mizukaze removed whatever enchantment had encased him before?

'Are you sure you want to do this?' Agamid asked Mantiss. 'Think about what will happen if this knowledge is revealed!'

'A wrong will be righted,' said Everand.

'Balance will be restored,' said Lamiya. 'It will be a new beginning.'

'Founded on truth and respect,' added Everand.

'Mage Mantiss,' said Lamiya softly, 'the untruth and deception have eaten away your spirit. You hold the opportunity to make things right. You would not be failing the first mage but instead freeing the Guild and future mages to a true new beginning.'

Astounded, Everand fidgeted on his chair. How could Lamiya possibly have such insight into Mantiss' mind so quickly? Had she soul-read his master when she held his hands to help him up?

Twisting to face him, Lamiya said, 'You and Tiliqua should read this notebook together because she needs to know too. I'll change places with her.' After giving his knee a brief squeeze, she stood up.

'Yes,' said Mantiss, his face brightening. 'Read it together. Quickly, then we can plan.'

Astonishment and then joy flitted across Tiliqua's face before she smoothly moved to the chair beside Everand. A faint smell of violets wafted past him. 'We work together, after all,' she murmured. Watching his face, she added, 'You should know, I intend to challenge Pelamis for the position.'

Seeing Lamiya's nod of satisfaction out of the corner of his eye, Everand met Tiliqua's look. 'Let us make sure you win, then.'

'You approve?' Tiliqua's eyes widened.

'I can't think of a better mage,' he said sincerely. 'Besides, things are changing and the boundaries are dissolving. Perhaps we *can* still work together, but from different sides of the granite wall.'

'Nicely put,' said Lamiya with a brief smile. 'But let's take one step at a time.'

Lazuli suddenly leaned forward, looking nervous. 'Speaking of steps … Dare I ask, what happened to Malach?'

Guilt flushed through Everand. How could he have forgotten about Malach!

'The half-mage is alive,' said Agamid quickly. 'Held in the prepared cage in the Great Hall. We agreed it appropriate that his fate should be confirmed by the new Head of the Guild, given the unprecedented scenario.'

'If you win the position, what will you decree?' Everand asked Tiliqua, observing her intently.

Taking her time to look around the table, her gaze hovering on Lamiya and Lazuli, Tiliqua finally fixed serious eyes on him. 'You can have Malach back, without his power, if that's what you want.' The edges of her mouth twitched. 'In the interests of inter-province relations.'

Everand noticed the pleased look on Lamiya's face. Surely that wasn't out of any relief on Malach's part … no, it was more to do with the prospect of peaceful relations. And Malach no longer having power. Surreptitiously, he observed Mantiss and Agamid. Both looked uncomfortable, but resigned. Did this mean they'd already accepted the idea of Tiliqua as the new Head of the Guild? He sat back, thinking it through.

Subtly, Tiliqua had managed to take control of this discussion. By offering up Malach was she just trying to guarantee his support to make sure she would win? The bigger question was whether she, and hence the Guild, would relinquish the Staropal. His gaze dropped to the slim notebook, still under Tiliqua's hand. Well, letting Pelamis win was not an option, so he and Lamiya should continue to tread this path. Warily.

'Shall we look at the notebook?' he asked Tiliqua respectfully.

'There are clues in there,' said Mantiss. 'Read quickly.'

Gently prising the ancient text from beneath Tiliqua's fingers, Everand admired the crumpled parchment cover and the elegant cursive script. His pulse raced: what was he about to learn from these long-guarded pages? Exactly what had the first mages done?

'Note-scrawl-Lapemis,' muttered Mantiss, and the cover sprang open to offer the first page.

Conscious of Tiliqua's warm breath close by and the hint of violets, Everand began to read. Soon enthralled, he read of the courageous escape of twelve mages and the same number of humans aboard the *Wavestrider*. His breath caught at the description of their landing and finding the tranquil, turquoise lake. So, the mages *had* actually landed at Riverplain! Before it became Riverplain. Glancing up, he found Lamiya watching him closely, absorbing his reactions.

At the description of the battle with the green serpent, he clenched his hands beneath the table. How could they chase and kill the river dragon, unprovoked! Holding his breath, he ploughed on, Lapemis' words filling his mind with vivid images.

The cave twisted around a bend, luminous lights refracting off the walls. I reinforced my ward and edged around the final curve, emerging into a smooth, rounded cavern with a kaleidoscope of light and energy dancing off the walls and roof. My eyes went straight to the enormous, pearly eggs collected against the back wall.

In their midst sat a star-shaped stone with all the colours known shifting inside it. About the size of my head, the stone oozed magic. Entranced, I stared. If we could access the magic inside that stone then we could magnify our power a hundredfold and reclaim much of what we'd lost.

The shadows by the wall shifted and my breath lodged in my throat when a red-and-gold serpent nudged into the light of the star.

Horror rising, Everand absorbed the telling of the stunning of the red dragon by Lapemis and Aclys and the deliberate theft of the stone. He swallowed. Small wonder the mages had fled from the ire of Akachi — all the way across Ossilis! The truth was far worse than he'd anticipated. Head bowed, he struggled to read on.

Hearing the distant roar of the red beast echoing across the lake, I pulled the cloak-wrapped stone to my chest, feeling the disturbance within it. Was the stone responding to the beast's rage? Did they have an unbreakable connection and the red beast would know where we took it, despite our efforts and distance? It occurred to me that we should wipe the memory of the theft of the stone from the humans' minds, and not pass this knowledge down to the next generation of mages.

Sadness clouding his thoughts, Everand read of the fake story concocted by Lapemis about finding the Staropal in the eternal spring. For the next three generations, this version of history had been taught without anyone, including himself, thinking to question it. What fools. He looked up into Mantiss' green eyes and gave a small nod. This knowledge was a mighty burden. It was not surprising that his master, who possessed integrity and foresight, was suffering.

Beside him, Tiliqua sat rigid with tension, her chest rising and falling in short, fast breaths. If she won the right to be the Head of the Guild, what would she do with this knowledge? He persuaded his reluctant eyes to read on.

Becoming bolder, I asked the stone about its origin. I received images of an enormous cradle-shaped shell in the depths of the cave in the turquoise lake. I was shown tears of the red serpent dropping into the base of the shell, glinting with colour and crystallising into a small, translucent orb. Over time, the tiny orb grew and the serpent licked at it with her forked tongue, teasing out the points and helping it to transform into this magnificent star.

The stone conveyed the term 'dragon' to me. Sadness whirled inside me when I realised the stone was born from the tears and innate power of the red dragon. Small wonder the creature had protected it.

Fear edged into my mind. Why had the dragon creature created it? Was it to do with the eggs, and was that why it was nestled among them? Surely, the dragon could not let us keep it.

A sob escaped his lips. Was the theft of the Staropal why there were only three dragons after all this time? Mizuchi had only managed to rear one egg: Mizukaze. And the single egg left with Akachi, thanks to Lapemis' small act of mercy, must be Hanachi, who was somehow connected to Lamiya. Raising his smarting eyes, he sought Lamiya's face to anchor him. He felt soiled, unworthy.

'We will make it right, my love,' said Lamiya immediately. 'That's why we are here.'

'First,' said Mantiss, his expression sharp, 'we must use the Staropal to choose Tiliqua over Pelamis. There is a passage about what happens when someone seeking power for themselves tries to handle the stone. When you find that, read it to all of us.'

Struggling to focus, Everand saw the table was adorned with cups of tea and plates with loaves and slices of fruit. When had that arrived? Gratefully, he took the cup and filled plate that Lazuli pushed his way. Sipping the strong tea, he glanced at Tiliqua to see if she was ready to continue. Face pale, she nodded, and he turned his attention back to the notebook. Only a few pages further on, he found the segment Mantiss must be referring to.

'Are you happy for me to read it out, or would you prefer to?' he asked.

'You do it,' came Tiliqua's whispered reply. 'I was not prepared for any of this.'

Tugging the notebook closer, Everand steadied his nerves, cleared his throat and read aloud:

One dark-fall, I jerked out of a deep sleep, an image of the stone flashing red behind my eyelids. With a gasp, I perceived a shadowy figure hunched over where I had placed the stone in a nook in the rocks next to me. I scrambled up, and a shrouded figure turned to face me: Nactus, with the stone gripped between his hands.

'Why should you be the only one to wield it?' he hissed, spittle forming on his lips.

Alarmed, I eyed the red streaks building inside the stone. Without the code words, Nactus could not access its power.

'Tell me how to use it! We should take more power.' Nactus' twisted face was lit with an eerie red glow.

In that instant, I perceived the danger attached to the stone. Its power could be used for good — or evil. Forcing calm, I stretched out my hands. 'Give it to me. See the lurid red it has become? It will not respond to you.'

Nactus clutched the stone to his chest, the lust for power glowing in his eyes.

Fear trickled into me. We needed a proper hierarchy and a set of rules immediately; clear order and protocol must be established. And once we had taken what power we needed to establish ourselves, the stone should be removed from sight and temptation. I kept my hands held out, waiting.

The stone pulsed with red light and heat, and suddenly Nactus handed it to me. The lust fading from his eyes, he turned on his heel and strode into the gloom.

Shaken, I caressed the stone and murmured to it until it resumed its tranquil blue colours, like the lake glinting in sunlight.

Looking up from the page, Everand blinked the faces of the others into focus. 'Lapemis goes on to write that those with ambition must never be let near the stone. For obvious reasons. He also says that the stone does not forget the red dragon.'

Tapping his fingers on the table, he looked at Mantiss and Agamid. 'Lapemis was right about another thing. The dragons do live for generations and the same red dragon, whose name is Akachi, still lives in that turquoise lake and has bound Lamiya and me to return the Staropal to her.'

Mantiss emitted a groan and clutched a hand to his chest.

'Will the granite wall and wardspell continue to protect us?' asked Agamid.

'They might,' said Everand slowly, choosing his words carefully and watching Lamiya's face to see if she approved. 'But in exchange for helping Tiliqua win the vote, we ask that the Guild give us the stone. We have vowed to return it.' He spread his hands. 'Think about it — all these unprecedented events have brought us to this very point.'

Silence stretched across the table, broken only by the clattering of Mantiss' teacup when he put it down with trembling fingers. Across from Everand, Lazuli was staring out the window as if he wished he were somewhere else. Gently, Everand closed the notebook and slid it across the polished table back to Mantiss. Lifting the notebook, his master clutched it against his chest, his expression vacant.

Schooling his features into a bland expression, Everand waited, relieved when Lamiya sat back in her chair, content to wait too. Mantiss, Agamid and Tiliqua must come willingly to this part of the plan. Coercing the mages would lead to unpredictability, and there was enough of that already in Pelamis and Malach.

Finally, just as Everand was starting to think about how much his body ached and how tired he felt, Tiliqua stirred in her chair.

Lifting her chin, she said crisply, 'Father, Agamid, do you support me seeking the position? Neither of you wish to lead?'

Agamid's hand stilled, mid-stroke of his beard. 'I am pleased to support you as senior mage. I do not wish to lead.'

Mantiss' green eyes gradually came back into focus, and the fingers clutching the notebook lost some of their tension. 'That upstart Pelamis must not lead.' Sitting straight and looking at Tiliqua, he said firmly, 'I am weary of leading. I should have noticed your strength earlier, and I am proud to support you.'

The rigidity eased in Tiliqua's neck and shoulders, and she turned to Everand, her eyes brimming with excitement. He dipped his head to her.

'Very well. Let us go to the Great Hall and raise the Staropal.' Standing, Tiliqua smoothed her hands down her dress.

A cold shiver coursing down his spine, Everand stood too. The mages hadn't *actually* said they agreed to give him the Staropal. Were they waiting to see if Tiliqua won and could persuade the other mages? Did they hope the answer would be taken from their hands? Once Tiliqua held the Staropal, would she become so captivated by its beauty and the power it could yield that she wouldn't relinquish it? The energy buzzing from her did not bode well.

At a gentle touch to his elbow, he looked down into Lamiya's sincere eyes. 'From what you've said, the stone will judge her, my love. She must hold true,' she murmured.

Breathing out, Everand found Agamid and Lazuli were observing him, foreheads pinched with concern. Indeed, matters could still go wrong. Taking a step to follow Tiliqua towards the door, he thought of Akachi's task: *Yes. You have touched the stone. It will come to you.*

He jolted to a stop.

What if the Staropal refused to go to either Pelamis or Tiliqua?

What if it chose him?

Chapter Twenty-four

Lamiya stepped on Everand's heel. Why had he stopped? The tell-tale set to his shoulders meant he'd thought of something else that could go wrong. Pushing down her sigh and desire to ask what he was thinking, she shoved his lower back so he resumed walking. Whatever he'd thought of would become apparent soon enough.

At the front door, they clumped together while the mages sorted out what order they should exit in. Lazuli hovered anxiously by her shoulder and she brushed the back of his hand with her fingers to show she was glad of his presence. His grey eyes lit up briefly, then resumed their troubled expression. Agamid moved off in the lead, followed by Mantiss, Tiliqua and Everand, leaving her and Lazuli to follow.

Once outside, Lamiya looked up. The dark sky was broken by splashes of pinks and yellows, the stars fading into mere hints of light. Everything was still and uncannily quiet. There were no birds calling a greeting to the sun, no buzzing or whirring of insects, no sounds of people. She shivered; this place was so subdued and ordered, as if living was not fully permitted.

Frowning at Everand's back as they followed the others, she couldn't help wondering at his transformation in the short time she'd known him. Sensing her attention, he looked over his shoulder and arched an eyebrow. She should smile, but the gravity of what they were about to do stole it away. When Everand arched the other eyebrow, she shook her head: it's nothing.

Too soon, she was climbing the steps to the imposing Great Hall. At the top, Agamid waved a hand and the two massive, ornate wooden doors swung open. She filed in after the others, jumping when the doors swung back closed with a loud click that echoed hollowly across the space. Orb lights flickered to life on the far wall, behind a long, polished table on a raised dais. Craning her neck, Lamiya took in the hall with its high, beamed roof, the intricate and colourful glass windows, and the smooth, opalescent marble walls. A serious place for serious decisions. She felt stifled.

Something moved near a bookcase and her gaze swung that way. Her hand flew to her mouth as Malach, grimy and dishevelled, came to the front of a tall, warded cage and mutely placed both hands on the glass, staring at them. Her heart twisted at the way his eyes fixed on Everand in shock, and then his face creased into a smile. Before Everand could rush over to the cage, she snagged his sleeve.

'The stone first.'

Everand opened and shut his mouth, before giving Malach a brief wave of acknowledgment and saying, 'Yes. The stone first. I need my power.'

At a slithering noise behind her Lamiya spun around to see the massive silk rug rumpling up and sliding away, directed by a spell from Agamid's raised hand. With a gasp, she stared at the gold star-shaped motif between a sun and a moon carved into the marble tile floor, elegant words in a gold, flowing script inscribed beneath it. Her pulse raced. What would these powerful mages be like once they held the stone which magnified their magic a hundred-fold?

Swallowing, she watched Everand's face, seeing the anticipation reflected there. Half-closing her eyes, she murmured a prayer to the spirits that his power would be restored — and he'd still be the same mage she fell in love with.

Moving to stand beside the star motif, Tiliqua held her hands out and said impatiently, 'Let's do this before Pelamis or any others arrive.'

Mantiss and Agamid promptly took up position around the star with Tiliqua, and the three mages had to reach their arms wide to hold hands to form a triangle.

'Will it work with just the three of us?' asked Tiliqua.

Mantiss' shoulders lifted in a shrug. 'It should come to me as the Head of the Guild, but we will find out soon enough.' He closed his eyes, straightened his arms and said loudly, 'I, Mage Mantiss, Head of the Guild, hereby summon the Staropal. Lake-cave-star-opal!'

Lamiya held her breath when a faint hum sounded from beneath the floor, but after a few more breaths it faded.

'I, Mage Mantiss, Head of the Guild, hereby summon the Staropal. Lake-cave-star-opal!' repeated Mantiss louder and shaking his arms out for emphasis.

Green, purple and turquoise auras spread around the three mages, and the humming resumed, but again faded and the floor stubbornly remained marble tiles.

'Wait.' Everand moved forward. 'I should join you, even without my power.' He stepped between Mantiss and Tiliqua and took their hands, forming a square, with their toes just away from the edge of the motif and inscription.

All four mages bowed their heads and closed their eyes, and Lamiya found herself reaching to take Lazuli's hand, grateful for his strong fingers closing over hers. Her heart beat loudly. Surely, if Akachi was right, the stone would come with Everand there? A shudder of unease rippled over her at the frown pinching Everand's forehead while he muttered the incantation with the other mages. Did he worry that he'd have to challenge Tiliqua for the stone? The back of her neck went cold. If Tiliqua snatched the stone *before* he resumed his power, what would happen then?

Huddling closer, Lazuli squeezed her fingers. 'We must trust that Everand has a plan,' he murmured. With a flash of his lopsided smile, he added, 'He usually does.'

Pushing away her doubts, Lamiya took a slow, deep breath, gathering energy and optimism, and focused on the mages. She must be ready for whatever was going to happen.

'Lake-cave-star-opal,' said Mantiss. 'I, Mage Mantiss, Head of the Guild, summon the Staropal.'

'Lake-cave-star-opal,' echoed Everand. 'I, Mage Everand, also call the Staropal, on behalf of the great dragon Akachi.'

The air thickened imperceptibly and the humming began under the floor, this time spreading upwards and outwards, until it teased at Lamiya's ears. The hairs stood up all along the back of her neck and down her arms. This magic felt primal, elemental beyond anything she'd seen or experienced. Gripping Lazuli's hand, she reached her other hand to the neck of her tunic. Whirr promptly climbed up and rubbed his head against her fingers. Her dear and loyal friends; her instinct was shrieking that she was going to need them both.

The humming increased until the air vibrated throughout the entire hall and the orb lights flickered and danced. Glancing quickly at the warded cage, she observed Malach still standing with his hands up against the cage wall, his gaze transfixed on the mages and the star motif. Unease prickled down her entire being: Malach must not be allowed anywhere near this precious stone. The result could be as disastrous as if Pelamis took it.

Drawing in another deep breath, Lamiya deliberately brought into her mind an image of Akachi rising up out of her lake and waddling forward to take the stone from Everand's outstretched fingers. The image wavered and shimmered and then burned bright and true, like a vision. *Yes! This must be.* Her hair began to float away from her neck and shoulders, riding the static in the air, and the vibrating and humming increased to such a crescendo it felt as if every part of her shook with it. Breathing steadily, she kept a firm hold of the vision, seeing Akachi's powerful legs wading through the water, seeing the pleasure lighting the dragon's golden eyes as she beheld the stone that Everand held out.

A brilliant, white shaft of light suddenly formed around Everand and she was forced to squint to keep watching. With a massive crack, the motif split apart, the shattered marble and gold shards vanishing down into the hole created. Lazuli's hand jumped around hers and Whirr gave a shrill peep, only her fingers stopping the bird from diving deep inside her tunic. *No, my friend. Stay ready.*

Her heart skipped and raced with delight when a fountain of silver light beamed out from below the floor, cascading and twisting into the air with flecks and glints in every colour imaginable, like a waterfall in sunlight tumbling towards the high roof. She felt her lips curving into a smile of pleasure and warm tears forming in the presence of such beauty. When Whirr broke into song, greeting the light, she released Lazuli's hand and flung both of her arms outwards and upwards to welcome this elemental magic.

Giving her a startled look, Everand smiled and lifted his arms outwards and upwards too. Tears rolled down her cheeks unheeded when a magnificent, head-sized stone shaped like a star made of swirling blue and jade lake water and refracting too many hues of colour to count, rose up through the hole in the floor and hovered at head height between the mages. No words could ever do justice to describe the Staropal.

I created it. It is mine, Akachi's voice said into her mind. *Bring it to me.*

For an eternity, the Staropal hovered and the entire hall pulsed and thrummed with pure, elemental magic. Silver and incandescent blue motes swirled around the mages like a swarm of dragonflies. Lamiya's chest ached with the intensity of the pull of the magic. Perched on her shoulder, Whirr continued his warbling birdsong. Blinking, Mantiss lowered his arms and took a step back. Agamid lowered his arms and took a step back.

Her hair prickling and crackling with static and flying about her, Lamiya could do nothing more than stare while the Staropal bobbed towards Tiliqua, then paused, altered course and bobbed towards Everand.

Waggling her outstretched fingers at the stone, Tiliqua slid away from Everand until they faced each other across the small chasm in the floor. 'Lake-cave-star-opal!' shouted Tiliqua. 'Come to me and I will lead the Guild.'

Sadness infusing his face, Everand flexed his fingers and called, 'Lake-cave-star-opal. Come with me and I will return you to Akachi.'

Bestowing Everand a vicious look, Tiliqua lifted her chin and began to glow with a bright turquoise aura, a golden halo forming above her golden-blonde hair. Her eyes flashed an icy, intense blue. 'Help *me*, Staropal. I will bring this Guild back to glory.'

Dismay flooding her, Lamiya watched Tiliqua, who looked radiant, strong and beautiful, surrounded by so much power, whereas Everand seemed diminished and pale, just a man without power begging a magnificent artefact to choose him. A sour taste oozed into her mouth. After all this … no … they *must* have the stone.

Focusing on Everand, she brought the vision of Akachi to the forefront of her mind. When Lazuli gasped and grabbed her arm, she peered through her fluttering eyelashes at the hazy spectre of the massive red dragon taking shape. The wraith-like Akachi loomed behind Everand and flicked a ghostly tongue.

'Come to me,' Everand said distinctly to the bobbing stone, 'and I will return you to your creator, for the benefit of the dragon species and not for the purposes of mages or mankind.' Tilting his chin high, he added, 'I am but a vessel for your passage, great Staropal.'

'No!' shrieked Tiliqua. 'You promised to help me first!'

With a flurry of wings, Whirr pitched off Lamiya's shoulder, zoomed at Tiliqua and darted around her face, disrupting her concentration.

'Shoo!' snapped Tiliqua, batting at Whirr with a hand.

Behind Everand, the spectre of Akachi released a mighty roar that bounced in rumbling echoes off the walls and roof. Mantiss and Agamid took several hasty steps away, and Malach began to slam his hands against his cage wall.

Whirr! Come back! commanded Lamiya, relieved when he dodged Tiliqua's flattened hand and sped towards her. With a booming crash, noise erupted all around. Whirr flew circles around her head peeping shrilly, Malach furiously battered his hands against the cage and the wraith-dragon's roar magnified off every surface possible. Mantiss and Agamid seemed to be shouting, their voices multiplying and discordant while flashes of colour tumbled into the space.

The air whooshed from her chest when Lazuli abruptly flung both arms around her, lifted her and leaped backwards. Disoriented, she blinked furiously, her heart hammering in her ears.

'Mages!' gasped Lazuli. 'Stay out of their way!'

Feeling as if time had become a turgid, turbulent river around her, Lamiya struggled to disentangle the commotion and cacophony. The crash was the doors shattering, the added colours were the mages' robes. There must be twenty of them! Amid a wave of dizziness, she saw the mage in a vivid orange robe stride towards Tiliqua and Everand. Pelamis! Then he caught sight of her and stopped, his startled expression transforming into a cruel grin.

Lazuli yanked her sideways as a bolt of power shot past where she'd been standing.

Her concentration disrupted, the spectre of Akachi dissolved, floating away like thousands of tiny red leaves on a chill breeze. 'Nooo!' she wailed.

Everand was unprotected!

Chapter Twenty-Five

Everand took his eyes off the Staropal to ascertain how many mages had burst in. Too many.

'You're supposed to be dead!' shouted Pelamis, advancing and shaking a fist. 'Yet more deception, you stinking traitor!'

A swarm of pointed shards followed Pelamis' accusation and Everand leaped aside, horrified when he heard grunts behind him. Had the shards hit someone else? No time to look though, with Pelamis following through with a death bolt. Behind him, another mage swore. Pelamis was beyond reason already!

'Desist!' yelled Everand. 'Before others get hurt.'

The irate mage flung another swarm of shards at him and then rounded on Tiliqua. 'And you! Another traitor, trying to take the Staropal before the vote.' Arms raised, Pelamis shouted, 'Mages, to me! We must protect the Staropal from these traitors!'

Gathering his courage, Everand sprinted to stand behind Tiliqua. 'Protect me,' he urged. 'We must work together to insist the vote be held.'

After a tight nod, Tiliqua raised a shield around the two of them.

Frantic, he scanned the room for Lamiya. After three sweeping gazes his heart beat wildly. Where was she? Shaking his head, he searched again. There! Up on the dais, behind the mahogany table, with Lazuli standing protectively beside her. Nearby, to their right, Malach was slamming his hands against the front of his cage and roaring. If Lazuli could free him ... that would give Pelamis something else to think about.

Flexing his fingers, Everand moaned at the weak, hollow feeling that resulted. What could he do without his power? Not much. He needed the stone. However, the mages had formed a large circle and the Staropal bobbed in the centre, hovering above the hole in the floor, red hues mingling with the blues and jades to indicate its displeasure. His throat clenching, Everand assessed the stone. What would happen if several mages called it to them?

He ran his eye around the circle, confirming the entire Outer Council of Twenty stood there. Agamid and Mantiss were next to Tiliqua, and she was whispering to Agamid, while Mantiss looked as if he were struggling to remain upright. Seeing Saiphos several mages away, Everand flapped a hand until he caught the young mage's eye, then tilted his head to indicate Tiliqua. Saiphos frowned, then calmly edged his way around the circle to stand near him and Tiliqua.

Repeating the sequence, Everand persuaded Hydrelaps, Caimanops and Neelaps to all stand by him and Tiliqua, in effect forming two factions across the hole in the floor. But they were eight, compared to Pelamis' twelve. He cast his eyes up to the warded cage. Malach's volatility could work to their advantage. If freed, he would surely go after Pelamis.

Guilt prodded Everand: that might be the last thing Malach ever did. Then again, eying the fury on Malach's face and the way he was brutally slamming his hands against the cage, he felt a flush of hope. Such intensity and determination ... anything could happen. He swallowed. Ideally, Malach would survive to return to Riverwood and Mage Beetal would live on through his son.

The desperation on Malach's face tugged at his heart. Being obliterated while helpless inside a cage would be jarringly unjust — whereas letting a true hunter, a raptor in man-form, decide his own fate — there was justice in that. His resolve returned: just as Mage Beetal had made his choices, he would free Malach and let the son determine his own fate. It was the best he could do.

'Can you shatter Malach's cage? he murmured to Tiliqua. 'We could use his help.'

'Maybe, if Agamid helps me,' she replied tersely.

'Mages of the Outer Council,' shouted Pelamis, 'I call upon you to vote immediately for a new Head of the Guild.' He flapped a hand dismissively. 'Mantiss is no longer fit to lead us. I offer myself as your new leader. I will be strong and tireless in leading the Guild forward. What say you?'

The mages all focused on Pelamis and Everand groaned. Now Tiliqua would have to take her stance against Pelamis instead of destroying the cage. If only he had his power! In the middle of them all, the Staropal bobbed in jerky movements and the blue seas swirled with waves of crimsons, reds and oranges. His mouth ran dry. What if he simply dashed forward and snatched it? Would the stone restore his power immediately? He became aware of Simoselaps watching him. Curse it, he'd never reach the stone in time.

Moving further behind Tiliqua, to where Simoselaps couldn't see his face, he glanced towards the dais. Lazuli and Lamiya were nudging their way closer to Malach's cage. What did they think they could achieve?

He was suddenly exposed again when Tiliqua took a step forward, her words strident. 'Mages of the Outer Council, I offer myself as your new Head of the Guild. Where does it say that the position must be filled by a man? We are in the midst of unprecedented events and it is time for a new approach, new ideas. I am as strong as Pelamis, with greater moral fortitude. I urge you to choose me.'

The mages gaped at Tiliqua, then swung their collective gaze to Pelamis.

With a sardonic sneer, Pelamis retorted, 'Don't waste our time. Unprecedented events need a leader of unprecedented strength, not a weakling woman trying on the role for the first time.'

Anger bubbling up, Everand stepped beside Tiliqua and cleared his throat. 'Actually, before the council votes, *both* candidates are required to pass a test.' Out of the corner of his eye, he saw Mantiss nod vigorously.

'What trick are you playing now, traitor?' accused Pelamis. 'Don't listen to him. He continues to deceive us, playing dead and saying he was leaving the Guild.' Pelamis' upper lip curled. 'Yet here he is, trying to influence things. Ignore him. His words are meaningless, and without his power he isn't even a mage anymore and his vote isn't valid.'

Holding his head high, Everand said firmly, 'I don't intend to vote. However, as Mage Mantiss, our *current* leader, will confirm, the Staropal is passed from one *worthy* Head to the next *worthy* Head.' His lips twitched with the desire to smile. 'And *worthy* is decided by the Staropal itself.'

Holding his hand out, palm facing the stone, he made brief eye contact with every mage standing in the circle. 'This is not my word. This is Guild *Law*. So, let's first ask the Staropal to confirm that the council does indeed have two candidates for the role.'

'Outrageous!' cried Pelamis. 'The stone confirms the choice of the councils, not the other way around! Don't listen to him!'

Everand held his breath. Enough needling, Pelamis was puce in the face and could act impulsively … *yes*, Pelamis flicked his wrists to shake back his robe sleeves and bounded two steps towards the Staropal, reaching across the hole for it.

Reds, crimsons and oranges erupted like flames within the stone, black smears appearing and whirring around with the lurid, angry colours. A discordant buzzing filled the air and the stone bobbed *away* from Pelamis, across the hole in the floor so he couldn't grasp it. The circle of mages muttered and shuffled uneasily.

'See?' called Tiliqua, flicking Everand a grateful look. 'Pelamis is deemed unworthy.' She held her hands out beseechingly. 'Come to me, stone of power. I am worthy.'

Taking a step sideways to give her space, Everand observed the Staropal. The base colours were returning to the tranquil blues and jades, but there were still splashes of red and orange. The discordant buzzing noise dissipated and he lifted his gaze to see what Lamiya was doing. She and Lazuli now stood beside Malach's cage, but she was staring down at him.

'Take it,' she mouthed.

He arched an eyebrow at her. Tiliqua would never forgive him.

'Take it, my love,' she mouthed again, moving her hands sinuously in front of her. 'For Akachi.'

The hairs on the back of his neck stood up and he perceived the hazy red dragon forming behind him again. Around the circle, the mages' expressions were filling with horror and a few stepped backwards, widening the circle. Everand shook his head at Lamiya; this wouldn't help. *If* the stone came, it had to come to him, not the dragon. The hovering presence of the dragon disappeared.

Tiliqua held her hands out again. 'Come to me, Staropal. Judge me worthy.'

The Staropal began to spin where it was, blues, greens, jades, purples all somehow mingling yet also distinct. Colours of acceptance. Hope growing, Everand watched an azure hue became more prominent, amid flashes of starlight yellow and pale gold. His heart gave a great jolt. *His* colours! Looking up, he registered Lamiya's smile and encouraging nod. Her melodic voice echoed in his head. *Take it. Not for yourself, for the dragons, for everything.*

Mutely, he held out his hands, palms up. An odd tingling started at the front of his mind and he stood straighter, narrowing his eyes when a tableau began to play out, as if he were looking down through the eyes of a bird in flight. Behind his eyelids, the turquoise lake by Lamiya's hut unfolded like a picture of the landscape in progress, complete with vibrant trees and shrubs below pale blue sky.

He saw himself walk to the edge of the water, the gleaming Staropal clasped between his hands. He watched himself bow respectfully, then wade out to thigh depth. Saw the swell of water of the approaching dragon. Saw Akachi rise up, water cascading over her burnished red-and-gold scales, felt her tongue lick the top of his head, then saw himself stand steadfast when the dragon put her massive head in front of his face and opened her jaws wide. He observed from on high as he gently placed the Staropal onto the dragon's tongue. The imagery was so real he felt warm air gushing over his cheeks. *This* was Lamiya's vision?

You are the one, my love. No avoiding it. Open your eyes and take the stone. Lamiya's words rolled amid the vision.

Fluttering his eyelashes up, he felt detached from the Great Hall, removed from the circle of mages, until only he and the Staropal existed. Breath floated into his body, and out of his body. His heartbeat thudded strong and true. The swirling star filled his vision, his spellbound eyes following the trails of colours, contentment flowing into his bones and whole being. Breath floated into his body, and out of his body. His heartbeat thudded strong and true.

The Staropal arced in smooth curves over the air to lightly touch Tiliqua's outstretched hands, swirling turquoise for a breath, before bouncing back up and bobbing to him.

I approve of her. A tinkling, brittle voice sounded in his head. *But I will come with you.*

His palms crackled and tingled with restless energies when the stone perched upon them. A great sob of joy built in his stomach and flowed up and out between his lips. *Thank you,* he thought, curling his fingers gently up around the base of the stone. A searing white light shot through him, freeing the two tiny dots of power he'd concealed in the pit of his stomach, and flinging incandescent silver-blue magic throughout his system. His body became static with power!

In a blink, he translocated to beside the warded cage. Lamiya beamed at him, a strange white light radiating off her face, and beside her Lazuli stood blinking like an owl in sunlight.

'See, the stone likes you.' Lamiya smiled again. 'What next?'

Oh, I like her too, the stone tinkled at him. *How do you find all these special women?*

The stone sounded so very female that Everand laughed. He was indeed surrounded by special women. Maybe everything would turn out well. 'First,' he said to Lamiya, also giving Lazuli a nod, 'we free Malach. Then we help Tiliqua.'

Turning, he found Malach staring at him, mouth open and hands held up poised for the next slam against the cage wall. Everand made a flapping motion and Malach scurried to the far wall of the cage. Focusing his thought, Everand chose a spot in the middle of the front wall of the cage and hurled the command: *disintegrate.*

The cage shattered, thousands of tiny shards cascading down to create a jagged square line of rubble on the floor.

Malach grinned and rubbed his hands together.

Everand stepped to the side.

The raptor was loose. Let him hunt.

Chapter Twenty-Six

Persuading his stiff leg muscles to take a large stride, Malach stepped over the shards. Unbelievably, he was free! And Everand was not dead. Unable to look at Everand's face because the mage was glowing with an eerie light, he gave a curt nod. His gaze was unerringly drawn to the pulsing stone between Everand's hands. *This* was the Staropal? *This* was what his father had been driven by and had stolen? The stone granted untold power — he should take it.

A voice in the back of his mind dryly prompted that taking the stone hadn't saved his father. Yet it was magnificent and *oozed* magic. He could use it to become a proper mage with full power, then the Guild wouldn't be able to touch him. His mouth felt dry and gritty.

Everand sternly speaking his name caught his attention, and blinking to break the allure of the stone he reluctantly looked up.

'The Staropal will not go to you, so don't even think about it.' No longer glowing, Everand half-smiled but his eyes and tone were cold. 'We need you. We must help Tiliqua become Head of the Guild.'

Yearning to gaze into the depths of the Staropal, to watch the colours shifting and shaping, Malach blinked harder. Tiliqua, the stunning woman mage? Become Head of the

Guild? He stole a sideways glance at Lamiya, whose grey-blue eyes were observing him warily, her body tensed ready for action. Riverplain was now led by a woman and the Guild was to be also? A chill swept across his nape. Atage should have left matters alone! Riverwood had been just fine without Riverfall's grand plans.

'You can't change that now,' said Lamiya. 'None of us can. We can only choose how we go forward.'

Had the cursed boatwoman read his mind? Had joining with the old guide's previous mind-read given her unfettered access to him?

Everand needs your help, slammed into his forehead. *Choose your actions carefully and don't scowl at me like that. If you must vent, exert your anger at Pelamis.*

'Malach?' prompted Everand, an eyebrow arched.

What to do? So far, Everand had proved to be an ally and true to his word. Could he put aside the fact Everand was also the former apprentice who had spent so much time with, and then betrayed, his father? His tongue was too dry and swollen to even lick his cracked lips. Stupid mages hadn't brought him any food or drink since he'd been captured.

'Hold out your hand,' said Everand, juggling the Staropal so that it rested on his left hand and extending his right one.

'Why?' asked Malach.

'Don't answer him,' said Lamiya when Everand opened his mouth to speak. 'He must learn to trust you.'

'You might want to move a little quicker,' said Lazuli, hovering by Lamiya's shoulder. 'The mages are arguing and we aren't safe up here.'

Everand pushed his hand closer. 'Take my hand. Hurry.'

Acutely conscious of the cursed boatwoman's eyes on him, Malach grunted then gripped Everand's hand. A beam of silver light ran down Everand's arm, flowed across his wrist, spread down his fingers and then flowed seamlessly into his own fingers. Malach felt magic and energy coursing into him, spreading up his arms and into his body. His hand felt hollow and cold when Everand released his hold.

'There. You are refreshed and a little stronger. Use your ability wisely.'

He trusts you. Don't betray him or you will answer to me and the dragons. Lamiya's words snipped into his mind.

His palms turning clammy, Malach asked, 'What do you want me to do?' He waited while Everand's face creased with concern, his eyes becoming a dark cobalt.

'Lamiya and I will stand with Tiliqua to support her during the vote.' Everand hesitated, his words slowing, sounding reluctant. 'We need you and Lazuli to keep an eye on Pelamis and be ready to … intercept him.'

Malach's chest swelled. Was Everand indirectly *asking* him to challenge that stinker Pelamis? He bit down his reply of 'with pleasure', changing it to, 'I can do that.'

Lazuli's grey eyes gleamed with anticipation.

'Good,' said Everand. 'Stay up here where you can see what everyone's doing and let's see how this unfolds. Ready?' he asked Lamiya.

Lamiya directed a last, assessing look his way and Malach's forehead tingled just before her projected words. *Yes, Malach. Do whatever it takes.* Then she followed Everand from the dais.

He stared at their receding backs. So much for a controlled Guild that didn't mingle with the provinces. Something hard pressed against his fingers and he looked down to see Lazuli pushing a short, viciously-honed stone dagger at him.

'Sometimes the unexpected can succeed against the odds.' Lazuli gave a grim smile. 'Especially if we throw together and from different places.'

Malach grunted. An impressive suggestion from a usually peaceful person.

Twisting his dagger in his hands, Lazuli said, 'One more thing … we protect Everand as best we can … but Lamiya *must* stay safe. Riverplain needs her.'

Ah. That's why the pacer was here. He should have guessed. Holding Lazuli's intense gaze, Malach did not nod. Lazuli's expression made it clear that Lamiya was his priority, and Everand cared for her too — but the boatwoman was annoying, far too smart and he did not appreciate having his mind read unasked. That made it far too difficult to choose his best path. Forcing a grim smile, he dipped his head fractionally. Let Lazuli assume he agreed. He turned to see what the mages were doing.

Everand and Lamiya had joined the mages near Tiliqua. The mage-woman had drawn herself up tall and was fiery and imposing with her startling blue eyes flashing and her coiled hair the colour of molten gold. Malach felt a surge of admiration.

On the other side of the hole in the floor, eleven mages crowded around Pelamis, who looked furious and deadly. Malach tilted his head to one side, stretching taut neck muscles, and thought hard. What would he do if he were Pelamis? Having the greater number of allies, he'd go for the Staropal. Except the stone had rejected Pelamis. Given this, he would remove the opposition so the councils didn't have a choice to vote on. Had Everand worked this out? He watched Everand move to beside Tiliqua and hold the Staropal out in front of them both. Yes, he had.

What was pesky Lamiya doing? His eyebrow lifted when he saw her go to the older mage in the green robe and support him with a hand under his elbow. Small wonder this mage wanted to hand over the leadership; the way he clutched at his chest he looked as if he were on his last legs.

In his mind, Malach heard Mage Beetal laughing: *Look at the doddery old fool. Look at all of them, buffoons in disarray, clueless about what to do. And Everand remains an annoying, moralistic idiot. He wants a woman to lead the Guild! My son, you must stop this nonsense.*

Malach's pulse raced. How could he test how much power Everand had given him? He assessed the mages supporting Pelamis. What if he attacked one using magic? The mage in brown robes was Pelamis' strongest supporter, *and* he'd been the one who'd held him captive with fiery snakes in Riverplain. Simoselaps. He'd do nicely. Give him a taste of his own medicine.

'I demand that the council votes!' shouted Pelamis, sweeping an arm to encompass the mages huddled around him. 'Guild Law states that the Head of the Guild is an elected position.'

'Guild Law also states the Staropal must pass to a worthy leader,' countered Tiliqua. 'Without the approval of the stone, any elected Head cannot lead.'

Interestingly, Agamid took a step and raised a hand. Malach eyed the purple-robed mage with contempt. Was he belatedly going to make a stand? Agamid had hardly come across as leadership material when the group of mages came to Riverplain.

'Before we do anything, I ask whether anyone else intends to challenge for the position? Or is the vote between Tiliqua and Pelamis?' called Agamid.

By the subdued murmuring and downcast faces, no other mage was even remotely considering offering their service. Mage Beetal laughing uproariously in his mind, Malach clenched and unclenched his hands, seriously tempted to stride down and offer himself. That would surely cause chaos! But he'd be too vulnerable down there, in their midst. It was time to wreak chaos another way, and he couldn't think of a better way than the pacer's suggestion.

Finding Lazuli regarding him in expectation, he said, 'Go to the other side of where the cage was. I'll create a distraction, then raise my arm. Count two beats, then we throw at Pelamis. Hard.'

Without a word, Lazuli slid away. He watched the pacer walk quietly and smoothly until he was some fifty paces away, half-concealed by the edge of the bookcase on the far side of where the cage had been. When Lazuli looked at him, he nodded. That should be far enough for the two daggers to come from such divergent paths that Pelamis would have trouble deflecting them both. Presumably the pacer wouldn't lose his nerve. His own throw must prove fatal, just in case.

Harsh voices reached his ears. Mages were calling comments from both sides, all sense of order vanished. Malach's lips twitched, but his amusement faded at the sight of Tiliqua and Everand standing steadfast with the Staropal glowing in front of them. *One thing at a time. Chaos first.* He tucked the dagger into his belt where he could reach it, then flexed his fingers. Faster, faster, drawing power until his hands were prickling with it, then he focused on his target. Simoselaps was alongside Pelamis, shouting and shaking a fist at the other group, totally absorbed.

His lips curving into a smile, Malach created a head-sized bolt of red, fiery energy, teased sharp points from it that would feel like stabbing needles of fire, drew his arm back, tensed his mighty paddling muscles — and hurled the bolt at the centre of Simoselaps' back. The mage shrieked when the bolt took him and the brown robe burst into flames. Unexpected, but welcome. Even better, Simoselaps staggered into the woman mage in a lilac robe beside him and her robe caught fire too.

Mages cursed and shouted, looking around wildly and backing away from the mages on fire. Too cowardly to even try to help them! His father was right, they were fools. None of them were worthy.

Malach yanked the dagger from his belt, spun it so he could send it with a twisting flick of his wrist, raised his arm and watched Lazuli's arm lift up.

'Oi! Pelamis!' shouted Lazuli.

One … two … with a savage flick of his wrist, Malach hurled the dagger. Pelamis was turning his head away to look back up towards Lazuli and the dagger took him in the neck. Pelamis' hands were scrabbling at the dagger handle protruding from his neck when Lazuli's dagger thudded into his back. Pelamis' body jolted and he staggered a step, blood spurting from the severed jugular vein, his groping hands failing to stem the flow.

'Help me!' gurgled Pelamis, weaving about with dark blood gushing over his hands and staining the front of his robe.

Malach grinned. If anyone had the fortitude to yank the dagger out, Pelamis' blood would gush faster. *Serves you right, stinker. A painful and not overly swift death.*

The other mages stared in horror, creating a hasty gap. One in red robes had the presence of mind to use a spell to douse the flames on the woman mage in lilac robes and then Simoselaps. The mage in lilac sank to sit on the floor, fanning at her face with a sleeve. Simoselaps curled into a ball, moaning.

Satisfied, Malach looked back at Pelamis, whose hands were glowing bright orange and a scarf of orange magic was appearing around his neck. The stinker was healing his wound! Hastily forming another spiked ball of fire, Malach aimed at Pelamis' chest, an easy target because the mage's hands were at his neck. *Intercept him … do whatever it takes …* He hurled the fire bolt and Pelamis went down with a ghastly, liquid, gurgling scream. And stayed down. In the bedlam, Pelamis' allies scattered.

Malach leaped from the dais and ran toward Everand, seeing Lazuli sprinting in from the far side of the chaotic gaggle of mages. Panicked shouts reverberated off the beamed ceiling and the marble walls, exponentially magnifying the cacophony. He slithered to a stop beside Everand and scanned what was happening. The mages who'd supported Pelamis were running in random directions. Simoselaps had crawled across the floor and was huddled over what was hopefully Pelamis' body.

Nearer him, Agamid was vainly shouting for order. Lamiya was fully occupied holding up the older mage, who might have fainted, the young mage in crimson hurrying to help her.

Before him, Tiliqua gaped at the chaos with her eyes wide and mouth open while Everand tried to speak to her, his attention on her face. The Staropal hovered a handspan above Everand's flat, open hands, the colours swirling hypnotically.

Malach gasped. The stone was just there. Right in front of him. Without further thought, he reached out and grabbed it. Nothing dreadful happened. The opalescent stone was smooth and slightly warm, firmly fixed between his fingers. Everand's hands were still open, flat and *unreacting.* Astonished, Malach blinked and translocated to the entry of the Great Hall, then translocated to the path outside.

Sunlight streaming down on his face and pebbles crunching beneath his sandals, he stared at his hands. Against all expectation, he held the stone! The Staropal had become a mix of blues, greens and hints of red and orange. Would it take him to Riverwood? Hurry, hurry, before Everand gave chase. He looked up, discerning the faint shimmer of the wardspell above.

'Take me through the wardspell and to Riverwood,' he commanded the Staropal, raising his hands to level with his face and looking skyward.

The Staropal glowed with reds and oranges and heat scorched his fingers and palms. And nothing else happened, as if the stone was sulking. His mouth gritty, Malach swallowed and lowered his hands, relieved when the burning against his fingertips reduced. So, the stone could refuse a command. But it didn't appear to be capable of direct action itself, or it would have taken him back inside the hall, taken itself back to Everand. *Think! Think!* He'd have to use his own power to escape. Where was Everand, anyway?

A shadow flitted over him and he jumped. What was that? A beetle with a mage aboard! Headed to the roof of a building not far away. Malach started to run, then translocated himself to the base of the building. Charging through the doors, he bounded up the curling flights of steps two at a time. Would his father's beetle recognise him? It would know how to take him to Riverwood.

By the time he reached the top floor his thighs were burning, chest heaving and sweat was running freely down his face and armpits. He burst through the open wooden doors and skidded to a stop at the sight of so many stalls containing massive beetles. A pungent peaty odour assailed his nose and a bevy of stableboys ceased what they were doing and gaped at him.

Ignoring the boys, who shrank away from him, he marched around the front of the cages peering in at the occupants. Most were large jet black or shiny orange beetles. Whoa! There. He backed up. A gigantic black-and-white staghorn waved its feelers at him. Was this the one? The beetle chirruped and came to the front of its stall. Yes. It recognised him. Juggling the Staropal, he drew back the bolts to the stall doors and stepped in.

The beetle waved its feelers again, and Malach translocated onto its back. Forget about the bridle. No time. Why hadn't Everand arrived yet? Surely, Everand must realise where he'd gone? Whatever could he be doing? *Never mind. Run with it.* He squeezed the Staropal up inside his tunic, making the fabric pull tight across his back and shoulders, but he didn't have a cloak so this would have to do. Securing the stone against his stomach with one hand outside his tunic, he gripped the edge of the carapace behind the beetle's neck joint with the other hand.

'Take me to Riverwood. Hurry.' The beetle walked with clacking feet out through the open stall door, rose to hover above the peaty floor and flew straight across the space in the centre to a ramp leading to the roof. Malach laughed aloud at the astounded looks on all the stableboys' faces.

The staghorn zipped up the ramp to emerge on a rooftop landing pad under crisp blue sky. 'To Riverwood. How my father Mage Beetal went,' repeated Malach. The staghorn swung to face north, its wings humming as it gained height and speed.

Glancing down, he saw the pebbled paths were still empty. His initial rush of glee faded. What did this mean? Why wasn't Everand in pursuit? Would he translocate ahead to the gap into Riverwood? Did he know where it was? Yes, he'd used it to come to warn him. Malach's pulse boomed in his ears. *Go! Try anyway.*

'Faster! Higher!' he yelled. His mount responded and he was enveloped by sunlight, cool air brushing his cheeks, ruffling his hair. He didn't look down again. Everand would undoubtedly pursue him to Riverwood, but he had a head start.

And he had the stone of power.

Time to gather his men and eagles.

Chapter Twenty-seven

Heart hammering, Everand stared across the gap in the floor at the twisted pile of orange and charred robe. Was Pelamis dead? His heart galloped faster. Out of the corner of his eye he saw movement at the dais; Malach winding his way down towards them with Lazuli running to catch up. By the way Simoselaps was crouched brokenly by the orange robe, Pelamis must be dead.

He tried to swallow his rush of guilt. Would anyone realise he'd sanctioned, no *sought*, Pelamis' death? Would Malach gloat and reveal his part in it? Numbed, he felt as if he stood outside of himself, a blank object with chaos raging around him.

Movement flitted around him, he felt a shift in the air and a lightness touch his hands. Blinking rapidly, he struggled to bring his mind back to the present. Tiliqua filled his vision, standing close in front of him with her blue eyes wide and her mouth open in shock. Her gaze lowered to his outstretched hands.

Everand looked down at his empty palms. What? Where was the Staropal? What just happened? Had Malach snatched the Staropal? After *everything* he'd done for him? The selfish idiot! Anger coursed through him and sour bile filled his mouth. Like father, like son — they couldn't help themselves. A great weight pressed on his shoulders. Why, oh why, didn't he see this coming?

'Help me!' Lamiya's distressed call reached his ears amid the general disorder.

'Father!' shrieked Tiliqua.

He spun around to see Lamiya holding up a slumped Mantiss by the armpits, with Lazuli and Saiphos trying to help her. His mind shrieking about the Staropal, he could only stare.

Tiliqua grabbed his forearm, her fingers pinching. 'Save him. Please,' she pleaded, her face white.

Shaking himself, Everand said to Agamid, 'Keep an eye on the others. Tell me if any become a threat.'

Agamid's expression grew more alert and he started to scan the hall. Everand hurried to Lamiya, despair rising at how limply Mantiss hung in her arms.

'Look at me.' Lamiya's tone brooked no argument.

Peering into her beautiful eyes, Everand saw compassion and concern.

'We will recover the stone because we know where Malach will go. But Mantiss needs you. Like Ejad after the viper bite, you have one chance to save him — and it is now.'

Torn, Everand fought to anchor himself in her wisdom, with all the colours of the Staropal swirling insistently in the front of his mind. In Lamiya's arms, Mantiss' body arched in a spasm and he moaned with pain.

'Your master's heart and spirit fail him.' Lamiya spoke urgently. 'Between us, we can bring him back. Look at me. You'll never forgive yourself if you don't save him.' Her voice wavered but her clear, grey eyes compelled him. 'I need you whole, my love. Do this for Mantiss, and for us.'

The colours of the Staropal ebbing from his mind, Everand focused on Mantiss, observing the deathly white face, cheeks and eye sockets hollowed by pain, the once-green, misted eyes rolled upwards. A sob built in his heart.

'Master.' He clasped Mantiss' limp, cold hands and looked at Lamiya. 'Can you sit on the floor with his head in your lap?'

'Yes, my love. Lazuli, help me lower him.' With Lazuli's help, she folded down to sit cross-legged with Mantiss' head resting in the crook of her lap.

Agamid came to stand nearby, his eyes still monitoring the activity of the other mages. 'Saiphos, help me keep a watch on the others.'

Saiphos positioned himself beside Agamid, the two of them providing a screen, protecting them from the sight of the others.

'What can I do?' asked Tiliqua.

Thinking hard, Everand said, 'Stand behind me with your hands on my shoulders and feed me some of your power.'

'Feed your love for your father through Everand,' added Lamiya. 'Give Mantiss reasons to stay. To live.'

Pushing down his amazement at Lamiya's insight and bowing his head, Everand drew in a sharp breath. He'd never told his father Tenuis that he loved him. He would not make the same mistake now.

'Mantiss feels he has failed everyone and is responsible for the fall of the Guild, for undoing everything the early mages worked for. You must convince his spirit this is not so.' Lamiya laid her hands over his. 'Tell him he was a leader with compassion during a time of great change.' She glanced up at Tiliqua. 'His daughter will carry forward his virtue, and she will lead wisely during a time of renewal.'

Everand felt Tiliqua's hands tighten on his shoulders and heard her swallow with a gulp. *Special women* ... wasn't that what the Staropal had said? Hope flared in his heart. Lamiya's visions tended to ring true, and Mantiss deserved to see his daughter lead the Guild. His heart thudded loudly. Everything would be alright. For now, save his master.

He placed his hands flat over Mantiss' heart. Lamiya rested her hands on top of his, and he perceived a triangle of connection through their linked hands and Tiliqua's on his shoulders. Easing in a long breath, he summoned the silver-blue magic the Staropal had released inside him, gathering with it the love seeping from Tiliqua and Lamiya. He could do this. He must do this.

Imperceptibly, he extended his perception through the wall of Mantiss' still and cold chest, seeking the vessels and pathways that carried blood, air and life to and from the barely beating heart. The currents of blood were sluggish and unwilling. A bead of sweat trickled a tickling path down his forehead. No wonder Mantiss struggled! It was as if his master's body had given up and no longer wanted to pump blood and life through his heart.

Persisting, Everand pushed along the artery near Mantiss' collarbone, looking for the valve that let the flow enter the top of the heart. Air was barely entering his master's body his breath was so shallow, and the blood was thickening and stagnating without oxygen.

A cloud of immeasurable sadness formed, pressing on his head and shoulders. Far worse than the external poison that almost took Ejad's life, this was an inexorable, slow and excruciating strangulation of life from within. Mantiss did not deserve this. The backs of his eyes prickled with tears.

'Master,' he said brokenly, 'hear me. I need you to live.' He swallowed. *Go on, tell him. Utter the words that are so hard to say.* 'Master, I have long served you, not only out of duty but also with love. Far more than my master, you are a father to me. You gave me purpose when I needed it.'

Lamiya's fingers twitched and he felt her approval. He crept his perception forward, tiring against the sluggish flow, until he came to the black sheath of despair surrounding Mantiss' heart and blocking the valves. Taking his time, he gauged it. Woven from dark, sticky, webbed strands, the sheath slowed the movement of blood and sifted out oxygen and life.

The pressure from Lamiya's hands increased and her presence infused his mind. *We must identify each fear and emotion and undo them one at a time. This is a trap set by the mind and spirit — and it is these we must free in order to save his body.*

Imagining his mind fingers as needles of blue-and-silver power, laced with love, Everand chose a strand. An orange-and-green mist coiled around his needle. *This strand is horror*, said Lamiya. *Grasp it and identify the incidents for me.* Unsure what she meant, Everand tentatively visualised his needle-like fingers of power clasping around the strand.

With a flash of black light, he was transported to eight seasons earlier, to when Mantiss stood in the Great Hall surrounded by Mage Beetal and his allies with the army of winged dragons descending outside. Dark emotions burst from the strand to assault him: terror, betrayal, powerlessness, despair, pain, guilt and self-loathing, all magnifying as mages died defending the Great Hall.

So much grief and loss. Everand's heart began to waver. 'More power,' he croaked at Tiliqua.

You are doing magnificently, my love, sent Lamiya. *You were there too, now redefine this strand for your master. Destroy the darkness with images of the victory and the positives.*

Warmth oozed into the backs of his hands and a hint of wild grasses and flowers filled his nostrils. At the same time, with a waft of violets, warmth seeped into his shoulders from Tiliqua's hands. Steeling himself, Everand directed a steady stream of silver-blue magic at the dark strand and lined it with images of the end of the battle: Mage Beetal dead, the farseers departed or dead, the dragons being returned through the sky rift to the volcano in Terralis. He showed Elemar and Rhyan joyously leaving to return to her village in Terralis, then he showed the entire gathered council affirming Mage Mantiss as their leader.

Frowning, he carefully constructed an image of himself bowing to Mantiss and saying, 'Well done, Master. It is over.'

Yes, I like that part. He sensed Lamiya's smile.

Abruptly, the dark strand dissolved like smoke blowing away from a freshly snuffed fire. Blood and oxygen trickled through the gap and into Mantiss' heart.

One down. Now tackle the next strand. The next two are the darkest, then it will get easier.

Everand rubbed his forehead on his sleeve to wipe the sweat away. This was hard work. Closing his eyes, he sought the next dark strand. He saw Mantiss repeatedly sitting at his study desk poring over Lapemis' notebook. Outside the windows it was dark. Always dark. Lapemis' cursive and commanding words danced in his mind and he felt stabs of dismay, guilt, shock and despair piercing Mantiss, overlaid with a growing fear of a massive red dragon until the creature loomed over his master like a death-knell.

The overwhelming sense of dread was so palpable that icy goosebumps shivered all over Everand and his chest grew stiff and cold. How long had his master struggled with this? Why hadn't he confided his fears?

Set that aside, my love, sent Lamiya tenderly. *This is not yet about you. Reassure Mantiss he was only keeping the deep secrets in accordance with Lapemis' wishes.*

With a shudder, Everand refocused and projected himself into the image. The study orb flared brighter at his approach. 'Master,' he said, waiting until Mantiss' green eyes studied him instead of the notebook. 'You did well. None of us guessed this information and no-one questioned the history we were taught. You upheld Lapemis' wishes. You also guarded the Staropal and kept it safe.'

Mantiss closed the notebook and gave him a considered look. 'I did, didn't I?'

The second dark strand dissipated and more blood and air dribbled into Mantiss' heart.

Beneath his hands, Mantiss' chest rose with a shallow breath, then fell flat again. Everand ran his tongue over his cracked lips. It was working, but his arms felt heavy, his heart felt tight and he was flagging.

One more, my love, sent Lamiya. *Be prepared. This one is for both of you.*

What did she mean? Apprehension coursing strongly, he so wanted to look up into her face, read her expression, let her boost his courage.

'His eyelids fluttered!' exclaimed Tiliqua, her fingers gripping his shoulder with excitement. 'Keep going!'

Overriding his trepidation, Everand bent his perception back into Mantiss and grunted in surprise. Mantiss' blood was flowing more steadily and the heart was beating in a shallow but even rhythm. The dark sheath had become grey, just one black thread defiantly challenging him. He crunched his fingers, coaxing his power, then grasped the thread with both imaginary hands.

Cold washing over him, he watched himself as a lanky, serious boy of twelve season-cycles open the door to let Mantiss and Agamid into his parents' quarters. The senior mages discussed the body of his father, Tenuis, while he stood behind them, a silent shadow.

Then Mantiss sent Agamid away and spoke to him alone, outlining an audacious plan to apprentice him to Mage Beetal and secretly train him in stealth spells. Fleeting images followed of his clandestine meetings with Mantiss in the shadowy library in darkness. He observed himself standing forlorn and broken-hearted when Elemar and her warrior lover Rhyan departed. She had left him. Just like his father and mother. No-one wanted him. A sob entered his ears. Was that sob then or now? Another sob. It was now.

Lamiya's fingers pressed into the back of his hands. *My love. Keep going.*

He watched the cold, aloof shell of himself going through the motions of attending council meetings, half-heartedly doing his research and spending much time staring blankly out the window of his favourite room at the library. Abruptly, the vision shifted and took on an ethereal hue. He sat there now, wan sunshine fingering the windowpane.

Mantiss entered and got down on one knee. 'My boy. Can you ever forgive me? I used you for my own ends at no thought of the cost for you. I saw an opportunity and I took it. I am abominable! I exploited an orphan and set you against dangers I was too cowardly to face myself. I am not worthy to lead, and I certainly do not deserve your loyalty and respect. You must despise me!'

Still on bended knee, Mantiss clutched his hands fiercely, green eyes moist with unshed tears. 'No wonder you want to leave the Guild. I free you and absolve you from everything you've done in my name. Farewell, my boy.'

Shock ripped through Everand and he couldn't catch his breath. *He* had caused his master this much pain? No! He couldn't bear it.

Tell him, urged Lamiya. *Tell him what you truly feel. Be whole, my mage.*

Jolted back into the sunny library, Everand grasped the kneeling Mantiss' hands fiercely and tugged him to his feet, standing too. 'Master! I served you willingly. I believed in you. You gave me purpose and identity.' The look on Mantiss' face was sceptical.

Wobbling between the perceived internal world and the external real world, Everand held onto Mantiss' cold hands for all he was worth. 'You are my *father* to me. I appreciate everything you've done for me and I wouldn't change any of it. Not even Elemar leaving. If she hadn't left, I wouldn't have found Lamiya. *You* gave me the mission that brought me to Lamiya. I love you for making me who I am, and I love you more for your integrity in setting me free.'

He paused for air, mustering strength. 'Master, there is *nothing* to forgive. Now *live*, because I want you to, as do Elytra, Tiliqua, Agamid, Saiphos, Hydrelaps … too many to name them all. We are not done yet. *You* are not done yet.'

The dark strand vanished in a puff of black particles. Mantiss' heart pumped several strong beats, vivid red blood coursed in through the valves and Mantiss' fingers pinched his.

Smiling down into Mantiss' watery, green eyes Everand said, 'Now stand up and help Tiliqua win the council over.' Tugging on Mantiss' hands, he pulled him upright.

'You did it!' Tiliqua threw her arms around his neck and kissed his cheek. Twice. Then she hugged Mantiss so tightly Everand worried she'd make him faint again.

Extending a hand, he helped Lamiya up from the floor and enveloped her in his arms, burying his lips in her hair. 'You are wonderful and amazing, but you know that. I can't thank you enough.'

Her arms squeezing his lower back, Lamiya murmured, 'I only nudged you to do what your heart knew was needed.'

Over the top of her head, Everand's eyes met Lazuli's. The pacer looked lost and uncertain. 'I owe you a great debt for your courage. When we get back to Riverplain, let's talk.'

Lazuli gave a half-smile and the creases smoothed from his forehead. 'I'd like that.'

Becoming aware of a poised hush surrounding them, Everand released Lamiya and looked around. The mages were gathered in a semicircle on the other side of the hole in the floor, all watching him. He swallowed. The dissenting mages had fallen sombre and silent without Pelamis to rally them. He noticed a mound of cloaks off to one side that probably covered the body. Guilt flushed through him. Would he ever get over his role in that? Simoselaps stood nearest the mound, his face cast down.

'I think I should address the council,' muttered Mantiss, wringing his hands nervously.

'Yes,' said Everand. 'But we must leave you. Malach has fled with the Staropal and we must go after him.'

'What?' Mantiss stared at him.

'Tiliqua can tell you what happened,' said Everand gently. 'We must find Malach before he gets organised to resist us.'

Lamiya linked her arm around his. 'We have friends waiting in Riverwood, and they won't be expecting Malach to arrive without us.'

Alarm prickled through Everand. That explained Lazuli's tension! They must move faster.

'Will you bring the Staropal back?' The sorrow in Mantiss' eyes suggested he knew the answer.

Shaking his head, Everand said, 'We will return it to Akachi. I'm sure Tiliqua will be voted the new Head of the Guild on her own merit and will be able to lead wisely without the stone.'

'Will I see you again, my boy?' asked Mantiss, with a wistful expression.

'I'd like that.' Everand included Tiliqua and Agamid in his smile. 'We have much to talk about, and you must visit Riverplain. Properly.'

'You will be welcome,' said Lamiya, inclining her head gracefully. She slid a sideways glance at Everand. 'Besides, there will be an important ceremony for you to attend.'

Chapter Twenty-eight

Lazuli's rising agitation drew Lamiya's attention away from the surprise on the mages' faces. Her pacer was shifting his weight from foot to foot and casting her anxious glances, worrying about their friends in Riverwood. She tapped Everand's arm. 'We should go.'

Relief chased across Everand's forehead before he grasped Mantiss' hands. 'We'll let you know. I can take two beetles?'

'Of course, my boy. Take yours and Beetal's staghorn,' replied Mantiss.

Lamiya nudged Everand's elbow and he released Mantiss' hands but then hovered in front of Tiliqua. They didn't have time for another discussion! Intervening, she said, 'Good luck, Tiliqua. I look forward to conferring with you as respective leaders of our people.'

Thoughts flickered in Tiliqua's eyes, which Lamiya noticed were almost the same blue as Everand's. Giving her an exasperated look, Lazuli began to stride towards the hall doors. She tugged at Everand's hand and although his fingers curled around hers, she perceived his inner turmoil; he wanted to know the outcome of the vote but knew they'd be unwise to give Malach more time.

Anxiety flitted into her. Could Malach wield the impressive Staropal? If so, he'd already be back in Riverwood. Would he dare threaten their friends to make them do what he wanted? Whatever that was. Surely, Everand now understood that Malach was not to be trusted! Ever.

Outside, she inhaled deeply, welcoming the sunshine and crisp air. Everand sped up, determined now they were on the move, and they jogged down the steps. Lazuli, already at the bottom, pointed upwards. She gasped at the sight of the transport beetle, barely a speck in the sky, speeding north.

'Curse it,' muttered Everand. 'He's probably taken Beetal's staghorn, and it knows the way to the tunnel. We must move faster. Take a hand each, I'll translocate us to the stables.'

Lamiya had just tightened her grip when her body surged forward with the uncomfortable sensation that she'd left her stomach behind. Eyes watering, she blinked, finding herself in a large, circular area in the middle of a ring of stables. Releasing her hand, Everand strode briskly across the peaty floor while, beside her, Lazuli stared around with wide eyes.

'That was a short trip,' she said. 'It's worse the further you go.'

Lazuli ran his hands through his hair as if his scalp itched, and turned thoughtful grey eyes on her. 'Why doesn't he translocate us all the way to Riverwood? Couldn't we get ahead of Malach if he did that?'

'Good question!' Across the peat floor, Everand was leading an orange-tinged beetle out of one of the stables. He spoke to a couple of young boys, who ran off to a stall further along. When Everand beckoned, her mouth ran dry. Ride the beetle high in the air? It didn't look very secure. Why didn't he want to use his magic? Persuading her feet to move, she tried to give Lazuli a bright, encouraging smile. He frowned back.

As soon as they reached him, Everand threw the reins over the beetle's head and said to Lazuli, 'This is Hover. He's obedient and will follow the other beetle. Grab the reins and I'll give you a leg up.'

'Wait,' said Lamiya, resting a hand on his arm. 'Wouldn't it be faster if you translocated us?'

Everand's forehead creased. 'It would, but I want to conserve my power.' His expression softened. 'I hope the Staropal will resist Malach, but I'm not sure so I want to be as strong as possible when we meet. And I plan to seal the tunnel, which will use energy.'

Before she could reply, a clacking sound distracted her. Two boys were leading a huge black-and-white beetle towards them. Closing her mouth, she eyed its curved, jagged horns and height with trepidation.

'You'll ride with me,' said Everand, a hint of a smile reaching his eyes. 'This beetle is even bigger than the one Malach took. Any advantage we might need.'

Hopefully he'd let her get off first! With a strangled swallow, Lamiya quelled her questions while Everand boosted Lazuli onto the back of Hover and explained how to sit and where to put his legs so the beetle could still breathe.

Once he was positioned, Lazuli looked down and grinned. 'How fast can it go?'

Next thing, Everand's hands closed around her waist and he levitated them both onto the staghorn's broad back, her legs not liking the stretch across her hips and thighs. Easy for him, being taller and having longer legs. The beetle lurched into an odd six-legged walk and she grabbed the rim of the hard carapace at the base of its neck, relieved when Everand held the reins in his right hand and circled his left arm securely around her. Better.

The beetle marched up the steep ramp leading onto the roof, and she took in the view from the circular landing pad. Below her, white marble domes sparkled in the early sunlight, interspersed with green lawns and vibrant shrubs and flower beds, everything ordered into straight lines and squares. Tilting her chin up, she squinted at the glinting shield far above. What did Everand call it? The wardspell?

Interpreting her gaze, he said, 'Another reason to go by beetle and the tunnel. Even with my restored power, I'm not strong enough to take three of us through the wardspell.' He kissed the back of her head. 'Besides, it hurts.'

He clucked his tongue and the beetle raised a gauzy set of wings, lifted into the air and swung around to head due north. Lamiya leaned into the wind rushing past, glad of the warmth of Everand's chest along her back. The ground sped by in a blur of colours and she concluded the beetles must be as fast as birds. His beak peeking out of the V-neckline of her tunic, Whirr had his eyes closed against the airflow. Peering over, she saw Lazuli was smiling and, if anything, coaxing his mount to go faster. Her lips twitched; her bold pacer loved to skim the water, and apparently the air too.

After a while, her stomach lurched when the beetle abruptly dropped height, and she averted her eyes from the granite boulders zipping past at dizzying speed. The darker patch ahead must be the tunnel already. The beetles alighted, and she yelped in time with Whirr's squawk when Everand scooped her up and jumped down. Lazuli laughed and she felt heat creep up her neck.

Everand looped an elbow through the beetle's reins and went to enter the tunnel.

'Wait,' called Lazuli, his expression serious. 'Have you named it? If we are to fight, you must name and honour your mount.'

A breeze stirred around Lamiya, and words flowed up her throat. 'The spirits will protect you if you honour your mount.' Placing a hand on the black-and-white beetle's face, she closed her eyes, trying not to wince at the prompt image of the beetle darting down to snap up a smaller insect. 'Dart,' she murmured. 'His name is Dart.'

Everand gave her an unfathomable look.

'Let's go,' said Lazuli, bouncing on the spot.

'Me first,' said Everand firmly. 'We don't know what waits on the far side.' He tugged the rein and Dart clacked after him into the gloom of the tunnel.

Lamiya followed, Lazuli clipping her heels in his eagerness. Eighty paces in darkness, guided by the solid walls and faint glints off the white parts of the beetle ahead. Another twenty paces and they emerged into the wide, grass expanse with the facing forest of pines — a clear marker of Malach's domain, the dense trunks and shadows concealing any activity within.

Everand turned to regard the entry to the tunnel, considering how to destroy it, and a cold shiver ran down her spine. What if they needed it to retreat from Malach? 'Wait,' she croaked. 'Should you ward it rather than destroy it?' Her numb lips refused to add *What if we need it?*

Without answering, Everand raised a hand, his lips moving, and a solid, blue shield stretched across the entry, pulsing with beams of light. Relief tumbled into her. Followed by an icy-cold thrill that spread across her back and shoulders. She spun around. 'Eagles!'

She stared at the dark trees. Nothing moved. Her forehead prickled. Where were Plummet and the other falcons? Hadn't she asked the bird to wait for them here? Her pulse began to race and her bones just knew Malach's eagles were coming. The way Whirr burrowed deep inside her tunic confirmed it. Was that why the falcons were absent, or well hidden?

The skin along her arms tingled and prickled and all the hairs stood up. 'Tree-moths! Malach is sending the moths!' Anxiety pinged into her.

'Where are the eagles?' asked Lazuli, shading his eyes with a hand.

Images flooding her, Lamiya licked her lips. 'Malach is sending the eagles and moths first.' Her mind saw weaponed men sliding through trees. 'His men follow. Malach will wait until we're tired.'

'Where are our friends?' asked Lazuli, his cheeks hollow with tension. 'Larimar?'

Frowning, Lamiya reached out, seeking the essences of Beram, Mookaite, Tengar, Larimar, Ejad … Solid branches laced together sprang into her thoughts and anger punched away her anxiety. How dare he! 'They're in the raptor cages.'

Lazuli gave her a level look, his shoulders tense. 'After everything we did …'

Seeing his suppressed fury, Lamiya nodded. Good, she was no longer alone in wanting Malach's downfall. Blinking, she realised the throbbing noise was not her pulse in her ears but the beating of large wings and she balanced on her toes and squinted at the tree-line. 'They come!'

Everand touched her arm, his face grim. 'Ride with Lazuli. Then Dart can do his job.'

As he turned away, she snagged his sleeve. 'Take care, my mage.' His face blotted out the sky and his lips closed over hers, his murmured *always* in her mouth. Then he leaped onto Dart.

The staghorn rose to the height of the wall and fifty eagles swooped over the treetops in a massive, pointed arrow, headed right at them. How had Malach regained so many of his eagles so quickly?

Lazuli's fingers closed over her forearm. 'Mount up.' He pulled her to Hover and cupped his hands so she could step up.

Reluctantly tearing her gaze away from Everand, she mounted, Lazuli leaping up behind and reaching both arms around her to take the reins. Hover fidgeted beneath them as Lazuli leaned forward so his mouth feathered her ear. 'Can you deflect Malach's eagles?'

The air whooshed out of her chest. Could she? Or had Malach gained more power from the stone? 'Position us so I can try.' Her heart hammered against her breastbone while Lazuli directed Hover higher. She fixed her eyes on Everand's ramrod straight back up ahead, astride Dart.

The eagles split into four groups and went wide. They were going to attack Everand from multiple directions.

Lazuli's heated words flowed over her shoulder. 'Stinking coward. To think I sheltered him!'

Lamiya shuddered, remembering the bloodied mess two eagles had made of the back of Everand's head before the boat races. And now there were fifty of them …

The air shimmered into a shield around Everand and Dart and she saw him coiling power into his right hand. The eagles circled warily, and a hint of musk teased her nostrils just before a swarm of tree-moths flew out from the northern edge of the pines. The moths hurled themselves directly at Everand and he disappeared among a flurry of large beige wings and a cloud of musky dust. Through the murk, she saw Dart rake a tree-moth's torso with his curved antlers while Everand hurled a bolt at another one.

The circling eagles closed in, waiting their opportunity. Observing them, Lamiya decided the one with darker feathers looked to be the natural leader. Half-closing her eyes she reached out to it, flinching when a wave of red anger and hate rushed back at her. But the bird's flight trajectory wavered and she sensed it considering whether to break away to attack her instead. 'So much hate,' she murmured sadly.

Lazuli squeezed her shoulder. 'You can do it.'

Pushing past the images in the bird's mind of tearing at her flesh with its talons and beak, she called it. *Come to me. I would set you free, with your flock, to soar the mountains and ride the ice currents in your true majesty.* Her mind filled with a snapping beak. *Why fight petty battles when you can rule the mountains? Go, be free. Take your flock.* She felt the bird hesitate and sent visions of tall, snow-capped mountains and fresh running streams filled with trout and sliver-fish.

Go away! Malach's voice roared into her head. *These are my birds!*

Her link with the eagle severed, she dragged the back of a hand across her mouth when four arrows of birds wheeled inwards at Everand with cries shrill enough to wake the dead.

Lazuli gripped her shoulder harder. 'You can summon a dragon; you can summon an eagle.'

Everand flung several blue bolts of energy and two eagles burst into flame and fell. The tree-moths renewed their efforts, and she saw him hurling what looked like spears of blue magic at their wings. Dart twisted to and fro, raking at the closest moths with his antlers and scratching with his forefeet. Injured, three moths dropped to the ground to lie writhing amid the grass, keening pitifully.

Lamiya squinted at the looping eagles until she identified the leader again. Closing her eyes, she drew deep, summoning her silver calling power, gathering it, gathering it. *Come to me! Why waste your flock on the whim of men? You are above this, you are the lord of the skies. Go behave so.*

Her lips curled in a smile when arrogance seared through the bird and a bright black eye turned her way. Forcing all thoughts of Malach away, she compelled the eagle. *Go, take your rightful position as lord of the skies and mountains. Go now.*

No! The bird flinched at Malach's shrieked command. *Kill them and rip their flesh!*

Choose your own prey, Lamiya pushed at the bird. *Be master of your own destiny.* She sensed Malach spluttering, forming his next command. Forcing her heart to steady, she sent as coldly as she could muster: *Come near me and I will kill you. All of you. I, too, have power over birds.*

The eagles flew a wide circle around Everand but did not attack him. This was the moment. A shrill cry sounded and Plummet and a flock of falcons wheeled into view from the southern edge of the pines. The falcons swooped to fly a loop above her, shrill cries echoing.

This one is true to her word, she heard Plummet cry. *She freed us. She respects us and will not use us for her own means.*

Lamiya watched the falcons fly elegantly between the circling eagles, repeating their shrill cries. Scrunching her eyes shut, she reinstated her link with the lead eagle. *I name you Skylord. Be free. May the currents lift your wings and guide your path.*

Malach's anger and frustration battered at her mind, trying to disrupt her. Calm stealing over her as if she were sinking through clear, embracing warm water, she blocked him and projected a compelling vision of the whole flock of eagles peeling away and heading north to the mountains.

Against her back, Lazuli's chest swelled with a mighty gasp. 'You did it!'

Peering through her eyelashes, her heart thudded in relief; the eagles were clearing the tops of the trees, heading due north. Tearing her gaze away from them, she lifted her arms in triumph. *Thank you, Plummet.*

May warm currents guide your path, responded Plummet. *Do you need anything more?*

Can you free my friends? They are in Malach's cage.

We will try. Plummet and the falcons sped above Everand and Dart and vanished into the dark-green foliage, heading to the cages.

Lamiya dropped her gaze and found Everand had felled all but three of the tree-moths.

'Our friends,' said Lazuli firmly, kicking at Hover's sides. The beetle whizzed towards the far line of trees and the raptor cages beyond them.

They should wait for Everand, but saying nothing Lamiya leaned forward, the rigid urgency in Lazuli's arms worrying her. Hover lurched up and she ducked to avoid the branch that came at her face, pine needles scraping over her hair and down her back. Lazuli uttered a muffled curse. Her stomach roiled when the beetle zipped sideways, narrowly missing a tree trunk. A spear thudded into the trunk. They were flying above Malach's men!

Shaking the reins, Lazuli called, 'Faster!'

Unbelievably, Hover shot forward. She'd thought they were at full speed! Tears sprang to her eyes at the air whooshing past while the beetle nimbly twisted and turned around and through the trees, avoiding spears and then arrows. The shouts of Malach's men reached her ears, then they were past.

The back of the cages loomed ahead. Her heart sank. Malach sat astride his staghorn, which hovered in front of the cages, a smile playing upon his lips. She just had time to glance down to see her friends recognise her and Lazuli and rush to the front of the cage.

'Boatwoman,' snarled Malach. 'You will pay for everything you've done.'

Chapter Twenty-nine

Malach glared at Lamiya. How dare she compel his eagles to leave him! And how unbelievably stupid of her to try to rescue her friends without Everand. Yet she stared back at him with her chin tipped up in defiance and anger flashing in her eyes. From behind her, Lazuli shot him a look of contempt, then gazed down at his friends, crowded by the door to their cage. Hah. Shame about Lazuli The paddler had courage and would be welcome among his hunters, but if he thought they could free their friends, he was sorely mistaken.

'Let the team go,' said Lamiya imperiously, chin still held high.

'Or what?' said Malach.

Incredibly, the orange beetle moved closer. 'You and Everand can fight if you wish. Leave the team out of it,' Lamiya said coldly.

'You *owe* them,' shouted Lazuli, waving a clenched fist at him. 'We protected you as best we could. And I helped you defeat Pelamis! Doesn't that count for anything?'

A wall of heat ran up Malach's body. 'You stupid meddlers started all this! Atage should have left matters alone. We don't need to trade.'

'Have you no shame? No honour?' called Lamiya. 'All you had to do was bring your team to the races, or you could have declined the invitation! It was *your* efforts at sabotage that led to Everand's mission. Without your stupid attacks we'd have had simple, glorious races and welcome trade.'

'Enough!' Malach's vision went black. How *dare* she? *Torrap!* He hurled a mind-command. *Bring the men back to the cages!* Bands of fury gripped his chest so tightly he could barely draw breath and his arms burned with the desire to throttle Lamiya. How could he make the Staropal listen to him with these people interfering all the time? Why couldn't they all just *go away*?

He blinked. What the …? The orange beetle dived away in a wide curve and, with a loud crack, Lazuli broke a branch off a tree. The beetle zipped back over the top of the cage, swooped low, and Lazuli leaned sideways, hanging impressively far over the side of the beetle to poke the branch down through the roof. The other pacer, the dark-haired one, caught it and ran back to the cage door. How would that help? Two paddlers pushed the branch through the door and jiggled it until the wooden latch on the outside lifted. A small flock of falcons — *his* falcons — dived down from nowhere and helped yank the cage bar up with their talons.

Where was Torrap when he needed him? 'Torrap!' he bellowed.

His men bolted into the clearing just as the wooden bar fell from the door. The paddlers tumbled out through the gap and split, sprinting away in several directions. 'Stop them!' Malach yelled. How else would he get Everand's compliance? A deep roar built in his stomach as he watched the paddlers running wild loops and curves, his men in pursuit but hindered by the falcons darting at their faces and clipping their heads with their wings. Had his birds all lost their minds? He ground his jaw, wanting to rip Lamiya apart one limb at a time.

His staghorn growled. By the stars! The orange beetle's horns were coming at his leg. Yanking his knee up so the short horns hit his mount's hard side instead, he fumbled to form a death bolt and threw it at Lamiya. She and Lazuli ducked and the bolt skimmed over them and dissipated.

'Charge them!' he yelled at his mount, a thrill running through him when it raised its antlers and forefeet aggressively. The orange beetle emitted a high-pitched chirrup and fled. The staghorn zoomed after it. Exhorting his mount, Malach tilted forward but a prickling heat jabbed into his stomach. The cursed stone! Ignoring the burning jabs, he flexed his fingers and crafted a spiked fire bolt, eying Lazuli's broad back up ahead. Just a bit closer … the orange beetle sped up and nimbly dived among the tree trunks, zipping above and below branches and twisting between narrow trunks and gaps. Finally, a decent hunt! His blood pumped through his veins.

'Faster,' he grunted, enjoying the instant surge of speed. A piny branch thwacked his face, then another. 'Be more careful,' he snarled.

The staghorn allowed more space around the foliage but couldn't catch the orange beetle, giving him annoying, tantalising glimpses of Lazuli's back, but not enough time to lob the fire bolt. A ball of heat scorched his stomach and he sat up with a gasp, immediately dodging a looming branch. He dropped the fire bolt, and the pine needles at the base of the tree smouldered.

'Slow down,' he instructed, fumbling under his tunic with both hands to draw the stone out, away from his skin. The tips of his fingers felt as if he'd plunged them into a bonfire but the scalding heat spreading over his stomach and up his chest was worse. Wisps of smoke were rising from his tunic. Finally, he got sufficient purchase to tug the Staropal out from under his tunic and hold it in front of him.

'Stop,' he commanded and his staghorn hovered where it was, wings whirring, front legs raised aggressively.

Between his hands, the stone glowed an eerie blood red, with oranges, yellows and golds spurting in agitated bursts like fireflies swarming before a storm. Wishing he had his hunting gloves on, Malach shook the stone. 'Stop that!' Pain lanced into his fingers and he shook the stone harder. He almost dropped it when his mount jolted forward, rammed from behind. The staghorn spun so fast he nearly lost his balance, clamping his legs inward just in time.

'Give it to me.' Everand's cold words washed over him.

Malach looked up into Everand's steely glare, from astride an even larger staghorn that faced his mount in the battle-ready poise. Powdered with tree-moth dust, the mage's robes were torn along one shoulder and down one sleeve, but none of this detracted from the determination and ire shining from Everand's eyes.

'It is not yours to keep. Give it to me.'

'You are as stupid as my father said!' yelled Malach, dizzy rage coursing through him. 'With the stone, we could do anything!' He gritted his teeth against the heat scalding his fingertips. The pain! He should smash the wretched stone, the source of so much trouble, against the nearest rock. No, no, no. That was not the path to power. What was he thinking? He must persuade Everand to help him. Or get rid of him.

'Listen to me,' Everand sat taller. 'The Staropal does not belong to *any* mage. *None* of us.' He spread his hands. 'We have power, we don't need it. But its rightful owner does.'

Movement flickered at the edge of Malach's vision; the orange beetle with Lamiya and Lazuli drawing closer.

'You have one last chance to do something good,' called Lamiya.

How could one woman be so incredibly annoying? He ground his back teeth together. She and Everand deserved each other.

'Your next action defines you, for eternity,' said Lamiya, tossing her hair back like a challenge.

'Choose wisely,' urged Everand.

That did it. 'Last time you said that you broke your promise!' The words roared up from the pit of his stomach and out through his stiff lips. Yet another broken promise! His father had promised to train him to be a mage and then vanished. Everand had stood on that hillside telling him if he chose wisely, *he* would train him. The inside of his mouth felt like he'd eaten a bowlful of sour green-tang fruit. Everand had promised — '*you have my word'* — and instead he'd run back to the Guild, then slunk back to Riverwood and made him hide in Riverplain like a coward. Why was it so hard to become a mage? With such a powerful mage as his father, it should be simple!

'For that I am sorry,' said Everand, sounding sincere. 'Events run beyond my control too. Yet here we are, one more time. One *last* time. Choose wisely and give me the stone so I can return it to Akachi.'

Give it to the dragon? Everand was surely mad, or enchanted by the beast. That must be it. Or the pesky boatwoman held him in thrall, *with* the dragon. Together, they'd made Everand betray his Guild — the precious Guild he'd previously betrayed his father for. Such utter — stupid — waste. And what were they offering? Nothing. Mage Beetal's swarthy, bearded face loomed behind his eyelids. *Everand will never help you, my son. You know this. Annihilate him. For me.*

The skin on Malach's fingertips crackled and started to burn. The stone! His gaze was drawn down and the colours in the Staropal whirled and swooshed to form a massive golden dragon's eye surrounded by red scales. The eye blinked. His vision distorted in the pull of the deep, textured iris, and feeling as if he were falling into the stone, into the fiery chasm, he clenched his body backwards.

'Aggh!' He stretched his arms out, pushing the stone further away. The staghorn fidgeted and clacked its mandibles. In his ears, Lamiya and Everand were laughing, although nothing but anxiety showed on their faces. Panic twinged in his chest. The dragons mustn't have the stone or they'd be all-powerful. And they didn't like him. Not one bit. What if he threw the stone into the deepest part of the lake? No, the dragons would find it. Or Everand would. If he couldn't have it, why should anyone else? What to do?

His mount growled and clacked its mandibles impatiently. What if he flew really high and dropped the wretched stone onto the granite rocks? Surely, it would smash. Yes. 'Go!' he shrieked at the staghorn, projecting an image of the rocky lip at the top of the waterfall, far, far above the lake.

The beetle zipped forward, winding through the trees. Below, his hunters were still in pursuit of the escaped paddlers, but had fanned out and were closing in on them. Good. Once he'd got rid of the stone, he'd use the captives to negotiate with Everand. No more distractions, just proper, accelerated training. Tiliqua seemed intelligent and reasonable. If she led the Guild maybe she'd accept him if Everand vouched for him. The staghorn growled and sped up. Glancing over his shoulder, he saw the other two beetles were in pursuit.

Balancing precariously, he held the stone against his beetle's hard back with one hand, ignoring the skin blistering on his palm, and tugged his tunic off over his head. Avoiding looking at the stone, he put the tunic over the top of it. The staghorn skimmed through the forest at breakneck speed, then banked sharply to ascend the first ledge of granite outcrop. The crisp, cooler air was welcome, and he held up his free hand to let the air cool his singed fingers. Wisps of smoke were rising from his tunic, and black patches were forming where the spikes of the Staropal touched it.

'Hurry,' he urged the staghorn. It chirped and found more speed. The rocks and cervices zoomed past below, the craggy outcrops becoming larger, the shapes bolder, the vegetation sparser. Light glinted ahead and the lake came into view, magnificent columns of waterfall thundering into it. The air grew moist, tinged with misty spray.

What if it bounced? What if the stone bounced and dropped into Dragon Lake? Malach cursed and rasped his parched tongue over his cracked lips. What if he rammed it with a death bolt as it fell? Would the stone protect itself? Could he use a spell of propulsion to make sure it landed with maximum impact? Maybe both. Propel it *and* blast it with a death bolt just as it hit the rocks. He'd have to be far enough ahead that Everand couldn't catch the falling stone or use a spell to draw it to him. He glanced over his shoulder; was he far enough ahead? Probably not.

The staghorn flew over the edge of the lake and headed straight for the cascading waterfall, banking sharply to fly upward. Malach revelled in the glistening, colourful droplets that showered him. Wait! Would Everand work out what he intended to do? Probably. He'd have to convince them he'd decided to surrender. Difficult, mid-air. 'Go as high as you can,' he commanded, worried the beetle had a limit. He gripped the rim of the carapace and clamped his legs tightly when the beetle banked more steeply and flew almost straight at the sun. The sunlight was blinding.

The air grew thinner, the light brighter and the lake and waterfall became like miniature pictures far below. The other beetles were following, now flanking his mount, Everand on his right and Lazuli and Lamiya on his left. A frown tugged at his forehead. Why wasn't Everand doing anything? No spells? He had got his power back, hadn't he? *The stone.* Was he worried about damaging the stone? Or was he clinging to a pathetic hope that he could yet dissuade him?

His mount's ascent began to slow, its air spiracles opening wide in a vain effort to draw in air and oxygen. Curse it. He couldn't form the spells with both hands occupied holding on and securing the stone! 'Level out,' he murmured. 'Hover directly above the rocky crest.'

As soon as the staghorn flattened out and turned around to face the waterfall and lake, he let go of the carapace and flexed his fingers, rapidly drawing power. Propulsion … he'd have to part the air molecules fast to create a vertical tunnel, then shove the Staropal downward with full force. Without falling off. The death bolt would have to follow. That could work, and might be useful if Everand dived to catch the falling stone. He eyed the smouldering tunic draped over the stone. The material was still intact — it would make a good slingshot.

Incredibly, although the other beetles were edging closer, Everand still wasn't doing anything. *Bumbling buffoon.* His father's words sprang to mind. Malach wrapped the tunic fully around the Staropal and bunched a handful of material at the top for purchase. He gave an experimental tug; it felt secure.

Surreptitiously glancing down, he cast the spell to form the vertical tunnel.

Far below, foaming water thundered over the rock crest, roaring between jagged ridges.

A particularly jagged lip stuck up like a row of fangs. *There.* Send it there.

Slowly, he grasped the top of the tunic ball with both hands.

CHAPTER THIRTY

'Malach! What are you doing?' Everand yelled, the thin air snatching and diluting his words. With his heels he nudged Dart a shade closer and tried to probe Malach's mind. A block rose immediately.

'I learn well,' said Malach with a feral grin.

'Really?' shouted Lamiya from the far side of Malach. 'You'd destroy the Staropal rather than give it up? You have no honour. You shame your people.'

Malach ignored Lamiya's goading and lifted the cloth-wrapped Staropal up high above his head. Alarmed, Everand extended his senses and detected the invisible tunnel falling straight down. Following its trajectory, he gasped. The rocks and waterfall were such a very long way below and the bundle would fall fast. Create a net? Try to snag it as Malach threw it?

When Dart chirped shrilly, he glanced back up. Hover was speeding straight at Malach, horns lowered ready to ram him. Malach promptly hurled the cloth ball downwards with full force. The Staropal! Everand zip-translocated Dart down to just above the rocky lip. The waterfall crashed and tumbled, spray soaked his legs and, subsumed by the noise and fluid movement, he ignored the ringing in his ears and trained his gaze on the ball of cloth hurtling right at him.

The blurred shape took on a shadow. What? His mouth ran dry. It was being chased by a massive death bolt. Barely a gap. Dart fidgeted and chirped in fright. 'Stay,' he commanded, hastily cobbling a spell to form a net — like the coarse fishnets that Acim and Zink wove — and flinging it into the base of the tunnel, just above his head height.

Steady … steady … his heart gave one mighty beat and the ball of cloth slammed into the net. Mind-pulling the net to him, he rammed the cloth ball against his chest while Dart beat his outer wings and flailed his legs, trying to fly backwards. The death bolt blasted past and exploded on the jagged rocks, spraying lethal shards everywhere. Dart reared with a teeth-grating, high-pitched shriek, feelers waving wildly, then fell, tumbling alongside the cascading waterfall. A sob lodged in his mouth, Everand clutched the Staropal to his chest and leaped away from Dart, momentum carrying him inexorably down to the churning lake. Arching backwards to distance himself from the body of the beetle, he hauled in a breath.

Cold, pounding, roiling water closed over his head and he sank, gripping the Staropal for all he was worth. Frantic, he kicked with his legs, swimming away from Dart's body to avoid being sucked into the vortex created by its mass as it sank. Water churned and rushed around him, pounding at his eardrums and snatching at his clothes. Wasn't this *exactly* how his mission had begun, being plunged into cold, powerful water and pushed around like a pebble in an eddy?

The outer edge of the net snagged on one of Dart's back legs and he was yanked downwards. Holding his breath, he wriggled furiously but the net was twisted around one of his arms. His heartbeat boomed in his ears, the rate rising. Streams of purple blood oozed from Dart's underbelly and drifted up into his face. Closing his eyes, forcing calm, he hugged the Staropal and dissolved the net. His body became lighter but his trousers were clamped around his legs. He kicked harder and not much changed, exactly like when he'd floundered in the river at the start of his mission while what he thought was a live dragon swam above him. *Just before you first saw Lamiya.* His lips twitched and bubbles seeped out, drifting gracefully upwards.

When you've finished reminiscing, you could take us to the surface. A tinkling female voice.

More bubbles seeped through his smile. *I could.* Focusing on which way was up, he strove for the surface. His trousers kept snagging between his legs but after a determined series of kicks he breached the surface and gulped in cool, fresh air. Treading water, he peered around to determine which way was the western shore. Fixing his gaze on a suitable spot, he began to murmur the spell of translocation. A scream shattered his concentration. His nape crawling with dread, he looked up.

Malach was plummeting downwards, arms and legs flailing. What happened? What did they do? With a gut-wrenching scrunch, Malach slammed into the rocky lip above the waterfall, his blood-curdling scream cut short. The water carried Malach's body through the jagged teeth and over the ledge so it plummeted again — straight at him. By the stars! Everand translocated backwards, water rushing around him.

With a massive splash, Malach plunged into the churning turbulence at the base of the waterfall.

Justice is served, said a muffled female voice.

Tucking the cloth ball under one arm and treading water, Everand eyed Malach's body, floating face-down, pummelled by the columns of water. Using another mind-pull, he brought the body out of the roiling mass to the calmer water near him. Grabbing a shoulder, he flipped Malach face-up, then translocated to the shore. Pebbles dug into his back and legs as he lay there, blinking at the bright blue sky.

A shadow flitted across his face and his ears registered the clacking of Hover's feet landing on the pebbles close by. Pebbles scrunched under running feet. Then Lamiya was leaning over him, grey-blue eyes wide and the ends of her hair tickling his face.

'Are you alright?' she asked, running her hands up and down his chest.

'I believe so.' But his limbs did not wish to move, his mind intent on piecing together what had happened. There was an awkward, uncomfortable lump under his left armpit. The Staropal. He had the stone. Intact. Dart! A pang of sorrow gripped his chest. The brave staghorn had perished. Malach! Was he dead too?

Urgency flooding his limbs, Everand sat up and twisted to regard the body lying beside him. Pale, slack lips open, Malach faced the sky, unmoving. Bare-chested, he was covered in gashes and bruises, one arm hanging at an unnatural angle and one leg bent back. Grief and shame piled into Everand. His mentor's son was dead, despite his best efforts. He'd failed them both.

'My love,' whispered Lamiya, putting a hand on his forearm. 'You tried. This is not your fault.'

Sorrow howled around his hollow chest. Not his fault … but Malach *had* fallen. How? He snapped his head up. 'What did you do?'

Sitting back, Lamiya said evenly, 'We charged him, to deflect him.' She swallowed.

Everand arched an eyebrow. 'And?'

Pebbles crunched as Lazuli crept over to squat beside Lamiya. Grey eyes miserable, the paddler said, 'We wanted to distract him so you could save the stone. But,' he looked to Lamiya and back, 'he was watching you and didn't see us.' Lazuli squared his shoulders. 'Hover hit his beetle so hard it tipped and Malach … just … slid off. He fell so fast.'

Averting his gaze from the pair of them, Everand fought to slow his racing pulse, to curb his anger and grief. *Be reasonable.*

He took a breath in and released it evenly. They didn't know about the invisible air tunnel. They hadn't mean to kill Malach. Or had they? Lamiya wouldn't mourn Malach's passing; she'd say it solved numerous problems. A wave of fatigue breaking over him, his limbs felt cold and heavy. What would he say to Torrap? His gaze was drawn to Malach's face. Without his beard he looked younger, more vulnerable, yet still achingly like Mage Beetal. He wanted to throw his head back in a howl to expel the sorrow battering inside him.

The eyelashes of Malach's nearest eye slowly lowered, fluttered, then half-opened.

Scrambling forward on his knees, Everand put his hand over Malach's heart. A weak, thready pulse met his fingers. 'He's alive!'

'Impossible!' said Lamiya.

'Are you sure?' Lazuli crouched closer and stared at Malach's face.

'There's a pulse. Let me check him.' Everand placed both hands over Malach's chest and leaned his concentration into the body. Five ribs were cracked and splintered, one edge poking into a collapsed lung. One collarbone was snapped, the organs were badly bruised, but none were bleeding internally … and several bones were crushed in his back. If he lived, Malach would be a cripple. But he sensed that Malach wouldn't live. Why not?

'There's blood oozing from the back of his head,' said Lamiya. 'I can see it spreading on the pebbles.'

She pointed, and Everand saw the dark stain. So, Malach's skull was cracked. He was dying. Unless he saved him. Peering into Lamiya's eyes, he tried to read her expression. She met his look, the blue flecks in her eyes jittering with thoughts. Lazuli fidgeted and glanced at them, not speaking, although his troubled expression suggested he would prefer they did not idly watch Malach die.

'He is nothing but trouble,' said Lamiya wistfully, 'but I know he means something to you. Riverwood needs a leader but can he ever be trusted?'

So, she was leaving it up to him. Sadness weighing heavily in his chest, he stared at Malach. He *was* trouble, and ambitious just like Mage Beetal, neither of them able to resist the lure of power. *Remove the lure.* Could he? He sat back on his heels. Malach's half-open eye swivelled, anchoring on his face. Everand's throat clamped with grief. Malach knew he was here; knew he could save him. Knew what else he could do.

Leaning closer, he looked into the dark-brown, almost black eye. Did Malach want to be saved or would he feel he'd lost too much honour? There was that too. Was that a twitch in the cold, slack lips? Was Malach trying to speak? He tilted his head from side to side, easing the threatening cramp in his neck. What to do?

'Rule Eleven,' murmured Lamiya. 'The choice was written there for a reason. It provides for an act of compassion. One the mages should have exercised the first time around.'

Love for her generosity of spirit brought burning tears to the back of his eyes. Even though she despised Malach, she would support his redemption. And wasn't this the very solution she'd negotiated with the mages back in Riverplain? Except Mantiss had only agreed on his behalf; not Malach's. But the Guild wasn't here now — he and Lamiya could decide.

'A compromise?' He met her serious eyes. 'He leads Riverwood as a man?'

Her beautiful face creased into a smile, the lights in her eyes dancing. 'You can do it?' She frowned. 'But don't absorb his power into you. Please. I couldn't stand it.'

A fair request, given everything. But where would he send the power to? He craned his neck around to regard the Staropal, resting on the pebbles. Would the stone agree to absorb Malach's power, given the half-mage's intentions were not pure?

'Ask it,' urged Lamiya.

'Hurry,' said Lazuli. 'His face is turning blue. And he kind of gurgled.'

Pulse racing, Everand said to Lazuli, 'Hold Malach's hand, as his friend. Squeeze it and anchor him so he knows we'll help him. He is not alone.'

Lazuli promptly gripped Malach's hand in both of his and huddled closer, speaking into the pale face. 'Hang on. Keep breathing.'

Spinning around on his knees, Everand gently tugged the singed, damp and rent tunic off the Staropal and put it to the side. Sunlight beamed onto the surface of the stone, and the reds and oranges retreated into the depths to be replaced by whirling blues, jades, greens and hints of gold and yellow. *Much better*, came the tinkling voice. Respectfully, Everand laid his hands on either side of the stone.

I have a request. His fingertips buzzed and tingled; the sensation ticklish.

Mage Everand, sighed the Staropal, gold and azure bands whipping around the surface, *since you are about to return me to Akachi, I will grant your request.*

Everand felt his eyebrows lift. *You don't want to know what it is first?*

Bell-like laughter rang in his ears. *Sometimes I think your mentor was so right! You are straitlaced beyond belief …* more bell-like peals rang in his ears … *but I have never encountered anyone so true to what is fair and just. So willing to sacrifice self. I see why she loves you.*

A warm blush spread up Everand's neck, crawling up behind his ears and making his scalp itch. Was the stone making fun of him? He stole a glance at Lamiya and she was grinning broadly. Was she listening somehow?

I will absorb the irksome half-mage's power and consider it a small repayment of the power taken by the Mages' Guild over time. All the colours of a sky-arch blossomed inside the stone and cascaded down like petals in a wind. *Don't worry, I will cleanse it to remove his taint. Proceed.*

Thank you, sent Everand, picking up the Staropal and putting it beside Malach's shoulder.

Lamiya shuffled to sit cross-legged at the top of Malach's head. 'I'll hold his head for you.' She arched an eyebrow. 'You'll start here?'

Dry-mouthed, Everand nodded. Start with the cracked skull, make sure Malach would live, remove his power and then heal the rest of him. Lamiya's gentle, encouraging smile showed she anticipated his plan. Lazuli gripped Malach's hand more tightly.

'The spirits will help you,' murmured Lamiya, sounding uncannily like U-Mali, 'given you do this for peace across the four provinces.'

The skin on Everand's shoulderblades twitched, as if patted by light hands, and the air around him grew subtly denser. If the spirits approved, this must be the right course to take. Closing his eyes, he placed both palms flat upon Malach's bare chest and nudged his senses into the body, past the clammy, chill and broken flesh.

Shaken, Everand pushed past the frenetic, buzzing disturbance of Malach's nerves shrieking in endless agony and reached his power into Malach's head. Pain and wrongness buffeting him, he cautiously probed his way until he found the crack at the back of the skull, a little above the base of the neck. Dark blood was edging out through the crack and oozing onto the pebbles below. Repressing a shudder, he meticulously repaired the crack then smoothed the bone and blended it seamlessly into the surrounding skull.

'The bleeding has stopped,' said Lamiya.

Travelling down, Everand checked the bones in Malach's neck, then took a breath and melded the broken ends of collarbone together, merging them back into each other and smoothing the result. Beneath his palms, Malach's chest lifted in a sigh. Not daring to look at Malach's face, Everand travelled lower, easing the cracked ribs back into place and gently taking the sharp end out of the collapsed lung. Next, he wove a patch over the tear in the lung, then blended that in.

Malach's chest rose in a more defined breath and the nerve-ends reduced their shrieking, settling into an incessant buzz, louder in the spine and broken limbs.

Pausing, Everand took a deep breath, expanding his lungs, storing power in his fingertips and filling his heart with resolve. Malach was conscious enough to understand his next action. *You should tell him.* What if he resisted? *You are stronger. Do not waver now.* Spirit hands squeezed his shoulders, encouraging him.

Heart heavy, he looked into the dark-brown eyes that were locked onto his face.

'Don't,' croaked Malach, his eyes growing darker.

Lamiya's lips pressed together and her fingers tightened around Malach's head.

'Malach.' Everand forced authority into his voice. 'The people of Riverwood need you as their leader. Above all, this is your purpose.' Swallowing painfully, he gathered his resolve. 'I wish you to live, as the son of my mentor Mage Beetal. However, by your own actions, you have shown yourself unworthy to become a mage.'

'No. Don't,' moaned Malach, feebly trying to lift his head.

Fighting his sorrow, Everand shook his head. 'In accordance with Guild Law, the mage councils have already judged that you have breached Rule Twelve and acted for your own ambition.' Malach started to fidget beneath his hands and he leaned on the bare chest more heavily. 'By stealing the Staropal and trying to destroy it, you have confirmed their judgement.'

Beside them, the Staropal became incandescent, like a sun-fade sky laden with stars twinkling all the colours of a sky-arch. *I am ready*, said the tinkling voice.

Ignoring the tremors ripping through Malach's body, Everand forced his words out. 'As the present mage and with Guide Lamiya, leader of Riverplain, we overrule the Guild's decree of punishment by obliteration.' Malach squirmed weakly. 'We decree instead that your power will be removed and given to the Staropal as recompense for past draws of power by the Guild.'

'No!' Malach gasped hoarsely. 'I want to be a mage!' His shoulders tipped up as he feebly tried to rise. With a grunt, he fell back when his broken arm and leg refused to take his weight.

His eyes dry and burning with emotion, Everand said, 'I will remove your power now. Lie still and it will hurt less.' He bit back the desire to apologise, to say he wished that things were otherwise.

'My love,' said Lamiya, 'he will never be ready. Continue.'

Malach's body went rigid with tension and the fingers of his unbroken arm flexed, perhaps trying to summon the power to resist.

Half-closing his eyes, Everand reached back inside Malach and gently probed down the torso until he found the pool of stored power. As Malach had described, it was dark brown, like a silty pond deep within a wood, the consistency of a thick soup. The edges of the pond fluttered and wavered. Malach was trying to raise a block but he was too damaged to draw the energy.

Clenching his throat against a building sob, Everand spread his fingers and began to draw the brown power into him. Once a steady stream flowed and his arms felt full, he lifted his left hand and reached sideways to press his open palm on the top of the Staropal. The stone warmed and the brown stream flowed down his arm and out through his palm as if into a funnel at the top of the stone, slipping down into the whirling colours. The brown sludge whirled a lap with the other colours, became green-brown, then green and then blue, before dissipating into the jades and azures.

It felt like an eternity before the brown stream became a trickle and then a reluctant drip. Malach had more power than he'd anticipated. Thinking of how he'd tricked Agamid, Everand probed all around the base of Malach's stomach, scraping at the vessel walls, until he was certain he'd taken it all. Fatigue and tremors coursing through his limbs, he bowed his head, his heart whispering an apology and final farewell to the power and legacy of his former mentor.

'You said you would train me,' hissed Malach, going limp.

CHAPTER THIRTY-ONE

Mantiss stared around the Great Hall. It looked like a battleground. The warded cage was a pile of shards, a jagged hole gaped in the floor where the emblem had been, the ancient silk rug lay crumpled against a wall, the broken ornate entry doors hung at an angle and bloodstains splattered the marble tiles. The mages stood in frightened huddles — and an awful, charred odour was rising from the cloak covering Pelamis' body.

'Father,' said Tiliqua, looming beside him. 'The council must vote immediately.'

Blinking, Mantiss tried to herd his thoughts and impose order on his memories of what had happened. Against all belief, Everand had appeared! Not dead, and in league with a feisty woman who was the leader of her people. He lifted a hand to his chest, feeling the strong steady heartbeat. Somehow, they had cured him. Gratitude gushed through him.

'Father,' said Tiliqua, an edge to her tone.

'Wait.' He scanned the room. Where was Agamid? There, talking with Hydrelaps and Saiphos. By the way they were nodding, perhaps he was asking them to formally record the events. Sensing scrutiny, Agamid looked over his shoulder, broke off and walked towards him.

'My friend,' Mantiss grasped both of Agamid's hands. 'I can't thank you enough for your role in all this.'

'It isn't over yet,' replied Agamid, brows furrowed. 'The half-mage has fled with the Staropal. Everand is in pursuit.'

A strange, unexpected calm oozed over Mantiss and his heart gave a steady beat. Above all others, and despite everything, he *could* trust his spy. 'We must presume Everand will prevail. We now know he will run true, consider the greater good.'

'But how will we know?' asked Tiliqua, chin held high.

'I suspect he'll find a way to tell us. Perhaps we should make it easier for him to do so?'

Agamid smiled. 'I see your sense of strategy has returned intact. What do you propose?'

Regarding his daughter, Mantiss replied, 'First, we vote. Once we have a new Head of the Guild, I suggest we consider some unprecedented ideas.'

'You're sure you wish to step aside?' Agamid asked, stroking his beard, his expression intent. 'You've been healed. You look strong again.'

His breath catching in the back of his throat, Mantiss looked from Agamid to Tiliqua. True, he had been healed. Externally and internally. Flexing his fingers, he relished the strength and power running through them. The Guild was entering a time of upheaval and change ... the next few events would be momentous in Guild history ... did he want to lead? Did he want the glory? Tiliqua's throat bulged with a swallow, hurt and disappointment growing in her eyes. Still, he hesitated. Agamid ceased stroking his beard and lifted an eyebrow.

Curling his fingers tightly into his palm, Mantiss wished Everand were present. What would his spy think? What would he recommend? Tiliqua's chin was edging higher, her eyes flashing with disappointment. He released a sigh. No, he'd hurt Tiliqua enough already by relying so heavily on Everand. And frightened Elytra with his failing health. It was not a requirement to die or be dying to hand over the leadership.

He gave Tiliqua a fond smile. 'Yes. The Guild will be better served by a change at the head of the table. We have an opportunity to elect a younger mage to chart us through what will be challenging times yet.'

Agamid smiled, then narrowed his eyes. 'You will remain on the Inner Council?'

'If invited.' Mantiss glanced at his fidgeting daughter.

'I'll call the mages to the table.' Agamid spun around and walked towards the nearest group.

'Come,' said Mantiss to Tiliqua. 'I'll open the meeting and call for the vote. Compose a few suitable words.' He set off towards the dais and on reaching the table, took his customary seat at the head of it. Tiliqua slid into her chair, two around from his.

Waiting for the other mages to settle into their chairs, he rejoiced in feeling control over his body. No longer did his hands tremble, or his legs threaten not to support him. His heart pumped blood and life through his veins. Whatever Everand and Lamiya had done was miraculous — achieved by an elemental, old form of magic that the mages did not understand. He drummed his fingers on the smooth tabletop. Perhaps the Guild would be wise to explore relations with the provinces — especially Lamiya and her people — with Everand as the conduit. He glanced at Tiliqua, sitting elegant and composed, hiding her nerves well. Perhaps she and Everand could continue to work together, but from different sides of the granite wall.

Bringing his focus to the table, he found eighteen mages seated; the two empty chairs glaring like empty eye sockets. Slumped sullenly in his bloodstained robe, Simoselaps refused to meet his eye. Menetia looked dishevelled and annoyed. The others appeared faintly anxious.

'Mages of the Inner and Outer Councils, we have experienced another round of unprecedented events.' Mantiss travelled his gaze over their faces. 'Nonetheless, we have important things to do to recover our equilibrium. Foremost, I abide by my decision to step down and we must elect a new Head of the Guild.' When the mages shuffled and a few mouths opened, he lifted a hand.

'Hear me out. I have led you for twelve season-cycles and much has happened in that time, not all of it good. Although I am perhaps not dying as I feared, it is time for younger blood to guide us and chart new courses through what will undoubtedly be a time of change. The river provinces have reached out, we have made contact and we must now find a safe way forward.' He swallowed. 'We no longer have the Staropal to draw upon, and we also know there are river dragons in Ossilis.'

He paused to allow the grimacing, muttering and exchanging of glances. 'I will explain the significance of the river dragons later. Already, we have much to absorb. Let's now vote on a new leader.'

Agamid placed his elbows on the table. 'The vote requires the support of both councils. We need to replace the two missing positions, especially as both are on the Inner Council.'

Curse it, Agamid was right. Mantiss ran his eye around the table, pausing on Hydrelaps. As the librarian and custodian of their history, it would be apt for him to take up a more important role. 'I move that Hydrelaps be promoted to the Inner Council of Ten. He has served us long and well as our librarian and custodian of our history. His perspective will be useful as we chart a new course, create new history. All those in favour, place your hand palm-up on the table.'

Many smiling at Hydrelaps' flapping hands and open mouth, everyone placed their palm upwards. Done. Mantiss' gaze was drawn to Everand's vacant chair. Was there a way they could retain Everand on the council, even if he lived in a river province? He looked into Tiliqua's steady gaze and she gave a barely discernible dip of her head. His pulse skipped; she was thinking the same thing, but it needed to be her proposal as the new leader. And would the mages agree to an Inner Council position? An Outer Council role would be more palatable.

He tapped his fingers on the table and once he held everyone's attention, said, 'Filling Everand's position is more difficult. Although he is not dead as we thought, and apparently retains his powers *despite* our decree and Agamid and Tiliqua removing them, he wishes to live in a river province.'

'Outrageous,' muttered Menetia. 'Why does he always get special consideration?'

Gently, Agamid said, 'This is a complex decision. If we sanction Everand's request, we are already agreeing to magic existing outside of Axis, out of the control of the Guild. These are decisions we should make under our new leader.'

'That would seem appropriate,' snapped Menetia. At the far end of the table Simoselaps nodded.

'Very well,' said Mantiss. 'I move that for now we demote Everand to the Outer Council, replace him on the Inner Council, and then vote on the leadership with the eighteen of us present. Everand has, in effect, already cast his vote. Is this acceptable to all?'

'Although not ideal, I concur,' said Agamid firmly. 'We must make several decisions, and quickly.'

'I agree,' said Tiliqua, with several mages then following.

Mantiss cast his eyes over the members of the Outer Council. One mage sat taller, waiting for his scrutiny. Aclys, named after his great-grandfather who had been a good friend to Lapemis, the original Head of the Guild. Mantiss arched an eyebrow and Aclys half-smiled. A fair option, the young mage reportedly had a quick mind and engaging manner.

'Mage Aclys, do you agree to be promoted to the Inner Council?'

With a short bow, Aclys said, 'I would be honoured, Mage Mantiss.'

'Anyone disagree with Aclys' promotion?' No-one spoke. 'I hereby appoint Mage Aclys to the Inner Council to replace Mage Everand, who is demoted to the Outer Council. Now we are positioned to vote for a new Head of the Guild and I hand over to Agamid to lead the proceedings.' His shoulders and neck feeling heavy, Mantiss leaned against his chair back. *Soon.* Soon he'd be free of the burden of responsibility and could spend time at the country estate with Elytra.

Flicking his sleeves back, Agamid put his hands on the table. 'Mage Mantiss, do you formally consent to your removal from the role of Head of the Guild and accept demotion to being a member of the Inner Council of Ten?'

'I do so consent.' Mantiss sat forward. 'I agree to relinquish the role of leadership and I consent to remaining in a position on the Inner Council.'

'Thank you,' said Agamid. 'I now ask the councils to formally thank Mage Mantiss for his extended leadership and guidance.'

Pleasingly, those around the table nodded deferentially and more than half murmured their gratitude. So far, this impromptu meeting was going well.

'Mage Tiliqua has offered herself as our new Head of the Guild. A short while ago, she was challenged by Mage Pelamis for the role and we agreed the Staropal would guide us whether either candidate was worthy.' Pausing, Agamid watched Simoselaps warily. 'At present Mage Tiliqua is our only candidate and she was blessed by the Staropal before it was taken. I ask now whether there are any further nominations?'

Breath held, Mantiss glanced around the table. Tiliqua waited with pride and dignity while the others regarded her thoughtfully, except for Simoselaps, who stared at the tabletop. Mantiss' gaze rested on Caimanops, scholarly in his silver-blue robe. Of them all, he was the only one he'd consider a possible candidate. The mage looked as if he were considering whether to stand, but then his shoulders relaxed and he nodded at Tiliqua. The concept of Caimanops as a potential partner for her flitted into Mantiss' mind. Not quite an Everand, but he had some merits.

'I take the silence to be an absence of any further nominations,' said Agamid. 'I move that we appoint Mage Tiliqua as our new Head of the Guild. Place your palms up on the table to indicate agreement or raise your hand to dissent.'

With a flurry of silk, all the mages placed their right hands palm-up on the gleaming table. A rosy blush crept up Tiliqua's neck and her eyes shone a deep sea-blue with delight. Pride coursed through Mantiss. Elytra would be thrilled; they should have a family celebration this sun-fade meal.

Agamid gave him a pleased look before saying, 'I congratulate Mage Tiliqua on her appointment as Head of the Guild. I further congratulate her on being the inaugural female leader. I now ask Mage Mantiss to vacate the chair and pass it to Tiliqua.'

Pushing the chair back, Mantiss rose and stepped back to allow Tiliqua to take the seat. Stepping sideways, he lowered himself into Tiliqua's old chair on the other side of Agamid. His friend gave him a subtle nod and the other mages ceased shuffling and sat straighter.

All eyes turned to Tiliqua.

Chapter Thirty-Two

Lamiya stared at the top of Everand's bowed head, her heart welling with pride. True as always, he'd taken an action he would rather not. Sliding her gaze to Lazuli, she found him staring at her with an inscrutable expression. How did he feel about what they'd done?

Between her fingers, Malach's head moved and he gave a low groan. His eyes were closed, his breath shallow and his face lined with despair. She caught at her lower lip with a tooth. He might not have his power any more but he could still prove to be difficult. Far simpler if he'd died in the fall. But she was being uncharitable. She should give him a chance as just a man, a young leader of his people. Squaring her shoulders, she lifted his head up a bit.

'Can you stand?' Lazuli slid a hand under Malach's shoulder. 'Come. Your people wait for you.'

Watching Lazuli coax Malach to sit up, she felt even more chastised by the way her pacer was determined to treat Malach with respect. Perhaps over time Malach would come to appreciate everything that had been done for him. For now, he fumbled to his feet, leaned heavily on Lazuli's shoulder and steadfastly refused to look at her or Everand.

With a shrug, Everand retrieved the Staropal and pushed to his feet, saying, 'Let's take Malach to his people, collect our friends, then go straight to Akachi.'

Tilting her head, she said, 'Go how?'

'Let's use the beetles to take Malach home, then I'll translocate us.' He scanned the beach and when he spied Hover foraging by the edge of the trees, he closed his eyes.

Within a heartbeat, Hover skimmed towards them. A few heartbeats later, the staghorn Malach had been riding emerged from the forest and made its way to them, weaving from side to side as if it would rather go elsewhere.

'Can I keep it?'

Lamiya jumped at Malach's croaked request, then her eyebrows lifted when Everand regarded Malach solemnly and nodded.

'Can I have Hover?' Lazuli said quickly.

The look on Everand's face! Lamiya's lips twitched with her effort not to smile.

'If you insist,' Everand replied.

Lazuli nudged Malach with his shoulder. 'I challenge you to a beetle race. As soon as you're ready.'

Bristling, Malach stopped leaning on Lazuli and thrust out a hand. 'I accept.'

By the stars, her pacer was clever! He knew it too by the smug glance he flicked her way.

'You two take the staghorn and we'll ride Hover,' said Everand. 'Malach, are you ready to be reunited with your people?'

Ignoring Everand, Malach clucked his tongue at the staghorn and said to Lazuli, 'I take the reins.'

Lamiya tried to read Everand's bland expression. Her gut was twisting and turning. What further havoc could Malach wreak? She swallowed. His hunters probably held her team captive, and they would be seriously outnumbered at his village. Malach had been planning a glorious and triumphant return as a powerful mage … Everand gazed back at her, his eyes a dark, turbulent blue. Would he yet be forced to kill Malach?

'I know,' Everand murmured. 'We give him one last opportunity, but he has your paddlers.' He blew out a breath. 'The sooner Akachi has the Staropal, the better. For everyone, in all of the provinces.'

Emotions tumbled through her: sadness, guilt, relief that he recognised the risk, frustration at Malach's stupidity, anxiety for her friends, fear they would fail Akachi … warm lips brushed her forehead, sweeping away her rising tension.

'We do our best and we do it together, my love.' His words echoed around her, bouncing in the air — and the vision fell swift and sharp.

She was back in her previous vision of Everand standing surrounded by a raging tempest, his robes billowing and a shadow lurking beside him. Her pulse throbbed in her wrists. The wind whipped unmercifully, snapping Everand's robes about his legs, whistling through his hair and buffeting his body. Shadowy figures encroached, surrounding him, threatening him. He raised his arms high and a woman stepped from beside him. Her throat clenched. The woman stood tall and proud, glossy mahogany hair flying wildly and obscuring her face, a magnificent green dress clinging to a lithe, strong body.

The woman lifted her arms and birdsong filled the air. The clouds ripped apart and brilliant sunshine rained down, highlighting them both. The wind blew the cascading hair back over the woman's muscled shoulders and Lamiya gazed, open-mouthed, at a face of stunning beauty, strength and energy, with dynamic grey-blue eyes. The shadowy figures advanced and the woman hurled birdsong at them while the gauzy spectre of a massive red dragon rose shimmering behind her.

The shadow figures vanished in puffs of grey matter. Lamiya blinked. She and Everand stood in a beam of incandescent sunlight, the air crisp, still and so, so blue. One shadowy figure remained, on bended knee before her. She blinked faster. Was *she* meant to tame Malach? Was this her final test? Her legs trembled. *Spirits of the skies and earth, if you love me at all, let this be the final test.*

Feathers tickled her breastbone and Whirr's fluffy body wriggled up until his face poked out of her tunic. He fixed bright eyes on her. Her unsteady pulse settling, she crooked a finger and stroked the back of his head. *My little guardian. We have more work to do.*

'Are you ready?' asked Everand.

Giving Whirr a last caress, she looked up to see Everand holding Hover's reins ready, and Lazuli and Malach sitting astride the staghorn, waiting. With a tug of air, she was lifted up onto Hover. Taking a firm hold, she lifted her chin and gave Malach a warning glare. He averted his face. From his perch behind Malach, Lazuli gave her an intense look and mouthed, 'Paddles up.' Her heart thumped; he was ready to help.

The two beetles rose simultaneously and the staghorn surged ahead. Lamiya gazed at Lazuli's back while the beetles flitted through the trees, then started the descent to the village. Everand remained silent, no doubt analysing all the possible scenarios. Thinking of the vision, she tipped her chin down until it touched the top of Whirr's head. *My friend, I need you to channel the voices of all our flocks. Can you do this?*

Whirr peeped and fluffed his wings. Reaching far inside, deep into her silver pond of calling power, she visualised not her flock itself, but their myriad calls and whistles. She thought of the sounds flowing into a melodious but invisible air current, reaching her, disappearing into her body, then seeping through her chest into Whirr. His feathers vibrated against her chest bone and she felt his breast puff out. He snapped his beak.

Ahead, the staghorn burst into the clearing where the raptor cages were. Everand's arms tensed around her as he directed Hover to follow the staghorn to the flat space at the front of the cages. She frowned. There, in the very cage she and Everand had been held captive, Beram sat propped against a wall with his arms around Mookaite while the others sat in a circle talking. When the shadows of the beetles flitted over them, the paddlers leaped up and ran to the front of the cage. In an eerie sense of having already lived this scene, she watched Lazuli give them a cheery wave and Larimar and Ejad wave back.

The staghorn landed, facing the cage door, and Malach yelled, 'Hunters! To me!'

Before Hover had all six feet fully on the ground, nearly a hundred hunters streamed from the trees to form a solid circle around them. All held a weapon and at least ten levelled crossbows at her and Everand, arrows nocked ready. Malach remained astride the staghorn and Lazuli firmed up his position behind him. Bitter bile edged into Lamiya's mouth. So, he wasn't even going to pretend he was changed. Everand would be so disappointed. His bowed head rested briefly on her shoulder and his sigh floated past her collarbone.

Torrap strode towards Malach, swarthy face creased in a smile. 'You return to us! What do you want us to do?'

Reaching down, Malach clapped Torrap on the shoulder. 'Guard the captives while I negotiate.' He glanced across at Everand. 'Kill them if needs be.' Nudging the staghorn with a heel until it turned to face them and ignoring her, he addressed Everand. 'You did not ask if you could remove my powers. Give them back. Now. Or …' He waved a hand at the paddlers milling restlessly inside the cage.

Everand's words rumbled against her back. 'You disappoint me. Have you learned nothing from all this? The Guild will never let you live if you have power. I gave you a path to life. For your people.'

'Your Guild is in disarray!' spat Malach. 'I can protect my people better with power — the power my father gave me! Give it back or you betray him yet again.'

Lamiya winced. Trust Malach to heap guilt on Everand, to aim for the weak point. It wasn't fair that he had to keep making decisions about Malach over and over. It was time to end it. Everand's chest expanded against her back as he prepared to speak. She jumped in. 'Wait. I want to talk to him. Leader to leader.'

'What? You despise him, and he you. Why would he listen to you?' Everand mumbled, sounding tired.

'Let me try. If it doesn't work, do whatever you have to do.'

'Lamiya … his men are armed …'

'Put one of your shields around him and me. Make it so others can't get to us or hear us.'

'Are you sure?'

Twisting around, she brushed his lips with hers. 'You've done enough for him. More than enough! He has no hold over me because, as you said, I despise him.' She shrugged. 'Let me try. I see only one path to a peaceful way forward and it doesn't involve you.'

'I don't like it,' Everand murmured. 'I'll be ready to protect you.'

Brushing his lips again, she said, 'Drop that shield over us as soon as we're both on the ground.'

'How do you propose to–'

Twisting forward, she nodded at Lazuli, slid down from Hover and ran several strides towards the staghorn. Lazuli grabbed Malach around the waist and fell sideways off the beetle. The two of them thumped into the dirt, with a yell from Malach. Lazuli jumped up first and flapped his arms at the staghorn. It growled and menaced him with a raking sweep of its antlers. Lazuli punched it hard on the nose, twice, and it scuttled backwards, chittering. Spinning around, Lazuli grabbed Malach's shoulders from behind.

Torrap and several hunters ran forward, blades hissing from knife sheaths. Lamiya opened her arms wide and Whirr flew up to flutter beside her face, opening his beak and blasting them with birdsong. Trill notes, bells and chirps radiated out from her palms and Whirr's beak in a wave of high-pitched sound until the men dropped their weapons to put their hands over their ears and staggered back a few paces.

A glittering shield dropped over the three of them. At a loud ker-thunk to her left, she grimly watched the arrow from Torrap's crossbow, at her head height, bounce off the shield and drop to the dirt. Lazuli gripped Malach under the armpits and staggered forward with him, stopping five paces away from her with a feral grin.

Shaking his fist at her, Malach yelled, 'Why you– ' Turning his face to Torrap, he shouted, 'Kill the captives!'

'He can't hear you,' said Lamiya.

With a rough twist, Malach yanked away from Lazuli's hands and advanced on her, his face dark with fury.

'Stop.' She held up her hand, palm outward, and took a deep breath, feeling the shades of the spirits past slithering and gathering behind her.

Malach faltered to a standstill, his eyebrows furrowed and dark eyes burning with hate.

'The spirits of Riverplain have no reason to like you and neither do I. Yet I offer you one *final* chance to be the leader of Riverwood that you should be.' Glaring, she added, 'I do this for Everand, not for you.'

'Spit it out, boatwoman. What do you want?'

'Sit down so your men understand we will talk. No rash moves.' Chin high, she held eye contact with him until he grunted and stiffly lowered himself to sit cross-legged on the dirt, Lazuli hovering tensely behind him. Gracefully, as if she had plenty of time, Lamiya folded down and kneeled sitting on her heels so she could jump up quickly if she had to. Out of the corner of her eye she saw Torrap waver, then slowly lower his crossbow. Good. Running her tongue across her dry lips, she wished they had brew and cakes to share.

'I propose that we speak, province leader to leader.' She indicated him with a hand, then touched it to her chest. 'We are both young, thrust unexpectedly into leadership of our people.'

'I am not like you,' growled Malach. 'Do not try to compare us.'

'True,' she agreed. 'But our context is similar. We both lost our family early,' she took a breath, 'and we are now both leaders of our people in a time that forebodes great change.'

Malach grunted, but at least he was listening.

'The four provinces have connected and the mages have come out of their Guild. The river dragons are on the loose. You and me,' she dared to flap a hand at him, 'we lead two of the four provinces. We can influence what happens.'

'I *was* influencing what happened.' Malach's scowl deepened.

Lamiya eased in a shaky breath, drawing courage from the spirits crowded behind her. 'You were influencing what happened to Riverwood, but not anywhere else.' Ignoring his look of affront, she ploughed on. 'Atage continued with the trade discussions, the other three provinces all signed, the mages still came out of their Guild and, most significant of all, the red dragon rose and seeks to influence us.'

Falling silent, she gave Malach time to absorb her words, grateful for Lazuli's sharp nod of support. Whirr flew down to land on her knee, tilting his head from side to side. Malach gazed around the clearing at his hunters, pausing on Torrap, who shrugged at him. Finally, his look rested above and behind her, presumably fixed upon Everand. Should she speak? Invisible hands pressed down on her shoulders. *Wait*, whispered U-Mali. *Let him grow to lead.*

'Did he tell you to say this?' rasped Malach, dropping his gaze back to her.

'He can't hear us either,' she said gently, shaking her head. 'Everand has relinquished his role at the Guild, and in Riverplain he will be my consort — this is between you and

me. I negotiate with you, leader to leader. You are strong.'
Where did that come from? 'You will be important, especially
as Riverwood is closest to Axis and the Guild.'

'Don't try to manipulate me, boatwoman.'

Although Malach sounded gruff, she could see him thinking.
Indeed, his was the province the mages would reach first if they
came out from behind their massive granite wall. And he'd lost
the trust of the male dragon, Mizukaze, so the dragons were
unlikely to help him. Surely, he understood he would need
friends? She put her hands in her lap and concentrated on
pressing her fingertips together to stop herself from speaking.

That's it, encouraged U-Mali. *You grew into your role far
faster than we anticipated, give him a chance to find his feet.*

Find his mind, more like it, Lamiya thought. Still, as a
hunter and boat captain Malach must have some common
sense. Somewhere. If he could get past his desire to be a mage.
Maybe it would have helped if Everand hadn't restored his own
powers because now Malach could never measure up to him,
his father's *other* apprentice, who was intent on changing the
world around them. A sigh escaped her as she understood the
extent to which Malach would need to redefine himself. Fast.
For now, Malach looked lost for words.

'Malach.' She caught his attention. 'I'm sure your people
are eager to welcome you home, and I imagine you're keen to
speak with them.' His eyes glinted in the light. 'I meant what
I said before, when you were with us in Riverplain. When you
are ready, we would welcome you as a true neighbour. If you
prefer, we can conclude our discussion in a sun or two.'

For several long breaths he stared solemnly at her. Outside
the shield, his hunters shuffled and gripped their weapons. She
wished she could see Everand's face but dared not remove
her focus from Malach. She'd offered him time to consider,
let him choose wisely. Anxiety niggled at her. He hadn't done
anything wise yet, why would he this time? Except in another

sun Akachi would have the Staropal and the balance of power would have shifted. Irrecoverably.

A moving speck above snagged her attention. An eagle. She felt a twinge of guilt. Sending all his birds away meant yet more loss of face for him. Half-closing her eyes, she projected a summons and the eagle wheeled and then spiralled down until it hovered above the shield, majestic wings beating. The shield crackled and the eagle flew through and landed next to Malach. The joy on his face tugged at her heart. Like her, he needed his birds. Was this the eagle that had accompanied him to the boat races? Whirr shivered and shook his feathers.

Sitting taller, Malach made eye contact. 'Two suns. You will come here.'

Anxiety rippling through her, she said, 'Agreed.'

The tight lines across his brow smoothed. 'Come at sun-high and we'll take food. Everand can be witness and scribe.' With a brusque nod, Malach brushed the dust from his hands and stood. 'I will release your paddlers now.'

With a faint tinkling, the shield around them dissipated like dew drops vaporising in sunshine. Standing on trembling legs, Lamiya half-bowed. 'I look forward to our discussion.'

Chapter Thirty-three

Everand's heart thumped erratically when Lamiya and Malach both stood, Lamiya bowing and Malach looking thoughtful. What had they agreed? *You must trust her*, advised his heart. She said she saw a peaceful way forward. *Yes, but what is it?* nudged his mind. *She's a leader*, replied his heart. *Let her lead.* He murmured the words to dissolve the shield, relieved when Malach waved a hand at Torrap who promptly marched to the raptor cage and opened the door.

The paddlers spilled out, legs and arms akimbo, grinning and calling 'Yosh' and 'Yo'. Warmth surged through him as Larimar and Lazuli embraced and swung each other around with wild whoops while Ejad, Acim and Zink did cartwheels around Lamiya, who laughed at them. Tengar clapped her on the shoulder before he was roughly elbowed aside by Luvu, who enveloped her in a fierce hug. Everand felt his eyebrows arch. Beyond the paddlers, Malach's hunters were greeting him with brisk nods. A number raised their fists aloft and called, 'Ki!'

Everand felt like an observer, seated astride Hover, a remnant from his life at the Guild. Where he no longer belonged. Would he ever belong here? Truly belong? He breathed in through his nose, trying to block the budding melancholy.

Someone tapped his knee and he looked down into Beram's broad grin, Mookaite beside him with pleasure radiating from her warm, brown eyes.

'Difficult to clap your shoulder all the way up there!' said Beram, tugging at his trouser leg.

Everand slid down and gasped when Beram hugged him so tightly the points of the Staropal dug into his stomach and his ribs creaked. Mookaite leaned in to plant a moist kiss on his cheek, and a flush flamed up his neck.

'Good to see you safe and sound,' said Mookaite. 'Welcome back.'

'What's the sharp thing?' asked Beram, releasing him and rubbing at his belly.

An inane urge to laugh romping in his chest, Everand held the Staropal up. 'My friend, this is the Staropal, the powerful, ancient artefact we must return to Akachi.' *The source of so much trouble.*

His ears tingled with tinkling words, *Be nice.*

Mookaite gently touched the stone with a finger, its colourful lights dancing across her face. 'It is beautiful beyond belief,' she whispered.

Pinks and pale blues whirled in the stone where Mookaite's finger had been. Everand smiled. 'There is only one, created by the tears of the red dragon four generations ago.'

Beram rested a firm hand on Everand's shoulder, his face wreathed in a smile. 'When I volunteered to go to the Guild to ask for help fifteen suns ago, which feels like a lifetime, I had no idea I would make a friend like you … no idea we'd become part of history!'

Mookaite kissed Beram's cheek. 'None of us did. Not even our undercover mage here.' She nudged Everand, her face serious. 'Go to her. You need to finish this mission for once and for all — so you can be together.'

His heart twisting painfully, Everand looked over their heads to see Lamiya disentangling herself from her exuberant paddlers. She was coming. To him. He drank in her smooth, graceful movement, lush mahogany hair gleaming in the sunlight, the threads of caramel and blue glinting, her grey-blue eyes locked on his face. Tucking the Staropal under an arm, he held the other arm open, his heart singing when she glided into his one-armed embrace. Kissing her hair, he breathed in the scents of grasses and wildflowers.

Leaning back, she tipped her face up. 'The paddlers are safe so we can go, but we need to return in two suns for negotiations with Riverwood.' She pressed a finger to his lips. 'I'll tell you more after we've seen Akachi. Let's finish this.'

Bending down, he brushed her nose with his lips. 'Agreed, my love.'

'Go,' said Mookaite. 'Beram and I will organise the paddle home. See you soon.' She gave him a push and Beram flapped a hand.

Everand pulled Lamiya a few paces away from them. 'Put both hands on my waist.' He gripped the Staropal firmly against his chest, waiting until Lamiya had grasped his tunic on both sides of his waist.

'Think of that flat spot on the shore by the tree with the red flowers, near the hills,' said Lamiya. 'Akachi will come there, where she bound us to this task.'

The back of Everand's right hand itched at the memory of the massive dragon taking it into her mouth and biting down. He expanded the memory to include the turquoise lake stretching to a distant shore shrouded in haze, the green hills rising to the east, and a few paces away loomed the distinctive, shapely tree adorned with vibrant red flowers. He focused on the water and the sense of a pond within the lake filled by deep, elemental magical water … the familiar chill mists of translocation swirled around them.

Goosebumps lingering on his arms, Everand eased out a breath. He was facing the mounded green hills and the glittering lake, rays of sunlight skipping over the tiny ripples hustled up by a gentle breeze. Lamiya shivered and let go of his tunic. A shoal of fish flashed by close to the surface and the last one, a beautiful silver fish with red splotches, jumped out of the water and flapped her gauzy tail before disappearing in a fountain of silver droplets. Everand blinked. Mizu? Had his fish just greeted him?

'See?' said Lamiya. 'Your fish is free and has friends but she still remembers you. One more good thing you achieved, my love.' She snuck a kiss onto his lips and hugged him. 'We'd better prepare for our greatest task.' Peering into his eyes, she blew at a random wisp of hair trying to crawl into her mouth and said, 'You might be confident but I am nervous … Akachi is so …'

'Imperious? Massive? Fearsome?' Everand's stiff lips failed to deliver a smile. 'What could possibly go wrong?'

'Don't even say that!' gasped Lamiya. 'We've been tested enough!'

Gathering her close, Everand planted kisses along the top of her head. 'I too am ready for this mission to end. It has been dramatic, exciting, inspiring, full of several boat rides too many …' His lips twitched. '… and enthusiastic paddlers who dream and talk of nothing else …' As predicted, she punched his arm. 'But best of all, it brought a mystical, gorgeous boat captain, bossy and impossible to deflect … the one aspect of this mission I can never have enough of.'

'Good recovery,' said Lamiya, her eyes bright. 'I pray the spirits are right and our reward is each other. For eternity.'

Everand leaned down to kiss her soundly, but quickly straightened up when small waves hissed and tumbled over the shore. 'They're coming. Already.'

Facing the lake, he eyed the fast-approaching swells of water and felt hopelessly unprepared. What should he say? Surely, there were special words for this momentous occasion? Should they hand over the Staropal together or was it his role, on behalf of the Guild? Should he ask? His chest grew tight.

Lamiya pushed her hair back over her shoulders before straightening her tunic. 'Perhaps we should have cleaned up,' she mumbled. After a couple of muffled peeps, Whirr crawled out of the front of her tunic and climbed up to sit on her right shoulder.

Edging closer to Lamiya, until their shoulders brushed, Everand stood as tall as possible. Pulling the remnants of cloth from the Staropal, he dropped the singed mess behind him, grasped the magnificent stone and held it out before him. Shuffling to firm up his balance, he felt the grimy tunic clinging to his back. Why hadn't he thought to grab his azure robe? He hardly looked like a representative of the Guild! *Which you are not*, snipped his mind. *No other mage would have taken this path.*

The stone grew warm in his hands and threads of deep azure and gold circled amid the array of bright colours. Soft cloth draped over his shoulders and ruffled, tickling, down his now bare chest. He gasped at the azure silk robe that fitted him perfectly, a fine gold thread woven along the collar and sleeve cuffs. Peering at one cuff, his breath quickened. The gold thread depicted tiny, lithe river dragons dancing in a line!

Now you look the part, came the tinkling voice of the Staropal. *You are right, this event deserves full pomp and gravity.*

'Nice,' croaked Lamiya. 'I like the gold trim.' Then she yelped and Whirr fluttered off her shoulder with a squawk.

Everand gaped at Lamiya, now clad in a long, green dress the colour of the Riverplain team trousers, with a silk sash of delicate orange leaves wound around her waist and flowing down one side. A wreath of silk orange leaves and tiny red flowers appeared in her hair.

The Eminent Mage and Mystical Bird Caller are now ready, announced the Staropal, edged with a giggle. *Dragons have standards, you know. Especially imperial red ones.*

'We need an audience,' whispered Lamiya. Perched back on her shoulder, Whirr lifted his head to trill a melodic song.

A breeze eddied behind them and Everand's neck prickled as the shades of all the past Riverplain guides materialised. Above, the sky became crowded with bustling, chattering birds who swooped around them and then settled into the elegant tree. Red petals showered down to create a fragrant red pool at its base, and Lamiya gave him a radiant smile.

Drawing in courage and hope, Everand watched the swells of water slow and then break apart. Mizukaze, Hanachi and Akachi rose from the lake, water cascading down their sides and legs in a hundred coruscating, swishing waterfalls.

Akachi edged ahead and all three dragons fastened intent golden eyes upon him. Blinking rapidly to prevent his vision from blurring, Everand tipped forward in a respectful bow.

Well met, Mage Everand and Guide Lamiya of Riverplain. Akachi's massive irises glittered like a casket of a thousand gems. *I see you have fulfilled your task. Impressive, although I have waited far longer than I would have liked for you two to find each other.*

His mouth dry and gritty, Everand pushed the Staropal forward. Lamiya placed her hands under his and together they waded into the water to Akachi. The red dragon blocked the sky and light, steam hissing from flared crimson nostrils. A feeling of total insignificance washed over Everand; he was *nothing* compared to these creatures of myth and legend. A mere blot upon the landscape. Lamiya's fingers trembled beneath his; perhaps she felt this way too.

Warm air blew around him when Akachi arched her neck, scales glistening blood-red in the sunshine, and lowered her head until one enormous, faceted eye was right beside him. *Place the stone under the crook of my neck.*

Lamiya following his movement with her hands beneath his, he reached up to position the Staropal in the angled space between Akachi's throat and the base of her jaw. The stone flared a dazzling white, brighter than a falling star, almost blinding him. Akachi subtly moved her head and the Staropal released from his fingers. Lowering his hands, he waded back a few steps, Lamiya with him.

Squinting against the brilliant white light, he found words pouring from his mouth, in exact time with Lamiya's words. *Great Akachi, we return the Staropal to you, its rightful owner. May it restore your species to true glory. With your blessing, we of the river provinces wish to live in harmony with you.*

A throaty rumbling came from Akachi, and Mizukaze and Hanachi crowded closer. Bouncy waves slapped around Everand's knees and Lamiya slipped her hand into his. The three dragon heads hovered above, sunlight radiating off their burnished golden horns. A shaft of incandescent light, fractured with all the colours of a sky-arch, beamed down upon him and Lamiya.

You two are special, and together you are unique, trilled the Staropal. *You are hereby blessed. We will live in harmony and friendship with you, the Eminent Mage and the Mystical Bird and Dragon Caller.*

Everand's skin itched all over and he felt as if a thousand tiny creatures were crawling through his hair. Lamiya shivered and gripped his hand.

'Thank you, Great Akachi,' she said. 'The people of Riverplain look forward to our friendship.'

We will race the boats and beat the drums? rumbled Mizukaze, tilting his head.

'Often,' said Lamiya, with a wide smile. 'All four provinces will come to race. Soon.'

Hanachi extended her green-orange nose to touch Lamiya with unexpected gentleness. *Sister, we must speak soon about your partnering ceremony. I have an idea.*

Everand swallowed his exclamation. Sister? Partnering ceremony? Lamiya flipped him a smug look and he swallowed again.

Better get used to it, said the Staropal, tinkling with delight.

The three dragons edged away and Everand bowed. Was this it? This was all most amicable. Did the Guild not need to apologise for stealing the Staropal and concealing it?

Indeed, your Guild will apologise. And grovel. Akachi turned baleful eyes on him. *When they come for your partnering ceremony, you will bring their leader to me.*

Everand bowed so deeply he almost got water up his nose.

How was he going to tell Tiliqua?

Chapter Thirty-Four

Joy flowing through her entire being, Lamiya watched the dragons swim away with a wave of their tails. They'd done it! Fulfilled Akachi's task! She felt like mimicking Ejad, Zink and Acim and doing cartwheels, but that would look most unseemly in this gorgeous dress. Which was now wet. Everand stood spellbound, gazing at the lake with an unfathomable expression. She sighed. What was his busy mind agonising over now?

'My love?' she threaded her elbow through his and tugged. He blinked and then smiled, his eyes turning the deep azure she so adored. 'Come along, *Eminent* Mage, we have things to do.'

'Indeed,' he murmured, 'Mystical Bird and Dragon Caller. Fancy titles to live up to.'

She slid both arms around his waist. 'No, we already lived up to them! We earned the titles. Now we get to live and enjoy ourselves. Together.' She reached up and kissed his jaw.

'Maybe,' he murmured. 'In the meantime, a small crowd awaits us.'

By the stars! She'd forgotten the shades of the guides had gathered. Planting another quick kiss on his stubbly jaw, she faced the shore and endeavoured to walk elegantly from the shallow water and to not trip over the sodden dress hem.

As soon as her feet touched dry ground, the spectres of the guides glided to her and the tree with red flowers erupted into warbling birdsong. Whirr flitted away to join the flock. Her heart swelling, she watched Whirr nuzzle his fluffy body between two vividly-plumed female birds. Every single branch was packed solid with feathered, bustling bodies. *Her* flocks.

Swallowing around the lump in her throat, she held Everand's hand and bowed to the gathered shades.

We are so proud of you. U-Mali's spirit hovered before her and a brief chill kissed her forehead. *You had so little time to prepare — but look what you achieved! You bring great glory to Riverplain.*

Out of the corner of her eye, she saw the shade of U-Lumin clap Everand's shoulder and drift in close to confer with him. Her eyebrows lifted at the intent look on Everand's face, then the rosy hint that edged along his cheekbones. Was U-Lumin advising him how to be her consort?

Daughter dear, our hearts sing for you! Her mother and father shimmered before her and puffs of air patted her forearms.

So, you tamed the fearsome beasts, grunted her father.

'Not quite,' said Lamiya hastily. 'Please don't use those words! We have reached an agreement with the dragons.'

See? said Lestaya. *She is a leader already. Consider yourself admonished.*

Huh, said Azuri. *She still has to get her man to like boats.*

The shade of Lestaya rolled shadowy eyes. *Can't you see he is teasing her? Her mage admires the boats. He well understands their importance.*

Lamiya stared at her mother's shifting outline. What? Everand, her unreadable mage, was teasing her all along? She compressed her lips. Well, two could play at that game.

Lestaya patted her arm again. *Don't be too harsh, my dear. He worships you.* Her mother's wispy form leaned in. *And he is most handsome and noble, an excellent choice. We'll see you again soon, for the ceremony to instate you as Guide of Riverplain.*

The familiar ache spread across her chest when the spirits of her parents, followed by those of U-Mali and U-Lumin and the others became fainter, dissolving until she was left looking at the ornate tree packed with birds. Whirr cheeped a farewell.

'What now?' asked Everand, silhouetted with the light behind him.

Wriggling her toes in her sandals, Lamiya considered. For once, they didn't have anywhere they had to be, something they had to rush off and do. It felt strange; she felt adrift. Did he feel lost too? Was that why he was standing there, absently flexing his fingers? Oh, he was waiting for her to decide. To lead. Her province. Her people. *Him.* She gulped. For so long she had followed him …

'No, my love, you did not follow me,' he said softly. 'Only at the outset. Once we'd found Mizukaze we did everything together, and even when we were apart you did your part and I did mine.' He stepped close, coming into focus in the light, his face angled down. 'What did the Staropal say? *Together you are unique.*' He tenderly took her fingers, lifting them to gently sweep his lips across her knuckles.

Love and desire flooded her, making her legs weak. 'I could do with a brew. Let's go to my hut.'

'I like that idea. Will there be food too?' He looked so hopeful that she laughed.

'I see the Eminent Mage still has hollow legs! I'm sure I can find some food …' She tried to keep her face straight. 'If you agree to wash me.'

The water and sky tilted around her and she stood at the entry to her hut with Everand's hands around her waist. 'My, my,' she said breathlessly. 'You are hungry!'

'Perpetually,' he agreed, leaning down to kiss her.

Entwined in his arms, she stumbled backwards through her feather curtain and guided him to her mattress. He mumbled something, his lips teasing hers, and she felt his hot, bare skin against hers. By the stars! What had he done with the special clothes?

'They're on the stool,' he murmured, pushing her down until the downy mattress met her back and buttocks.

'Neat trick,' she said, relishing the touch of his long, lean body. His tongue probed into her mouth and her next quip fled. She groaned as his tongue found hers, stroking it, and his fingers began to trace circles around one nipple. Heat flaring, she shifted her legs apart, revelling in his pulsing manhood rubbing against her. Pressing her weight into her feet, she tipped her hips up and he slid inside her. She clung to him, lost in pleasure, for what seemed an age.

Finally, he lay beside her, sweat trickling down his torso, hair dank against his forehead, azure eyes lingering on her face. He looked so happy, so content, her heart wrenched and she wanted to cry. He'd changed so much. Had she really brought him this much joy?

A twinkle in his eyes, he said, 'I'd be even happier if the promised food was delivered.'

Laughing, Lamiya rolled off the mattress. She lit her hearth, put water on to boil and snatched up a cloth to rinse herself. No sooner had she lifted the cloth to her shoulder than it was tweaked from her fingers and the heat of Everand's body pressed against her back. Closing her eyes, she released a long sigh while he gently sponged her with what seemed to be a wonderfully steaming cloth. Her skin tingling, she reached for her training tunic, then paused. No, something more formal. Her gaze rested on the moonlight-coloured skirt just before Everand plucked it from the rack and handed it to her, followed by the turquoise tunic.

Dressed, she turned to find he was already clad in a pale-grey tunic above storm-grey trousers. 'Do you remember the changing area in Melanite's hut?' she asked.

'How could I forget?' he replied softly. 'My second glimpse of you. And even though I was invisible you *knew* I was hiding there, knew *exactly* where I was.' He scrubbed at his jaw. 'I couldn't believe what I was seeing.' His lips twitched. 'But I knew I was in trouble, right then.'

'Absolutely.' She wagged a finger at him. 'No-one should try to hide in a woman's change area! Not even a mighty mage.'

'That's *Eminent* Mage, thank you. One with hollow legs.' Regarding her shelf of jars and baskets, he said, 'Surely one of these contains food?'

Relenting, she handed him a plate and piled it high with food then poured them both a ginger brew. Sipping at hers, she ran her mind over the things that needed to be done. Greet the boat when it returned, call a meeting of all the people, agree when they should hold the ceremony to instate her as Guide of Riverplain. Should the partnering ceremony be at the same time or have its own ceremony? How would they invite Tiliqua and Agamid? Her next sip went down the wrong way and she coughed. Malach! She'd agreed to meet with him in Riverwood only the sun after next. What had she been thinking?

Waving a chunk of bread at her, Everand said, 'I see this affliction you call overthinking might be contagious. Need any help? From an apparent master.'

Her eyes still watering, she croaked, 'Yes. Good practice for my consort-to-be. Let's map out a proposed order of events. What? It's not meant to be funny.'

'You think we might have a say in what happens when from now on? I admire your spirit.'

Sniffing, she held her head high. 'We'd better. What's the point of being a leader of a province if–'

Everand leaned low over the table, pretending to grovel.

'Stop it,' she snarled, but her lips curved into a smile and her heart grew warm.

How was it possible Everand had evolved so far from the closed-off shell he was when he arrived? The subtle tension she hadn't realised was present eased from her shoulders.

The future seemed so bright.

CHAPTER THIRTY-FIVE

Malach strode around the clearing. The sun, already high in the sky, was warm on the back of his neck. They would arrive soon. Was everything in order? A table and two benches had been dragged closer to the firepit. The residual embers glowed muted charcoals and oranges, giving an ambient mood. It should look as if he'd gone to some trouble.

A bead of sweat trickled down his brow and he swiped it away. His people were surprised when he told them he would meet with the new leader of Riverplain to discuss forward relations. Torrap remained sceptical, but the other hunters were interested to know what Riverplain would offer, saying they'd like to participate in the boat races again. With a faster boat. Hemma had slyly asked him whether some trade might be possible.

Stopping by the table, he tipped his face up to the empty, pale blue sky and clenched his fists. Where were his eagles? Without his power, everything was subtly harder. Turning to face north, to the trees beyond the raptor cages, he reached with his mind for the one eagle that had returned. His favourite. At least his affinity with birds had proved to be an innate ability, like Lamiya's, and was not connected with his father's mage power. Perhaps other abilities would reveal themselves over time. He should experiment.

For a few disconcerting breaths he sensed nothing, then the eagle's face appeared in his mind. It cocked its head in query. *Go to the cages and tell me when the mage and woman arrive.* The eagle blinked, dipped its beak and vanished.

The tantalising smell of roasting vegetables wafted under his nostrils. Good, Hemma and the women were preparing the high-sun meal. He flexed his fingers, so tempted to serve roasted small birds as well and watch the horror rise on Lamiya's face. His father would approve but it would be a petty action. He grunted. Perhaps Everand's persistent polite manners had rubbed off somewhat. *Everand* … did he want to be friends with him? Could he? A burning sting crossed his chest: how dare Everand remove his power without consent. He, of all people, knew how much his power meant to him! *You must live to lead your people. I give you this chance.* Curse it, he could still hear Everand's words bouncing around in his head.

A shrill cry echoed from the woods near the raptor cages. Malach unclenched his fingers. They were here. A sour taste filled his mouth. Get this over with and see what emerges. The boatwoman was arrogant and annoying, but admittedly she was clever. And fair. Like Everand. He should at least listen to what they proposed.

Footfalls sounded and his eyebrows quirked when Lamiya strode from behind the closest cabin with Everand and Lazuli flanking her — and Torrap and Tiek following. So much for his hunters escorting her! So, she was indeed determined to lead. He felt a pang of pity for Everand, demoted from mage to consort — but *he* still had his power. His jaw clenched.

He waited until Lamiya stopped a few paces away before saying, 'Welcome to Riverwood.'

Lamiya nodded respectfully, elegantly clad in a long green skirt and a flowing orange top with a neat braid coiled around her head. Lazuli was wearing the Riverplain team colours too and Everand wore his usual azure robe. Malach rubbed at the stubbly regrowth on his chin, wishing his beard would grow faster. Shaving it off as part of his disguise hadn't helped at all in the end.

'Take a seat.' Malach indicated the bench on the near side of the table so he could take the far side and retain a clear view across the meeting space. Lamiya sat and slid to the middle, leaving Everand and Lazuli to perch on either side of her. She looked composed and serious; Everand and Lazuli looked wary. Why was the pacer here?

Malach chose the middle seat and Torrap slid onto the bench beside him, opposite Everand. Tiek hovered until he motioned for him to sit opposite Lazuli to balance the table. As soon as they were all seated, Hemma and Fenchi appeared, carrying trays. Hemma circled the table placing four plates and forks down, while Fenchi put four mugs on the table then hovered uncertainly with the jug of spiced wine.

'Put the jug down and fetch two more mugs and plates,' said Malach.

Understanding his presence wasn't anticipated, Lazuli shifted uncomfortably and opened his mouth but Lamiya elbowed him to silence.

'Let's eat,' said Malach. 'Then you can tell me what you propose.'

An awkward pause ensued until the two women returned with the extra plates and mugs and Hemma circled again, using a long-handled ladle to place an assortment of char-baked vegetables on each plate, surreptitiously observing the visitors. Fenchi poured the dark wine into each mug, lingering when she poured his mug, her ample breasts swelling pleasantly above the neckline of her top. Amused, he saw Lazuli trying hard not to look. Fenchi was indeed skilled at deploying her curves … perhaps he'd invite her to his cabin at dark-fall. A celebration if things went well.

When the women straightened up, Malach nodded brusquely.

Lamiya arched an eyebrow at him, then looking at the women said, 'Thank you. I am Lamiya, this is Everand and Lazuli. What are your names?'

'Hemma,' responded Hemma, with a short smile, casting Malach a smug look.

Fenchi slid her eyes to Malach seeking permission to answer, and at his subtle nod she replied, 'Fenchi.'

'Thank you, Hemma and Fenchi,' said Lamiya with a brief smile.

'You may go,' said Malach, flapping a hand. Lamiya's eyes narrowed, presumably at his dismissal of the women, but Everand reached under the table and patted her leg, warning her not to say anything. Malach gave her a challenging look. His province; his customs.

Hemma and Fenchi walked away in tandem. Everand averted his gaze from the way Fenchi's hips swayed. Lazuli did not and Lamiya elbowed him in the ribs again.

Malach speared a potato with his fork. 'Eat, and tell me about your new boat.'

Everand gave him an incredulous look: *You want to talk about the new boat?* Then he reached for his mug, took a sip and swallowed with a gulp, his throat bulging as he struggled not to cough. Lamiya picked up her mug, wrinkled her nose and put it back down. Lazuli lifted his mug to take a good pull, then thunked it down, spluttering. Lamiya patted him on the back. Malach burst out laughing, Torrap laughing with him and Tiek looking down at his plate to hide his smile.

'Not a hunter yet, Lazuli,' Malach said, waving his mug at the pacer. 'This is what we drink before we race.'

Lazuli gasped, then replied, 'Hah! We don't need it. We bring our own inner fire.'

Malach laughed again. The pacer had spirit and a quick mind; no wonder Lamiya had brought him along. He looked at her and she gave him an amused, somehow superior, smile.

Everand spoke. 'To answer your question, the new boat progresses well. Lapsi and Lepid have finished the design and they are beginning to carve out the … shape.'

'Hull,' corrected Lazuli. Waving his hands animatedly, he added, 'Akachi will be similar to the boat Mizuchi, with a slightly broader base and a longer head and tail. And she will be red and gold.'

Malach grunted. 'I see. Riverwood will build a new boat too. Lighter and faster.'

'Does this mean you'll come to our races?' blurted Lazuli, ignoring Lamiya's nudge to his ribs.

Transferring his gaze to Lamiya, Malach said, 'If we reach agreement, yes, we will come.' He tilted forward. 'And we will be stronger and faster.'

'Excellent,' said Lamiya, looking him in the eye. 'Fast, hard-fought races are the best ones.' She carefully put down her fork. 'What specific things would you like to discuss?'

Malach drank the rest of his wine, put his mug down and turned it around a few times while he thought. He and Torrap had discussed taking a slow introduction, a cautious approach in mind. Deciding to adhere to this tactic, he addressed Lamiya. 'We weren't present at the trade discussions so perhaps you could outline what was agreed between the three provinces.'

Her eyes narrowed and her lips compressed, no doubt recalling her kidnap by his pacers. Squaring her shoulders, she said, 'Fair enough.' To Everand, she said, 'You'll record the discussion from here?'

Everand placed his cupped hands on the table and murmured low words until a clear ball appeared between his palms. 'This is a memory ball. It will show us speaking and record the words. I will make a copy so you and Lamiya both have one.'

Fighting the rush of irritation that he would never be able to work this magic, Malach said, 'Agreed. Continue.'

Lamiya composed herself and spoke evenly. 'Riverfall, Riverplain and Riversea all agreed to interact and trade with each other regularly. We decided to take it in turns to host a sun of boat races followed by a sun of trading and discussions between our leaders. These will be held at the end of every second season, with the host province changing. We agreed to host in the order of from north to south so Riverplain is next, followed by Riversea.'

Malach tapped his fingers on the table when she paused. This meant Riverwood would not need to be the host for a further six seasons. *If* they agreed to be a host. Did he want others visiting their terrain and influencing his people? He repressed a shudder.

'And,' said Lamiya, waiting until he looked at her squarely, 'we further agreed that Riverwood would be welcome to join us whenever you wished to be a good neighbour.'

A *good* neighbour? What did she mean by that? Malach felt the back of his neck stiffen and beside him, Torrap sat up straighter.

'May I?' said Lazuli with a disarming smile and not waiting for Lamiya to respond. 'For the boat races, we agreed to appoint an organiser — that's me for the Riverplain races — who would provide an advance list of the races to be held to the other provinces so all teams could train fairly.'

'We also agreed,' said Lamiya, racing on and giving him no time to ask what a *good* neighbour was, 'that each province would provide a list of the range of wares they'd bring to trade. Each province will determine its own prices and bring people to manage their stalls. The host will provide the trading place, tables, stalls and benches. The host will also provide a welcome feast and a celebration after the boat races.'

'Sounds fair,' grunted Malach. None of this was unexpected. But what did she mean by a good neighbour? Was this a way for the other provinces to turn on Riverwood with some arbitrary decision about them not exhibiting *good* behaviour? Did all the provinces have to show this good behaviour? Who defined what it was? His gaze slid to Everand, who was watching him intently.

Everand cleared his throat. 'In the spirit of cooperation and friendship, the races and trade are based on the idea that the provinces will respect each other's values and customs and not interfere with one another, and will support each other should the need arise.'

Such as the mages interfering again? Malach bit down the retort. So, this was what they meant by a *good* neighbour. Riverwood was closest to Axis, as Everand had so readily pointed out, and Riverwood lands covered most of the northern coastline. Would this agreement oblige him to protect them too? Given their weaknesses, this was not a surprise. Even without his power he and his hunters would do a better job.

Lamiya gave him a disconcertingly astute look. 'This principle works all ways. This means the other provinces must respect and value the Riverwood customs too.'

'Is this principle defined in the agreement?' asked Malach.

The sides of Lamiya's neck took on a pale pink hue and she looked searchingly into his face. 'Actually, I don't think it is. It is implied … but we could add it as a guiding principle at the beginning if you think this is important. Atage holds the original agreement.'

Malach refilled his mug while he thought, then passed the jug to Tiek to offer more wine around the table. He took a sip, noticing that everyone except Lazuli declined the wine. Allowing the spicy bite to sear his taste buds, he told his mind to focus. The two-way respect would be welcome … visitors less so. Lamiya had granted a concession by offering to define the principle, which would protect his province better. Could they agree to participate but not be a host? Torrap gave him a subtle nod, indicating he thought it opportune to table this compromise. Malach took a large swig of wine, swilled it around his mouth, swallowed and put the mug down.

To Lamiya he said slowly, 'The agreement is fair. The mutual respect is important and I prefer it is stated clearly at the outset. Ask Atage to add it.' Part of his mind gave a silent shriek. *What are you saying? What are you thinking? Can you ever respect these people?*

Everyone sat very still, all focused on his face. 'I propose a two-step approach to Riverwood's participation.' He noted the way Everand's fingers gripped the memory ball more tightly and the slight drawing down of the blond eyebrows. Lamiya's eyes widened fractionally.

'Riverwood agrees to participate in the Riverplain boat races and trade festival and then we propose a further discussion. At that time, we will determine whether Riverwood wishes to participate further.' He sat back and placed his hands flat on the table. This was a good test of the depth of their offer and whether they were indeed prepared to respect Riverwood's values, including that of isolation.

Lamiya tossed her head, even though the braid already kept her hair away from her face, and gave him a serious look. 'We will be pleased to welcome you to Riverplain.' She drummed her fingers on the tabletop and her tunic bulged as her small bird poked its head out of her tunic neck. 'Can I propose you agree to participate in both the Riverplain *and* the Riversea hosted races and trade? They might be quite different experiences and this would give *all* parties time to become comfortable.'

Malach's heartrate sped up. This was like being in a boat race with looming choppy currents and Lamiya's boat crowding his into them. What to do? Should he insist on one festival only? Take a firm stand or appear to compromise? Torrap and Tiek both sat stiffly, their faces neutral. Everand dipped his head imperceptibly, encouraging him to agree. What did Lazuli think? The pacer looked hopeful and flashed him a smile.

'I can't wait to see Riversea,' said Lazuli. 'Imagine racing in the waves of a sea! That will be a real test of skill and courage.'

Remembering the way the Riversea boat had ploughed up the massive wave created by Mizukaze at the end of the long race in Riverfall — with the paddlers *laughing* and *singing* — Malach felt a stir of interest. His respect for Lazuli rose a notch; the pacer had given him a way to accept Lamiya's counter offer without losing face.

'Will you challenge me on the sea?' The blue flecks in Lamiya's eyes were dancing, daring him.

Pride gushing through him, Malach smashed his fist down on the table. 'I accept your challenge. Riverwood agrees to participate in the Riversea races as well.'

'Ki!' shouted Torrap and Tiek together, indicating their support.

With a quick glance at the memory ball cupped in Everand's hands, Malach said loudly, 'Let the records show that Riverwood agrees to participate in the races in Riverplain *and* Riversea. At their conclusion, we will decide whether to commit further. Let the records also show that Riverwood reserves the right not to be a host.' He sat up. There. What would they do now?

'Participate in the races *and* trade for the next two festivals? For clarification?' asked Everand.

Malach flapped a hand. 'Races and trade.' They could put more effort into the races and take token wares to trade.

'You don't wish to be a host?' asked Lamiya. 'May I ask why not?'

His good humour fading, Malach tried to keep his dislike for her forthrightness from showing, and considered how to answer without undoing the agreement so far. He spread his hands. 'My people have lived in isolation since we arrived here in my great-grandfather's lifetime. I must give them time to adjust.'

The disappointment remained on Lamiya's face and Lazuli gave him a sad look.

Torrap leaned in to whisper, 'Give them a little more.'

Malach clasped his hands together on the table. 'After the Riversea festival, I will put the option to host the next races and trade to my people and let you know Riverwood's decision within three suns.' He held the assessing look Lamiya gave him, waiting her out. No-one else moved or spoke. She said the principle works all ways. Fine words. Let's see if she means them.

Lamiya's sudden smile was like the sun coming out from behind a cloud, and she reached across the table to shake one of his hands. Her grip was firm, decisive. 'On behalf of Riverplain, and I think I can speak for the other provinces too, I accept your terms. You are right, we must respect your people's values too.'

When she stood up Malach hurriedly did too. Cursed woman, it wasn't her role to indicate the discussion was ended! He still felt as if he were gliding a boat through choppy currents, despite the agreement they had reached. In hindsight, he liked negotiating with Everand better, as slippery as the mage was! At least he knew Everand listened to and evaluated what he said; with Lamiya he wasn't so sure. The boatwoman was determined and difficult to deflect. He stood straighter. Perhaps this made it more important that he, as leader of Riverwood, participated. She'd run rings around Atage in Riverfall, and Chiton and Conch in Riversea could be beguiled by her too.

Looking down at Lamiya with the advantage of his height, he said, 'If Everand has everything required for the formal records, I'll introduce you properly to our boat team.' He turned to Tiek. 'Gather the paddlers and bring them.' The young man hurried away and everyone hovered, unsure whether to sit. To Torrap he said, 'Ask Hemma to bring fruit and water, enough for the whole team.'

Torrap grunted and strode away.

Malach sat and waved a hand for them to sit too.

Lamiya arranged her skirt tidily, then sat. 'I'm glad we reached agreement,' she said frankly. 'Although we've had our differences, it will be good for the four provinces to be friends.' She put her elbows on the table. 'So much has happened so fast, and we don't know how events may unfold from here.'

Squashing his instinctive response to reply with a grunt, Malach said, 'True.' He looked at Everand. 'What do you think will happen? Will the mages come again?'

Everand gave him that sincere look that always irked him. 'We, I mean Riverplain, will invite the mages to attend the ceremony to instate Lamiya as Guide of Riverplain. I hope they will come in friendship.'

'Does the woman mage lead?' asked Malach. A bud of hope blossomed. What if he could befriend that stunning woman mage? What could he negotiate for … down the track?

'I assume so, but I don't know for certain.' Everand regarded him steadily and began to drum his fingers on the table. 'You did everyone a favour by dealing with Pelamis. We healed Mage Mantiss, but I think Tiliqua will still have been voted in as Head of the Guild.'

For a moment Malach couldn't breathe. Was that Everand's way of thanking him for killing Pelamis? Everand was looking at him with that ever-so-serious face, as if he wanted to say more. 'Speak.' That came out as a croak.

'While the others are not here … I hope you can come to forgive me for taking your powers.' Everand paused and Lamiya reached out to place a hand over his, encouraging him. 'I couldn't see any other way and despite everything, I wanted you to live. I owed it to Mage Beetal to protect you, once I knew who you were.'

Malach closed his eyes, feeling as if he were tumbling down that waterfall, arms and legs flailing, heart shrieking with despair, towards the jagged rocks waiting below all over again. His skull, back and ribs prickled with echoes of the agony he'd endured. These very three people had killed him but brought him back to life. With conditions. And now they sat at his table wanting him to forgive them? Go forward as if none of this had happened? Be *friends*? His father would be appalled. Or would he? He brought his father's face to mind, silently asking.

His father's dark eyes glittered and the black beard bristled as usual. *I have failed you*, thought Malach. *I can never be a mage now. I can't change your Guild. I can't avenge you.* His chest tightened.

'Malach?' said Everand softly. 'You did change the Guild. We did it together. No, I'm not reading your mind, I can see the despair and bitterness on your face. I can imagine what you are thinking.'

Keeping his eyes firmly closed, Malach let Everand's ever-so-annoyingly-sincere voice wash over him.

'You lead your people in a time of change. The mages will come, and we will influence them to change their ways.' Everand's words wavered. 'You pushed me. Without your actions things would not be as they are now, with new possibilities opening for us all. Including the Guild. You are a strong leader. You can still make Mage Beetal proud of you.'

In his mind's eye, Mage Beetal patted his shoulder. *My apprentice was always teeth-gratingly annoying, but on occasion he was also irritatingly right.* His father's image sighed. *Perhaps I should have listened to him, on occasion, as you have done.* The image grew fuzzy, then vanished.

His chest hollow, Malach sat feeling the breath entering and leaving his body, becoming aware of the pine trees rustling in a faint breeze. Were the others still there? He assumed so. They were silent, waiting, granting him space. Everand's words were true, he *had* altered events from the moment his team had arrived at the Riverfall boat races. He and Everand had clashed, over and over, but change had slowly been wrought. And they were all still here.

He became aware of the chatter of his paddlers approaching, heard Torrap telling them to hurry. They would look forward to the races. Perhaps he could beat Lamiya's skill and team next time, with a new boat and proper training.

Could he work with Everand and the pesky Lamiya to persuade the Guild to make further changes? Wait. What if Lamiya and Everand produced a *child*? His heart skipped and bounded. The Guild Law would *have* to be changed to allow half-mages! Yes, he should work with Everand, prove his worth, become known to Tiliqua, succeed in bringing about change where his father had failed.

He became aware of the warm sunlight caressing his face. Opening his eyes, he stared deep into Everand's azure ones and smiled.

This time, from his heart.

Chapter Thirty-Six

Lamiya stared into the almost darkness. Tendrils of silver light caressed the edges of the door curtain feathers. Sun-up was nigh. She flexed her feet a few times to dispel the restless energy in her legs. Perched beside her head, Whirr gave a soft peep. Was Everand awake? A shiver zig-zagged down her spine; by dark-fall she would formally be the Guide of Riverplain, the cloak of responsibility for her province and all her people resting snugly on her shoulders.

Warm, soft lips brushed her bare shoulder. 'You're awake already?' murmured Everand.

Twisting, she kissed him gently. 'I think I'll go to the lake.'

'The lake?' He sounded surprised. 'To watch the sun rise? I'll come too.'

Gladness washing through her, she sat up and fumbled for her clothes, hearing the blanket rustle with his movements. Whirr chirped happily, pecking at the edge of her tunic. She pulled the tunic from his beak, slipped it on, followed by her trousers, and rummaged for her sandals. Carrying these, she went outside. She'd barely finished lacing her sandals when Everand loomed out of the gloom and wordlessly took her hand, his grip firm and reassuring.

The water glimmered with hints of silver and translucent blue, like looking down into a starry sky, and absolute quiet wrapped around them. The trees huddled along the lakeshore, the branches mutely reaching for the pending light and warmth. Lamiya stopped at the water's edge and peered across the expanse of lake to the boat dome, shrouded in hazy gloom waiting for the sun. Restless energy coursed through her legs and arms, but there was no time for training.

'No boat this sun,' said Everand, as if he'd read her mind. 'The whole team will be twitching by the feast.' He squeezed her hand. 'I'm sure you can drive them harder next sun to make up for it.' When she didn't react, he slipped an arm around her shoulders and gently turned her to face him. 'Nervous?'

'I thought I was ready, but now I worry,' she chewed at her lower lip, her stomach rolling as if she were riding choppy waters. 'I know we agreed we should wait until the boat races to have the partnering ceremony and instate you as my consort, but I feel so … responsible. For everything and everyone.'

'I am here with you for every step, my love.' Everand kissed her forehead. 'And dynamic, determined boat captain and glide that you are, you'll be a wonderful Guide of Riverplain.' He kissed her forehead again, pale light contouring his cheekbones and putting glints in his eyes. 'Your people love and respect you; they will follow you anywhere.'

'*That's* what I'm afraid of,' muttered Lamiya, her forehead tightening. 'They will follow whether I make wise choices or not.'

'So far, your choices have been seriously wise. The dragons like and respect you, and you've even persuaded Riverwood to participate in the races and trade discussions!' He squeezed her shoulder. 'As for your choice of consort … what can I say? Who else could snare a mage from Axis?'

Her lips crinkled into a smile, warmth filling her. 'I was fortunate to find the one that was different from the rest.'

'True,' said Everand, feigning modesty. 'What do you want me to do before the ceremony?'

Lamiya slid her arms around his waist. 'Keep me company until I have to get ready. Let's go and see how far Lepid and Lapsi have got with the new boat.' She tilted her head. 'Thinking of boats, we need to plan for and invite the other provinces to our boat races and trade. This is the last sun of planting season, then sixty suns for growing season … so the races should be in sixty suns, meaning the trade and leader discussions will be in sixty-one suns.'

She studied Everand's face in the growing light, loving the set of his jaw and the high-planed cheekbones. 'Do we hold our partnering ceremony on the same sun as the trade and discussions or is that too much?'

He reached up to play with a strand of hair that had fallen in front of her shoulder. 'I think the same sun, if you're happy with a ceremony in the golden light leading to a feast at dark-fall. Everyone will be here and three feasts in a row …' A shudder rippled across his shoulders. 'Could be a bit much. Let's make the second feast one to remember.'

Standing on tiptoes, she kissed him. 'Sixty-one suns it is, consort-to-be.' Dropping down, she added, 'I'm glad the spirits of the guides said my ceremony should be for Riverplain alone. As much as I love seeing our friends from Riverfall, the spirits are right. This sun is for me and my people.'

'See?' Everand said with a crooked smile. 'Another wise decision.' His smile faded. 'Are you sure I can be present?'

Her heart ached at the fleeting anxiety in his face. 'Yes, my love. Riverplain is your home now.' Her lips twitched. 'You are one of *my* people. Never forget that!'

Everand bowed with an exaggerated flourish.

☪

'May I enter?' called Lulite from the doorway.

It was time already? Her mouth running dry, Lamiya said, 'Of course!'

Everand retrieved his azure robe from the clothes rack and gave her a brief peck on the cheek. 'See you at the Meeting Place.'

As soon as he'd exited, Lulite came in, the magnificent green silk dress with the orange silk belt and trail hung neatly over her arm. 'I washed it and pressed it straight.' Lulite's face creased in a broad smile. 'I hope the spirits will appreciate this.'

'Brew?' asked Lamiya, standing.

'Please,' said Lulite, carefully draping the dress over the top of the clothes rack.

'Let me look at you.' Lamiya eyed Lulite's belly and the small swell forming there. 'How's the queasiness?'

'Tiresome.' Lulite smoothed her hands down her moss-green skirt. 'I'm deeply honoured you asked me to be your escort.'

'Who better, dear friend?' A sharp pang of loss rocketed through Lamiya. *Mother should be here. And Father.* She released her clenched grip on Lulite's mug and handed it to her then sat, preparing to be patient while her hair was braided and adorned.

Whirr flew through the door curtain with something red dangling from his beak. Eyes bright, he landed on the table with a screech of talons, dropped his parcel in front of her and preened his chest feathers. Astonished, Lamiya blinked at the three, large red flowers on stems. These were from the tree near Akachi's' favourite spot in the lake! Where she'd first met the dragon. Picking one up, Whirr fluttered up to hover above her head and plopped it onto her hair.

'He wants me to weave these into the braid!' exclaimed Lulite.

Lamiya swallowed a knot of emotion. Was this Akachi's idea? Were the flowers intended to be a symbol of their friendship? Certainty swept through her. 'Can you place one in the centre at the front, then one to each side in a kind of crest?'

'Yes, that will work. I'll put the wreath of smaller, silk flowers behind them so they're prominent.'

Lamiya's mind drifted while Lulite's deft fingers worked on her hair. Snippets of her planned words wafted in and out and she sifted them into what felt like a logical order. Her people would be pleased and supportive, but they'd also expect an indication of leadership, some directions for the immediate future — especially given the traumatic events leading to her early rise to the role.

'Done.' Lulite's hands rested on her shoulders. 'Dress and rinse your mouth. Lazuli is no doubt on his way with the cart.'

She'd barely donned the dress and refreshed her mouth and face when she heard the clop of approaching hooves. Taking a deep breath, she lifted the hem of the dress and headed to the door with Lulite following. Outside, she stopped dead, her mouth dropping open. Both the cart and the two hopeepa were draped in multiple wreaths of orange flowers and cascading trails of green leaves.

From the driver's seat Lazuli gave her a lopsided grin, looking particularly pleased with himself. 'Like it?'

'Love it!' she breathed, laughing when the nearest hopeepa swung its head her way and the wreath around its horn slipped over an eye. The creature bellowed and tossed its head, somehow landing the wreath back where it was supposed to be.

'An auspicious omen,' declared Lazuli, flicking the reins. 'Crystal, behave. No licking the face of either our illustrious guide or the consort-to-be.'

Trust Lazuli to defuse her tension. Lamiya climbed up onto the seat beside him and Lulite gingerly climbed up on his other side.

'You look magnificent,' said Lazuli, admiration radiating from his grey eyes.

Words failing her, Lamiya cast her gaze over the tranquil turquoise lake, the vibrant bushes and trees along the foreshore, the sun rising to its highest point and hovering above the Meeting Place that stood so proudly upon the crest of the slope ahead. The heart of her land, her people.

While the hopeepa clopped sedately along the track following the lake's edge, Lazuli kept casting her sideways looks, but remained uncharacteristically silent. Glad to be left with her thoughts, Lamiya focused on the Meeting Place. The stone steps and elegantly carved gateway with its intricate symbols representing their lifestyle, their beliefs, and all those that had been guides before her, loomed closer and higher.

People were gathering in curved rows to either side of the steps, and the boat team in their vivid orange-and-green uniform was hurrying to form ranks of honour. A knot formed in her throat and her eyes grew warm. She gulped, and Lazuli put the reins in one hand and patted her knee. Blinking, she held back her tangled emotions while he expertly guided the cart to the end of the neat ranks of honour, her team's paddles forming an arched path to the base of the steps. Lepid's wife hurried to take the reins and Lazuli scrambled down and jogged to his place at the head of the team, deftly catching the paddle that Larimar threw to him.

Lulite came to her side and carefully picked up the back of her dress so the hem wouldn't trail. Lamiya waited for Lazuli's hint of a smile then walked under the arch as smoothly and elegantly as she could muster. Pride and joy threatening to overwhelm her, she nodded to each fit, strong and ever so dear paddler in turn — Lazuli and Larimar, her trusted pacers — Laza and Lopa, her quick second row — Levog and Lattic the burly, strong middle of the boat — Lepid and Lapsi, more strength and power — Luvu and Latog! Her heart soared to see Latog standing in position with a wooden cane in one hand and the other hand determinedly raising his paddle.

'Yo,' the team said respectfully when she cleared the final pair of arched paddles.

Her legs wavered on seeing Everand in his azure robe, his spun-starlight hair bound back with a matching thong, and such love and pride reflecting in his deep-blue eyes. He dipped his head and she had to persuade her legs to keep moving her to the first stone step rather than run her into his arms. Lulite's faint sigh of relief reached her ears.

The rows and rows of people clasped their hands before their chests and bowed, casting her warm smiles. So many familiar and dear faces. All counting on her. Her heart thudded against her breastbone.

Lifting the front of her dress, she ascended the steps, the rising breeze sending a shiver across her nape. The spirits were coming. Finally reaching the top step, she gladly used Lulite's offered elbow for support while she unlaced her sandals and put them on the shelf. Turning to the bowls of pure water, she picked up the long-handle ladle. The tinkling water sent a rush of anticipation through her. Was it her imagination or was there more water than usual flowing from the top bowl?

While she trickled water across her left hand, she lifted her eyes to stare across the expanse of shimmering turquoise lake with coruscating beams of golden light. The water running over her hand was searing cold, sharp, refreshing, enhancing her senses. A current moved in the lake centre, creating a path of darker water amid the golden tints — heading towards the Meeting Place. A shroud of cold encased her, inciting goosebumps along her arms. She trickled water over her right hand, the guiding hand, and her entire body went so cold she gasped. The hairs on the back of her neck lifted at the presence of the spirit crowd gathering behind her. Before her, the approaching current gained height to become a distinct wave.

Her people murmured and shuffled when Akachi's red-and-gold head breached the wave, followed by Mizukaze's blue-and-gold head and Hanachi's green-and-orange one. Putting the ladle down, Lamiya pressed her hands together in front of her chest and bowed deeply to the three dragons. Below, Lazuli turned to face the lake, the entire team following him and bowing in one fluid movement. A thrill raced through her as *all* of her people — every single one, from knee-high to stooped with age — acknowledged the dragons. She felt humbled, unworthy.

Steam wafting from her nostrils, Akachi dipped her nose. *Greetings, Lamiya of Riverplain. We come to celebrate with you.*

Overcome, Lamiya bowed again, hoping the dragon would understand her failure to respond. A shiver travelled down her legs. It was time. Straightening up, she nodded to Lulite to say she could go, then slowly turned to face the gathered spirits. Tears prickling the backs of her eyes, she nodded respectfully to U-Mali and U-Lumin, Lestaya and Azuri, her beloved mother and father, U-Hyalite and U-Lode, U-Molda and U-Geode and, finally, the founding guides Aura and Spinel. Each wrinkled, wise face gave her a bird-like nod and a warm smile. Lamiya blinked away her tears; she must hold strong. The shades of U-Mali and U-Lumin glided forward.

Lamiya, dear heart, U-Mali's voice sounded in her head. *U-Lumin and I will anoint you as our successor. Move to the front of the matting so we will be seen and heard by the people.*

The chill dissipating from her body, Lamiya moved to the rim of the matting and gazed out over the lake and people. The spirits of U-Mali and U-Lumin, now a little more solid, came to stand on either side of her. Quickly running her tongue over her lips and forcing moisture into her mouth, Lamiya glanced down. Everand stepped up onto the bottom step and cast a brief look at U-Mali. So, he was preparing to project their words. What would happen next? If only she'd thought to ask her mother what the ceremony to anoint U-Mali was like! Would the words she'd prepared be suitable? Too late now.

U-Mali's spirit raised her arms high above her head, an elegant bright blue feather materialising in each hand. Her words rang out as clearly as if she stood there still alive. 'People of Riverplain, we gather this sun to anoint Lamiya, daughter to Lestaya and Azuri, as the Guide of Riverplain. Lamiya will guide you well. She is strong in heart and spirit.'

Lamiya focused on U-Mali, acutely aware of so many upturned faces filled with hope and joy watching and hanging on to every word, every action. Breathing in, she fought to steady her racing heartbeat, so wishing that Everand stood with her. *Be calm, be strong. You were born for this, my love.* She imagined his gentle but firm words, knowing he would not presume to project to her during this, her time, her ceremony. Her heartrate steadied.

U-Mali faced her and held her right hand high, a vivid sky-blue feather catching the light. A jolt ran through Lamiya. Surely that was the feather U-Mali had worn hanging down beside her face for as long as she could remember?

'I bestow upon Lamiya the blue feather of ancient wisdom.' The shade's fingers tickled as UMali reached over and tucked the feather into her braid, just below the red flower on the right side.

Brimming with wonder, Lamiya allowed the words that flowed from her very core to spill from her lips. 'I thank you, U-Mali, departing Guide of Riverplain. I will do my best to serve and guide our people with the wisdom of all the previous guides, to always make choices with the best interests of the people in my mind and heart.' Her words echoed uncannily across the water, carried by a breeze that ruffled the surface.

U-Mali lifted her left arm, a second sky-blue feather in her fist, then stepped close to place this feather in Lamiya's braid, just below the red flower on the left side of her head. 'I bestow upon Lamiya the blue feather of love and compassion.'

Her heartbeat resounding against her ribcage, Lamiya said passionately, 'I thank you, U-Mali, departing Guide of Riverplain. I will do my utmost to care for our people with compassion and nothing but love in my heart. I will cherish each and every person with my heart and soul and always act to protect, nourish and love them.' Energy coursed through her body, and all of her limbs tingled.

U-Mali and U-Lumin stood by her shoulders and lifted their arms. The sky was blotted out by flittering, fluttering bodies as the entire flock of birds, every colour of the sky-arch after fresh rain, swooped towards the Meeting Place and flooded in under the roof to perch on every rafter. The chattering and chirping drowned out all other sound.

'Hush now,' commanded U-Mali and silence fell.

Lamiya's heart galloped when U-Mali and U-Lumin closed in beside her and wispy, ethereal yet somehow firm fingers pinched hers and both of her hands were lifted with theirs.

U-Mali's words bounced into the air: 'People of Riverplain, we give to you U-Lamiya, Guide of Riverplain. Strong of heart and mind, she will be a guide to remember for all eternity. Welcome her and always follow her wisdom and words.'

'Yo!' Her team rattled their paddles and shouted their team cry, joined by every man, woman and child present until Lamiya's ears were ringing.

A massive roar rent the air and the three dragons reared up, jaws open, spitting flames of fire and guttural words that everyone could understand: 'Welcome, U-Lamiya, Guide of Riverplain, Bird Caller and friend of dragons.'

Lamiya bowed low, pulling U-Mali and U-Lumin's hands and arms down with her.

'Nice touch from your mage,' whispered U-Mali.

U-Lumin grunted. 'I'm glad I'm not the consort following *your* consort-to-be. Such massive shoes to fill.'

Lamiya giggled. Then snapped her lips closed. Seriously? The Guide should not giggle.

'You may giggle as much as you like, dear heart,' murmured U-Mali. 'The people will love you even more for it.' The shade hugged her. 'The spirits will leave you now. Bid us farewell, but know that we are watching over you and will come whenever you need us.'

Her heart aching, Lamiya said, 'Wait, I must farewell the dragons first. Stand with me in recognition of our renewed friendship.' She took a step so she teetered on the edge of the floor, pleased to see Everand watching her, anticipating a request. She mouthed, *My love, we need to honour the dragons' presence and release them.* He nodded and flexed his fingers.

Raising both arms high, Lamiya threw her words as far as she could. 'Great Akachi, beloved Mizukaze and Hanachi, I thank you for attending the ceremony. As Guide of Riverplain, I am honoured and overjoyed by our friendship. We of Riverplain look forward to working with you — and racing you in our boats!'

The birds in the rafters burst into full song and red, blue and yellow-gold petals showered onto the water around the dragons. A massive gasp erupted from her people as ghostly images of a blue-and-gold boat racing a blue-and-gold dragon chased across the water, followed by echoes of drumbeats and fading cries of 'Yosh' and 'Yo'.

Mizukaze and Hanachi loosed pleased-sounding roars and dived under the water to chase the ghostly boats. Her paddlers clapped and the people pointed at the racing dragons and cheered. Lazuli and Larimar were laughing.

Akachi reared higher, steam coiling from her nostrils. 'I look forward to our next meeting, Guide U-Lamiya.' The red dragon's eyes flared a blindingly bright gold, then she submerged her body and a mound of water sped away.

Pushing down a knot of concern about what the dragon might ask for next, Lamiya observed her people hugging and celebrating. Turning to farewell the spirits, she found them lined up from distant past to more recent, with Lestaya and Azuri forming the final pair. Her heart twisted and clenched with each gauzy, chill embrace and the kisses to her cheeks that felt like falling flakes of snow. After their kiss, each pair of guides dissipated into a spray of grey mist.

We are so proud of you, dearest daughter. Lestaya's words washed into her while the shade of her mother pressed her fingers with love.

Glide and boat captain and now the Guide! croaked Azuri, wiping his eyes with a gauzy hand. *With a mage for a consort. Who'd have thought?*

Lamiya gripped their hands tightly, refusing to let go. Couldn't they stay a while? Come to the celebrations? She heard water tinkling behind her as someone purified their hands, then soft footsteps and Everand's strong hands landed on her shoulders.

Look after our daughter, won't you? croaked Azuri.

As if she needs looking after! snorted Lestaya.

'With all my heart,' replied Everand seriously, speaking over her head.

Before she could decide what to say, Lestaya and Azuri kissed her cheeks and faded, their joyous faces lingering like an afterglow. Her heart panging with such pain she thought it would burst, Lamiya touched her cheeks, savouring their kisses.

Whirr flew down from the rafters and she held up a crooked finger for him to perch on. 'Yes, the flock may go now. Thank you.' Whirr peeped several times. 'Of course you can all come to the feast. There will be special bowls of nuts and seeds for you.' Whirr peeped again. '*Lots* of bowls. Now go, you greedy bird!' She flung her hand up, and with a flash of jade and gold, Whirr zoomed out the front of the Meeting Place and, fluttering and chirping, the flock followed. An array of tiny feathers wafted around her.

Her heart singing, she spun and clasped her arms around Everand's waist, tilting her chin up. His warm lips closed over hers and she leaned into the kiss, his hands pulling her closer until their bodies met. Too soon, he pulled away.

His voice deep, he said, 'Come, U-Lamiya, your people are waiting for you.'

Chapter Thirty-Seven

Sharp talons marched across his scalp. Everand yawned and batted Whirr off his head. 'Cheeky bird.'

Lamiya mumbled something and burrowed into his shoulder, her hair tumbling deliciously over his chest. Whirr strutted insistently back over his head and squawked into his ear. Waking properly, Everand looked at the golden sunlight sluicing through the feather door curtain. In one swift move, he sat up. Lamiya grumbled when he shook her shoulder.

'Wise and revered U-Lamiya, your people await you, and your messengers must be away in accordance with your first instructions as Guide of Riverplain.'

Sitting up, Lamiya gave him a look full of reproach, augmented by her tousled hair. Laughing, he said, 'Perhaps guides should not try to drink more jugs of feeja wine than their people.' The opportunity too good to resist, he wagged his finger under her nose like she often did to him. 'I thought the Guide of Riverplain was supposed to be a role model?'

'Very funny, envoy to the Mages' Guild of Axis who is late for his first task for said revered Guide.' She sniffed and tossed her head. 'I'll have to retitle you the Not-So-Eminent Mage if you can't complete my orders.'

His expression mock-serious, Everand wagged his finger again. 'This sun, you said. Go to the Guild to invite them to the races and our partnering ceremony this sun. You did not specify when, and it is still *this* sun.'

Grabbing his finger, Lamiya said pertly, 'Next time I will be precise. I intended you and Lazuli to go and return in the same sun.'

He kissed her. 'I know you did. I'm going.' Pushing the covers off, he stood.

'Wait!' called Lamiya, the corners of her mouth curving up. 'My envoy must be dressed in a fitting robe!' She ran her eyes over his naked body.

Bending over, he grabbed the edge of the blanket and threw it over her head. Whirr ran up and down the blanket, peeping loudly over her muffled giggles.

Everand filled the wooden tub with water, murmured the spell of heating and washed quickly, reflecting on the revelry of the previous dark-fall. His mouth tasted of stale feeja wine and his armpits felt gritty after so much dancing and whirling people around. He scrubbed harder than usual and once his skin was tingling, dried off and pulled on his azure robe. It would have been nice to impress the mages by wearing the special robe the spirits had given him with the dancing gold dragons lining the sleeves but that, no doubt, also needed a good scrub.

He sensed a shadow flit over the hut just before Lazuli called, 'Yo!'

Collecting the invitation message balls he'd created from the table, Everand went to the door. Outside, in the already bright sunlight, Lazuli and Larimar sat astride Hover. The beetle being the fastest option, Lamiya had readily agreed to Lazuli's request to use Hover to travel to Riverfall and Riversea to issue the invitations to the races. The orange beetle flexed its antennae at him and Everand patted its nose.

'Are you leaving soon?' asked Lazuli.

Approaching the side of Hover, Everand held up two message balls for Larimar to take. 'Yes. The balls will activate once in the hands of either Atage or Tengar in Riverfall, and Chiton or Cowrie in Riversea. Make sure you tell them they can listen to the message whenever they cup their hands around the ball and think of the races.'

Lazuli picked up the reins and adjusted his weight ready for the flight. 'Tell Malach I said hello. And find out if he is practising for our beetle races.' Grinning, he said over his shoulder to Larimar, 'I can't wait to test how fast we can go.'

Larimar hastily tucked the message balls deep into his trouser pocket and gripped the back of Lazuli's tunic with both hands.

Everand stepped away when the beetle raised its outer wings and rose to hover above his head. Lazuli flashed him a wild grin before Hover shot forward and disappeared beyond the trees. Shaking his head, Everand put his two message balls into separate pockets in his robe, then faced north and visualised the space beside the fire pit in the clearing Malach used for meetings. *Mori.* Wasn't that what the people of Riverwood called their …. village. Calling it a town seemed a stretch given the absence of any structures other than dwellings.

He materialised beside the fire pit just as a curvaceous young woman was walking past and she dropped her basket of breads with a yelp. 'Sorry.' Grimacing, Everand helped her to retrieve the scattered loaves.

Taking the bread from him, she said, 'You want Malach? I'll get him.'

Watching the woman walk away, he remembered her name was Fenchi. He looked around the clearing, seeing little activity other than a couple of curious faces peeking from behind the nearby cabins. The atmosphere was subdued. He felt a frown forming. Would Malach and his people be able to adjust to mingling with others?

'Everand?' Malach strode up from behind him. 'Is something happening?'

He spun to face Malach, gave a respectful nod and produced a message ball from his pocket. 'U-Lamiya, Guide of Riverplain, invites you and your people to participate in the boat races sixty suns from now.' He held the ball out to Malach. 'This is your formal invitation. You're also invited to the trade discussions and our partnering ceremony the sun after the races.'

Taking the ball, Malach said, 'My team will be there, as agreed.'

When Malach said nothing more, Everand flexed his fingers and said lightly, 'Lazuli said to warn you he is training for your beetle race.'

Malach laughed. 'Good. Tell him in return he will need to train hard. Very hard.' Rolling the message ball between his hands, he added, 'Would you like food or drink?'

'No, but thank you. I must go to the Guild to deliver their invitation.'

Alertness flooded Malach's face and his eyes brightened. 'Does the woman mage now lead, do you think? If so, I'd like to meet with her … as a *good* neighbour.'

Alarm crawling across his nape, Everand said, 'I expect Tiliqua has been elected. I'll find out.' He took a breath; he and Lamiya were encouraging openness and communication so despite his reservations, he should assist Malach. 'I can tell Tiliqua you would like to meet with her.'

'Do. Please.' Malach shifted his weight from one foot to the other and nimbly tossed the message ball between his hands. 'You will stop again on your return?'

The prickling across his nape now itching, Everand said evenly, 'If I have time. I don't know what matters the Guild will want to discuss. I'll let you know Tiliqua's answer somehow though.'

Malach stopped tossing the ball. 'The tunnel in the wall. What will the mages do about that?'

An excellent question. Trust Malach to think of this already. 'The tunnel is one of the matters I expect the mages will wish to discuss. I'll let you know what is said about that too.' Everand's palms felt clammy. So much for being the envoy Eminent Mage; he was rapidly becoming a general message-boy! He took a step back and flapped a hand in farewell before Malach could ask anything else.

Materialising in front of the blue shield across the entrance to the tunnel with his shoulderblades tingling, Everand glanced over his shoulder. Surely, Malach wouldn't have followed or sent someone to spy on him? Seeing no movement, he faced the wall. His ears caught a faint crackling and he swept his gaze to the top of the wall.

His breath hitched. The wardspell was visible, glinting myriad colours and crackling as if it were breaking. Wait. It *was* breaking! Several small chips broke off, tumbled down and vanished before they reached the grass. His heart thudded loudly. Why break now? *The Staropal!* For generations, the mages had used the powerful stone to help feed energy into the wardspell — and he'd given it to Akachi. A crushing weight pressed on his shoulders. The Guild would have to rely upon the granite wall for protection, which made the future of this tunnel critically important. He groaned. If only it led somewhere other than Riverwood!

Feeling a sense of urgency, he parted the blue barrier, slipped through and recreated the barrier behind him. When he reached the Axis side of the tunnel he paused, then created a barrier across that entrance too. The barriers would keep others from entering Axis, but if the wardspell failed completely, there would be nothing to stop the mages translocating, or even flying their transport beetles, out into the provinces. Did Tiliqua and Agamid know this? They *must* have noticed.

Flexing his fingers to draw more power, he considered where was best to arrive. Mantiss' home? The Great Hall?

Maybe the library, where Hydrelaps could fill him in on what had happened since he'd left before he put his foot in it somehow. Visualising the steps of the library, he translocated again.

He shimmered onto the polished redwood steps, hurried up them and strode into the library. 'Hydrelaps? Are you here?' His call echoed off the marble walls but the librarian did not appear. Where could he be? Everand strode across the entry hall and peered into the administration office. Nobody. He spun around and stopped his forward stride just in time. A young mage stood there. One of the recent apprentices?

The young mage bowed. 'Mage Hydrelaps is at a council meeting. Can I help you with a book?'

'A council meeting?' So, the mages were conveniently already gathered. Everand took a step sideways. 'No, I don't need a book.' He rushed past the perplexed apprentice and jogged along the path to the Great Hall.

He took the steps two at a time, hurried through the doors — noticing they'd been fixed already — and marched across the silk rug. Stopping at the edge of the dais, he regarded the astonished faces. Tiliqua … good, she was seated in the Head of the Guild's chair. She and Agamid leaped to their feet, concerned eyes upon him. Mantiss pushed himself upright, relief all over his face.

'Everand! Fortunate timing,' said Tiliqua. 'We've just started and your update will be crucial.' She ran her eyes over him and a small frown tugged her eyebrows together. 'You don't have the Staropal?'

'So, we can't fix the wardspell,' murmured Agamid, looking disappointed.

Everand's heart sank. Would they hold him responsible for this?

CHAPTER THIRTY-EIGHT

Swallowing hard, Everand forged ahead. 'I apologise for arriving unannounced.' He winced. They needed a better form of communication than him lobbing in unexpected. 'Before we discuss other matters, I'm here to bring you an invitation from U-Lamiya, Guide of Riverplain.' He fished in his pocket for the message ball and, retrieving it from a deep fold, mounted the dais and handed it to Tiliqua.

'U-Lamiya …' His tongue tangled over the title, which still felt odd to say, '… has appointed me envoy to the Mages' Guild to support communication between us.' He waved a hand at the ball that Tiliqua was handling as if it were a fragile lizard egg. 'The invitation is to attend the inter-province boat races in sixty suns, and then our partnering ceremony. Please play the message and advise me of your answer.'

Tiliqua arched a fine blonde eyebrow. 'I am glad Lamiya has arranged for communication between us.' Moving both hands, with the ball, she indicated the far end of the table. 'The council has just decided to give you a position on the Outer Council of Twenty and you will be invited whenever the full council meets.' Her gaze sharpened. 'This is acceptable to you?'

Squashing his surprise, Everand looked across the table at the faces of Agamid and Mantiss, who were both watching him expectantly. Clearing his throat, he replied, 'I would be honoured to continue to assist the Guild.' His mind added, a*s long as it doesn't intend harm to the provinces. Or the dragons.* But a seat at the table would position him to influence them. Whose idea was this? No matter, it was a welcome step.

'Good,' said Tiliqua. 'Take your seat. I'll ask you for an update, then the council can proceed with the agenda better informed.'

Everand swiftly moved to take the chair she'd indicated, between Aclys and Caimanops. They both nodded at him before returning their attention to Tiliqua.

Sitting, Tiliqua put the message ball on the table, rested her hands on either side of it and swept an intent gaze around the mages. 'Let's hear Everand's update and discuss matters relating to the provinces while he is here.' She turned piercing blue eyes upon him. 'The half-mage fled with the Staropal and you left straight after. What happened to the stone, and to Malach?'

Placing his palms on the table, Everand took a deep breath and rapidly outlined his pursuit of Malach, the recovery of the Staropal and his removal of Malach's mage power.

'Are you saying Malach is no longer a half-mage?' said Tiliqua. 'He has no power?'

'I have removed his pool of mage power,' confirmed Everand. 'However, he may retain other abilities not related to it.'

'Such as?' Tiliqua looked taken aback.

Resisting the urge to drum his fingers on the table, Everand said, 'Not many but a few of the people in the provinces have unexpected abilities. For example, both Malach and Lamiya can summon and communicate with birds, and others have an innate healing ability. The Guide of Riverplain can communicate with the spirits of the past guides … it is important the Guild knows that these different forms of ability exist outside of Axis.'

A stunned silence palled over the table. Clasping his hands together, Everand waited. The bigger shock was yet to be delivered.

Tiliqua blinked a few times. 'And the Staropal? What have you done with the stone?'

Breathing out through his nose, Everand gathered his courage. 'I did what I said I would. With Lamiya's help, I returned the Staropal to Akachi, the red dragon.'

Several mages gasped and Saiphos dropped his pen, slapping a hand on it when it rolled across the tabletop. Mantiss turned deathly pale and Agamid shook his head sorrowfully. Tiliqua regarded him through angry, narrowed eyes. So, she hadn't told them the full background yet and he'd put her in a difficult position.

Gently, Everand said, 'Does the council know the context or would you like me to tell them?'

Tiliqua opened her mouth, then closed it.

Mantiss fidgeted, then spoke. 'This part belongs to me to tell as the previous Head of the Guild and custodian of Lapemis' notebook and the Staropal.' His voice wavering, Mantiss gave the council a short version of the account in the notebook about what had happened when the initial mages first arrived.

'I am sorry you were all deceived,' Mantiss concluded. 'The burden of keeping this secret was passed to me and I carried it.' He looked at Everand. 'It has been a great weight on my shoulders and spirit. Knowing I would soon need to pass over the burden of responsibility, I sent Everand into the provinces, hoping that he wouldn't — but fearing he might — find the dragon … and he did. Now we know the red beast called Akachi still lives, even after all this time.'

Warmth spread up Everand's neck when all eyes swivelled to him. 'Mage Mantiss has led you well,' he said, eying his former master. 'By returning the Staropal to Akachi a past wrong has been righted and the Guild has the opportunity to go forward, to forge new friendships, to gather new knowledge.' He stopped. Tiliqua should be the one to drive the council.

Sitting stiffly, Tiliqua said sharply, 'Is the dragon a risk to us? What will it do with the Staropal?'

'Are we safe?' interjected Agamid. 'Especially now the wardspell is failing.'

Palms sweaty, Everand spoke slowly. 'First, the dragon is a she. Akachi is a superior dragon, with sharp intellect and strong, ancient powers. She is the mother of Hanachi, a female dragon. There is also Mizukaze, a male dragon whose mother was Akachi's sister, the blue dragon that Lapemis let leave unharmed. As far as I can tell, these three are the only dragons left and they need the Staropal for their species to continue.'

The mages fidgeted and muttered to each other until Agamid raised a hand to quieten them, and asked, 'Do *we* need the species to continue?'

Everand put his hands below the table and clenched his fingers. 'It is not a decision the Guild can make. The dragons were here first and have befriended the provinces, Riverfall and Riverplain in particular.' He ignored the bead of sweat trickling down his forehead. 'The dragons are important to Ossilis as a whole. They control the weather with elemental magic and hence the people of Riverfall please them with offerings and boat races in exchange for good rain for their crops.'

The mages stared at him sceptically. Tiliqua frowned, and he could see her thinking furiously. With a sigh, he added, 'The dragons are not an aggressive species, although they are fearsome if they need to defend themselves. Or a friend. They do not represent an outright risk to the Guild, but ...' He took a breath, *here goes*. 'Akachi has asked that the Guild formally acknowledge her and apologise for taking the Staropal. When you come to the Riverplain races.'

Fear infusing her face, Tiliqua stared at him with her mouth open. Mantiss shut his eyes and wobbled in his seat and even Agamid turned pale.

'What do you advise?' Tiliqua asked, her voice tight.

Holding eye contact, Everand said, 'I honestly advise you, from whatever position I look at it, to acknowledge Akachi and apologise *on behalf of* the *ancient* Guild. You–' He swept an arm around the table, '–this council, this Guild are not personally responsible for what was done. You didn't even know until now. I urge you to explain this, and to seek Akachi's friendship.'

The silence was so resounding he could hear his heartbeats booming in his ears. 'Everything rests on this, Tiliqua. It will be uncomfortable but the moment will quickly pass.' She sat ramrod straight gaping at him. 'If you do not do this, the Guild will remain set apart when the other four provinces have united.'

Tiliqua swallowed with an audible gulp, and out of the corner of his eye he saw Agamid grimace. How else could he persuade her? The dragon trusted him. Maybe he could make it easier, one final role in this unrelenting mission. 'I will stand with you while you speak to Akachi, if you like.'

Her throat moving in an even larger swallow, Tiliqua ran her eyes around the table before latching her gaze on his face. 'Very well, I will do it. You will help me with the wording?'

Inclining his head in respect for her courage, Everand said, 'It will be my honour. Lamiya will contribute suggested phrases too.' A wave of relief breaking over his shoulders, he said, 'Can I suggest you now play the message ball invitation for the council?'

Tiliqua blinked at him like an owl in sunlight and then peered at the ball on the table in front of her as if she'd forgotten it was there. Slowly, she cupped her hands around it and frowned in concentration.

Lamiya's head and shoulders appeared within the ball, the image smiling and nodding a greeting. 'Greetings, Mage

Tiliqua. With pleasure, I invite you and chosen representatives of the Mages' Guild in Axis to attend and observe the inter-province boat races in sixty suns, on the last sun of growing season.' The image tossed her hair. 'There will be a feast that dark-fall, which you are also welcome to join us for.'

Tiliqua was gripping the ball so tightly her knuckles were turning white. Everand shifted his weight on his chair. Did Tiliqua harbour any resentment to his partnering with Lamiya? Would this influence her reactions? He watched Lamiya's image intently, wondering how she had phrased the partnering ceremony. He'd been so intent on sustaining the message ball he hadn't really listened to her words. In the ball, Lamiya's image took a breath and spread her hands.

'The sun after the boat races, we will hold a day of trading. This may not be of interest to the mages but you, as Head of the Guild, and two other representatives are invited to participate in the discussions to be held among the leaders from all the provinces.' Lamiya smiled encouragingly. 'I hope you will join us.' Lamiya looked down, fluttered her eyelashes and then looked up, gazing uncannily directly into Tiliqua's eyes.

'The third part of the invitation is from me and Mage Everand. When the sun is descending after the trade and discussions, Riverplain will hold the formal ceremony to instate Everand as my consort and partner.' Sincerely, Lamiya said, 'I thank the Guild with all my heart for releasing Everand to be with me.'

Warmth rushed up Everand's neck and beads of sweat formed at his temples. He dared not look at the mages' faces, imagining amusement or perhaps horror. He heard Agamid clear his throat and Tiliqua sniffed. Lamiya's next words floated past him.

'We would be pleased if the Guild council, and any mages who are friend to Everand, would join us for this important and unprecedented ceremony. Please advise Everand of your answer to all parts of my invitation.'

Everand's eyes grew hot and moist. By the stars, Lamiya was clever and generous — she'd moved from disliking and distrusting the Guild to *this*? Her heart and spirit knew no bounds. Slowly, he lifted his gaze to find every mage at the table looking at him in wonder.

Tiliqua ceased clasping the message ball and passed it to Agamid. Smoothing her robe sleeves, she said crisply, 'I move that the full Council of Twenty, plus any others that Mage Everand suggests, accept the invitation to attend the partnering ceremony. Do any council members disagree, or not wish to attend?'

Astounded, Everand gaped at Tiliqua, then at the faces around the table. Admittedly, Pelamis was no longer present, but that was far easier than he'd expected. Agamid was stroking his beard with a broad smile and Mantiss was dabbing an eye with a lace handkerchief. Hydrelaps was smiling and nodding and seated beside him, Caimanops looked oddly pleased.

Everand cleared the lump from his throat. 'That's wonderful. Thank you.'

Tiliqua gave him a brief smile. 'I move that I, Mage Agamid and …' She looked around the table, '… Caimanops represent the Guild at the leader discussions. Anyone disagree or propose alternatives? No? Please record this too, Saiphos.'

'Lastly,' Tiliqua opened her hands, 'I move that the Inner Council of Ten attend and observe the boat races.' She looked at Everand. 'This is when I will speak to Akachi?'

'Most likely,' agreed Everand. 'I will confirm this. Perhaps we should create a communication sphere for me to use?'

'Agreed. Before you leave, I'll create one for you to communicate directly with me.' She looked around the gathering again. 'We have other pressing matters to discuss. While Everand is here, I propose we discuss the failing wardspell and the existence of a tunnel that apparently links Axis to a river province.'

Everand glanced up at the highest stained-glass window. By the way the light was refracting strongly through the middle of the oblong, he guessed the sun was already past its zenith. *I intended you and Lazuli to go and return this sun.* Lazuli was probably already home ... *home* ... he would go *home* to Riverplain. But it might barely be *this* sun by the time the Guild agreed any action on these major issues, which would necessitate an open discussion about the forward level of interaction with the provinces.

Just as well he was here.

☾⋆

Everand materialised on the grassy area in front of Lamiya's hut. He brushed dust from his robe, seeing that the tip of the sun had just sunk behind the western hills, the final tendrils of golden glow retracting over the hilltops like reluctant fingers letting go. The purple haze of dark-fall folded down from the sky, casting shadows and gloom. The lake lapped quietly at the shore behind him, an insect chirped nearby. He became aware of a presence.

Lamiya was standing outside her doorway, tapping a foot. 'I suppose the final rays before the sun sinks behind the hills could count as this sun. *If* I were feeling generous.'

Ignoring the pout on her lips, sure she was mocking him, Everand took swift strides, pulled her into a fierce hug and kissed the top of her head. Then he held her at arm's-length and smiled. 'Your envoy to Riverwood reports that Malach and his team will attend the boat races.' He paused for effect, watching her eyebrow lift in query.

'And, revered and wise Guide of Riverplain, the Guild has accepted all three parts of your invitation.'

'They will come? To *everything*?' Lamiya's eyes widened and she gripped his arms. 'You are truly an Eminent Mage, my trusted envoy.' She peered searchingly into his eyes. 'They come willingly?'

Everand nodded. 'Tiliqua is indeed the Head of the Guild and the others already follow her.' He thought of the expressions of those gathered and realised fully what he'd been seeing. 'My influence was timely and useful, but the current council is filled by sensible and reasonable mages.' Hope gushed into his chest. 'I am optimistic. They even agreed to not replace the wardspell, for now anyway, and to leave my barriers in place across the tunnel.'

His astonishment rising anew, he kissed her hair before continuing in a rush. 'There will be further council meetings to review the Guild Laws, but first they will come to the races — *your* races — to meet everyone and to hear all the province views.' He gazed at her, adoring the contours of her face, silhouetted by the pale light shimmering off the lake. 'Tiliqua has boldly agreed to apologise to Akachi but only with our help, my love. We have achieved the impossible. Ossilis will have a true new beginning.'

'This is wonderful,' breathed Lamiya, hugging him fiercely. Against his chest, she murmured, 'Did they feed you, my Eminent Mage, or do those hollow legs require sustenance?'

'My toes still feel hollow ...'

Lamiya curled her fingers around his. 'You will enjoy the meal I have ready, then.'

Everand followed her into the hut, his nostrils twitching at the aroma of baked fish and spiced vegetables. On her low table were plates and a covered pot, with Whirr perched on top of it trying to pry the lid off with his beak.

Lamiya batted Whirr with her palm. '*You* did not fly to two other provinces this sun as my envoy. You get your usual grains and seeds.' She nudged Whirr towards his bowl, the bird trying to dig his talons into the table to resist.

Amused, Everand sat on his favourite yellow cushion and watched while Whirr, feathers all fluffed up and beak snapping, dodged Lamiya's hands. His fingers twitched, tempted to translocate the bird to the bowl of grain so Lamiya could serve the meal. He focused on the wriggling, bustling bird.

Wait! *He* could serve the meal. He was no longer at the Guild, relying on the humans to prepare and serve his meals. A jolt rocketed through him. Tiliqua had also said the council had agreed to leave his Guild quarters assigned to him, so he and Lamiya had a place to stay when they visited. He'd thanked her and promptly translocated back to Riverplain, without any thought — none whatsoever — of going to see his rooms! No need, since Mizu was swimming free in the lake. He thought of the pretty fish coming to greet him, gauzy fin and tail waving, happy among a shoal of similar fish.

Here, he too was among friends. Soon to be family. No need for formality.

Contentment flowing into him, he picked up the ladle and lifted the pot lid.

Chapter Thirty-nine

A light breeze brushed the loose hairs away from Everand's cheeks and ruffled the dazzling feather streamers hanging along the entire side of the Meeting Place that faced the lake. The whole flock must have donated plumage! Tightening his hair thong and peering down from the top step, his heart skipped in anticipation at the sights unfolding below.

The four dragon boats were pulled up onto the shore in a neat row, proudly displaying their province team colours. Down to his right, the bright-green start flag and burnt-orange finish flag were fluttering in the breeze. Beyond the flags, four fishing boats were ready to be rowed out as the turn markers for the races. He watched Lazuli, tailed by Larimar, hurrying along the shore checking everything and speaking animatedly to his helpers.

Down to his left, were orderly rows of dining tables and benches set out on a level area hugging the flatter shoreline to the north of the Meeting Place. Wood for a massive bonfire was piled high in the middle for the post-races feast. A tingle ran across his nape. What would the mages think of all this compared to the magnificence of the marble Great Hall? Still, the hall did not have commanding views across a stunning turquoise lake surrounded by vibrant foliage and set against a backdrop of verdant, rounded hills.

The sun eased over the crest of the downy hills and primrose tendrils of light crept down the slopes to tentatively caress the far edge of the lake. Surely, the mages would arrive imminently. The air prickled with static and the feather streamers danced wildly, the ends of those nearby tickling his cheeks. Uncannily perceiving the change in the atmosphere, Lamiya, clad in her racing uniform, bounded up the steps, purified her hands far more quickly than usual, flashed him a smile and leaped beside him just as the first mages shimmered into being.

'Welcome to Riverplain,' said Lamiya, bowing to Tiliqua and nodding to Mantiss, Agamid, Caimanops and Hydrelaps. 'I and my people are honoured by your presence.'

'We look forward to learning about your customs,' said Tiliqua, inclining her head at Lamiya and flicking a glance laced with apprehension at Everand.

Everand stepped forward. 'We'll do the Guild apology first, before we awaken the boats and begin the races.'

Relief chased across Tiliqua's face. 'Yes, that would be best.'

Lamiya tilted her head as if listening to a distant call. 'The dragons are on their way.' Touching Everand's arm, she smiled at Tiliqua and said, 'I have a few things to do, so I'll leave my trusted envoy to welcome the rest of you and take you down to the lake.' On her way to the steps, she stopped to grasp Mantiss' hands. 'You look well, Mage Mantiss.' Before the mage could respond, she skipped away.

'She will race?'

Everand met Tiliqua's incredulous look. 'Yes, as the team captain and the all-important glide who steers the boat.' When Tiliqua's eyes widened further, he smiled. 'Don't worry, I won't be in a boat! The mages can stand near me while I help Atage and Lyber judge the race finishes, and afterwards I'll escort you everywhere and explain as much as possible.'

Tiliqua swallowed, her gaze now tracking Lamiya's movements down near the boats. Mantiss and the others were staring around with interest when the air bubbled behind them and the other five mages of the Inner Council materialised. Everand greeted Saiphos, Neelaps, Menetia, Aclys — and paused at Acanthopis. Wasn't he only recently appointed to the Outer Council? Why was he here and where was Simoselaps?

'Simoselaps chose not to come,' murmured Tiliqua, coming to stand by his side. 'In the interests of keeping the peace with Lamiya and Malach, he agreed to be replaced on the Inner Council by Acanthopis.'

'Wise decision,' said Everand, feeling a subtle tension leave his shoulders. Lamiya would be relieved and Malach … would no doubt be disappointed not to have the opportunity to cause Simoselaps discomfort. To the group he said, 'Gather close and I'll explain the order of events.'

He'd barely had time to point out which boat belonged to which province and to outline the four proposed races when the water behind the boats swirled vigorously and Akachi's head and shoulders appeared, followed by those of Mizukaze and Hanachi. The red dragon immediately looked to where he and Tiliqua stood and her golden eyes gleamed, small flames flickering from her jaws.

Seeing the colour leach from Tiliqua's face, Everand gripped both of her hands. 'You can do this. You *must* do this.' He leaned in close, his lips brushing her ear. 'You are Mantiss' bold and talented daughter. There is no-one better to achieve this moment in history.'

Noting the glint of moisture in her eyes, and a momentary longing, he released her hands and stepped back, feeling her fingers reluctantly trail loose from his. 'Come, we do this together.'

Mantiss edged closer and mumbled, 'I, too, will apologise. I bear culpability as the previous Head of the Guild.'

Warmth spread across Everand's chest. Having *two* Guild leaders apologise would surely appease Akachi? But when he glanced at the dragon, rising high in the water with her neck in a proud arch and her tongue flicking out between small flames, his hope gave way to doubt. Perhaps they were unwise to start with the apology. What if Akachi was *not* appeased and things went sour? His mouth ran dry. Lamiya was so certain it would be fine, a fitting way to open the festival, but if the dragons became angered the races and everything could be at risk. Tiliqua was watching him, still pale and possibly detecting his uncertainty. *Appear confident.*

Summoning a reassuring smile, he gestured to the steps. 'Let's go down.' He deftly laced on his sandals and then paused by the two bowls of water, the surfaces glinting prettily in the pale gold and wan blue light. The Guild's learning of Riverplain customs could start here. Picking up the ladle, he looked over his shoulder into Tiliqua's uncomfortably close face.

'It is customary to purify your hands and soul with this sacred water before entering the Meeting Place, which is a place of the spirits.' He ignored the mages' collective lifting of eyebrows. 'You arrived directly inside the space, so let's do it now as a sign of respect before we greet Akachi.' He trickled the cool water over his hands and passed the ladle to Tiliqua, watching as she mimicked his actions.

'It is refreshing,' she murmured. 'And calming.'

As soon as they were all done, he led the mages down the steps and made his way towards the boats. People parted at his approach, nodding shyly at the mages as they passed. On reaching the shore, he heard the mages' footsteps behind him slow and become hesitant. Not surprising, given that even he felt awed by the four dragon boat heads peering at him, seemingly tracking him with their eyes — especially Riverplain's new boat built in the likeness of Akachi. The shapely blood-red head with large golden orb eyes and golden spiral horns looked imperious and commanding.

'Even the boats are fearsome, and the dragon is so much bigger than I thought,' whispered Tiliqua, her shoulder brushing his as she came to stand on his right. Her fingers pinched his forearm. 'We don't have to apologise in front of all these people, do we?'

Everand prised her fingers open. 'No, Lamiya thought of this and you will have some space. Lazuli will call the paddlers into a huddle to outline the rules of racing and the other people will be taken to the far side of the boats.' Dropping her hand, he gave a wry smile. 'We don't want this to be any harder than it already will be.'

Tiliqua ran her hands down her robe, smoothing it. 'When do we start?'

'When Lamiya joins us. You have rehearsed the words?' At her curt nod, he faced the lake and mentally ran over the words that had taken them so many attempts to form into an apology that was coherent and sounded sincere. May it be sufficient. Let Akachi not decide to make the mages suffer.

'I'm ready.' Lamiya strode into position on his left and he blinked at the cloak flowing over her shoulders, a vivacious green cloth patterned with tiny orange birds flitting above ornate red flowers. Where had she conjured that from? The spirits? The cloak solved the matter of her looking formal enough for the apology without needing to change out of her race uniform.

Silence cocooned them when the people of Riverplain melted away, gently herded by Lamiya's paddlers. A chill brushed across Everand's shoulders and Lamiya's mouth curved into a soft smile at the spirits forming a gauzy, shadowy crowd behind her. The mages subtly rearranged themselves until Tiliqua, Mantiss and Agamid stood on his right and the other seven formed a line behind them. Out of the corner of his eye, he saw Caimanops lean forward to lightly touch Tiliqua's shoulder and noted her brief smile of gratitude. Interesting.

Mantiss looked across and Everand dipped his chin in a nod. *We begin.*

The three dragons waded fully from the water to tower before them, lit from behind by the strengthening yellow-gold rays of sunlight. Rivulets of water trickled crooked paths between their intricately patterned, glistening scales and dripped onto the ground. Somewhere deep in Everand's soul prompted how fitting it was that the mages faced east, towards Akachi's cave, to where the theft had happened. Had Lamiya anticipated this or was it a natural consequence of the layout for the festival? Before he could look at her, she brushed his hand with her fingers. She knew.

Lamiya bowed, and he hastened to match her depth and flourish. Then she began. 'Greetings and welcome, Great Akachi. Welcome, Mizukaze and Hanachi. This sun and the next, many magnificent things will happen, but we open this festival with a matter of significance to all of Ossilis.'

Everand marvelled at how strong and clear Lamiya's words were. Akachi stretched her sinuous body taller, her eyes glowing as if stoked from within by molten fire. Wisps of steam coiled from her nostrils and the talons at the end of her powerful forelegs flexed and curled. Mizukaze, expression fierce and intent, edged closer. Everand tried to swallow his niggling disquiet, the back of his right hand prickling where Akachi had bitten it to bind them to the task of recovering the Staropal.

As if nothing worried her, Lamiya spread her hands open and said calmly, 'Everand and I have fulfilled our task of returning the Staropal to you. I now invite Mage Everand to introduce the Head of the Mages' Guild in Axis. He and she wish to speak of how the Guild came by the Staropal and to acknowledge it was not rightfully theirs.' Lamiya clasped her hands before her, indicating she had finished speaking.

Squaring his shoulders, Everand projected his voice. 'Great Akachi, I introduce to you Mage Tiliqua, recently elected as

Head of the Mages' Guild in Axis, and her father, Mage Mantiss, the outgoing Head of the Guild.' He waited while Tiliqua and Mantiss stepped forward and bowed.

As soon as she had straightened up, Tiliqua said, 'Great Akachi, thank you for hearing us. We recently came to understand that our ancestors, Mage Lapemis and his colleagues, performed a great wrong.' She stopped, her throat moving in a massive swallow.

Everand edged closer to Tiliqua, worried by her pallor and the faint tremble he could see in Mantiss' legs. May their rehearsals get them through this! Akachi brought her head closer to Tiliqua, nostrils flaring a dark crimson and eyes burning far brighter than any feast bonfire. Not helpful! However, Tiliqua retained the presence of mind to not look directly into the dragon's eyes, as he'd instructed. On cue, he began to speak the agreed apology in time with Tiliqua, their voices mingling to sound like an echo from the past.

'We have come to learn that Mage Lapemis and his cohort of ten mages arrived on the east coast of Ossilis, not the west coast as we thought. We have learned that the mages discovered this very lake, encountered your mate and killed him. We have learned that they found your cave, stunned you and stole the Staropal from you.' They both paused to draw in a breath, Everand trying not to look at the darker, denser steam rising from Akachi's nostrils, nor at the dark shadows writhing in the dragon's eyes. They must finish this.

'We have learned that the mages fled to the west coast and buttressed themselves and the Staropal in Axis.' As practised, he and Tiliqua took another measured breath. Despite her stilted posture, her words were measured and strong and he felt a brief surge of admiration. 'For this, the Mages' Guild is deeply remorseful. We are sorry that our ancestors took the stone. We apologise for the grief and loss caused to you.'

Everand, Tiliqua and Mantiss bowed low. Then Everand said, 'That was the past. Great Akachi, the Guild wishes to speak of the future.' He tilted his head just enough to give Tiliqua a look of encouragement. Although Akachi had not reacted so far, other than to stare down at them with smouldering intensity, the next part would be revealing.

'The current Guild wishes to make amends.' Tiliqua and Mantiss spoke together. 'We wish to repair the relationship with you. Now that the Staropal has been returned to you, its rightful owner, we seek your forgiveness.'

The words hung in the crisp air. *We seek your forgiveness.* Everand became conscious of his heart beating in his chest and felt an odd sensation of looking down from above, as if they were a tableau of small figures set out on a strategy board somewhere, waiting for someone to make the next move. Unconsciously, he reached out with his left hand and Lamiya's fingers stole into his.

Akachi's heavy leathery eyelids closed slowly over her smouldering orbs then lifted again. Jets of steam hissed from her nostrils. Fixing her gaze on Tiliqua, she rumbled, *You said "we have learned". Why did you not know?*

His legs shaking, Mantiss shuffled forward and cleared his throat. 'Great Akachi, sadly Lapemis and the original mages concealed what they had done and forbade anyone to speak of it. The only ones who knew the truth, recorded in a secret notebook, were the appointed Heads of the Guild. Since Lapemis, four of us.' He rasped in a breath. 'I say *us*, because as the previous Head of the Guild, *I* knew.' Akachi hissed and Mantiss' legs shook harder.

'However, I was bound to secrecy by the outgoing head as part of my oath to accept the leadership. I am deeply sorry for perpetuating the deception.' Mantiss spread wobbling hands. 'Concealed in Axis as we were, we did not know whether dragons still existed.'

Everand's pulse rose a notch. Mantiss spoke the truth and meant well but he was straying into dangerous terrain by seeking forgiveness for deliberate ignorance. He went to step forward but Lamiya's fingers pressed his and her command sounded in his mind. *No, my love. Wait. Your time to speak will come.* He put his foot back down and clamped his tongue to the base of his mouth.

I see. Akachi's words were grave, ominous. *You hid and lied to each other. Why?*

Mantiss swayed and Tiliqua put a hand under his elbow, saying, 'Fear, Great Akachi. Fear.'

Bravely, Mantiss continued with, 'The original mages had fled violence and arrived with fear in their hearts. The records tell that a sea serpent attacked and nearly sank their boat … when they saw dragons their fear rose afresh.' Mantiss licked his lips. 'I wish they … we … all of us, had more honour.'

Akachi snaked her head close to Mantiss and breathed hot air over him until he closed his eyes and hunched into himself. Her tone was rasping, harsh, bordering on a growl. *They smashed my eggs. All except one. They were ruthless and cowardly. I see no honour in your kind.*

Everand's heart hammered against the base of his throat when Akachi opened her mighty jaws wide enough to swallow Mantiss whole. Cowering, Mantiss wrung his hands and mumbled incoherently. The other mages looked as if they would faint or dissipate back to the Guild. Hydrelaps was being supported by Saiphos and Tiliqua was standing her ground but repeatedly smoothing her robe with clenched hands.

Tearing his fingers from Lamiya's, Everand took two steps. 'Great Akachi, may I speak?' When the dragon turned baleful eyes on him and hissed, he clasped his hands before his chest. 'That is the past. You are right, Lapemis and the early mages acted dishonourably and although fear might be the reason it does not sanction their actions.' He could feel everyone's eyes drilling into the back of his head, even those of the shadowy spirits. 'The Guild does not ask you to condone or forgive what was done back then; not at all.'

Sweeping his right arm open, he indicated Tiliqua, Mantiss and the other mages. 'However, *these* mages did *not* commit the crime, although they *are* guilty of perpetuating the crime out of ignorance and residual fear.' He snatched a breath. 'Perhaps we should have been bolder. Perhaps we should have asked more questions.'

He ran a hand over his hair. 'I wish *I* had asked more questions! But we didn't. I didn't. Until recently. For *unknowingly perpetuating the crime*, the current Guild seeks your forgiveness. *I* seek your forgiveness for being part of it, for failing to realise what must have happened even after I met Mizukaze and then you.'

Akachi glared at him, flexing her long, sharp talons, and blinked slowly. Twice. Everand felt hope building. *You, I forgive. You have made amends. You returned the Staropal to me.* Akachi blinked again and stared down at Tiliqua, who stood rigidly, hands fisted by her sides. Akachi flared her nostrils and steam hissed up.

Then she swung her massive head lower and growled into Mantiss' face: *He knew. He lied. He cannot be forgiven.* Behind her, Mizukaze edged forward, his whiskers bristling threateningly and even Hanachi arched her neck and growled at Mantiss with flames flickering in her jaws.

Heart thudding so hard he could barely breathe, Everand watched Mantiss clasp his hands together and tuck his head down, anticipating a swift death. *No!* In two strides, he pushed Tiliqua aside, reached Mantiss and stared defiantly into Akachi's face. Eyes watering and vision blurring, he blinked furiously, refusing to allow the dragon's thrall to take him.

'*No!*' He hurled his words at Akachi. 'Listen to me. Mage Mantiss did perpetuate the lies but at the end *he* is the one who took action to bring us to this point. *He* is the one that sent me, his spy, out into the provinces.' To Mantiss, he barked, 'Stand tall, Master. Meet the dragon properly.'

Spinning back, he swept his gaze over Akachi, Mizukaze then Hanachi. 'This outgoing Head of the Guild is the one that *broke* Guild Law to send me into the provinces, something *no* other Head has done. He *wanted* to know if there were dragons. His spirit and body failing, he did not want to hand over the burden and guilt of sustaining the lie to his successor. Do you understand? *This* mage is the one that sought to break the lie.'

Lamiya slid to his side. 'Eloquent, my love,' she murmured. 'Now speak fully from your heart.'

What? Everand compressed his lips. Speak from his heart? Why would Akachi care about that? His pulse raced when Akachi stretched out her neck and nosed at Mantiss, who endured, eyes pressed shut and quaking from head to toe. The red dragon flicked her tongue, then swung her head at him. Everand focused on the glinting red scales on her forehead while she pushed at him with her nose, bracing his legs when her nudges became more forceful.

Hmmmn. Akachi reared back and blinked ponderously, the flecks and textures shifting in her massive gold eyes. *The other mage does not smell of evil, yet you are the one the Staropal trusts. You are the one who found and respected us. Do you overplay his role?*

A bone-deep ache creeping up his legs, Everand dredged deep for the right words. Lamiya squeezed his fingers: *The truth, my love. Nothing less.* Squaring his shoulders, he looked into the depths of the dragon's burnished gold eyes, summoning the power to deflect her thrall.

'We worked together. Mage Mantiss could not have taken action without me — but he trusts me and I trust him. I *know* he works for the greater good. He is my master, my teacher, the father I never had.' Everand strengthened his tone. 'Lamiya and I returned the Staropal to you and we brought the mages to speak with you. Now I, Mage Everand, your friend, ask you to forgive Mage Mantiss, who is so important to me.'

Lamiya tilted her head and smiled confidently at Akachi. 'Great Akachi, the Guild hid from the river province people all this time too. Yet this sun, we *all* have an opportunity to start anew. To go forward with honesty and a willingness to learn about each other and to live in harmony with each other. Will the dragons be part of this? Will you let go of the past and work with us to make the suns ahead shine bright?'

Akachi glared at Lamiya, clamped her jaws closed and thrashed her tail from side to side. Scalding steam coiled from her nostrils.

Undaunted, Lamiya broadened her smile and transferred her attention to Mizukaze. 'Will you not race our boats while we beat the drums?' To Hanachi, she said, 'You called me "sister". Will you not remain my sister? I could use your help next sun for my … partnering ceremony.' She smiled coyly at Everand.

Bringing her focus back to Akachi, she said, 'Great Akachi, we, the people of Riverplain, and you dragons share this lake. We have built a new boat in your likeness because we admire you and are so proud of your friendship.' She gripped Everand's hand.

Taking her cue, he held their entwined hands up high and called out, 'The Staropal told us "Together you are unique". She said Ossilis needs us. *Together,* we beg you to be part of this new beginning. We invite you to lay the first slat in the bridge for the future by accepting the Guild's apology and agreeing to go forward. All of us in Ossilis will be stronger together.'

This was it; he ached all over, no more words or emotion to give. The three dragons loomed, frozen, staring unblinking at him and Lamiya. Everand's mind drifted to his wild ride on Mizukaze, to the exuberance of the blue-and-gold dragon racing the boat, to how Mizukaze and Hanachi had saved him from Pelamis. Sadness welled in his heart. How he could he lose their friendship? His gaze rested on Mizukaze. The dragon was watching him intently, his gold whiskers pricked forward. Did Mizukaze feel the same? Mizukaze blinked, then nudged Akachi's shoulder with his nose.

Giddy hope rising, Everand took slow breaths while the red dragon put her nose to Mizukaze's nose and then to Hanachi's. Lamiya's excitement tingled through her fingers into his.

Ponderously, Akachi brought her head back to the centre, bestowing a softer golden gaze upon Mantiss and Tiliqua. Her jaws dropped open in what could be a smile. *Very well. Mage Tiliqua, Head of the Mages' Guild in Axis, I accept your apology on behalf of your Guild. We will initiate a friendship and see how it evolves.*

Tiliqua bowed deeply, a flush staining her cheeks. 'Thank you, Great Akachi. The Guild is honoured and humbled.'

To Mantiss, Akachi said, *Mizukaze reminded me that Everand saved him not that long ago and they are friends. Although I do not fully absolve you, in recognition of Everand's friendship and loyalty to you, I declare a truce between us.*

Ignoring Mantiss' shaky bow and stuttered reply, Akachi trained her gaze on Everand and Lamiya. *The Staropal considers that together you two are unique; I find that together you two are difficult to refuse.* Steam curled from the dragon's nostrils and red glints appeared in her eyes.

Mizukaze arched his neck and swished his tail, sending up a cloud of dirt. *We race the boats now?*

Joy flooding his entire being, chasing away all fatigue and doubt, Everand lifted Lamiya and swung her around. Blocking out the hubbub and movement around them, he put her down and kissed her soundly.

Pulling back, Lamiya beamed at him. 'My mage, your meandering mission is finally ended.'

Chapter Forty

Lamiya snatched a breath, excitement buzzing through her veins. The apology had proved unexpectedly fraught, but they'd done it! Everand was finally free to be with her. Standing on tiptoes, she kissed him soundly, revelling in the warmth of his lean body pressed hard against hers and the ardour of his response — until someone coughed close by.

'Can we start now?' Lazuli was hopping from foot to foot, a frown etched across his forehead. 'The paddlers are waiting by the boats. So are Atage and Lyber.'

'Great glide, your team needs you,' said Everand with a crooked grin. He held out his hand. 'I'll take your cloak. Glide well.'

Lamiya unclasped and handed him the cloak, shivers of anticipation racing down her arms. 'See you after, enjoy the races.' She walked backwards, still speaking. 'Can you ask the dragons to stand behind the boats while we awaken them?'

'Lamiya!' said Lazuli, striding out. 'Let's go.'

Spinning around, she jogged past Lazuli. 'Hurry up, esteemed pacer.' She laughed when he sprinted by her and ran all the way to the assembled lines of paddlers.

'One way to warm up,' she murmured on reaching the team. Lulite promptly handed her the pouch of clover and flowers to awaken her boat and she eyed her friend fondly. 'Are you feeling alright? Good to drum?'

'Wouldn't miss it,' said Lulite, her eyes shining. 'There'll be time enough to be a mother soon.' She returned to her place at the front of the team, beside Lazuli and Larimar.

Lamiya waited until Atage approached, accompanied by Lyber who was clutching the wooden tally board he'd used to keep score for the races in Riverfall. Her pulse lifted a notch. Could her team win as best boat overall again? She beamed at them both. 'I'll welcome the teams, then Atage can lead us through the awakening ceremony.'

She stood before the teams, waves of pride surging through her. The lake glittered blues, silvers and golds and the four boats looked magnificent, only overshadowed by the three formidable dragons poised by the boat tails. Akachi peered at each boat then nuzzled the red boat's tail. Lamiya's heart lifted: Akachi liked their boat! Surely, that bode well? The paddlers were splendid in their vivacious team colours, standing neatly to attention, eager eyes upon her. So many familiar and dear faces: Beram, Mookaite, Tengar, Ejad, Clommus … they were all here.

From the head of the Riverwood team, Malach gave her a wry smile. His new boat, still named Raptor, looked less chunky, lighter and faster. She swallowed and Malach's smile turned to one of challenge. She did a double-take on noticing Fenchi standing in the drummer position just behind Malach. The grey tunic and brown shorts highlighted the woman's curves, but there was muscle in her arms and legs. Lamiya nodded and Fenchi gave a surprised smile in return. Then Malach scowled and Fenchi lowered her eyes.

Lamiya gazed beyond the paddlers, tears burning the back of her eyes at the colourful crowd of hundreds of happy people — *her* people — chatting excitedly and holding feathers and streamers ready to cheer the boats on.

Don't let it go to your head. U-Mali's amused words appeared in her mind. *We're all here, in the Meeting Place so*

we can see everything and everybody. Glide well, dear heart.
The presence vanished.

We are so proud of you. Lestaya sounded as if she we crying.

Race hard and well, said Azuri gruffly.

Blinking back tears, Lamiya glanced over her shoulder, her heart swelling with joy at Everand standing tall and prominent with the mages, his eyes locked upon her. *Stronger together.* His deep voice sounded in her mind. *My reason for being.*

Almost overcome, Lamiya took a breath and spread her arms wide. 'Welcome to Riverplain!' she cried. 'Dearest of friends, we and the dragons welcome you to our shore. May this sun be filled with friendship and joy and long remembered in our hearts. I thank you all for being here, for being part of a gathering of *all* of Ossilis.'

Her next words were drowned out by the cheering and whooping from her people and the cries of 'Yosh' and 'Yo!' and 'Ki!' and 'Ee-ahh!' All four teams waved their paddles and clapped each other's shoulders. With a rapid fluttering of wings, Whirr swooped in to perch on her shoulder. 'There you are,' she murmured. He peeped twice then scrambled down the front of her tunic. Now she felt ready.

When she lifted her arms again, the noise ebbed away. 'I ask Atage of Riverfall to lead us through the awakening of the boats.' She skipped down the gentle slope to take her position at the front of her team. Lazuli squeezed her shoulder, his face dancing with excitement.

'First, I thank U-Lamiya and the people of Riverplain for hosting these races and trade festival.' Atage gestured to the dragons and then to the collection of mages. 'I echo U-Lamiya's joy that this sun, for the first time, all of Ossilis is gathered together.' He held up a hand to forestall any crowd reaction.

'I ask that we acknowledge the dragons, Akachi, Mizukaze and Hanachi, and thank them profusely for giving us good rainfall. A cartload of offerings will be brought to the shore for them once the races are finished.'

While everyone bowed, Akachi roared and Mizukaze swished his tail, making the back end of the four boats wobble in the water. Tears burning the back of her eyes again, Lamiya clutched the pouch of clover.

Atage beckoned. 'I now invite Glide Lamiya to awaken her boat.'

Stepping past her team, Lamiya looked into the intricately carved red-gold face of the boat Akachi. Lapsi, Lattic and Lopa had done an incredible job. Boat Akachi was imperious and commanding yet elegant and mystical at the same time. The red scales with golden rims painted along the boat's sides were flawlessly uniform and the boat looked sleek and fast. Built to skim the water. They'd only trained in her twice, but the boat had felt good. The races would be the true test.

Looking to the back of the boat, Lamiya gave the real Akachi a coy smile. *May we bring you honour, this sun.* Then she held the posy of clover and red flowers up for Jibo to light with his torch. Waving the smouldering and divinely sweet-smelling bouquet under the boat dragon's nose, she cried, 'Great Akachi, come fly the water with me. Skim the light and dance the waves. Bring Riverplain to glory.'

Taking the small bowl that Lulite passed her, she dipped her right forefinger into the red dye made from crushed petals of the red-flower tree near Akachi's cave, and pressed a red dot into the centre of the boat's golden left eye. The eye became textured like an iris and shimmered. Hiding her smile, Lamiya stepped to the right of the boat and repeated her moves to dot the other eye.

From beneath her lowered eyelashes, she watched Akachi breathe gently into the back end of the boat. For a single heartbeat, the whole boat rippled and the scales looked real — a dragon readying to race. Her heart thudding against her breastbone, Lamiya twisted around, seeking Lazuli. He was staring at her, wonder highlighting his grey eyes. The corners of his lips curved up and he gave her a crisp nod. Clasping the empty pouch, she stepped away from the boat and moved to beside Lazuli, her heart still thudding wildly.

Tengar, Cowrie and Malach all wakened their boats. Lamiya observed intently, but just like at the races in Riverfall, although the boats became somehow more vibrant, none shimmered like hers had. A strange quivering rippled through her and Lazuli shook himself with a soft grunt. 'You felt it?' she whispered, awed when he nodded and shivered again. His grey eyes bored into her, and she felt an invisible connection bind them: the front and the back of the boat. What just happened?

'Paddlers,' called Atage. 'You may board.'

The shore exploded into activity and the four teams swiftly boarded. From her stance at the glide platform, she waved to Everand as he walked briskly towards the finish flag with the group of mages following him, their flapping robes making her think of a gaggle of ducks. He waved back, then listened to a question from Tiliqua. Keeping the boat steady, she watched eight fishermen, clad in the Riverplain orange-and-green uniform, row the four turn-marker boats away from the shore. Two headed south towards the nearer end of the lake and river inlet, and the other two rowed north towards the boatshed. From there, she knew one would head east to the wetlands near Akachi's cave to mark the distant turn for the long race.

Atage moved closer to the water, and she focused on him. Although the teams knew what the races would be, and the order of the races, only Lazuli and the three judges knew the line-up order for each race. Lazuli had planned the races meticulously, making sure that, as host, Riverplain held no unfair advantage. A shiver ran down her bare arms. What had Akachi done when she breathed into the boat? What would she — and Lazuli —

feel when they raced in earnest? Lamiya chewed her lower lip. No unfair advantage.

'The first race is from the marker near the boatshed back to the finish flag in front of the Meeting Place,' called Atage. 'Boats must line up on the *far* side of the marker boat, in the deeper water, in the following order: closest to the marker boat is Riverfall, then Riverwood, then Riversea and Riverplain on the furthest side. Everyone got that?' Atage waited until all four glides had acknowledged.

'Remember that no boat must cross directly in front of or interfere with another. Hold your line as straight as possible until you pass the orange finish flag.' He indicated the flag, where Everand and Lyber stood ready. 'Jibo will sound the horn as each boat nose passes the flag. Do not stop paddling until your *whole* boat is past. Paddle well, and may the best boat win. The start will be when the rear rower in the marker boat drops the green flag.'

'Paddles back,' called Lamiya. 'We lead the way to the marker.' The boat reversed smoothly, and she turned the nose towards the boatshed. 'Paddles up. Go.' She grinned when Lazuli and Larimar plunged their paddles in as hard as a race start and the red boat surged forward. After twenty strokes she called, 'Steady. Save your energy.'

A bubble of water slipped by on her right and Mizukaze's head poked briefly out of the water. She tightened her grip on the oar, hoping the exuberant dragon had listened to Everand's command that they not impede any of the boats. Not even Malach's. The team working steadily, Lamiya glanced ahead. Lazuli had planned a first race of about five hundred strokes and the paddle out to the marker boat provided a solid warm-up.

'Slow the rate.' She eased her boat past the marker boat, nodding at the two rowers, and turned in a broad curve until they faced back towards the Meeting Place, allowing sufficient space for the other three boats.

'Pretty lake,' said Cowrie when Seasprite eased into position. 'There be no waves though.'

Lamiya laughed. No doubt Riversea would find a way to introduce waves when it was their turn to host. Working to keep her boat straight, she admired the elegant, flowing artwork along the side of Seasprite. Weren't they the artists, Charonia and Clama, towards the back of the boat? Charonia smiled shyly, patting the base of her neck and Lamiya beamed back. At the feast she would indeed wear the beautiful necklace Charonia had designed; her special gift from Everand. How could she not? The necklace would also proudly adorn her neck when he and she became joined forever in the partnering ceremony. A tingle of anticipation trickled down her spine. *Focus on the races.*

The sunlight bounced off the water while they waited for Raptor and Mizuchi to line up. Lamiya uncurled her fingers then curled them tightly around the top of the oar. There was virtually no current and little breeze; this would be an honest and fast race. Her quick peek suggested the four boat heads were in a neat line, she gulped in a breath and adjusted her balance.

The rower in the rear of the fishing boat stood and held up a green flag. 'Paddlers, sit ready. Take a breath. Go!' The green flag swung down.

The four boats ploughed forwards, the paddles splashing deep and strong, the four dragon heads vying to outdo each other. Five deep strokes, followed by ten quick ones, then Lazuli and Larimar stretched forward, reaching longer, adding more power, the team all leaning in time. Her boat nudged ahead.

'Yosh!' cried Tengar, and the Riverfall paddlers reached longer too.

Halfway, and the red and blue boats still led on the outer lines by a narrow margin. On her right, Seasprite's nose was back level with her glide platform, Cowrie yelling for lifts. Raptor was aligned with Seasprite, Malach's mouth set in a grim line. Lamiya looked at Lulite and gave a clear nod. Lulite lifted her drum rate and the pacers followed seamlessly. Her boat edged ahead, water slapping merrily against the bow and silver bubbly wash gushing past on both sides.

Joy coursing through her, Lamiya nodded again. Then again. The boat skimmed the turquoise water, the slapping waves gurgling like a dragon song from the deep. Lamiya blinked when a dark shadow sped past on her outer edge with a splash of a red-scaled tail. Peering out the neck of her tunic, Whirr snapped his beak.

'Yosh! Yosh!' The blue-and-gold head of Mizuchi was coming through on the far side. A respectful distance away but beside it, Mizukaze was frolicking through the water with Hanachi behind him.

'Ki! Ki! Ki!' The paddlers in Raptor strained hard, Fenchi leaning forward, drumming fast and yelling at them. Raptor nudged ahead of Seasprite.

The Meeting Place loomed on Lamiya's right and she focused on the orange finish flag fluttering on the shore with the judges standing behind it. Pulse racing, she screamed, 'Yo! Yo! Go *now*!' The boat shot forward. *Whoa*! She righted her balance, then the red-and-gold boat, feeling light as a feather, hurtled past the orange flag with the blue-and-gold Mizuchi nose two strokes behind. Yes! They'd done it. Just.

At the front, Lazuli and Larimar high-fived each other, then doubled over, breathing hard. The rest of the team patted each other's backs, grinning broadly.

'Great work!' called Lamiya. 'Cheer for the other teams.'

Tengar glided Mizuchi towards them. 'Well done, Lamiya.'

'That was close,' she replied. 'Great work by Riverfall too.' She waved at each paddler and grinned at Ejad, glad to see him accepted into the Riverfall team.

While the paddlers took the opportunity to drink from their bottles, she lined the boat up to face the finish flag and judges. Tengar slid Mizuchi in on her left, then Malach aligned Raptor and Cowrie brought Seasprite in. Was this the finish order to be confirmed by the judges?

'Good work,' said Latog, looking up at her from the back seat. 'I see I've lost my glide spot forever.'

'I was taught by the master,' said Lamiya, bending forward. 'How's your leg?'

'Stiff. But it'll do,' replied Latog, rubbing at his left thigh. 'Glad to be on board.'

'No more climbing trees?' asked Lamiya sweetly, smiling when Luvu grunted and elbowed Latog in the ribs.

'Well done paddlers!' Atage's words rang across the gap. 'An exciting first race, as hard-fought as anticipated. The results are as you have lined up, Riverplain by a mere nose from Riverfall, then Riverwood by less than a boat length and Riversea just a nose behind them.' The crowd clapped and waved their feathers and streamers.

Lamiya looked at Everand, who was busy explaining the results to the mages, pointing at Lyber's tally board. Sensing her gaze, he glanced up and gave her a quick smile. Tiliqua glanced across too and dipped her head in respect.

'The second race,' began Atage, reading from notes Lazuli had given him, 'is a test of technique and skill. It is a short race, just a hundred strokes, from the marker boat to my right,' Atage waved a hand at the fishing boat some two hundred paces away, close to the shoreline, 'back to the finish flag. The catch? No glide. The paddlers must steer the boat.'

Atage paused while the crowd muttered and oohed. 'The glides will remain in position and can call directions to the paddlers, but the glide oar must be taken out and laid in the boat.'

Lazuli stood up. 'I suggest the glides do this now to practise on the way to the marker, and so the judges can confirm the oars are out and it will be an equal contest.' He sat and Larimar handed back his paddle.

'Very well,' said Atage. 'Reverse your boats to face the start boat, then remove the oars. Wait — before you go, remember that any boat crossing in front of another or bumping another will be disqualified. If this looks likely, the infringing boat must stop. Got it?' The glides all nodded.

Lazuli stood again. 'Paddlers, acknowledge. Use your skills wisely and stop if you need to.' He twirled his paddle between his hands as he roamed his eyes over the paddlers in each boat, waiting for them to nod.

Lamiya watched the tension leave Lazuli's shoulders. He'd insisted he wanted to include this race but it held some risk of bumping and tipping, as did the next one. She agreed with his reasoning though, that the races should be a test of all-round skill and technique as well as strength and stamina, and the races should be different to those held by Riverfall. All the teams had been given forty suns' notice to practise; she hoped they had.

Reversing until the boat nose faced the start boat, she pulled the oar from its socket and carefully slid the blade end down the centre of the seats between the paddlers. Adjusting her balance without the oar to lean on, she watched the other glides follow suit.

As soon as the four glides were ready, Atage spoke. 'The line-up order for this race is, from the wider lake side of the start boat, Riverwood, Riverplain, Riversea then Riverfall.'

Lamiya grimaced; they were next to Riverwood. Recalling the tight turn and narrow canal that the Riverwood paddlers navigated each time they took their boat in and out, Raptor could be the boat to beat. 'Paddles up, go,' she said absently, her mind running over the drills they'd practised for the paddlers to keep the boat straight.

Without the glide oars, it took some toing and froing before the boats were lined up straight and equal distances apart.

Lamiya squinted at the orange finish flag. Not far, but far enough if the boat nose wavered. Malach gave her a confident, smug look and she arched an eyebrow at him. *We'll see.*

'Paddlers, get ready,' called the rear rower, holding up the green flag.

Lamiya kneeled on the glide platform with her right leg bent up; less chance of losing her balance but she could still see what was happening. Lazuli would direct the team from the front, Lulite relaying his orders. She suppressed a smile when Malach gave her a confused look, remaining standing but putting his right leg forward, bent at the knee.

'Take a breath, go!' The rower swung the flag down.

On her right, Raptor surged forward, Malach leaning easily into the movement and his team pulling hard. Her boat head became aligned with his first row of paddlers, Lazuli having taken a more cautious start to make sure they were straight. After twenty strokes she felt the boat lift and they crept forward beside Raptor. She glanced left, seeing Mizuchi and Seasprite had also started cautiously. She frowned. Was it her imagination or were their boats' noses drifting towards the shore? Yes. Tengar and Cowrie both called for the front right paddlers to paddle stronger to correct the angle.

Her boat lifted again and she concentrated. Raptor seemed to be edging towards them and she swallowed, remembering Malach's efforts to run her into the bank in one of the races in Riverfall. She glared at him and he frowned, then realised and yelled for his front right paddlers to draw water for five strokes. Raptor straightened, and her boat head crept forward to be level with Fenchi in the drummer seat. Lulite bent forward, listening to Lazuli. Then she picked up her drum rate and the team stroked faster, digging their paddle blades deep. Paddling straight and true, they were bringing it home already! Lazuli had drilled them over and over, and had even swapped a couple of paddlers to ensure equal power on both sides. It was working.

'Ki! Ki!' shouted Malach, swinging a clenched fist forward. 'Take them!' Fenchi drummed harder and the Riverwood team gave a massive lift, the muscles in the burly hunters' arms and shoulders bulging. Raptor clove through the water, straight as an arrow.

Lamiya watched her team reaching and pulling, saw the white bubbles increase down the sides of the boat, but they couldn't regain any ground. Raptor passed the flag with boat Akachi's nose still level with Fenchi. The curvy woman did a drum roll, hair slicked back and sweat running down her face and the Riverwood paddlers all punched a fist up. 'Ki!'

'Nicely done,' Lamiya said to Malach, astounded by the warm grin he returned.

'Good race,' said Malach. 'Good test.'

Pushing to her feet, Lamiya allowed the paddlers to feed the oar back to her. 'Great work, team. Lazuli, well done.'

Lazuli twisted around to check where all the boats were, relief crossing his face that all four had finished.

'That be tough, Lamiya,' called Cowrie, guiding Seasprite past in a curve to face the finish line and judges. 'We be planning something tricky for when you come to us.' But he was grinning.

The four boats lined up and Lamiya detected a frown on Tengar's face when his boat was announced equal third with Riversea, two points each. She chewed her lower lip. Was it possible there was a bit of current towards the shore? Just as well they were rotating the line-up order. Lazuli's arm muscles rippled as he drained his water bottle. Was he happy with how the races were going? He was doing incredibly well to focus on his races when he must be worried about the overall event and whether all the teams were happy.

She wriggled her toes.

Two races down, two to go.

Chapter Forty-one

In no time, the four boats were back at the same marker boat. Lamiya worked the oar while her paddlers reversed the boat into position between Mizuchi and Raptor. One hundred strokes backwards. Her shoulders prickled with discomfort at not being able to see the course, despite all the drills they'd done for this race. Suppressing a shiver, she watched Lulite, who was frowning and perched tensely in the drummer seat. Lulite would help tell her if the boat was not travelling straight.

Running her eyes over the solid torsos of the hunters from Riverwood and the naturally strong-boned build of the paddlers from Riversea, she sighed. Their strength would be an advantage. Lazuli had insisted this was fair, given that the leaner frames of the paddlers from Riverplain and Riverfall gave them an edge in the longer races. And it wasn't that long since they'd done the epic paddle all the way to Riverwood so she and Everand could retrieve the Staropal. The ultimate training for a long race.

Gripping the oar, she pulled it up to just above the water, keeping it ready to dip in to correct their line if necessary, and adjusted her balance ready to go backwards. *It won't take long. Nothing will go wrong.* Whirr clawed his way up her tunic to lean snugly against the side of her neck, facing backwards. His feathers tickled. 'Nice,' she whispered. 'You too can tell me if we're not straight.'

The green flag dropped and her team plunged their paddles in behind them and pushed the blades forward through the water. Lazuli and Larimar set a steady, solid rate, one that could be sustained given the massive effort required. After thirty strokes, Lulite drummed with her right hand but held her left one out and flapped it inward, indicating the boat was drifting to Lamiya's right. Whirr peeped near her ear, barely audible over the splashing paddles and drumbeats. Peering over her shoulder, Lamiya dipped the oar in for a quick correction and then checked back for Lulite's nod.

At fifty strokes, Lazuli and Larimar began to chant, 'Yo!' with each stroke, coaxing the team to maintain time, to keep plunging and pushing. Lulite lifted the drum rate. The air filled with a cacophony of 'Yosh' 'Yo' 'Ki' and 'Ee-ahh' that made it hard to concentrate. Lamiya winced; the uneven drumbeats sounded discordant.

At seventy strokes, the 'Ki' and 'Ee-ahh' were louder, faster. Her heart sank. Raptor and Seasprite were pulling ahead, the paddlers thrusting their blades in behind with impressive force and churning them through the water. On her right, Tengar stood in perfect alignment with her, their boats surging together with each stroke. She ground her teeth and nodded at Lulite to lift again. They must beat Mizuchi or they'd lose too many points overall.

By ninety strokes, the backs of her legs were burning from balancing against the reverse surges and she felt the team's stroke rate falter. Lulite flapped her left hand, and Lamiya hurriedly corrected their line.

Tengar frowned at her then yelled, 'Yosh! Go!' His team lifted.

On the bank, Jibo blew the horn sharply twice, indicating the first two boats were past the finish flag. Lazuli shouted, 'Yo! Yo! Yo!' and her paddlers rallied for the final few strokes. Jibo blew the horn sharply — twice again.

Lamiya put the oar blade in the water and leaned on the oar haft while her paddlers stopped the boat. By the spirits, it was good that race was over! Who'd have thought the four boats would be so close going backwards? Her legs trembling, she eyed her groaning, sweating team. Their arms and legs must be filled with afterburn. They needed those fire cakes before the last race.

Tengar, also leaning on his oar, grimaced at her. 'That was not fun, but I understand why you included it.' He nodded at Lazuli, who was listening in. 'Well designed races. I look forward to the next one most of all.'

Lazuli brushed sweat from his forehead and grinned at Tengar. 'May the best boat win.'

'Team,' called Lamiya, 'stretch and have a drink. Lulite, pass around the fire cakes.'

'Paddlers!' Atage boomed from the shore. Lamiya saw Everand was beside him, amplifying the words. 'Go for a cooldown paddle and then line up for the results. The judges need a short discussion.'

Lazuli twisted right around to look at her and held up his water bottle, upside down to indicate it was empty. Lamiya thought hard. They couldn't possibly start the long race without having a drink. And more fire cakes. She turned the boat's nose towards the shore. 'Lazuli, paddle us in and we'll get more water.' He nodded and set a gentle rate to take them in.

'Whirr,' she murmured, 'tell Everand we need people to bring water and snacks to each team. Quickly.' Watching her bird zip towards the shore she cursed under her breath. They should have thought of this. Tengar and Cowrie were watching her, so she called out they should wait near the shore too. By the time the four boats were holding position in shallow water, six people were running towards them carrying baskets. Four women briskly handed each drummer parcels of cakes and bowls of sliced fruit, and two men splashed between the boats handing in extra water bottles.

Sipping her drink, Lamiya gazed around checking everything, noticing Lazuli doing likewise. The sun was halfway to sun-high, coating her face, arms and legs with a gentle warmth befitting the end of growing season. The lake was smooth, except for the swirls where the dragons were swimming, waiting for the long race. The breeze was no more than a sigh against her skin, and the leaves of the trees and bushes along the shore were tinged with the oranges and reds of the imminent colour-leaf season.

She nibbled her fire cake, enjoying the zesty burst over her tongue. One more race. The one they wanted. Lazuli was rolling his shoulders and stretching his neck from side to side. He and Larimar had trained mercilessly with extra running, swimming and lifting rocks. She'd never seen him so fit and strong. Her heart skipped a few beats. Lazuli so wanted this race; so wanted to snatch the endurance race victory back from Riverfall.

Finishing her cake, she rubbed her palms down her trouser legs to dislodge the sticky crumbs. The other boats were preparing to go for an easy paddle given the judges still hadn't called them. What could be taking so long? She thought of Jibo's double horn-toots. Were they deciding how to distribute the points to tied boats? That must be it, given the importance of the total scores in determining who was the best boat overall.

'Let's do a loosener,' she called. The paddlers tucked their water bottles under their seats, vigorously rubbed their palms up and down their shorts legs and retrieved their paddles. 'Paddles up!'

While they paddled a slow circle, she did the sums. Her team had four points for winning the first race and three for second place in the second one. Their tie with Riverfall in the third race gave them two points, and a total of nine so far. Riverfall had three and two points, and another two for the tied third, giving seven points. Her pulse lifted. They were two points ahead of Riverfall! If they won *or* came second in the last race, they could still win overall. Had Lazuli worked this out?

What about the other teams? Riversea had one point for a fourth, two for a third and probably four for equal first backwards, giving them seven points too. So, they were level with Riverfall. Unexpected. And Malach's team? Riverwood had two for a third, four for winning the no-glide race and probably another four for the backwards race, giving them ten points. Wait. What? Malach's team was in the lead! To win overall she'd need to beat Raptor by *two* boats in the long race! Lazuli's efforts to design fair races had certainly achieved this.

The horn sounded a long blast, calling the boats. Lamiya ran her tongue over her lips as the boats lined up, wishing she could confer with Lazuli. You've set your strategy, she told herself. You can't change it now. Her team had the stamina and they'd drilled and drilled their corner turns. The best boat would win. She brushed a loose hair from her eyelashes as Atage started to speak.

'The judges are impressed with the variation in these races, resulting in a tight contest. The backwards race yielded two sets of tied boats and we had to determine the fairest way to distribute the points. While it was tempting to award points for two first and two second places, in the end we decided awarding two firsts and two thirds would be more consistent with the overall intention of testing skill, technique, strength and stamina.' Atage stopped to clear his throat.

Everand stepped forward. 'Accordingly, we have awarded four points to Riverwood and Riversea for incredible skill in reversing so straight and with such power, and two points to Riverfall and Riverplain.'

Lamiya swallowed. *No unfair advantage*. Giving her team and Riverfall three points each for a second instead of a third would have given them the edge going into the final race. This way, it was open. She nodded at Everand and he smiled. He'd known she would understand. Lazuli's shoulders slumped, then he straightened up and whispered to Larimar, whose expression turned serious. Lulite gave the pacers an incredulous look then glanced up at her and shrugged. Lamiya's pulse raced. Lazuli was determined; Malach had better be ready!

'Paddlers,' called Atage, 'Lazuli estimates the final race will require around two thousand strokes, with four tight turns in it. This race will test everything — strength, technique, skill and stamina. The four marker boats are in position and you must paddle on the outside, or right-hand side, of each boat. In other words, each marker will be on your *left* when you pass it. You start here, in front of the Meeting Place, and travel towards the nearest marker first.' He waved an arm. 'That way.'

Pausing, Atage reviewed Lazuli's notes. 'From there, you head due east, towards the distant wetlands, turn left and travel the entire length of the lake, turn left again for the second shorter side, then left again at the marker near the boatshed. So, the final leg will be the same as race one — from the boatshed back to the Meeting Place.'

Everand added, 'You must not cross in front of or impede another boat, especially as you make the turns. The boat reaching the marker first has the inside run and the other boats must turn wide of it. If you are to pass another boat, go to the *right* of it.' He smiled. 'The rowers in the marker boats will be watching, as will the dragons. Do not give them cause to roar at you!'

Atage lifted his notes. 'The line-up for the final race is Riversea furthest out on the left, Riverfall, Riverwood and Riverplain nearest the shore. Remember, you must go *right* of the first marker, which will come up quickly. Please align your boat noses with Jibo and the start flag. Paddle strong and hard and may the best boat win!'

The crowd cheered and clapped, many waving cloth-and-feather streamers of orange and green. Children shrieked and skipped, waving flags and an array of coloured feathers.

Lamiya moved her boat to nearest the shore, her heart sinking. They'd have to go widest for the first turn then try to make up ground. Had Lazuli put Riversea on the inside for the first turn anticipating Seasprite might need an edge by the final race, or had the judges varied the order? No matter, the order was fair. Too fair. They'd have to travel further than the other boats, at least for the first half.

Closing her eyes, she breathed deeply, imagining courage and determination flowing in and seeping down her arms, body and legs, all the way to her toes. Her chest expanded, and the wood beneath her feet softened and felt like scales. Resisting the temptation to peek, she absorbed the sensation. Akachi was with them in spirit. A large, rolling pulse travelled through the boat and she felt another heartbeat at the front echo hers — Lazuli. *Don't think, accept. Fly the water, skim the light and dance the waves.* A single, warm tear trickled down her cheek and she opened her eyes.

The crowds along the shore hooted and clapped and Lamiya dared not look at Everand, fixing her eyes on Lazuli's back. Glowing admiration filled her. Such a magnificent pacer. And friend. They must win, for him. A sudden silence descended; the flag was up.

'Paddlers, sit ready … take a breath … go!'

The water bubbled and churned as the boats ploughed towards the first marker. Knowing the water was deep enough near the river inlet, Lamiya took them wide. Better to stay out of trouble at the first turn when the boats would be together and get a clear run in the straight. Seasprite was awkward around the turn, the tail spinning wide, and Tengar yelled at his team to draw water on the back outside so Mizuchi's tail wouldn't hit them. Malach started his turn, his team paddling short and sharp on the inside while the outside paddlers ploughed their blades through the water in long and strong strokes. Raptor's nose spun in a sharp turn and despite her team's efforts, they lost ground.

As soon as she'd straightened the boat, Lamiya called, 'Lift!' Seamlessly, her team reached, stretched and pulled in their sustainable powerful stroke. The boat's nose lifted and waves slapped the bow. Better. After two hundred strokes, they were gaining on Raptor, the red-gold head drawing level with Riverwood's second row of paddlers. Further over, Mizuchi was level with Raptor and, on the inside, Seasprite was already dropping back. Lamiya jumped when the massive shadowy form of Akachi glided past underwater. *Fly the water.* Her team subtly quickened, inspired by the dragon, and she lost herself in their strong, steady rhythm.

Blinking back her focus, she found the second marker was close, the two rowers holding onto the boat sides, anticipating the choppy washes. Fully ahead of Seasprite, Tengar was holding Mizuchi's lead on the inside but Malach was edging Raptor closer to the blue-gold boat. Lamiya swallowed; he intended another super-tight turn. Go wide or go tight? Wide. There were still two turns to go. 'Turning wide!' she yelled, watching Lulite repeat her call to Lazuli. Then the marker was upon them.

Mizuchi slewed around the fishing boat, the front inside paddlers slamming their paddles into the water while the outside ones powered the boat around. Lamiya's heart leaped into her mouth when Raptor copied, the Riverwood inside paddles almost mingling with the outside paddles of Riverfall. That was bold!

'Front left draw water at pace!' she yelled, and Larimar, Lopa and Lattic leaned out on the inside front and thrust water under the boat. Boat Akachi nimbly swept around the turn, not losing any ground. Lamiya worked the oar hard and yelled, 'Yo! Go! Yo! Go!' The boat clove through the water, her team finding their rhythm before the others did.

Squinting against the sunlight, Lamiya fixed her intention on the silhouette of the third marker way, way ahead. It would be easy to lose trajectory and waste effort on this long, open stretch. She glanced at Malach, standing fierce and strong at the back of Raptor; she must not let him force her wider. *Get ahead.* Barely had she thought it when Lazuli and Larimar increased their power and the boat lightened. Yes! The water bubbled and Akachi, moving fast, came alongside, swimming with the boat. *Skim the light, dance the waves.*

Lazuli, Larimar, Laza and Lopa added more power for twenty strokes, then Levog, Lattic, Lapsi and Lepid joined in. The waves sang a merry chorus against the prow and the wash rushing down the sides became pure silver. Another twenty strokes and Luvu and Latog added power at the back. The boat edged forward beside Raptor until she was standing level with Malach and the red-gold dragon head vied for supremacy over Raptor's vicious eagle head.

'Ki! Ki!' yelled Malach and his paddlers strained harder. Fenchi flicked her hair back over her shoulders then drummed hard and fast, sweat glistening on her forehead.

'Hold the pattern!' called Lamiya. They still had half the race to go. Her paddlers reverted to their sustained strong rate for twenty strokes then power-lifted for twenty, repeating this seamlessly, as they'd drilled. Over and over. Each time they added power, the boat crept forward until she stood level with the middle of Raptor. The red-gold head and neck stretched away before her, enjoying its lead. Peeking over her shoulder, she saw Seasprite was a boat length behind, and Tengar was driving his team hard to keep his inside run at the third marker.

The sun grew warmer on Lamiya's cheeks, arms and legs. Her tunic clung to her back and sweat trickled down the back of her legs. Her plaited hair felt heavy and she longed to lift it up to cool her neck and back. A lump clogged her throat. Her team was paddling magnificently, sodden tunics gripping their backs, their arms glistening with rivulets of sweat. Snapping arms up and plunging down deep, snapping arms up and plunging down deep, their timing was impeccable and enormous silver bubbles were flowing away from everyone's blades. In the back row, Luvu and Latog were paddling powerfully, no sign that Latog had been injured. *One team, one heart, one spirit.* They deserved to win.

But Raptor was still positioned annoyingly on her inside. No way she'd get past before the third marker. Checking on the others, her pulse raced. Mizuchi was dropping back, the blue-gold nose now level with Raptor's fanned eagle tail. How had this happened? Work it out, work it out! Or you'll lose and Lazuli will never forgive you. Shaking her head to dislodge the stinging droplets of sweat from her eyes, she narrowed her focus to Raptor. What had changed?

The boat sat higher in the water than the one they'd raced at Riverfall, so it was definitely lighter. The prow was more curved, less square, so it glided better. She eyed Fenchi. The woman would be a lot lighter than whoever had drummed at Riverfall. Was that why Malach chose her? Wait, no. Pelamis killed one of the hunter-paddlers so Malach had to replace him. Was Fenchi his favourite? She skimmed over the entire team. Still muscle-bound, their torsos and arms were more streamlined, less chunky. And their timing was good. They'd trained. Far harder than expected. She swallowed. Lazuli had challenged Malach to make him agree to come — and Raptor was now the team to beat.

Chewing at her lower lip, she thought hard. Was there *anything* she could improve? They were still lighter, that was their edge. And they had Lazuli's sheer willpower. The final leg was where these would count. Keep calm until then. *Skim the light, dance the waves.*

Lazuli and Larimar's shoulders were tightening as they reached further, striving to pull ahead. 'Hold the pattern!' she shouted. 'Hold our position!' After a few strokes they resumed their sustained rate and she sensed the team take a breath.

'Great work!' she called. 'We've got this. Stay calm.' Lulite tipped forward and repeated her words to the front rows.

The third marker boat loomed. Malach held Raptor's line so he couldn't be accused of cutting in front of Mizuchi. Another wide turn for her team but she'd be turning slightly ahead. Whatever they did, they must not cross Raptor's path. What to do? Her breath caught. She couldn't turn early, too much risk of cutting across, but they could race the *entire* turn. No short paddling. She uncurled her fingers from the oar and flexed them several times, then took an extra firm grip. Leave the paddlers *all* powering around while she took the full brunt of the turn with the oar. The boat would lean a little, but they'd manage.

'Lazuli!' she yelled, seeing his head lift a notch and Lulite's attention focus on her. 'Paddle hard the entire turn. No matter what.' Lulite missed a few beats as she tilted forward and repeated the command. Lazuli and Larimar nodded and firmed their grip on their paddles. Lamiya smiled grimly as the effect rippled down the boat and every paddler tightened their grip, adjusted their balance, braced their legs and feet ready. *Please let this work.*

'Ki! Ki! Ki!' Malach exhorted and Raptor sped towards the marker on a tight angle.

As she'd anticipated, Malach's paddlers dug in shorter, sharper on the inside, powering longer on the outside, and Raptor turned sharply but slowed, the eagle's beak still midway down her boat. Yes! They were out of the way. She hauled on the oar and, cleaving the water at full-pace, boat Akachi sheered in an impressively fast curve, the boat leaning inwards with the momentum and her team powering hard to Lazuli and Larimar's 'Yo! Yo! Yo!'

As soon as they were around, she straightened the nose. 'Lift! Lift!' Unbelievably, the team found more speed and power and the eagle head slipped back to level with her.

'Lift again!' The boat skimmed the glinting water, air rushed past her face and goosebumps rose along her arms. *Skim the water, dance the waves.* It worked! Clear water in front of them. So tempting to pull away hard. She blinked. Did Lazuli just shake his head as if he'd heard her thought?

Go now, she thought, watching him. He shook his head and maintained his rhythm. Beside the boat, Akachi humped a few times, the red-gold scales of her back and golden spines catching the light. *Fine. We wait for the final leg.*

A light breeze stirred, chasing the stray hairs away from her cheeks, and the boat's nose bounced over the surface ruffles. The boatshed was already coming up on her right, so maybe fifty strokes to the final marker. In her peripheral vision, she could see the beak of Raptor's eagle head behind her.

'Repeat the last turn!' she yelled. 'Go in hard!' Hurriedly wiping each clammy hand down her trouser leg, she gripped the oar for all she was worth and firmed up her balance. Whirr gamely climbed up onto her shoulder and dug his talons in.

'Ki! Ki!' Raptor surged, trying to force her wide. She could feel Malach's glare boring a hole in her back.

Scowling, she nudged the boat nose slightly to the right to give Raptor space. 'Lift!' The boat drove forward, giving the margin she needed. 'Power! Power!' Her team power-paddled the fastest curve imaginable, the boat tilting inward with the force. The ruffled water gurgled and sang against the boat's prow and Whirr burst into melodic peeping and chirping.

They came out of the turn further ahead. 'Yo! Yo! Fly the water!' she shrieked, elation zinging through her, making her fingers and toes tingle. Akachi surged ahead, humping through the water and waving the tip of her tail. The water burbled on Akachi's far side as Mizukaze and Hanachi swam up. Mizukaze lifted his head out of the water and roared with pleasure. Her heart singing, Lamiya yelled, 'Go for home. Power pattern!'

Encased in a timeless bubble of blue sky, sunlight, glinting water and joy, Lamiya steered straight, revelling in the power of her team, the tempo of the drumbeat and the sheer magic of racing the dragons. The paddlers reached, plunged and drove, the boat skimming the light and dancing the waves. The platform felt warm and scaly beneath her feet, the sensation that the boat was a dragon stealing over her. More magic. *One team, one heart, one spirit.* Her chest swelled with pride and happiness until it hurt to breathe.

Too soon, the Meeting Place was towering on her right and the chaos of the crowd intruded, bursting her bubble. People were running along the shore, shrieking and waving. She fixed her eyes on the orange flag. 'Bring it home! Now!'

Lazuli and Larimar exhorted a final burst from their arms, the team valiantly following and boat Akachi sprinted past the flag, Jibo's horn blaring loud in her ears. Her heart hammered. They'd done it! Lazuli and Larimar punched their fists high, and the people of Riverplain screamed and shouted and clapped. The air above the crowd was sprayed with tossed streamers and flags, like a flock of vividly plumed birds, multiplying as real birds swooped in, caught the streamers and flags and swirled in loops before dropping them. *Her* people. *Her* birds.

Oh my! U-Mali's strangled gasp sounded in her mind.

The horn sounded again and Lamiya twisted to observe Raptor finishing hard with Mizuchi a boat length away and Seasprite another length behind them.

'Team,' she croaked. 'You are magnificent. Words fail me.' The boat had drifted well past the finish so she turned to face the shore. The paddlers took a few easy strokes, then stopped the boat in shallow water. Lamiya shook her head, tears mingling with droplets of sweat. Nothing would ever be more memorable. She dragged the back of her hand across her eyes, watching her paddlers laughing, crying and hugging each other. Above the crowd, the air was still a riot of colourful birds chittering and zooming around, dropping petals and feathers to the people dancing below.

Wait. Lazuli was getting out of the boat. Why? He splashed into the water and waded to her, his face contorted. Was he laughing or crying? Uncertain, she held onto the oar. Until Lazuli threw his arms around her waist and yanked her off the platform. She grabbed at his shoulders then clasped her arms around his neck. 'Don't you dare dunk me!'

Next thing, she was crushed against his quivering body, his chin resting on her head while he heaved in breaths. His heart pounded against hers, their heartbeats racing together. *The front and the back of the boat.* Words eluding her, she hugged him fiercely. Her special pacer, best friend, magnificent, bold Lazuli … this moment was for him and her. Disentangling herself, she kissed both of his salty cheeks, her heart wrenching at the love gleaming in his eyes. There was nothing she could say.

Gripping Lazuli's hand, she turned to the crowd. With the broadest smile ever, she held their entwined hands aloft and yelled, 'Yo!'

The shore erupted into total chaos.

And weaving his way among the mayhem was Everand.

Coming to her.

Chapter Forty-Two

Everand sipped his feeja wine, trying again to persuade his shoulders to relax. The noise was making his ears ring. So many people crammed into the feast area drinking, laughing, calling out and making a merry racket. In the centre, the bonfire burned bright, throwing sparks and smoke toward the velvet, star-laced sky far above. The air was crisp against his cheeks and nose with the promise of the encroaching cooler season.

Once more, he was alone in a crowd. The mages had returned to the Guild, declining the feast on the grounds they'd stay for the one to celebrate his partnering ceremony instead. He eased a crick in his neck on one side, then the other. The races had been a challenge for the mages; so much activity and revelry. But he was glad they'd come, and immeasurably relieved the apology was done. His nape still turned ice-cold whenever he thought of Akachi towering over Mantiss with her massive jaws open wide.

Taking another sip he rolled the smooth wine under his tongue, watching Lamiya, skirt bunched in one hand, climb the short steps to the wooden platform they'd built for the race awards, tailed by Lazuli and Lepid. His throat tightened. Standing between the brothers, Lamiya was as stunning as ever in her turquoise top and skirt the colour of spun moonlight, the pearly shells of her necklace, his precious gift to her, catching the firelight and glinting like fireflies perched on her collarbones. His eyes growing warm and moist, he slipped the feeja wine down his throat. If only he could swallow the raw emotions rising.

Squeezing his eyes shut, he recalled with crystal clarity the sight of Lazuli ploughing through the water to swing Lamiya off the boat. Observed again their fierce, emotional embrace. Felt again the stabbing pain in his heart. How could she be his when she so belonged with her people; no … was the heart and soul of her people? He gasped at the pain searing his heart.

Her heart-shaped face and gorgeous, intent grey-blue eyes appeared behind his eyelids, peering at him, concern puckering her elegant eyebrows. He opened his eyes. She *was* looking at him. Her lips moved and Whirr climbed out of her tunic. The bird flew from the dais straight to him, landed on his shoulder and rubbed his downy head against the side of his neck. How could she possibly know of his pain? Heart thudding, he smiled, the depth of love in her return smile almost toppling him from the bench.

His arm was jostled, spilling his wine, and he was bumped and shoved by Beram and Mookaite sliding onto the bench on both sides of him. With much elbowing and laughter, Ejad, Acim and Zink crowded onto the bench opposite.

'Traveller!' said Beram, clinking his mug against Everand's.

'Traveller no more,' said Mookaite firmly, squeezing his forearm with slender, elegant fingers. 'He belongs here now.'

'I have a question,' said Beram, twisting to regard him and flapping a hand at the younger paddlers opposite. 'We were wondering–'

Jibo's horn blared from the wooden platform; a longer blast blaring when the shambolic merriment continued unabated. Lamiya clapped her hands. Still too much noise. She clapped again and Everand added the effects of sonic thunderclaps. The noise ceased and people shuffled and fidgeted until they were facing the platform, all eyes upon Lamiya.

'Good people,' cried Lamiya, 'it's time to present the medals for the races and declare the overall winner.' Once the team cries and the rumbling of people stamping their feet finally stopped, she beckoned to Lazuli, who stepped forward with an array of medals on bright ribbons hanging over one arm. 'First, we thank Lazuli, who organised the races with such skill, insight and effort.'

The applause was deafening. Lazuli almost dropped the medals trying to bow with a flourish, his face crimson with embarrassment.

Mookaite wriggled closer and Everand saw she was making room for Tengar to slide onto the bench. Whirr peeped and hopped up and down on his shoulder, then settled again. Everand looked at their beaming faces. What was going on? Had Lamiya asked them to keep him company?

The presentations for the individual races passed quickly, the glides climbing up the dais when called to collect the medals for their team. In a nice touch, Lamiya asked Latog, the previous glide for Riverplain, to collect the team's medals on her behalf. Malach accepted the gold medals on red ribbons for first place in the second race with a broad grin. Lamiya and Lazuli hadn't prepared for tied results, and Everand's eyebrow quirked when Malach graciously let Riversea have the gold medals for the third race and his team took the silver medals on blue ribbons. Well, well. Perhaps Riverwood could become a good neighbour, after all.

Lamiya clapped her hands, speaking as soon as she had everyone's attention. 'I now announce the overall best boat at the races.' She smiled fondly at Lazuli. 'Our race organiser cleverly arranged the mix of races to test as many aspects of great paddling as possible. Every race was *incredibly* close, but at the end there was a clear winner with a total of thirteen points. The best boat is Raptor — I call glide Malach and his entire team from Riverwood to the dais to receive the best boat medals!'

Malach and his team clomped up the steps, punching their right arms in the air and shouting 'Ki!' They formed a line facing the crowd.

Lamiya and Lazuli went to each paddler, starting at paddler ten, calling out their name as they handed them a boat-shaped gold medal on a dark red ribbon. When they reached Malach, Lamiya shook his hand and he grasped both of hers fervently. Malach mumbled something that Everand couldn't decipher, but Lamiya's smile suggested it was a compliment. Malach then grabbed Lazuli's shoulders and hugged him like a brother. Everand lip-read his words: *Glad I accepted your challenge?* Laughing and shaking his head, Lazuli stepped back.

With more punching of arms and team cries, Malach and his team filed down from the dais and returned to their table. Everand watched Fenchi nestle against Malach, who put an arm around her, kissing her soundly while his men congratulated each other and refilled their mugs. Everand buried his nose in his mug. Fenchi would be paddling by the next races. Things were changing faster than he'd thought.

'I now call Clommus and his band to the dais.' Beaming, Lamiya pointed to Clommus, seated at the Riversea table. 'I hear he has a new ballad. I urge you to listen carefully.' She put her hands on her hips. 'Or I'll ask him to sing it again.'

Laughter filled the air, mingled with excited chattering as Clommus took up a stance at the front of the dais, while Conch settled behind him with the large drum. Pippel stood beside Conch, playing sweet notes on his slender horn while Clama positioned herself and began to shake her disk with bells and Limpel blew deeper, resonant notes on a shorter horn.

Everand wriggled on the bench to get comfortable. Lamiya looked unaccountably pleased, so this ballad must be special. Just as Clommus opened his mouth to sing, he remembered Lamiya humming at the back of the boat on their epic paddle. Ah hah. Would Clommus use the opening words she'd sung?

The band settled into a jaunty rhythm, reminiscent of a boat surging through water and Clommus' mellow voice sprang into the air:

'In a risky, bold audacious move
ten paddlers and skilled glide did hove
an epic paddle up Dragonspine they strove
sneaking under darkness into a warded mages' cove

Three brave souls did enter the mages' lair
freeing the doomed glide held captive there
Save him they did from a fate most unfair
with scant breath and heartbeat to spare

The mages into chaotic turmoil did erupt
'til the paddlers felled the mage corrupt
In justice meted and most abrupt
a plot to overthrow the Guild they did disrupt …'

Everand stared at the sea of rapt faces. Just as well the mages weren't present to hear this! The tune was the one Lamiya had hummed. Did she compose the whole song, or just tell Clommus the key events?

Warm hands squeezed his shoulders. 'I like the last verse best,' Lamiya murmured into his ear. A flowery scent drifting over him, he leaned back against her while Clommus tapped his feet and the band played more vigorously.

'For our heroes this not be enough
of legends they wanting to be the stuff
Retrieving the stone of dragon's tears be tough
but this they did and call the mages' bluff

Returned to Akachi the stone now be
the dragons, people, mages all friendly
the whole of Ossilis united in harmony
the whole of Ossilis united in harmony!'

Clommus shouted the last line and everyone leaped to their feet, cheering, hooting, clapping, stamping and shouting, 'In harmony!' The band bowed low, grinning from ear to ear.

Taking the opportunity to turn around while they were standing, Everand crushed Lamiya to him and kissed her. 'I like it too, my love.'

Breaking the kiss, Lamiya peered up at him. 'Shall I ask him to sing it again?'

Wincing at the calls and whistles coming from the crowd, Everand said, 'No need.'

The tune started again and people moved to the space in front of the dais and began to dance, their twirling limbs highlighted by the flickering glow from the bonfire. Everand held his arm out so Lamiya could slide onto the bench beside him. He was still getting comfortable when Beram walked around the table, used both elbows to part Ejad and Acim and shoved his way between them to sit directly opposite. Oh yes, Beram had a question. Everand arched an eyebrow at him.

As soon as Clommus stopped singing the second rendition, Beram leaned forward. As did Ejad and Acim. And Zink and Mookaite. Everand's pulse lifted a notch. What now?

'My question is, will you train me to be a spy?'

'And me,' said Ejad, Acim and Zink concurrently, their faces earnest.

Everand started to laugh, then realised that they weren't. 'You're serious?' He looked at Lamiya, who merely shrugged. 'You knew about this?'

'I might have.' She lifted her chin in a way that suggested she was not inclined to compromise.

'I see.' Everand steepled his fingers together, eyeing the row of anxious faces over the peak. 'Why do you need to be spies?'

'Well,' said Beram, licking his lips and glancing at the others for support, 'you never know when *things* might happen.'

'And we saw how useful you were,' said Acim.

'You saved me!' added Ejad.

Confused, Everand pressed his fingertips together harder. 'What do you expect me to teach you? I can't teach you any spells or magic!'

'Slinking,' said Zink promptly.

'Hiding,' said Acim.

'Pretending to be someone else,' said Beram. 'You're really good at that!'

'Concealing what you're thinking,' said Zink.

'Reading people, checking for sabotage, things that aren't right,' contributed Acim.

'Deep healing,' Mookaite said suddenly on his right.

'Asking questions.' Beram pointed at him. 'You *always* know what to ask, and *when*.'

Astounded, Everand sat back. 'You sanction this?' he asked Lamiya. 'A Riverplain school for spies?'

'I do,' said Lamiya primly. 'We have among us the most skilled teacher imaginable, and …' She lifted her finger at him but changed her mind and lowered her hand. '… as Beram aptly put it, you never know when things might happen.' *Especially with you around*, appeared in his mind.

'I see.' Everand rubbed at his jaw. 'In that case, I agree.'

Beram promptly stood up and yelled over his shoulder, 'He said yes! He said yes!'

His mouth open, Everand blinked rapidly as Lazuli and Larimar ran up with Persaj and Zeol close on their heels. Just how many paddlers wanted to be spies? Lamiya was laughing so hard she was clutching at her side. He poked her in the ribs.

'How many spies do you think you're going to need? Do you know something I don't?'

Pulling him close, she nuzzled the side of his neck, still giggling, then murmured into his ear, 'They want a reason to spend time with you, my love. You are their friend and they admire you.' She licked his ear with her warm tongue. 'And you never know when we *might* need a spy. Or two.'

Breathing deeply, he leaned his forehead against hers. Indescribable joy whirled through him. What had he done to deserve her, deserve such friends? An idea taking hold, laughter bubbled in his chest. 'I *like* this idea. It means someone else can take on the next mission!'

'Wait,' said Lamiya, trying to peer into his face. 'I'm not sure–'

'Oh yes.' He wagged his forefinger at her, dangerously close to the tip of her pert nose. 'I will train them well. *Very* well. Then they can do all the sleuthing, leaving me to be with you.' Forcing his laughter to wait, he said seriously, 'Isn't this what you want?'

'No, I mean yes …' Lamiya punched his arm. 'You're impossibly devious! What was I thinking?'

Enjoying her squirming, Everand said across the table to the others, 'You're prepared to go on missions, aren't you?'

'Yes!' they all shouted, eyes shining.

'It's what spies do!' Lazuli nodded, his lips twitching but failing to stop his excited grin.

'See?' Everand smiled smugly at Lamiya. 'I'll start their training straightaway … oh. Maybe not next sun. I *might* be busy then. Remind me, is there something I'm supposed to do next sun?'

Lamiya whacked his arm so hard she then wrung her hand. The table exploded into guffaws, Tengar and Beram banging their fists on the table and Mookaite wiping away tears of laughter.

Leaning close, Lamiya rasped her tongue up the side of his neck and around the edge of his ear, provoking an immediate response in his groin. His grin faded and she pulled him closer, whispering, 'You will pay for this next dark-fall when we are alone, *consort*.'

Gently moving her hair back, he planted his lips against her ear. 'Oh, I hope so.'

Chapter Forty-three

How much longer? Everand scrunched his toes inside his sandals. For an eternity he'd been peering across the lake, the surface awash with glints of deep golds, reds and oranges from the setting sun. Still no activity near Lamiya's hut, tucked away behind a row of trees hinting at the hues of colour-leaf season. What *could* she be doing? Anticipation shivered through him. What would she be wearing?

A breeze hustled across the lake, stirring the surface into a cross-thatch of ripples and fluttering his silk robe against his body. The azure material, hints of starlight silver woven through it, caressed his thighs and whispered across his groin. Imagining how Lamiya's fingers might explore there, he pressed his lips shut when blood rushed to the area. *Later. Soon.*

To distract his body from the promise, he roved his gaze over those assembled. On his left, Mage Mantiss waited patiently to give him away to be consort to Lamiya. Mage Agamid, clad in his signature purple robe, stood on the far side of Mantiss, with Tiliqua in turquoise next to him and the other mages stretching away in a long line of colourful, flapping robes. He swallowed, humbled that both councils had come.

Unease rippled through his stomach. The shadow spirits of all the previous Riverplain guides were clustered in the Meeting Place up high behind him. Last time the spirits met the mages it had not gone well. U-Mali and U-Lumin had died. *It will be alright.* Pelamis was gone, and they were all here for a common purpose — a joyous purpose.

In front of him, the four dragon boats were neatly lined up on the shore, ornate and fearsome heads facing him. He smiled. Somewhat less fearsome when decorated with wreaths of leaves and trails of colourful feathers. Beside the boats, the teams had combined to form one long tunnel of paddlers, ready to salute with their paddles and release their team cries when Lamiya arrived. His eyes rested on the red-and-gold scaled boat. If she wasn't making a grand entrance by boat, where was she? Lazuli glanced at him then looked down, but not fast enough to hide his smile. So, the pacer knew what she was doing.

'Oh,' said Tiliqua suddenly, stepping out of line and coming to him. She rummaged in her robe pocket and held out, of all things, several small stones of the white marble the Guild buildings were made of. 'Lamiya asked me to bring these. I nearly forgot.'

'She did?' Receiving the faceted stones into his open palm, Everand frowned at them. 'What are they for?'

Tiliqua arched an eyebrow. 'She didn't say. You don't know?'

Shaking his head, Everand slipped the stones into his pocket. Tiliqua smiled and went back to her position. Although the stones were only small, he felt unbalanced, uneven. Weighted down by curiosity. What *were* they for?

A stronger breeze chased across the water and the azure robe swirled, an eddy of air brushing up his legs, ruffling the material as if a thousand butterflies were crawling up his skin. He clamped the robe to him, wishing it were Lamiya's caress wafting over his manhood. His mind leaped to the idea of trailing the end of the silken sash across her body. Gently, like the feet of a thousand tiny butterflies … his body responded and he bit down a moan.

Agamid tipped forward to peer at him. 'Are you alright?' The mage's brow creased into a frown. 'Is the new material uncomfortable?'

'No,' said Everand quickly. 'The cloth is sen–' He grit his teeth to catch the word. He was not going to tell the senior mage in charge of the silk moths that the new material was sensual! 'Soft,' he concluded.

'Sen-soft?' Agamid lifted a brown eyebrow. 'Is that a province term?'

Feeling an inane urge to giggle, Everand shook his head. *Mages do not giggle.* Although, he'd do his best to make sure that Lamiya giggled later. Among other things. She'd insisted he wear his new azure robe for the occasion, a gift from the Guild. And by the stars, the fabric was … astounding. The silk slipped and slid through his fingers, following his movements with sibilant whispers. The colour was of azure sky on the cusp of dark-fall, with subtle stars shining through, as if greeting the onset of true darkness. Soon, Lamiya would pinch the cloth between her long, slender fingers and slide it off over his shoulders … *Focus.* Can't be much longer.

Movement on the far shore caught his attention. The water swelled and the three river dragons emerged and stopped on the dirt beach near Lamiya's hut. His fingers twitched. *At last.* The paddlers formed straight rows and held their paddles, blades up, in their right hands. Beside and behind him, he heard excited mutters from the crowd, all three hundred of Lamiya's people, clustered along the shore. His mouth ran dry. So many people to witness their joining; who somehow considered he was worthy of their special Lamiya, adored by all.

Closing his eyes, he cherished the memory of his first sight of her, standing up at the back of the boat steering, balanced impeccably, muscles rippling and gorgeous mahogany hair flying in the wind while he floundered helplessly in the river. Insatiably curious, she'd followed him everywhere, determined to be helpful. Before he knew it, he was helplessly entwined in her aura and she'd unravelled his undercover disguise — captured his heart — diverted his destiny.

A murmur travelled through the paddlers and he opened his eyes. The dragons were swimming across the lake, most of their bodies above the water. Was she riding a dragon? Given how interwoven their fates seemed, that would make sense. Squinting, he watched the dragons draw closer. His eyes widened. Lamiya was standing with perfect balance on Akachi's arched back! Mizukaze and Hanachi swam at Akachi's shoulders. He blinked. The dragon outlines looked somehow bobbled, blurred.

Lamiya lifted her arms and swept them open in a wide arc and the stunning green dress sleeves opened at her shoulders, revealing her bare arms. With a melodious chorus, hundreds of vividly-plumed birds flew up from their perches on Mizukaze's and Hanachi's backs and heads. Everand jumped when Mantiss clutched at his left arm.

'My boy,' croaked Mantiss. 'This … she … is magnificent.'

Everand looked into his master's dear, lined face, reading wonder and compassion.

'*Now* I understand.' Mantiss squeezed his arm. 'How could you not choose this path, this life?' Mantiss squeezed his arm again. 'I am glad you worked with me for so long. My boy, I truly wish you well.'

'Master.' The words queued in Everand's throat, his chest throbbing with emotion. 'Thank you. For *everything*.' Imagining Lamiya nudging his ribs, the words tumbled out. 'I wouldn't change any of it. Not a thing.' He had to look away from the moisture clouding Mantiss' eyes.

Lulite, an elegant moss-green skirt swishing around her legs and a pale orange top billowing above, walked briskly to the front of the tunnel of paddlers, preparing to bring Lamiya to him. His heartbeats thudded louder. Another breeze hustled across the water, whipping up the surface until it glowed like a horde of fireflies in the setting sun. Everand rubbed at his brow. Wait. Were those red, orange and yellow petals floating in a wide path before and around the dragons? Where had they come from? Combined with the chirping, swirling birds and the darkening sky — if Lamiya wanted a grand appearance, she had it.

Akachi glided to the shore, wading from the water on powerful legs and washing an array of petals and feathers onto the neatly-raked dirt. Chin held high, Lamiya beamed down at him. Everand's lips twitched. Impressive. But how did she plan to get off the dragon? Slide down the side with her dress bunched up? He almost laughed. Did she expect him to translocate her down? He began to mutter the spell. *No. Wait.* Lamiya crouched down, facing sideways. Was she going to jump?

Smoothly, Akachi curled her neck around for Lamiya to sit sideways on her long snout, then the dragon sinuously slid her head back around and held it close to the ground while Lamiya fluidly stepped down. The crowd gasped and uttered low oohs and aahs, but no-one clapped or cheered to break the magnificence of the moment. Lamiya smoothed her dress skirt, then stood while Lulite arranged a pale-green scarf with orange birds and red flowers around the trim across her shoulders. Then, fluttering her eyelashes at him, she placed a hand on the elbow that Lulite offered.

'Yo!' The paddlers snapped their paddles up to create an impossibly neat tunnel of decorated blades, with Lazuli and Larimar at the front, closest to him.

Everand's heart slowed, each beat taking forever, an eerie stillness and silence enveloping him. All he saw was Lamiya, warm, pink, so-kissable lips curved in a coy smile, grey-blue eyes sparkling with love, walking so elegantly and determinedly toward him. Nothing else mattered. Nothing else existed. He was paused in time, breath easing in, breath easing

out, heartbeat, breath easing in, breath easing out, heartbeat …
until Lulite placed Lamiya's silky soft hand in his right hand
and peeled away to stand on his right. As if in a dream, he
felt Mantiss grasp his left hand and place it into Lamiya's, her
fingers curling around his as if she would never let go. In a
trance, he eased closer to her, their heartbeats meeting through
their linked fingers.

Unable to stop gazing deep into her eyes, indescribably
textured with greys and blues, Everand sensed the paddlers
peeling away from their tunnel and forming a large circle
around them, with a gap facing the shore. Dreamily, he watched
Mizukaze and Hanachi emerge from the water and stand like
guardian sentinels for Akachi to pass between. The red-gold
dragon loomed closer, a massive, radiant presence, her golden
spiral horns catching the last rays of the sun.

Lamiya's fingers gripped his fiercely. 'The spell, my love.
So all can follow.'

Shaking off his awe, Everand spoke the spell to translate
Akachi's words as she uttered them so everyone present could
understand.

The air shifted beside him and the spirits of the previous
guides came, misty wraiths deepening the gathering gloom,
contrasting with the radiant red dragon. Whatever he'd
expected, it wasn't this — this perception of him and her as the
centre of the darkening sky and fire of life. He curled his fingers
protectively around Lamiya's when Akachi's moist, heated
breath floated over them, sending shivering tingles throughout
his being. Lamiya's breast moved in a gasp.

*Well met, U-Lamiya, Guide of Riverplain and Mage
Everand of Axis.* Akachi's voice reverberated in the air, in his
heart, in his bones.

*Well met, U-Lamiya, Guide of Riverplain and Mage
Everand of Axis,* echoed the spirits of the guides, whispers
floating in the gloom.

The land has long waited for you two to bring forth a new beginning. All of Ossilis rejoices in your love and your union. Akachi's words sounded huskier. Did the dragon feel emotion?

All of Ossilis rejoices in your love and union, whispered the guides of ages past.

Akachi breathed a long flush of warm air over them and Everand felt his fingers, no, his *being*, blending with Lamiya. Hands, skin, heartbeat, breath, their souls flowed seamlessly into each other. Lamiya's moist lips parted and his body seared with an excruciatingly intense longing to kiss her, to crush her against him and fill her until their blending was complete.

His mind abruptly shifted to a vision of the Staropal, shining resplendently in a wide, pearly shell in a deep underwater cavern. The stone's tinkling voice merged with the husky, gruff words of Akachi: *I pronounce U-Lamiya, Bird and Dragon Caller, and Everand, Eminent Mage from Axis, together. You are now together — and together you are unique. Love each other for eternity, and lead these lands wisely and with compassion. We are all with you, in body, soul and in spirit.*

A hot tear collected in the corner of Everand's eye and Lamiya's eyes shone with tears too.

Akachi gave a rumble, then lifted her great head and roared: *The Staropal has spoken. I declare U-Lamiya and Mage Everand to be Guide of Riverplain and Consort. May their lives be long and endowed with love, joy and harmony.*

Did he need permission to kiss her? Leg-trembling desire rocked him. Releasing Lamiya's hands and sneaking his beneath her luscious hair to cup them around the back of her neck, he drew her tenderly to him, melding his lips over hers. Her fingers pressed against his nape and the kiss became so ardent his heartbeats were pounding against hers. The air filled with noise and mayhem. Was everyone cheering? Wait. Was everyone chanting their names? Heat flamed up his cheeks.

When you are ready, came Akachi's amused voice, *there is another part to this ceremony.*

Everand pulled away — difficult with Lamiya's lips somehow following his — until they stood holding hands and staring at the red dragon.

Akachi moved her head close to Lamiya, opened her jaws and flicked out her tongue. In the fleshy groove rested six gleaming, perfect pearls. *U-Lamiya, take these pearls from the heart of Riverplain.*

With trembling fingers, Lamiya prised the six pearls from the dragon's tongue, cupped them gently in her palm and looked at him with eyes bright with wonder.

Your pocket, said Akachi, looking at Everand pointedly.

The marble stones! Everand fished them from his pocket and tipped them into his palm, seeing there were six. Undoubtedly not a coincidence. What did six stones mean?

Now call Mage Tiliqua of Axis, Malach of Riverwood, Atage of Riverfall and Cowrie of Riversea to us, commanded Akachi.

'Me?' asked Everand.

Yes, you. And when they are here, hold both of your hands out, palms up.

'Me?' said Everand.

Akachi pushed her nose close to his face and blinked ponderously. *You are the bridge. Are you not?*

Bridge? He glanced sideways at Lamiya, who shrugged, then smiled coyly.

'Just do as she says,' she murmured. 'It will become clear, my love.'

Fine. Augmenting his voice, Everand said loudly, 'I call to us Mage Tiliqua of Axis, Malach of Riverwood, Atage of Riverfall and Cowrie of Riversea.' With sudden insight, he added, 'Bring your stones.' Four river provinces, one Mages' Guild and the dragons. Six peoples of Ossilis.

While the others approached, Everand realised his breath was misting before his face. Although the sky retained the residual soft ambers of fading sunlight, the purple haze of dark-fall was pressing down upon them. Far, far above, the first pinpoint star winked at him. He looked down at the marble stones in his palm. Should he give them back to Tiliqua, or were they his? The air rustled around him.

'Congratulations,' said Malach gruffly.

'This be a ceremony for another ballad,' said Cowrie cheerfully.

'Heartfelt congratulations to you both,' said Atage, smiling broadly.

Tiliqua smiled warmly at him and nodded at Lamiya.

Your hands, Eminent Mage, came Akachi's instruction.

Everand held out his hands, blinking when Akachi breathed a cold, white-gold flame over them and an intricate, lacy basket of slender white strands materialised beneath and around his marble stones.

Mage Everand has laid the foundation stones of purity for the new beginning for Ossilis, declared Akachi. *U-Lamiya will now lay the pearls of wisdom.*

Lamiya gently tipped her six pearls into the lacy basket, giving him a smile of pure joy.

Atage of Riverfall will now lay the stones of prosperity.

With a brisk nod at Everand, Atage placed six terracotta tokens into the basket.

Malach of Riverwood will now lay the stones of strength.

Guessing the stones would be granite, Everand watched Malach drop in six dark-grey chips.

Cowrie of Riversea will now lay the shells of compassion.

Six opalescent, coiled shells gleamed like moonlight and tinkled as Cowrie plopped them in.

Mage Tiliqua of Axis will now lay the stones of transparency and honesty.

Her expression unreadable, lips thinned, Tiliqua stepped forward and dropped six clear crystals into the basket. *Transparency. Honesty.* Not things the Guild excelled at. Was the dragon making a point?

On behalf of the dragons of all time, I now place the six eggs of longevity. Akachi opened her jaws and six tiny luminous eggs fell out and floated down into the basket.

His eyes drawn to the perfect eggs, Everand swallowed. His chest thrummed with emotion. Had he and Lamiya really guaranteed the continuation of the dragon species by returning the Staropal? He looked up into Lamiya's star-filled eyes.

Mage Everand. You are the bridge that brought the peoples together. I ask you to mingle the stones so the people can truly be joined in purity, wisdom, prosperity, strength, compassion, transparency and honesty for all longevity. Akachi puffed steam from her flared nostrils, her eyes glowing in the waning light.

Beyond the dragon, the crowd was fading to grey silhouettes in the gathering gloom. This ceremony was important and everyone should see it. Everand created several silver-yellow orbs of light and floated them into a circle above him and Akachi, bringing their outlines into silvery focus. Lamiya's face lit up in delight and Akachi rumbled her approval. In the shadows, the crowd murmured and there came the sounds of shuffling as people jostled to see better.

Carefully, Everand tilted the lacy basket this way and that, watching the stones clink and mingle and a new pattern form — one with the stones nestling alongside each other, each type connecting to all the others. A chill brushed up his arms when the spirits of the past guides crowded closer, hazy figures whispering and peering into the basket.

U-Mali's voice sounded in his mind. *Hold the basket out so U-Lamiya can hold it with you.*

Everand pushed his hands forward, grateful for the warmth of Lamiya's fingers covering and caressing his and the way her eyes lingered on his face.

Akachi lifted her head, eyes glowing like beacons, ornate scales glinting red-silver from his lights, and roared so all could hear: *Mage Everand has bridged the people. Guide U-Lamiya is the custodian of the union of Ossilis. This symbol will be placed in the water bowls at the Meeting Place so all who come to this sacred place are reminded of this new beginning.*

The dragon lashed her tail, sending those nearby scurrying. *You may now celebrate!*

Anticipating instant chaos, Everand whisked himself and Lamiya to the top step of the Meeting Place. Below, the darkening shore teemed with people streaming towards the feast tables. The bonfire flared to life, crackling sparks fountaining up and dancing daintily towards the dark sky. Several people cheered.

'Clever mage,' said Lamiya. 'Place the symbol first.' She tugged the lacy basket, pulling him sideways with her until they were next to the bowls of cleansing water.

'I still don't understand where the water comes from,' said Everand, admiring the crystal clarity, the surface sheened with scant moonlight and the soothing trickling of the rivulet spiralling into the bottom bowl.

'The spirits provide,' murmured Lamiya. 'It is not for us to question how.' She closed her eyes, breathed deeply, then opened them. 'We are to place the symbol in the top bowl, so the attributes wash into the water and will be ladled over the hands of all those who come.'

Tentatively, they lowered the lacy basket into the centre of the top bowl. Everand smiled. 'It fits perfectly. Why am I not surprised?'

Lamiya slid her arms around his waist. 'There is much about Riverplain that will cause you wonder yet, my love.' Gripping him tightly, she tipped her face up.

'I can't wait to show you. Everything.'

Chapter Forty-four

The moon had passed her zenith and was beginning her downward arc. Everand rubbed at his arms; the air was chill despite the press of bodies in the feast area and the glow from the waning bonfire. Sitting by himself, he gathered his thoughts. The ceremony had gone well. Lamiya's grand entrance was fitting and magnificent, and the mingling of the stones was a pleasant and moving surprise. Akachi was most clever. Like the stones in the basket, the six peoples had mingled and made merry, united in celebration.

The dragons had roared with pleasure at the cartload of offerings brought to the water's edge for them, and had hovered for a while so people could approach and admire them. Then they'd glided away in the dark water. The mages had returned to the Guild a while ago, after much grasping of his hands and good wishes. Mantiss had gripped both of his hands, reluctant to let go and murmuring, 'my boy,' over and over until Tiliqua had gently prised him away and Everand had promised to visit soon. Clommus and his band had ceased playing, and were no doubt enjoying well-earned mugs of wine.

But many people remained, huddling together with happy murmurs, some with drunken grins. Acim, Zink and Ejad had fallen off their bench and been propped back up several times, amid guffaws from their team. Everand roved his gaze through the crowd. Lamiya was still passing among her people, clasping hands and chatting animatedly, receiving kisses on her cheeks. Did she never grow tired? Even his bones felt weary … until he thought of returning to Lamiya's hut. Soon. Let it be soon.

Feeling a presence, he glanced up at the hovering shadow, backlit by the bonfire's dying embers. Smudgy-blond hair curling on broad, muscled shoulders. Lazuli. He waved a hand at the seat opposite and the pacer slid onto the bench, regarding him with a grim twist to his mouth. Alertness flooding in, Everand flapped a hand. 'Speak your mind.'

Lazuli brushed hair back from his face and leaned forward, deep-set grey eyes earnest. 'I wanted to say … you know how lucky you are …' The pacer took a breath, finding courage. 'I wish she'd chosen me and nothing will ever change that, but you need to know I respect you.' Lazuli smiled wryly. 'I wish you both well.' He shrugged, his eyes ringed with sadness. 'I will do whatever you need me to do to keep her happy, to make things easy between us.'

Everand's shoulders tensed. Such directness! He must frame his response carefully. Of all the people in Riverplain, this brave, smart, handsome pacer was the one who mattered most to Lamiya. Pushing away the unwelcome memory of the two of them brawling on the beach when he first arrived in Riverplain, he conjured a smile. 'Lazuli, I in turn respect you. I know how much you mean to Lamiya, and to your team and the people. I would value friendship between us.'

Lazuli's eyebrows lifted sceptically. 'You would?'

Feeling an unexpected rush of warmth, Everand nodded. 'You were important during the mission. I'm not sure Malach would have come around without your nudges.' His smile came more readily. 'I might be a mage, but I can learn things from you too.'

An eyebrow still raised, Lazuli relaxed his stilted posture and a grin crept across his lips. 'True. Better paddling, for example.'

Everand groaned, tempted to say he was thinking of more important or useful things, but that would be unwise.

'Or swimming,' added Lazuli, now grinning openly. 'You never know when a spy might need to slink underwater!'

'Slink underwater? Who? Why?' Lamiya materialised from the shadows behind Lazuli. Putting her hands on her hips, she looked at Lazuli and then him. 'Well?'

Even in the gloom, the flush highlighting Lazuli's cheekbones was discernible. Everand said, 'We're talking about things we can learn from each other.'

Lamiya put a hand on Lazuli's shoulder and bent down to kiss his cheek. 'I am glad to hear so. Most excellent pacer, my consort and I must retire. Can you plan a recovery training session for the sun after next?'

Standing, Lazuli placed both hands on Lamiya's shoulders and squeezed them. 'Yes, mighty glide.' Suddenly looking uncomfortable, he stepped back, nodded to Everand and melted into the press of people passing by.

Anticipation running through his veins, Everand stood. Lamiya fluttered her eyelashes and his pulse galloped.

'Is my consort ready to take me to our hut?' she teased.

'More than ready,' he croaked, loving the way she came to snuggle under his arm.

Nodding pleasantly at the stragglers they passed, they soon reached the small bridge across the inlet to the lake. On the crest of it, Everand stopped, facing across the lake to the eastern hills. The air was crisp and brittle, slender spirals of mist coiling up from the lake like pale silver dancers in the light of the half-moon. High above, the sky was sprayed with twinkling stars. Lamiya nestled closer and he tugged the scarf tighter around her shoulders.

'Are you happy?' he murmured.

'Deliriously so.' She gave a deep sigh. 'Everything was *just* as I dreamed.'

'You looked magnificent, my love. Surpassing all my dreams.'

'Do you think the dragons are asleep?' Lamiya said wistfully, looking to the base of the hills, where Akachi's cave was concealed.

'Maybe.' Everand planted a kiss on her head. He thought of the six tiny luminous eggs. 'Or maybe they are busy making larger eggs.'

'I can't wait to see a baby dragon,' said Lamiya, peering up at him. 'How big do you think it would be?' Excitement shivered through her.

'About the size of a hopeepa?' guessed Everand.

Lamiya laughed. 'A hopeepa! I forgot to tell you, Riverfall has another gift for us. Persaj is going to bring Crystal for you.'

Everand instinctively winced at the prospect of the hopeepa rasping her tongue across his face. Regularly. 'Nice, but what am I supposed to do with a hopeepa? Where will we keep her?'

'You'll think of something,' said Lamiya, nudging him to resume walking. 'Lazuli has offered to run her with his herd.'

Shrouded in comfortable silence, they passed along the lake shore, crept quietly past Lulite and Lapsi's hut, and then the hut that was now for Lattic and Lopa. Would he learn how to read people like Lamiya did? She'd predicted they'd be a couple by the time of the races. His heart beat louder and faster when the familiar copse of trees surrounding Lamiya's hut came into view. *Finally*, they would be alone. In *their* home.

'Whirr is with the flock,' murmured Lamiya, reading his mind. 'Just us, together and unique, my love.'

Everand lifted a hand to part the feather curtain when an idea took hold. 'Wait.' He muttered a spell to create a small arched bridge, paved with dragon scales the colour of spun starlight, edged on both sides by small azure shrubs.

'The bridge to our future together!' Lamiya's eyes shone. Twisting sideways, she leaped up so he had to catch her in his arms. 'Take me across, my love.' She nibbled at his jaw. 'Show me how much you love me.'

Blood pulsing in his groin, Everand held her tight and marched across the bridge, vanishing it behind them. Lamiya twined her arms behind his neck and pulled him into a hot kiss. He barely made it to the edge of the mattress before he stumbled, both of them landing on the bed with a thump.

'Elegant as ever,' giggled Lamiya. She ran her tongue all the way up the side of his neck. Reaching behind his head, she tugged loose the hair thong and his hair swished forward around his face. Tenderly, she tucked some strands behind his ear. 'I do so love your hair.' Next, her fingers pinched at his shoulders, trying to grasp the silk cloth, which slid and slipped through her fingers. 'What was Agamid thinking?' Her lips formed a determined pout.

'Try the sash instead,' he breathed into her ear, shuddering with anticipation when she purposefully walked her fingers down his chest and to his waist, groping for the knot. 'That tickles!' he gasped when her hands fumbled across his stomach.

'Oh, is this better?' She smiled wickedly and walked her fingers over his manhood.

Everand groaned and, propping himself up on an elbow, tugged the scarf free from her shoulders and dropped it on the bed beside them. He tried to tug the dress down over her shoulder, then understood it was tied at her back.

'Got it,' said Lamiya triumphantly waving the silk sash under his nose.

'I need that.' He grabbed it from her. 'Roll sideways so I can undo the dress.' She complied and he cursed his awkward fingers as he undid not one but ten ties holding the dress tightly to her curves. Parting the back of the dress, he trailed his fingers up and down her spine until she squirmed.

'Enough!' she gasped, sitting up so he could slip the dress down over her shoulders, wriggling to help him shuffle it down her legs and off over her feet.

He folded the dress and put it aside, then unlaced her sandals and dropped them off the end of the mattress. Putting the silk sash between his teeth, he eased out of his robe, shivering as the material slithered sensuously down his back, undid the top laces of his sandals and kicked them off. Glancing at her shelf above the cooking area, he squinted to ascertain where the candle was, then murmured it alight. A mellow glow highlighted the sheen on Lamiya's forehead, and the cloth wrap binding her breasts. She lay back and put her hands above her head, inviting him to undo it.

Smiling around the sash, he mind-uttered a spell and the wrap and her loincloth both disappeared.

Eyes widening, her lips parted. The soft light flickered across her features and he drank in every hollow, curve and fold of her. She was so gorgeous, so perfect. Pinching his robe sash between his thumb and forefinger, he let one end trail down and, as delicately as possible, wriggled it from the base of her throat down her breastbone then across the mound of her breast to the nipple. Feather-light, he wafted it across the hardening nipple until she moaned and clenched her jaw.

He danced the sash across to the other nipple, playing with her until she moaned again. Her fingers reached for his loincloth and impatiently yanked it loose. His erect manhood sprung free, and he bit down his groan. 'A thousand butterflies,' he murmured and the sash dissolved into a thousand tiny azure silk butterflies. He imagined them fluttering down her stomach and crawling around her womanly parts.

'Oooh. Aaaah.' Lamiya wriggled and arched her hips invitingly, her breath coming in sharp bursts. 'Make them stop!'

Leaning over, he brushed his mouth across hers, directing the butterflies between her legs again, fluttering them over her moist folds to dance around and over the nob that gave her such pleasure. 'Make it stop? Are you sure?'

'It's unbearable! Stop!' Lamiya writhed against him, planting her mouth on his and diving her tongue into his mouth.

He hungrily absorbed her tongue and kissed her so hard he felt their teeth connect. The butterflies vanished. Lamiya writhed and arched beneath him, her moist opening slicking over the top of his manhood sending shafts of pleasure through him. Probing deep into her mouth with his tongue, he felt her legs shift apart, then drove himself into her warmth and love as deeply as possible. He was scorched by endless waves of joy and pleasure.

He and she were blended.

Utterly.

Completely.

Bodies, minds, hearts, souls.

Mage. Bridge. Best of all, consort.

He was where he was meant to be.

ABOUT THE AUTHOR

Kaaren lives on the South Coast of New South Wales in Eurobodalla Shire — land of the Yuin Nation — a place of many beautiful waters entirely suitable for kayaking and dragon boat paddling. An avid lover of stories, as a child she was often sprung reading under the sheets by torchlight long after 'lights out'. One of her most vivid childhood memories is of sitting in the sun-filled, wood-panelled library at high school while her English teacher read aloud *The Hobbit*. From then on, she wanted to write fantasy.

The Mage and the Bird Caller is her third fantasy with romance series. As well as being an author she is a professional freelance editor, and a volunteer judge for several of the Romance Writers Australia competitions. Her short stories 'The Bridge' and 'Lollipops up!' were published in the Sweet Treats anthologies in 2022 and 2023. When she isn't writing, she is editing fiction — or paddling.

Fascinated by the history and mythology of oriental culture, Kaaren has a B.A in Asian Studies, specialising in East Asian Civilisations with Honours in Japanese language. Kaaren was immediately intrigued by the origins of dragon boating in Chinese mythology, and hooked by the camaraderie and mental and physical discipline of the sport. She soon discovered that as a breast cancer survivor, she could also be a 'pink' paddler and joined Dragons Abreast Australia.

The time created by the Covid lockdowns, combined with her new passion for paddling, led to this fantasy trilogy containing romantic elements, enchanting river dragons and several teams of dragon boat paddlers …

Dragons Abreast Australia

Many tears are shed over a breast cancer diagnosis. The disease robs us of many things — our energy, our appearance, our confidence. Once a survivor has had surgery and other treatments, we need hope and connection with those who understand and others who have this lived experience. We need to be physically active; to tread a new life by learning something new; to attain peace through mindfulness. And we can give advice and support to help other survivors. Then the tears will be of happiness, while we power down many rivers and waterways of the world.

Founded in 1998 on the principles of participation, awareness and inclusiveness, Dragons Abreast Australia is a national charity with groups spread across the country. We are a network of paddling groups comprising breast cancer survivors of various ages from a great variety of backgrounds, athletic abilities and interests. High on our list of priorities is having fun and travelling across the rivers, lakes and harbours of the world to help us restore ourselves.

Being able to paddle and socialise in the company of others who have travelled the same path helps to restore the confidence, spark and sense of adventure we need to permit a full and active life after treatment.

We invite you to join us in the boat at www.dragonsabreast.com.au

Many regattas hold designated 'pink' races, where paddlers combine to form 'pink' teams and meet new people. There are numerous Dragons Abreast Clubs around Australia. To find a club near you, go to https://dragonsabreast.com.au/location/

The author participated in 'pink' races at the Masters Games in Adelaide in 2019, and had an absolute ball! After major surgery for metastasised cancer in her spine in 2021, Kaaren is thrilled to be back in a dragon boat and once again able to participate in 'pink' regattas. An absolute highlight of 2023 was paddling for Dragons

Abreast Australia Team 'Hope' at the International Breast Cancer Paddlers Commission regatta held on Lake Karapiro in New Zealand.

She is delighted to donate some of the proceeds from book sales to support DAA.

How to find out more about dragon boat paddling in Australia

The Dragon Boat Festival, also known as the Double Fifth Festival, is one of the oldest festivals in China with a history of 2,500 years, and is now celebrated throughout the world.

Revered as the controller of water, the water dragon is a symbol of divine power and energy and is one of the most important creatures in Chinese mythology. In ancient times, fishermen would pray for abundant rain for their harvests. From the second century onwards, the festival also became associated with the commemoration of the poet Qu Yuan, a well-loved poet and patriot of the Chu dynasty.

The first modern dragon boat races were held in Hong Kong in 1976, and following their success other nations began to hold races. The International Dragon Boat Federation (IDBF) was founded in 1991 and by 2021 had a membership of 87 countries. The IDBF principles are intended to maintain the Chinese traditions and culture of the sport.

For more information visit www.dragonboat.sport

The first Australian involvement occurred in 1980 when the Penang Tourist Development Corporation invited the WA Surf Life Saving Association to send a team to the Penang Festival. The next year WA and NSW sent teams to what was then considered the unofficial world championships on Hong Kong Harbour. As interest grew, state dragon boat bodies sprang into being, and in 1997 voted to start a national body, the Australian Dragon Boat Federation. More information can be found at www.ausdbf.com.au/about-us/

There are numerous dragon boat clubs around Australia, and paddlers join for fitness, fun and camaraderie as well as competitions. Visit the Australian Dragon Boat Federation website and follow the link to your state Dragon Boat Federation, which will have details about the clubs in your states and the calendar of regattas and other events.

Paddles up! Give it a go.

Undercover Mage

Book One of The Mage and the Bird Caller

A simple mission ... with twists and meanders that capture his heart and divert his destiny.

A grumpy river dragon withholds rain. Their crops wilting in unrelenting sunlight, the provinces plan a festival of dragon boat races to appease the dragon. But someone doesn't agree … As the incidents of sabotage mount, Riverfall sends a desperate messenger to the aloof Mages' Guild hidden behind its deadly warded wall.

Mage Everand, a spy, is astounded when his master sends him to Riverfall to find out what is going on. The catch? *'Under no circumstances, none whatsoever, must you reveal your powers.'* The undercover mission unfolds with layer upon layer of intrigue, until Everand starts to question everything he believes. The alluring boatwoman, Lamiya, insists on helping him, making it increasingly difficult to conceal his purpose — and retain control of his heart. Everand faces an irate dragon, a rogue half-mage and, worst of all, a legacy of treachery and secrets underpinning the foundation of his beloved Guild.

Can he save the provinces and make things right without sacrificing his soul and sense of self?

Undercover Mage has a silver book award from Literary Titans, and was a top 3 finalist in the Romance Writers Australia RuBY Award, speculative fiction category, in 2023.

Fugitive Mage

Book Two of The Mage and the Bird Caller

A simple mission ... with twists and meanders that capture his heart and divert his destiny.

His heart captured, Everand decides to forego his mage status to stay with Lamiya in Riverplain. When she is kidnapped by the rogue half-mage, a complex set of lies is revealed. Worse, the Mages' Guild recalls him, and to find his way back to Lamiya he must deceive his master, the Head of the Guild.

Meanwhile, in the provinces, Lamiya awakens Akachi, the

superior red dragon, who sees her and Everand as the means to settle a generations-old score with the Guild.

Fugitive Mage picks up the pace from Undercover Mage as Everand faces one dilemma after another. Is nothing he ever believed in true? How can he spend time getting to know Lamiya with the Guild unravelling around him, the rogue half-mage causing chaos and the river dragons intervening? His mission has developed unimaginable layers!

Fugitive Mage has a gold book award from Literary Titans.

What readers are saying

Sutcliffe writes an engaging narrative that combines excellent prose and showstopping scenes.

Reader's Favorite, US ★★★★★

Undercover Mage will keep readers guessing and holding their breath with its intense suspense.

Reader's Favorite, US ★★★★★

Fugitive Mage is an action-packed story of escape, subterfuge, and romance… In a marvellous feat of character development, those who were initially framed as enemies become allies or those in need of protection.

Literary Titans, US ★★★★★

Fugitive Mage accomplishes what most middle books in a trilogy cannot: the ability to fully immerse a reader with the same strength and tenacity as its first book. Sutcliffe has no weak runners and her story races all of the way through.

Reader's Favorite, US ★★★★★

Just So Fiction